ALDOUS HUXLEY

*

Those Barren Leaves

By ALDOUS HUXLEY

Novels

CROME YELLOW
ANTIC HAY
THOSE BARREN LEAVES
POINT COUNTER POINT
BRAVE NEW WORLD
BRAVE NEW WORLD REVISITED *
EYELESS IN GAZA
AFTER MANY A SUMMER
TIME MUST HAVE A STOP
APE AND ESSENCE
THE GENIUS AND THE GODDESS *

Short Stories

LIMBO
MORTAL COILS
LITTLE MEXICAN
TWO OR THREE GRACES
BRIEF CANDLES
COLLECTED SHORT STORIES *

Biography

GREY EMINENCE
THE DEVILS OF LOUDUN *

Essays and Belles Lettres

ON THE MARGIN
ALONG THE ROAD
PROPER STUDIES
DO WHAT YOU WILL
MUSIC AT NIGHT &
VULGARITY IN LITERATURE
TEXTS AND PRETEXTS (Anthology)
THE OLIVE TREE
ENDS AND MEANS (An Enquiry
into the Nature of Ideals)
THE ART OF SEEING *
THEMES AND VARIATIONS
THE PERENNIAL PHILOSOPHY *
SCIENCE, LIBERTY AND PEACE *
THE DOORS OF PERCEPTION
HEAVEN AND HELL
ADONIS AND THE ALPHABET *

Travel

JESTING PILATE
BEYOND THE MEXIQUE BAY (Illustrated)

Poetry and Drama

VERSES AND A COMEDY
(including early poems, Leda, The Cicadas
and The World of Light, a Comedy)
THE GIOCONDA SMILE *

* Not yet available in this Collected Edition

ALDOUS HUXLEY

Those
Barren Leaves

A Novel

1960
Chatto & Windus
LONDON

PUBLISHED BY

Chatto & Windus

LONDON

*

Clarke, Irwin & Company Ltd

TORONTO

Applications regarding translation rights in any
work by Aldous Huxley should be addressed
to Chatto & Windus, 40 William IV Street,
London, W.C. 2

FIRST PUBLISHED 1925
FIRST ISSUED IN THIS COLLECTED
EDITION 1949, REPRINTED 1950 & 1960
PRINTED IN GREAT BRITAIN
ALL RIGHTS RESERVED

CONTENTS

෪

Part I: An Evening at Mrs. Aldwinkle's   *page* 1

II: Fragments from the Autobiography
of Francis Chelifer   83

III: The Loves of the Parallels   175

IV: The Journey   272

V: Conclusions   339

THOSE BARREN LEAVES

PART I

AN EVENING
AT MRS. ALDWINKLE'S

Chapter I

THE little town of Vezza stands at the confluence of two torrents that come down in two deep valleys from the Apuan mountains. Turbulently—for they still remember their mountain source—the united streams run through the town; silence in Vezza is the continuous sound of running waters. Then, gradually, the little river changes its character; the valley broadens out, soon the hills are left behind and the waters, grown placid as a Dutch canal, glide slowly through the meadows of the coastal plain and mingle with the tideless Mediterranean.

Dominating Vezza itself, a bold promontory of hill juts out like a wedge between the two valleys. Near the top of the hill and set in the midst of ilex trees and tall cypresses that rise up blackly out of the misty olives, stands a huge house. A solemn and regular façade, twenty windows wide, looks down over the terraced cypresses and the olive trees on to the town. Behind and above this façade one sees irregular masses of buildings climbing up the slopes beyond. And the whole is dominated by a tall slender tower that blossoms out at the top, after the manner of Italian towers, into overhanging machicolations. It is the summer palace of the Cybo Malaspina, one-time Princes of Massa and Carrara, Dukes of Vezza, and marquesses, counts and barons of various other villages in the immediate neighbourhood.

The road is steep that leads up from Vezza to the palace of the Cybo Malaspina, perched on the hill above the town. The Italian sun can shine most powerfully, even in September, and olive trees give but little shade. The young man with the peaked cap and the leather wallet slung over his shoulder pushed his bicycle slowly and wearily up the hill. Every now and then he halted, wiped his face and sighed. It was on an evil day, he was thinking, on a black, black day for the poor postmen of Vezza that the insane old English-woman with the impossible name bought this palace ; and a blacker day still when she had elected to come and live in it. In the old days the place had been quite empty. A couple of peasant families had lived in the out-houses ; that was all. Not more than one letter a month between them, and as for telegrams—why, there had never been a telegram for the palace in all the memory of man. But those happy days were now over, and what with letters, what with packets of newspapers and parcels, what with expresses and tele-grams, there was never a day and scarcely an hour in the day when some one from the office wasn't toiling up to this accursed house.

True, the young man went on thinking, one got a good tip for bringing a telegram or an express. But being a young man of sense, he preferred leisure, if a choice had to be made, to money. The expense of energy was not to be compensated for by the three francs he would receive at the end of the climb. Money brings no satisfaction if one has to work for it ; for if one works for it one has no time to spend it.

The ideal, he reflected, as he replaced his cap and once more started climbing, the ideal would be to win a big prize in the lottery. A really immense prize.

He took out of his pocket a little slip of paper which had been given him only this morning by a beggar in exchange for a couple of soldi. It was printed with rhymed prophecies of good fortune —and what good fortune ! The beggar had been very generous. He would marry the woman of his heart, have two children, become one of the most prosperous merchants of his city, and live till eighty-three. To these oracles he gave small faith. Only

2

the last verse seemed to him—though he would have found it difficult to explain why—worthy of serious attention. The last verse embodied a piece of specific good advice.

Intanto se vuoi vincere
Un bel ternone al Lotto,
Giuoca il sette e il sedici,
Uniti al cinquantotto.

He read through the verse several times until he had got it by heart; then folded up the paper and put it away again. Seven, sixteen and fifty-eight—there certainly was something very attractive about those numbers.

Giuoca il sette e il sedici
Uniti al cinquantotto.

He had a very good mind to do as the oracle commanded. It was a charm, a spell to bind fate : one couldn't fail to win with those three numbers. He thought of what he would do when he had won. He had just decided on the make of car he would buy —one of the new 14-40 horse-power Lancias would be more elegant, he thought, than a Fiat and less expensive (for he retained his good sense and his habits of economy even in the midst of overflowing wealth) than an Isotta Fraschini or a Nazzaro—when he found himself at the foot of the steps leading up to the palace door. He leaned his bicycle against the wall and, sighing profoundly, rang the bell. This time the butler only gave him two francs instead of three. Such is life, he thought, as he coasted down through the forest of silver olive trees towards the valley.

The telegram was addressed to Mrs. Aldwinkle; but in the absence of the lady of the house, who had driven down with all her other guests to the Marina di Vezza for a day's bathing, the butler brought the telegram to Miss Thriplow.

Miss Thriplow was sitting in a dark little Gothic room in the most ancient part of the palace, composing the fourteenth chapter of her new novel on a Corona typewriter. She was wearing a

3

printed cotton frock—huge blue checks ruled, tartan-fashion, on a white ground—very high in the waist, very full and long in the skirt; a frock that was at once old-fashioned and tremendously contemporary, school-girlish and advanced, demure and more than Chelsea-ishly emancipated. The face that she turned towards the butler as he came in was very smooth and round and pale, so smooth and round that one would never have credited her with all the thirty years of her age. The features were small and regular, the eyes dark brown; and their arched brows looked as though they had been painted on to the porcelain mask by an oriental brush. Her hair was nearly black and she wore it drawn sleekly back from her forehead and twined in a large knot at the base of her neck. Her uncovered ears were quite white and very small. It was an inexpressive face, the face of a doll, but of an exceedingly intelligent doll.

She took the telegram and opened it.

'It's from Mr. Calamy,' she explained to the butler. 'He says he's coming by the three-twenty and will walk up. I suppose you had better have his room got ready for him.'

The butler retired; but instead of going on with her work, Miss Thriplow leaned back in her chair and pensively lighted a cigarette.

Miss Thriplow came down at four o'clock, after her siesta, dressed, not in the blue and white frock of the morning, but in her best afternoon frock—the black silk one, with the white piping round the flounces. Her pearls, against this dark background, looked particularly brilliant. There were pearls too in her pale small ears; her hands were heavily ringed. After all that she had heard of Calamy from her hostess she had thought it necessary to make these preparations, and she was glad that his unexpected arrival was to leave her alone with him at their first introduction. Alone, it would be easier for her to make the right, the favourable first impression which is always so important.

From what Mrs. Aldwinkle had said about him Miss Thriplow

4

flattered herself that she knew just the sort of man he was. Rich, handsome, and what an amorist! Mrs. Aldwinkle had dwelt, of course, very lengthily and admiringly on that last quality. The smartest hostesses pursued him; he was popular in the best and most brilliant sets. But not a mere social butterfly, Mrs. Aldwinkle had insisted. On the contrary, intelligent, fundamentally serious, interested in the arts and so on. Moreover, he had left London at the height of his success and gone travelling round the world to improve his mind. Yes, Calamy was thoroughly serious. Miss Thriplow had taken all this with a grain of salt; she knew Mrs. Aldwinkle's weakness for being acquainted with great men and her habit, when the admittedly Great were lacking, of promoting her common acquaintances to the rank of greatness. Deducting the usual seventy-five per cent. rebate from Mrs. Aldwinkle's encomiums, she pictured to herself a Calamy who was one of Nature's Guardsmen, touched, as Guardsmen sometimes are, with that awed and simple reverence for the mysteries of art, which makes these aristocratic autodidacts frequent the drawing-rooms where high-brows are to be found, makes them ask poets out to expensive meals, makes them buy cubist drawings, makes them even try, in secret, to write verses and paint themselves. Yes, yes, Miss Thriplow thought, she perfectly knew the type. That was why she had made these preparations—put on that masterpiece of a fashionable black dress, those pearls, those rings; that was why she had donned, at the same time, the dashing manner of one of those brilliant, equivocal-looking, high-born young women at whose expense, according to Mrs. Aldwinkle, he had scored his greatest amorous triumphs. For Miss Thriplow didn't want to owe any of her success with this young man—and she liked to be successful with everybody—to the fact that she was a female novelist of good repute. She wanted, since he was one of Nature's Guardsmen with a fortuitous weakness for artists, to present herself to him as one of Nature's Guardswomen with a talent for

5

writing equally fortuitous and unessential. She wanted to show him that, after all, she was quite up to all this social business, even though she *had* been poor once, and a governess at that (and, knowing her, Miss Thriplow was sure that Mrs. Aldwinkle couldn't have failed to tell him that). She would meet him on level terms, as Guardswoman to Guardsman. Afterwards, when he had liked her for her Guardish qualities, they could get down to art and he could begin to admire her as a stylist as well as a brilliant young woman of his own sort.

Her first sight of him confirmed her in her belief that she had been right to put on all her jewellery and her dashing manner. For the butler ushered into the room positively the young man who, on the covers of illustrated magazines, presses his red lips to those of the young woman of his choice. No, that was a little unfair. He was not quite so intolerably handsome and silly as that. He was just one of those awfully nice, well-brought-up, uneducated young creatures who are such a relief, sometimes, after too much highbrow society. Brown, blue-eyed, soldierly and tall. Frightfully upper class and having all the glorious self-confidence that comes of having been born rich and in a secure and privileged position ; a little insolent, perhaps, in his consciousness of good looks, in his memory of amorous successes. But lazily insolent ; the roasted quails fell into his mouth ; it was unnecessary to make an effort. His eyelids drooped in a sleepy arrogance. She knew all about him, at sight ; oh, she knew everything.

He stood in front of her, looking down into her face, smiling and with eyebrows questioningly raised, entirely unembarrassed. Miss Thriplow stared back at him quite as jauntily. She too could be insolent when she wanted to.

' You 're Mr. Calamy,' she informed him at last.

He inclined his head.

' My name is Mary Thriplow. Everybody else is out. I shall do my best to entertain you.'

6

He bowed again, and took her extended hand. 'I've heard a great deal about you from Lilian Aldwinkle,' he said.

That she'd been a governess? Miss Thriplow wondered.

'And from lots of other people,' he went on. 'Not to mention your books.'

'Ah; but don't let's talk of those,' she waved them airily away. 'They're irrelevant, one's old books—irrelevant because they're written by some one who has ceased to exist. Let the dead bury their dead. The only book that counts is the one one's writing at the moment. And by the time that it's published and other people have begun to read it, that too has become irrelevant. So that there never is a book of one's own that it's interesting to talk about.' Miss Thriplow spoke languidly, with a little drawl, smiling as she spoke and looking at Calamy with half-closed eyes. 'Let's talk of something more interesting,' she concluded.

'The weather,' he suggested.

'Why not?'

'Well, it's a subject,' said Calamy, 'about which, as a matter of fact, I can speak at the moment with interest—I might almost say with warmth.' He pulled out a coloured silk handkerchief and wiped his face. 'Such an inferno as those dusty roads in the plain I never walked through before. Sometimes, I confess, in this Italian glare I pine for the glooms of London, the parasol of smoke, the haze that takes the edge off a building at a hundred yards and hangs mosquito netting half-way down every vista.'

'I remember meeting a Sicilian poet,' said Miss Thriplow, who had invented this successor of Theocritus on the spur of the moment, 'who said just the same. Only he preferred Manchester. *Bellissima* Manchester!' She turned up her eyes and brought her hands together with a clap. 'He was a specimen in that glorious menagerie one meets at Lady Trunion's.' That was a good name to drop casually like that. Lady Trunion's was one of the salons where Nature's Guardsmen and Guardswomen encountered the

7

funnies and the fuzzy-wuzzies—in a word, the artists. By using the word ' menagerie,' Miss Thriplow put herself, with Calamy, on the Guardsmen's side of the bars.

But the effect of the talismanic name on Calamy was not what she had expected. ' And does that frightful woman still continue to function ? ' he said. ' You must remember I 've been away for a year ; I 'm not up to date.'

Miss Thriplow hastily readjusted the expression of her face, the tone of her voice. Smiling with a knowing contempt, she said : ' But she 's nothing to Lady Giblet, is she ? For real horrors you must go to her. Why, the house is positively a *mauvais lieu.*' She moved her jewelled hand from side to side with the gesture of a connoisseur in horror.

Calamy did not entirely agree ' Vulgarer, perhaps, at the Giblet's ; but not worse,' he said—and in a tone of voice, with an expression on his face that showed Miss Thriplow that he meant what he said and didn't at the bottom of his soul secretly adore these social delights. ' After having been away, as I have, for a year or so, to come back to civilization and find the same old people doing the same idiotic things—it 's astonishing. One expects everything to be quite different. I don't know why ; perhaps because one 's rather different oneself. But everything is exactly the same. The Giblet, the Trunion and even, let 's be frank, our hostess—though I 'm honestly very fond of poor dear Lilian. There 's not the slightest change. Oh, it 's more than astonishing —it 's positively terrifying.'

It was at this point in the conversation that Miss Thriplow became aware that she had made a huge mistake, that she was sailing altogether on the wrong tack. Another moment and she would have consummated a hideous error in social judgment, have irreparably made what she called, in her jovial undergraduatish moments, a ' floater.' Miss Thriplow was very sensitive about her floaters. Memories of floaters had a way of sticking deep in

her spirit, making wounds that never thoroughly healed. Cica-
trized, the old scars still hurt from time to time. Suddenly, for no
reason, in the middle of the night, or even in the middle of the
jolliest party, she would remember an ancient floater—just like
that, *à propos de bottes*—would remember and be overcome by a
feeling of self-reproach and retrospective shame. And there was
no remedy, no spiritual prophylaxis. One might do one's best to
invent triumphantly right and tactful alternatives to the floater
—imagine oneself, for example, whispering to sister Fanny the
mollifying instead of the bitter, wounding phrase ; might walk in
fancy with the airiest dignity out of Bardolph's studio into the dirty
little street, past the house with the canary hanging in the window
(an exquisite touch the canary), away, away—when in fact (oh
Lord, what a fool one had been, and how miserable, afterwards !),
in actual fact one had stayed. One could do one's best ; but one
could never really persuade oneself that the floater hadn't happened.
Imagination might struggle to annihilate the odious memory ; but
it never had power to win a decisive victory.

And now, if she wasn't careful, she'd have another floater
rankling and suppurating in her memory. ' How could I have
been so stupid ? ' she thought, ' how could I ? ' For it was obvious
now that the dashing manner, the fashionable disguise were entirely
inappropriate to the occasion. Calamy, it was clear, didn't
appreciate that sort of thing at all ; he might have once, but he
didn't now. If she went on like this she'd have him putting her
down as merely frivolous, worldly, a snob ; and it would need time
and enormous efforts to obliterate the disastrous first impression.

Surreptitiously Miss Thriplow slipped the opal ring from off
the little finger of her right hand, held it for a moment, clenched
out of sight in her left ; then, when Calamy wasn't looking, pushed
it down into the crevice between the padded seat and the back of
her chintz-covered arm-chair.

' Terrifying ! ' she echoed. ' Yes, that 's exactly the word.

9

Those things *are* terrifying. The size of the footmen !' She held up one hand above her head. 'The diameter of the strawberries !' She brought both hands (still far too glittering, she regretfully noticed, with their freight of rings) to within a foot of one another in front of her. 'The inanity of the lion hunters ! The roaring of the lions !' It was unnecessary to do anything with her hands now ; she dropped them back into her lap and took the opportunity to rid herself of the scarab and the brilliants. And like the con-juror who makes patter to divert attention from the workings of his trick, she leaned forward and began to talk very rapidly and earnestly. 'And seriously,' she went on, putting seriousness into her voice and smoothing the laughter out of her face, so that it was wonderfully round, earnest and ingenuous, 'what rot the lions do roar ! I suppose it 's awfully innocent of me ; but I always imagined that celebrated people must be more interesting than other people. They 're not !' She let herself fall back, rather dramatically, into her chair. In the process, one hand seemed to have got accidentally stuck behind her back. She disengaged it, but not before the scarab and the brilliants had been slipped into the cache. There was nothing left now but the emerald ; that could stay. It was very chaste and austere. But she would never be able to take off her pearls without his noticing. Never—even though men are so inconceivably unobservant. Rings were easy enough to get rid of; but a necklace. . . . And they weren't even real pearls.

Calamy, meanwhile, was laughing. 'I remember making the same discovery myself,' he said. 'It 's rather painful at first. One feels as though one has been somehow swindled and done in. You remember what Beethoven said : " that he seldom found in the playing of the most distinguished virtuosi that excellence which he supposed he had a right to expect." One has a right to expect celebrated people to live up to their reputations ; they *ought* to be interesting.'

Miss Thriplow leaned forward again, nodding her assent with a child-like eagerness. 'I know lots of obscure little people,' she said, 'who are much more interesting and much more genuine, one somehow feels, than the celebrated ones. It's genuineness that counts, isn't it?'

Calamy agreed.

'I think it's difficult to be genuine,' Miss Thriplow went on, 'if one's a celebrity or a public figure, or anything of that sort.' She became very confidential indeed. 'I get quite frightened when I see my name in the papers and photographers want to take pictures of me and people ask me out to dinner. I'm afraid of losing my obscurity. Genuineness only thrives in the dark. Like celery.' How little and obscure she was! How poor and honest, so to speak. Those roaring lions at Lady Trunion's, those boring lion huntresses . . . they had no hope of passing through the needle's eye.

'I'm delighted to hear you saying all this,' said Calamy. 'If only all writers felt as you do!'

Miss Thriplow shook her head, modestly declining the implied compliment. 'I'm like Jehovah,' she said; 'I just am that I am. That's all. Why should I make believe that I'm somebody else? Though I confess,' she added, with a greatly daring candour, 'that I was intimidated by your reputation into pretending that I was more *mondaine* than I really am. I imagined you as being so tremendously worldly and smart. It's a great relief to find you're not.'

'Smart?' repeated Calamy, making a grimace.

'You sounded so dazzlingly social from Mrs. Aldwinkle's accounts.' And as she spoke the words she felt herself becoming correspondingly obscurer and littler.

Calamy laughed. 'Perhaps I was that sort of imbecile once,' he said. 'But now—well, I hope all that's over now.'

'I pictured you,' Miss Thriplow went on, straining, in spite of her obscurity, to be brilliant, ' I pictured you as one of those people in the *Sketch*—" walking in the Park with a friend," you know; a friend who would turn out at the least to be a duchess or a distinguished novelist. Can you wonder that I was nervous?' She dropped back into the depths of her chair. Poor little thing! But the pearls, though not marine, were still rather an embarrassment.

CHAPTER II

MRS. ALDWINKLE, when she returned, found them on the upper terrace, looking at the view. It was almost the hour of sunset. The town of Vezza at their feet was already eclipsed by the shadow of the great bluff which projected, on the further side of the westernmost of the two valleys, into the plain. But, beyond, the plain was still bright. It lay, stretched out beneath them like a map of itself—the roads marked in white, the pinewoods dark green, the streams as threads of silver, ploughland and meadowland in chequers of emerald and brown, the railway a dark brown line ruled along it. And beyond its furthest fringes of pinewoods and sand, darkly, opaquely blue, the sea. Towards this wide picture, framed between the projecting hills, of which the eastern was still rosily flushed with the light, the western profoundly dark, a great flight of steps descended, past a lower terrace, down, between columnar cypresses, to a grand sculptured gateway half-way down the hill.

They stood there in silence, leaning their elbows on the balustrade. Ever since she had jettisoned the Guardswoman they had got on, Miss Thriplow thought, most awfully well. She could see that he liked her combination of moral ingenuousness and mental sophistication, of cleverness and genuineness. Why she had ever thought of pretending she was anything but simple and natural she couldn't now imagine. After all, that was what she really was—or at least what she had determined that she ought to be.

From the entrance court on the west flank of the palace came the hoot of a motor horn and the sound of voices.

' There they are,' said Miss Thriplow.

' I rather wish they weren't,' he said, and sighing he straightened himself up and turned round, with his back to the view, towards the house. ' It's like heaving a great stone into a calm pool—all this noise, I mean.'

Mentally cataloguing herself among the tranquil charms of evening, Miss Thriplow took the remark to be complimentary to herself. 'What smashings of crystal one has to put up with,' she said. 'Every other moment, if one's at all sensitive.'

Through the huge echoing saloons of the palace the sound of an approaching voice could be heard. 'Calamy,' it called, 'Calamy!' mounting through the syllables of the name from a low to a much higher note, not, however, through any intervals known to music, but in a succession of uncertain and quite unrelated tones. 'Calamy!' It was as vague and tuneless as the call of an articulate wind. There were hurrying footsteps, a rustling of draperies. In the huge pompous doorway at the head of the steps leading down from the house to the terrace appeared the figure of Mrs. Aldwinkle.

'There you are!' she called in a rapture. Calamy walked to meet her.

Mrs. Aldwinkle was one of those large, handsome, old-masterish women who look as though they had been built up from sections of two different people—such broad shoulders they have, so Junonian a form; and growing from between the shoulders such a slender neck, such a small, compact and childish head. They look their best between twenty-eight and, shall we say, five-and-thirty, when the body is in its perfect maturity and the neck, the little head, the unravaged features seem still to belong to a young girl. Their beauty is made the more striking, the more attractive by the curious incongruousness of its components.

'At thirty-three,' Mr. Cardan used to say of her, 'Lilian Aldwinkle appealed to all the instinctive bigamist in one. She was eighteen in the attics and widow Dido on the floors below. One had the impression of being with two women at the same time. It was most stimulating.'

He spoke, alas, in the past tense; for Mrs. Aldwinkle was no longer thirty-three, nor had been these twelve, these fifteen years or more. The Junonian form—that was still stately and as yet not too massive. And from behind, it is true, the head still looked like a child's head set on those broad shoulders. But the face, which had once been so much the younger member of the partner-ship, had outstripped the body in the race through time and was old and worn beyond its years. The eyes were the youngest feature. Large, blue and rather prominent, they stared very glitteringly and intently out of the face. But the setting of them was pouchy and crow's-footed. There were a couple of horizontal wrinkles across the broad forehead. Two deep folds ran down from the corner of the nose, past the mouth, where they were partially interrupted by another system of folds that moved with the movements of the lips, to the lower edge of the jaw, forming a sharp line of demarcation between the sagging cheeks and the strong, prominent chin. The mouth was wide, with lips of rather vague contour, whose indefiniteness was enhanced by Mrs. Aldwinkle's very careless reddening of them. For Mrs. Aldwinkle was an impressionist; it was the effect at a distance, the grand theatrical flourish that interested her. She had no patience, even at the dressing-table, for niggling pre-Raphaelite detail.

She stood there for a moment at the top of the steps, an imposing and majestic figure. Her long and ample dress of pale green linen hung down in stiff fluted folds about her. The green veil tied round her wide straw hat floated airily over her shoulders. She carried a large reticule over one arm and from her waist there dangled at the end of little chains a whole treasury of gold and silver objects.

' There you are ! ' she smiled at the approaching Calamy, smiled what had once been a smile of piercing sweetness, of alluring enchantment. Its interest now, alas, was chiefly historical. With a gesture at once theatrically exaggerated and inexpressive, Mrs. Aldwinkle suddenly stretched out both her hands in welcome and ran down the steps to meet him. Mrs. Aldwinkle's movements were as inharmonious and uncertain as her voice. She moved awkwardly and stiffly. The majesty of her repose was dissipated.

'Dear Calamy,' she cried, and embraced him. 'I must kiss you,' she said. 'It's such ages since I saw you.' Then turning with a look of suspicion to Miss Thriplow. 'How long has he been here?' she asked.

'Since before tea,' said Miss Thriplow.

'Before tea?' Mrs. Aldwinkle echoed shrilly, as though outraged. 'But why didn't you let me know in time when you were coming?' she went on, turning to Calamy. The thought that he had arrived when she was not there, and that he had, moreover, spent all this time talking with Mary Thriplow, annoyed her. Mrs. Aldwinkle was perpetually haunted by the fear that she was missing something. For a number of years now the universe had always seemed to be conspiring to keep her away from the places where the exciting things were happening and the wonderful words being said. She had been loth enough, this morning, to leave Miss Thriplow behind at the palace ; Mrs. Aldwinkle didn't want her guests to lead independent existences out of her sight. But if she had known, if she had had the slightest suspicion, that Calamy was going to arrive while she was away, that he would spend hours *en tête à tête* with Mary Thriplow—why then she would never have gone down to the sea at all. She'd have stayed at home, however tempting the prospect of a bathe.

'You seem to have made yourself extremely smart for the occasion,' Mrs. Aldwinkle went on, looking at Miss Thriplow's pearls and her black silk with the white piping round the flounces.

Miss Thriplow looked at the view and pretended not to have heard what her hostess had said. She had no wish to engage in a conversation on this particular subject.

'Well now,' said Mrs. Aldwinkle to her new guest, 'I must show you the view and the house and all that.'

'Miss Thriplow's already very kindly been doing that,' said Calamy.

At this piece of information Mrs. Aldwinkle looked extremely annoyed. 'But she can't have shown you everything,' she said, 'because she doesn't know what there is to show. And besides, Mary knows nothing about the history of the place, or the Cybo Malaspinas, or the artists who worked on the palace, or . . .' she waved her hand with a gesture indicating that, in fine, Mary Thriplow knew nothing whatever and was completely incapable of showing any one round the house and its gardens.

'In any case,' said Calamy, doing his best to say the right thing, 'I've seen enough already to make me think the place perfectly lovely.'

But Mrs. Aldwinkle was not content with this spontaneous and untutored admiration. She was sure that he had not really seen the beauty of the view, that he had not understood it, not known how to analyse it into its component charms. She began to expound the prospect.

'The cypresses make such a wonderful contrast with the olives,' she explained, prodding the landscape with the tip of her parasol, as though she were giving a lantern lecture with coloured slides.

She understood it all, of course; *she* was entirely qualified to appreciate it in every detail. For the view was now her property. It was therefore the finest in the world; but at the same time, she alone had the right to let you know the fact.

We are all apt to value unduly those things which happen to belong to us. Provincial picture galleries are always stuffed with Raphaels and Giorgiones. The most brilliant metropolis in Christendom, according to its inhabitants, is Dublin. My gramophone and my Ford car are better than yours. And how pathetically boring are those poor but cultured tourists who show us their collection of picture postcards with as much pride as if they had been the original paintings themselves.

With the palace Mrs. Aldwinkle had purchased vast domains unmentioned in the contract. She had bought, to begin with, the Cybo Malaspina and their history. This family, whose only claim to fame is to have produced, a little before its extinction, that Prince of Massa Carrara to whom the Old Woman in ' Candide ' —when she was young and a Pope's ravishing daughter—was once engaged to be married, had now become for Mrs. Aldwinkle as splendid as the Gonzaga, the Este, the Medici, or the Visconti. Even the dull Dukes of Modena, the tenants of the palace (except during the brief Napoleonic interlude) between the extinction of the Cybo Malaspina and the foundation of the Kingdom of Italy, even the Dukes of Modena had so far profited by their connection with the place that for Mrs. Aldwinkle they were now patrons of letters and fathers of their people. And Napoleon's sister, Elisa Bacciochi, who had, while Princess of Lucca, passed more than one hot summer on these heights, had come to be credited by the present owner with an unbounded enthusiasm for the arts and, what in Mrs. Aldwinkle's eyes was almost more splendid, an un-bounded enthusiasm for love. In Elisa Buonaparte-Bacciochi Mrs. Aldwinkle had acquired a sister soul, whom she alone under-stood.

It was the same with the landscape. It was hers down to the remote horizon, and nobody but she could really give it its due. And then, how she appreciated the Italians ! Ever since she had bought a house in Italy, she had become the one foreigner who knew them intimately. The whole peninsula and everything it con-tained were her property and her secret. She had bought its arts, its music, its melodious language, its literature, its wine and cooking, the beauty of its women and the virility of its Fascists. She had acquired Italian passion : *cuore*, *amore* and *dolore* were hers. Nor had she forgotten to buy the climate—the finest in Europe—the fauna—and how proud she was when she read in her morning paper that a wolf had devoured a Pistoiese sportsman within fifteen

miles of home !—the flora—especially the red anemones and the
wild tulips—the volcanoes—still so wonderfully active—the
earthquakes. . . .

'And now,' said Mrs. Aldwinkle, when she had polished off
the view, 'now we must look at the house.'

She turned her back on the view. 'This part of the palace,'
she said, continuing her lecture, 'dates from about 1630.' She
pointed upwards with her parasol; the coloured slides were now
architectural. 'A very fine specimen of early baroque. What
remains of the old castle, with the tower, constitutes the eastern
wing of the present house. . . .'

Miss Thriplow, who had heard all this before, listened none the
less with the rapt expression of interest that one sees on the faces
of children at Royal Institution lectures; partly to atone in Mrs.
Aldwinkle's eyes for the offence of having been at home when
Calamy arrived, and partly to impress Calamy himself with her
capacity for being frankly, totally and uncritically absorbed in
the little affairs of the moment.

'Now I'll show you the inside of the palace,'said Mrs.Aldwinkle,
mounting the steps that led from the terrace to the house; her
treasures jingled at the end of their chains. Obediently Miss
Thriplow and Calamy followed in her wake.

'Most of the paintings,' proclaimed Mrs. Aldwinkle, 'are by
Pasquale da Montecatini. A great painter—dreadfully under-
rated.' She shook her head.

Miss Thriplow was somewhat embarrassed when, at this remark,
her companion turned to her and made a hardly perceptible grimace.
Whether to smile confidentially and ironically back, whether to
ignore the grimace and preserve the Royal Institution expression—
that was the question. In the end she decided to ignore the tacit
confidence.

On the threshold of the great saloon they were met by a young
girl dressed in a frock of pale pink linen, with a very young round

19

face (otherwise ingenuous than Miss Thriplow's) looking out of a rectangular window cut in a short smooth bell of copper-coloured hair. A pair of wide-open pale blue eyes looked out from beneath the straight metallic fringe. Her nose was small and delicately snubby. A short upper lip made her look at once pathetic and merry, like a child. It was Mrs. Aldwinkle's niece, Irene.

She shook hands with Calamy.

' I suppose,' he said, ' that I ought to tell you that you 've grown up tremendously since I saw you last. But the truth is that I don't think you have at all.'

' I can't help my appearance,' she answered. ' But inside . . .' Inside Irene was older than the rocks on which she sat. It was not for nothing that she had passed the five most impressionable years of her life under her Aunt Lilian's guardianship.

Mrs. Aldwinkle impatiently cut short the conversation. ' I want you to look at this ceiling,' she said to Calamy. Like hens drinking they stared up at the rape of Europa. Mrs. Aldwinkle lowered her gaze. ' And the rustic work with the group of marine deities.' In a pair of large niches, lined with shell-work and sponge-stone, two fishy groups furiously writhed. ' So delightfully *seicento*,' said Mrs. Aldwinkle.

Irene, meanwhile, feeling herself excused by long familiarity from paying much attention to the marine deities, had noticed that the loose cretonne covers of the arm-chairs were crumpled. Being naturally tidy—and since she had lived with Aunt Lilian she had had to be tidy for two—she tiptoed across the room to smooth them out. Bending down to the nearest of the chairs, she took hold of the loose cover near the front of the seat and gave it a smart pull down, so as to loosen it completely before she tucked it tidily in again. The stuff came forward like a suddenly bellying sail and with it there was shot out—from nowhere, as though Irene had been doing a conjuring trick—a glittering shower of jewels. They rattled on the floor, they rolled over the tiles. The noise disturbed Miss Thriplow in her rapt and child-like contemplation of the sponge-stone niches. She turned round just in time to see a scarab ring racing towards her, with the limp of an eccentric hoop, across the tiles. Arrived within a few feet of her it lost speed, it staggered, it fell on its side. Miss Thriplow picked it up.

'Oh, it's only my rings,' she said airily, as though it were the most natural thing in the world for her rings to come jumping out of the chair when Irene straightened out the cover. 'That's all,' she added reassuringly to Irene, who was standing, as though petrified by surprise, looking down at the scattered jewels.

Mrs. Aldwinkle was fortunately absorbed in telling Calamy about Pasquale da Montecatini.

CHAPTER III

DINNER was served in the Saloon of the Ancestors. In Mrs. Aldwinkle's enthusiastic imagination what marvellous symposia had been held within those walls—centuries even before they were built—what intellectual feasts! Aquinas, here, had confided to an early Malaspina his secret doubt on the predicability of rollations, had twitted the robber marquess, over a goblet of wine, with the feebleness of his synderesis. Dante had insisted on the advantages of having a Platonic mistress whom one never met and who could, when necessary, be identified with Theology. Peter of Picardy, meanwhile, on his way to Rome had recited from his rhymed version of *Physiologus* the lines on the Hyaena, a beast which, besides being an hermaphrodite, carries in its eye a stone which, held by a man in his mouth, permits him to see the future; it symbolizes moreover avarice and lasciviousness. Learned Boccaccio had discoursed on the genealogy of the gods. Pico della Mirandola, over the boar's head, quoted the kabbala in support of the doctrine of the Trinity. Michelangelo had expounded his plans for the façade of San Lorenzo in Florence. Galileo had speculated why it is only up to thirty-two feet that Nature abhors a vacuum. Marini had astonished with his conceits. Luca Giordano, for a wager, had painted, between the roast and the dessert, a full-sized picture of Hannibal crossing the Alps. . . . And then, what brilliant ladies heightened the lustre of these feasts! Lovely, perennially young, accomplished as the protagonists of Castiglione's *Courtier*, amorous in the extreme—they inspired the men of genius to yet higher flights, they capped their hardiest sallies with a word of feminine grace.

It had been Mrs. Aldwinkle's ambition, ever since she bought the palace, to revive these ancient glories. She saw herself, unofficially a princess, surrounded by a court of poets, philosophers and artists. Beautiful women should swim through the great

22

saloons and the gardens, glowing with love for the men of genius.
And periodically — for the apartment of the dwarfs, which the
Cybo Malaspina, in imitation of the Gonzaga, had included in
their palace, demanded appropriate inhabitants to furnish it—
periodically they should bring forth, painlessly, children to the men
of genius—all curly-headed, fully toothed and two years old on the
day of birth, and all infant prodigies. Rows of little Mozarts.
In a word, the palace of Vezza should re-become what it had
never been except in Mrs. Aldwinkle's fancy.

What it had been in fact one could only guess by looking at the
faces of the Ancestors who gave the banqueting-hall its name.

From circular niches set high in the walls of the huge square
room the lords of Massa Carrara looked out, bust after bust, across
the intervening centuries. Right round the room they went,
beginning on the left of the fireplace and ending, with the penultimate Cybo Malaspina, who arranged the room, on the right.
And as marquess succeeded marquess and prince, prince, an expression of ever profounder imbecility made itself apparent on the
faces of the Ancestors. The vulture's nose, the formidable jaw of
the first robber marquess transformed themselves by gradual
degrees into the vague proboscides of ant-eaters, into criminally
prognathous deformities. The foreheads grew lower with every
generation, the marble eyes stared ever blanklier and the look of
conscious pride became more and more strongly marked on every
countenance. It was the boast of the Cybo Malaspina that they
had never married beneath them and that their heirs had always
been legitimate. One had only to look at the faces of the last three
Princes to feel sure that the boast was amply justified. Were
these the Muses' friends ?

' You can imagine the splendour of the scene,' said Mrs. Ald-
winkle rapturously as she entered the Saloon of the Ancestors on
Calamy's arm. ' The innumerable candles, the silks, the jewels.
And all the crowd manœuvring in the most stately manner accord-

ing to the rules of etiquette.' The last representative, albeit adoptive, of these gorgeous beings, Mrs. Aldwinkle lifted her head still higher and with a still more swelling port sailed across the huge room towards the little table where, in shrunken splendour, the successors of Cybo Malaspina were to dine. The train of her coral-coloured velvet dress rustled after her.

' It must have been very fine,' Calamy agreed. ' Certainly, from the point of view of picturesqueness, we 've lost by the passing of etiquette. One wonders how much further informality will go. Mr. Gladstone, in his old age, paid a visit to Oxford and was horrified to observe the new fashions in undergraduates' dress. In his young days every young man who respected himself had at least one pair of trousers in which he never sat down for fear of making them bag at the knees, while the outfit in which he normally walked about the streets was never worth less than seventy or eighty pounds. And yet, in the time of Mr. Gladstone's visit, the undergraduates still wore stiff collars and bowler hats. What would he have said if he could have seen them now ? And what shall we say fifty years hence ? '

The company disposed itself round the table. Calamy, as the new arrival, occupied the place of honour on Mrs. Aldwinkle's right.

' You 've broached a very interesting subject,' said Mr. Cardan, who sat opposite him, on their hostess's left. ' Very interesting,' he repeated, as he unfolded his napkin. Mr. Cardan was a middle-sized, thickly built man. The upper hem of his trousers followed an ample geodesic ; his shoulders were very broad, his neck short and powerful. The red face looked tough and knobbly like the head of a cudgel. It was an enigmatic and equivocal face, whose normal expression was at once gross and sensitively refined, serious and sly. The mouth was small and its thin lips fitted tightly together, as though they were the moving parts of a very well made piece of furniture. The line that marked the meeting of the lips was almost straight, but at one end its horizontal gravity was deflected a trifle downwards, so that Mr. Cardan seemed to be for ever in process of suppressing a wry smile that was for ever importunately troubling his demureness. The hair was smooth, silvery and saintly. The nose was short and straight, like a lion's —but a lion's that had become, with time and good living, rather bottled. Looking out from the midst of a web-work of fine wrinkles, the eyes were small, but bright and very blue. As the result, perhaps, of an illness—or perhaps it was merely under the weight of five-and-sixty years — one white eyebrow had settled down permanently lower than the other. From the right side of his face Mr. Cardan looked at you mysteriously and confidentially through the gap in a kind of chronic wink. But from the left the glance was supercilious and aristocratic, as though the western socket had been stretched by an invisible monocle a size or so too large for it. An expression of benevolence mingled with malice shone in his glance while he was talking ; and when he laughed, every polished red facet of his cudgel's face twinkled with mirth, as though suddenly illumined from within. Mr. Cardan was neither a poet nor a philosopher ; nor of a remarkably brilliant family ; but Mrs. Aldwinkle, who had known him intimately for many years, justified his inclusion among her courtiers on the ground that he was one of the obscure Great : potentially anything he chose to be, but actually, through indolence, unknown.

Mr. Cardan took a couple of spoonfuls of soup before proceeding. ' A very interesting subject,' he repeated yet again. He had a melodious voice, ripe, round, fruity and powdered, as it were, with a bloom of huskiness—the faint hoarseness of those who have drunk well, eaten well and copiously made love ' Formality, external pomp, etiquette—their practical disappearance from modern life is really a most extraordinary thing, when you come to think of it. Formality and pomp were one of the essential features of ancient government. Tyranny tempered by transformation scenes—that was the formula of all governments in the seventeenth century, particularly in Italy. Provided you treated your people to a procession or some similarly spectacular function once a month or thereabouts, you could do whatever you pleased. It was the papal method *par excellence*. But it was imitated by every grand seigneur, down to the most piddling little count in the peninsula. Look how all the architecture of the period is conditioned by the need for display. The architect was there to make backgrounds for the incessant amateur theatricals of his employers. Huge vistas of communicating saloons to march down, avenues for processions, vast flights of steps to do the Grand Monarch descent from the skies. No comfort—since comfort is only private—but an immense amount of splendour to impress the spectator from outside. Napoleon was the last ruler to practise it systematically and scientifically on the grand scale. Those reviews, those triumphal entries and exits, those coronations and weddings and christenings, all those carefully prepared stage effects —why, they were half his secret. And now these pomps are no more. Are our rulers so stupid and so regardless of the lessons of history that they neglect these aids to government ? Or can it be that tastes have changed, that the public no longer demands these shows and is no longer impressed by them ? I put the question to our political friends.' Mr. Cardan leaned forward, and looking past Miss Thriplow, who sat on his left, smiled at the young man who sat beyond her and at the older man occupying the corresponding place on the opposite side of the table, next to Irene Aldwinkle.

The young man, who looked even younger than he really was— and at best it was only two or three months since Lord Hovenden had attained his majority—smiled amiably at Mr. Cardan and shook his head, then turned hopefully to the person who sat opposite him. ' Ask me anover,' he said. Lord Hovenden still found it difficult to pronounce a th. ' What do you say, Mr. Falx ? ' An expression of respectful attention appeared on his boyish, freckled face as he waited for Mr. Falx's answer. Whatever the answer might be, it was obvious that Lord Hovenden would regard it as oracular. He admired, he revered Mr. Falx.

Mr. Falx, indeed, invited admiration and respect. With his white beard, his long and curly white hair, his large dark liquid eyes, his smooth broad forehead and aquiline nose, he had the air of a minor prophet. Nor were appearances deceptive. In another age, in other surroundings, Mr. Falx would in all probability have been a minor prophet : a denouncer, a mouthpiece of the Lord, a caller to salvation, a threatener of wrath to come. Having been born in the middle of the nineteenth century and having passed the years of his early manhood in the profession which, between three and seven, every male child desires to embrace—that of the engine driver—he had become not exactly a prophet, but a Labour leader.

Lord Hovenden, whose claim to figure in Mrs. Aldwinkle's court was the fact that she had known him since he was a baby, that he was descended from Simon de Montfort, and that he was immensely rich, had added a further merit : he had become an ardent Guild Socialist. An earnest young schoolmaster had first apprised him of the fact—hitherto but very imperfectly realized by Lord Hovenden—that there are a great many poor people whose lives are extremely disagreeable and arduous and who, if justice were done, would be better off than they are at present. His generous impulses were stirred. Youthfully, he desired to precipitate an immediate millennium. Perhaps, too, a certain egotistical ambition to distinguish himself above his fellows had something to do with his enthusiasm. Among persons born in privileged positions and in the midst of wealth, snobbery often takes a form rather different from that which it commonly assumes. Not always, indeed ; for there are plenty of rich and titled persons who regard wealth and title with the same abject respect as is shown by those whose acquaintance with the nobility and the

plutocracy is only in fiction and the pages of the weekly papers.
But others, whose ambition it is to climb out of the familiar surroundings into, at any rate intellectually, higher spheres, become
infected with a passionate snobbery in regard to the artistic or
political world. This snobbery—the snobbery of blood towards
brain—had mingled without his being conscious of it with Lord
Hovenden's purely humanitarian ardour, and had given it added
strength. Lord Hovenden's pleasure at being introduced to
Mr. Falx had been enormous, and the thought that he alone, of
all his friends and relations, enjoyed the privilege of Mr. Falx's
acquaintance, that he alone was free of the exciting political world
in which Mr. Falx lived, had made him more than ever enthusiastic
in the cause of justice. There had been occasions, however—
and they had become more frequent of late—when Lord Hovenden
had found that the demands made on him by a strenuous social
life left him very little time for Mr. Falx or Guild Socialism. For
one who danced as long and often as he did it was difficult to pay
much attention to anything else. In lulls between the merry-
making he remembered with shame that he had not done his duty
by his principles. It was to make up for arrears in enthusiasm
that he had cut short his grouse shooting to accompany Mr. Falx
to an International Labour Conference in Rome. The conference
was to be held towards the end of September; but Lord Hovenden
had sacrificed a month's more shooting than was necessary by
suggesting that, before the conference, Mr. Falx and he should
go to stay for a few weeks with Mrs. Aldwinkle. ' Come when
you like and bring whom you like.' Those were the words of
Lilian's invitation. He telegraphed to Mrs. Aldwinkle to say
that Mr. Falx needed a holiday and that he proposed to bring him;
Mrs. Aldwinkle replied that she would be delighted to have him.
There they were.

Mr. Falx paused for a moment before answering Mr. Cardan's
question. He turned his bright dark eyes round the table, as

though collecting everybody's attention ; then spoke in the penetrating musical voice that had stirred so many audiences to enthusiasm. 'Twentieth - century rulers,' he said, 'respect the educated democracy too much to try to bamboozle it and keep it falsely contented by mere shows. Democracies demand reason.'

'Oh, come,' protested Mr. Cardan. 'What about Mr. Bryan's agitation against Evolution ? '

'Moreover,' Mr. Falx went on, ignoring the point, 'we in the twentieth century have outgrown that sort of thing.'

'Perhaps we have,' said Mr. Cardan. 'Though I can't imagine how we should have. Opinions change, of course, but the love of a show isn't an opinion. It's founded on something deeper, something which has no business to change.' Mr. Cardan shook his head. 'It reminds me,' he went on after a little pause, 'of another, similarly deep-rooted change that I can never account for : the change in our susceptibility to flattery. It's impossible to read any ancient moralist without finding copious warnings against flatterers. "A flattering mouth worketh ruin"—it's in the Bible. And the reward of the flatterer is also specified there. "He that speaketh flattery to his friends, even the eyes of his children shall fail "—though one would have thought that the vicariousness of the threatened punishment rendered it a little less formidable. But at any rate, in ancient days the great and the prosperous seem to have been fairly at the mercy of flatterers. And they laid it on so thick, they did their job, from all accounts, so extremely coarsely ! Can it be that the educated plutocracy of those days was really taken in by that sort of thing ? It wouldn't be now. The flattery would have to be a great deal more subtle nowadays to produce the same effect. Moreover, I never find in the works of the modern moralists any warnings against flatterers. There's been some sort of change ; though how it has come about, I really don't quite know.'

'Perhaps there has been a moral progress,' suggested Mr. Falx.

Lord Hovenden turned his eyes from Mr. Falx's face, on which, while he was speaking, they had been reverently fixed, and smiled at Mr. Cardan with an air of inquiring triumph that seemed to ask whether he had any answer to make to that.

'Perhaps,' repeated Mr. Cardan, rather dubiously.

Calamy suggested another reason. 'It's surely due,' he said, 'to the change in the position of the great and the prosperous. In the past they regarded themselves and were regarded by others as being what they were by divine right. Consequently, the grossest flattery seemed to them only their due. But now the right to be a prince or a millionaire seems a little less divine than it did. Flattery which once seemed only an expression of proper respect now sounds excessive ; and what in the past was felt to be almost sincere is now regarded as ironical.'

'I think you may be right,' said Mr. Cardan. 'One result, at any rate, of this slump in flattery has been a great alteration in the technique of the parasite.'

'Has the technique of the parasite ever altered ?' asked Mr. Falx. Lord Hovenden passed on his question to Mr. Cardan in an interrogating smile. 'Hasn't he always been the same— living on the labours of society without contributing to the common stock ?'

'We are speaking of different sorts of parasites,' Mr. Cardan explained, twinkling genially at the minor prophet. 'Your parasites are the idle rich ; mine are the idle poor who live on the idle rich. Big fleas have little fleas ; I was referring to the tapeworms of tapeworms. A most interesting class, I assure you ; and one that has never really had its due from the natural historians of humanity. True, there's Lucian's great work on the art of being a parasite, and a very fine work too ; but a little out of date, particularly where flattery is concerned. Better than Lucian is Diderot. But the *Neveu de Rameau* deals with only a single type of parasite, and that not the most successful or the most worthy of imitation. Mr. Skimpole in *Bleak House* isn't bad. But he lacks subtlety; he's not a perfect model for the budding tapeworm. The fact is that no writer, so far as I'm aware, has really gone into the question of parasites. I feel their remissness,' Mr. Cardan added, twinkling first at Mrs. Aldwinkle, then round the table at her guests, 'almost as a personal affront. Professing as I do—or perhaps trying to profess would be a more accurate description—the parasitical mystery, I regard this conspiracy of silence as most insulting.'

'How absurd you are,' said Mrs. Aldwinkle. The complacent references to his own moral defects and weaknesses were frequent in Mr. Cardan's conversation. To disarm criticism by himself forestalling it, to shock and embarrass those susceptible of embarrassment, to air his own freedom from the common prejudices by lightly owning to defects which others would desire to conceal —it was to achieve these ends that Mr. Cardan so cheerfully gave himself away. 'Absurd!' Mrs. Aldwinkle repeated.

Mr. Cardan shook his head. 'Not at all absurd,' he said. 'I'm only telling the truth. For alas, it is true that I've never really been a successful parasite. I could have been a pretty effective flatterer; but unfortunately I happen to live in an age when flattery doesn't work. I might have made a tolerably good buffoon, if I were a little stupider and a little more high-spirited. But even if I could have been a buffoon, I should certainly have thought twice before taking up that branch of parasitism. It's dangerous being a court fool, it's most precarious. You may please for a time; but in the end you either bore or offend your patrons. Diderot's *Neveu de Rameau* is the greatest literary specimen of the type; you know what a wretched sort of life he led. No, your permanently successful parasite, at any rate in modern times, belongs to an entirely different type—a type, alas, to which by no possible ingenuity could I make myself conform.'

'I should hope not,' said Mrs. Aldwinkle, standing up for Mr. Cardan's Better Self.

Mr. Cardan bowed his acknowledgments and continued. 'All the really successful parasites I have come across recently belong to the same species,' he said. 'They're quiet, they're gentle, they're rather pathetic. They appeal to the protective maternal instincts. They generally have some charming talent—never appreciated by the gross world, but recognized by the patron, vastly to his credit of course ; (that flattery's most delicate). They never offend, like the buffoon ; they don't obtrude themselves, but gaze with dog-like eyes ; they can render themselves, when their presence would be tiresome, practically non-existent. The protection of them satisfies the love of dominion and the altruistic parental instinct that prompts us to befriend the weak. You could write at length about all this,' went on Mr. Cardan, turning to Miss Thriplow. 'You could make a big deep book out of it. I should have done it myself, if I had been an author ; and but for the grace of God, I might have been. I give you the suggestion.'

In words of one syllable Miss Thriplow thanked him. She had been very mousey all through dinner. After all the risks she had run this afternoon, the floaters she had stood on the brink of, she thought it best to sit quiet and look as simple and genuine as possible. A few slight alterations in her toilet before dinner had made all the difference. She had begun by taking off the pearl necklace and even, in spite of the chastity of its design, the emerald ring. That's better, she had said to herself as she looked at the obscure little person in the simple black frock—without a jewel, and the hands so white and frail, the face so pale and smooth —who stood opposite her in the looking-glass. 'How frankly and innocently she looks at you with those big brown eyes !' She could imagine Calamy saying that to Mr. Cardan ; but what Mr. Cardan would answer she couldn't quite guess ; he was such a cynic. Opening a drawer, she had pulled out a black silk shawl

—not the Venetian one with the long fringes, but the much less romantic bourgeois, English shawl that had belonged to her mother. She draped it over her shoulders and with her two hands drew it together across her bosom. In the pier glass she seemed almost a nun ; or better still, she thought, a little girl in a convent school— one of a hundred black-uniformed couples, with lace-frilled panta- lettes coming down over their ankles, walking in a long, long crocodile, graded from five foot eight at the head to four foot nothing at the tail. But if she looped the thing up, hood fashion, over her head, she 'd be still more obscure, still poorer and honester —she 'd be a factory girl, click-clicking along on her clogs to the cotton mill. But perhaps that would be carrying things a little too far. After all, she wasn't a Lancashire lass. Awfully cultured, but not spoilt ; clever, but simple and genuine. That was what she was. In the end she had come down to dinner with the black shawl drawn very tightly round her shoulders. Very small and mousey. The head girl in the convent school had all the accomplishments ; but, for the present, wouldn't speak unless she were spoken to. Modestly, then, demurely, she thanked him.

' Meanwhile,' Mr. Cardan continued, ' the sad fact remains that I have never succeeded in persuading anybody to become completely responsible for me. True, I 've eaten quintals of other people's food, drunk hectolitres of their liquor '—he raised his glass and looking over the top of it at his hostess, emptied it to her health— ' for which I 'm exceedingly grateful. But I 've never contrived to live permanently at their expense. Nor have they, for their part, shown the slightest sign of wanting to take me for ever to themselves. Mine 's not the right sort of character, alas. I 'm not pathetic. I 've never struck the ladies as being particularly in need of maternal ministrations. Indeed, if I ever had any success with them—I trust I may say so without fatuity—it was due to my strength rather than to my feebleness. At sixty-six,

B*

however . . .' He shook his head sadly. 'And yet one doesn't, by compensation, become any the more pathetic.'

Mr. Falx, whose moral ideas were simple and orthodox, shook his head; he didn't like this sort of thing. Mr. Cardan, moreover, puzzled him. 'Well,' he pronounced, 'all that I can say is this: when we 've been in power for a little there won't be any parasites of Mr. Cardan's kind for the simple reason that there won't be any parasites of any kind. They 'll all be doing their bit.'

'Luckily,' said Mr. Cardan, helping himself again to the mixed fry, 'I shall be dead by that time. I couldn't face the world after Mr. Falx's friends have dosed it with Keating's and vermifuge. Ah, all you young people,' he went on, turning to Miss Thriplow, 'what a fearful mistake you made, being born when you were!'

'I wouldn't change,' said Miss Thriplow.

'Nor would I,' Calamy agreed.

'Nor I,' Mrs. Aldwinkle echoed, ardently associating herself with the party of youth. She felt as young as they did. Younger indeed; for having been young when the world was younger, she had the thoughts and the feelings of a generation that had grown up placidly in sheltered surroundings—or perhaps had not grown up at all. The circumstances which had so violently and unnaturally matured her juniors had left her, stiffened as she already was by time into a definite mould, unchanged. Spiritually, they were older than she.

'I don't see that it would be possible to live in a more exciting age,' said Calamy. 'The sense that everything's perfectly provisional and temporary—everything, from social institutions to what we 've hitherto regarded as the most sacred scientific truths—the feeling that nothing, from the Treaty of Versailles to the rationally explicable universe, is really safe, the intimate conviction that anything may happen, anything may be discovered—another war, the artificial creation of life, the proof of continued existence after death—why, it 's all infinitely exhilarating.'

34

'And the possibility that everything may be destroyed?' questioned Mr. Cardan.

'That's exhilarating too,' Calamy answered, smiling.

Mr. Cardan shook his head. 'It may be rather tame of me,' he said, 'but I confess, I prefer a more quiet life. I persist that you made a mistake in so timing your entry into the world that the period of your youth coincided with the war and your early maturity with this horribly insecure and unprosperous peace. How incomparably better I managed my existence! I made my entry in the late fifties—almost a twin to *The Origin of Species*. . . . I was brought up in the simple faith of nineteenth-century materialism; a faith untroubled by doubts and as yet unsophisticated by that disquieting scientific modernism which is now turning the staunchest mathematical physicists into mystics. We were all wonderfully optimistic then; believed in progress and the ultimate explicability of everything in terms of physics and chemistry, believed in Mr. Gladstone and our own moral and intellectual superiority over every other age. And no wonder. For we were growing richer and richer every day. The lower classes, whom it was still permissible to call by that delightful name, were still respectful, and the prospect of revolution was still exceedingly remote. True, we were at the same time becoming faintly but uncomfortably aware that these lower classes led a rather disagreeable life, and that perhaps the economic laws were not quite so unalterable by human agency as Mr. Buckle had so comfortingly supposed. And when our dividends came rolling in—I still had dividends at that time,' said Mr. Cardan parenthetically and sighed—'came rolling in as regular as the solstices, we did, it is true, feel almost a twinge of social conscience. But we triumphantly allayed those twinges by subscribing to Settlements in the slums, or building, with a little of our redundant cash, a quite superfluous number of white-tiled lavatories for our workers. Those lavatories were to us what papal indulgences were to the

35

less enlightened contemporaries of Chaucer. With the bill for those lavatories in our waistcoat pocket we could draw our next quarter's dividends with a conscience perfectly serene. It justified us, too, even in our little frolics. And what frolics we had! Discreetly, of course. For in those days we couldn't do things quite as openly as you do now. But it was very good fun, all the same. I seem to remember a quite phenomenal number of bachelor dinner parties at which ravishing young creatures used to come popping out of giant pies and dance *pas seuls* among the crockery on the table.' Mr. Cardan slowly shook his head and was silent in an ecstasy of recollection.

' It sounds quite idyl-lic,' said Miss Thriplow, drawlingly. She had a way of lovingly lingering over any particularly rare or juicy word that might find its way into her sentences.

' It was,' Mr. Cardan affirmed. 'And the more so, I think, because it was so entirely against the rules of those good old days, and because so much discretion did have to be used. It may be merely that I'm old and that my wits have thickened with my arteries ; but it does seem to me that love isn't quite so exciting now as it used to be in my youth. When skirts touch the ground, the toe of a protruding shoe is an allurement. And there were skirts, in those days, draping everything. There was no frankness, no seen reality ; only imagination. We were powder magazines of repression and the smallest hint was a spark. Nowadays, when young women go about in kilts and are as bare-backed as wild horses, there's no excitement. The cards are all on the table, nothing's left to fancy. All's above-board and consequently boring. Hypocrisy, besides being the tribute vice pays to virtue, is also one of the artifices by which vice renders itself more interesting. And between ourselves,' said Mr. Cardan, taking the whole table into his confidence, ' it can't do without those artifices. There's a most interesting passage on this subject in Balzac's *Cousine Bette*. You remember the story ? '

36

'Such a wonderful . . .!' exclaimed Mrs. Aldwinkle, with that large and indistinct enthusiasm evoked in her by every masterpiece of art.

'It's where Baron Hulot falls under the spell of Madame Marneffe: the old beau of the empire and the young woman brought up on the Romantic Revival and early Victorian virtues. Let me see if I can remember it.' Mr. Cardan thoughtfully frowned, was silent for a moment, then proceeded in an almost flawless French. ' " Cet homme de l'empire, habitué au genre empire, devait ignorer absolument les façons de l'amour moderne, les nouveaux scrupules, les différentes conversations inventées depuis 1830, et où la ' pauvre faible femme ' finit par se faire considérer comme la victime des désirs de son amant, comme une sœur de charité qui panse des blessures, comme un ange qui se dévoue. Ce nouvel art d'aimer consomme énormément de paroles évangéliques à l'œuvre du diable. La passion est un martyre. On aspire à l'idéal, à l'infini de part et d'autre ; l'on veut devenir meilleur par l'amour. Toutes ces belles phrases sont un prétexte à mettre encore plus d'ardeur dans la pratique, plus de rage dans les chutes (Mr. Cardan rolled out these words with a particular sonority) que par le passé. Cette hypocrisie, le caractère de notre temps a gangrené la galanterie." How sharp that is,' said Mr. Cardan, ' how wide and how deep ! Only I can't agree with the sentiment expressed in the last sentence. For if, as he says, hypocrisy puts more ardour into the practice of love and more " rage in the chutes," then it cannot be said to have gangrened gallantry. It has improved it, revivified it, made it interesting. Nineteenth-century hypocrisy was a concomitant of nineteenth-century literary romanticism: an inevitable reaction, like that, against the excessive classicism of the eighteenth century. Classicism in literature is intolerable because there are too many restrictive rules ; it is intolerable in love because there are too few. They have this in common, despite their apparent unlikeness, that they are both matter-of-fact and unemotional. It is only by inventing rules about it which can be broken, it is only by investing it with an almost supernatural importance, that love can be made interesting. Angels, philosophers and demons must haunt the alcove; otherwise it is no place for intelligent men and women. No such personages were to be found there in classical times; still less in the neo-classic. The whole process was as straightforward, prosaic, quotidian, and *terre à terre* as it could be. It must really have become very little more interesting than eating dinner—not that I disparage that, mind you, particularly nowadays; but in my youth'—Mr. Cardan sighed— ' I set less stock in those days by good food. Still, even now, I have to admit, there 's not much excitement, not much poetry in eating. It is, I suppose, only in countries where powerful taboos about food prevail that the satisfaction of hunger takes on a romantic aspect. I can imagine that a strictly-brought-up Jew in the time of Samuel might sometimes have been seized by almost irresistible temptations to eat a lobster or some similar animal that divides the hoof but does not chew the cud. I can imagine him pretending to his wife that he was going to the synagogue; but in reality he slinks surreptitiously away down a sinister alley to gorge himself illicitly in some house of ill fame on pork and lobster mayonnaise. Quite a drama there. I give you the notion, gratis, as the subject for a story.'

' I 'm most grateful,' said Miss Thriplow.

' And then, remember, the next morning, after the most portentous dreams all the night through, he 'll wake up tremendously strict, a Pharisee of the Pharisees, and he 'll send a subscription to the society for the Protection of Public Morals and another to the Anti-Lobster League. And he 'll write to the papers saying how disgraceful it is that young novelists should be allowed to publish books containing revolting descriptions of ham being eaten in mixed company, of orgies in oyster shops, with other culinary obscenities too horrible to be mentioned. He 'll do all that, won't he, Miss Mary ? '

'Most certainly. And you forgot to say,' added Miss Thriplow, forgetting that she was the head girl in the convent school, 'that he'll insist more strictly than ever on his daughters being brought up in perfect ignorance of the very existence of sausages.'

'Quite right,' said Mr. Cardan. 'All of which was merely meant to show how exciting even eating might become if religion were brought into it, if dinner were made a mystery and the imagination thoroughly stirred every time the gong sounded. Conversely, how tedious love becomes when it is taken as matter-of-factly as eating dinner. It was essential for the men and women of 1830, if they didn't want to die of pure boredom, to invent the *pauvre faible femme*, the martyr, the angel, the sister of charity, to talk like the Bible while they were consummating the devil's work. The sort of love that their predecessors of the eighteenth century and the empire had made was too prosaic a business. They turned to hypocrisy in mere self-preservation. But the present generation, tired of playing at Madame Marneffe, has reverted to the empire notions of Baron Hulot. . . . Emancipation is excellent, no doubt, in its way. But in the end it defeats its own object. People ask for freedom; but what they finally get turns out to be boredom. To those for whom love has become as obvious an affair as eating dinner, for whom there are no blushful mysteries, no reticences, no fancy-fostering concealments, but only plain speaking and the facts of nature—how flat and stale the whole business must become! It needs crinolines to excite the imagination and dragonish duennas to inflame desire to passion. Too much light conversation about the Oedipus complex and anal erotism is taking the edge off love. In a few years, I don't mind prophesying, you young people will be whispering to one another sublime things about angels, sisters of charity and the infinite. You'll be sheathed in Jaeger and pining behind bars. And love, in consequence, will seem incomparably more romantic, more alluring than it does in these days of emancipation.' Mr. Cardan

39

spat out the pips of his last grape, pushed the fruit plate away from him, leaned back in his chair and looked about him triumphantly.

'How little you understand women,' said Mrs. Aldwinkle, shaking her head. 'Doesn't he, Mary?'

'Some women, at any rate,' Miss Thriplow agreed. 'You seem to forget, Mr. Cardan, that Diana is quite as real a type as Venus.'

'Exactly,' said Mrs. Aldwinkle. 'You couldn't have put it more succinctly.' Eighteen years ago, she and Mr. Cardan had been lovers. Elzevir, the pianist, had succeeded him—a short reign—to be followed by Lord Trunion—or was it Dr. Lecoing? —or both? At the moment Mrs. Aldwinkle had forgotten these facts. And when she did remember, it was not quite in the way that other people—Mr. Cardan, for example—remembered them. It was all wonderfully romantic, now; and she had been Diana all the time.

'But I entirely agree with you,' said Mr. Cardan. 'I unequivocally admit the existence of Artemis. I could even prove it for you empirically.'

'That's very good of you,' said Mrs. Aldwinkle, trying to be sarcastic.

'The only figure on Olympus whom I have always regarded as being purely mythical,' Mr. Cardan went on, 'as having no foundation in the facts of life, is Athena. A goddess of wisdom—a *goddess*!' he repeated with emphasis. 'Isn't that a little too thick?'

Majestically Mrs. Aldwinkle rose from the table. 'Let us go out into the garden,' she said.

CHAPTER IV

MRS. ALDWINKLE had even bought the stars.

'How bright they are!' she exclaimed, as she stepped out at the head of her little troop of guests on to the terrace. 'And how they twinkle! How they palpitate! As though they were alive. They're never like this in England, are they, Calamy?'

Calamy agreed. Agreeing, he had found, was a labour-saving device—positively a necessity in this Ideal Home. He always tried to agree with Mrs. Aldwinkle.

'And how clearly one sees the Great Bear!' Mrs. Aldwinkle went on, speaking almost perpendicularly upwards into the height of heaven. The Bear and Orion were the only constellations she could recognize. 'Such a strange and beautiful shape, isn't it?' It might almost have been designed by the architect of the Malaspina palace.

'Very strange,' said Calamy.

Mrs. Aldwinkle dropped her eyes from the zenith, turned and smiled at him, penetratingly, forgetting that in the profound and moonless darkness her charm would be entirely wasted.

Miss Thriplow's voice spoke softly, with a kind of childish drawl through the darkness. 'They might be Italian tenors,' she said, 'tremoloing away like that so passionately in the sky. No wonder, with those stars overhead, no wonder life tends to become a bit operatic in this country at times.'

Mrs. Aldwinkle was indignant. 'How can you blaspheme like that against the stars?' she said. Then, remembering that she had also bought Italian music, not to mention the habits and customs of the whole Italian people, she went on: 'Besides, it's such a cheap joke about the tenors. After all, this is the only country where *bel canto* is still . . .' She waved her hand. 'And you remember how much Wagner admired what's-his-name. . . .'

41

' Bellini,' prompted the little niece as self-effacingly as possible. She had heard her aunt speak of Wagner's admiration before.

' Bellini,' repeated Mrs. Aldwinkle. ' Besides, life isn't operatic in Italy. It 's genuinely passionate.'

Miss Thriplow was, for a moment, rather at a loss for an answer. She had a faculty for making these little jokes ; but at the same time she was so very much afraid that people might regard her as merely clever and unfeeling, a hard and glittering young woman. Half a dozen smart repartees were possible, of course ; but then she mustn't forget that she was fundamentally so simple, so Words-worthian, such a violet by a mossy stone—particularly this evening, in her shawl.

However much we should like to do so, however highly, in private, we think of our abilities, we generally feel that it is bad form to boast of our intelligence. But in regard to our qualities of heart we feel no such shame ; we talk freely of our kindness, bordering on weakness, of our generosity carried almost to the point of folly (tempering our boasting a little by making out that our qualities are so excessive as to be defects). Miss Thriplow, however, was one of those rare people so obviously and admittedly clever that there could be no objection to her mentioning the fact as often as she liked ; people would have called it only justifiable self-esteem. But Miss Thriplow, perversely, did not want to be praised or to praise herself for her intelligence. She was chiefly anxious to make the world appreciative of her heart. When, as on this occasion, she followed her natural bent towards smartness too far, or when, carried away by the desire to make herself agree-able in flashing company, she found herself saying something whose brilliance was not in harmony with the possession of simple and entirely natural emotions, she would recollect herself and hastily try to correct the misapprehension she had created among her hearers. Now, therefore, at the end of a moment's lightning meditation, she managed to think of a remark which admirably combined, she flattered herself, the most genuine feeling for Nature with an elegantly recondite allusion—this last for the benefit particularly of Mr. Cardan, who as a scholarly gentleman of the old school was a great appreciator and admirer of learning.

' Yes, Bellini,' she said rapturously, picking up the reference from the middle of Mrs. Aldwinkle's last sentence. ' What a wonderful gift of melody ! *Casta diva*—do you remember that ? ' And in a thin voice she sang the first long phrase. ' What a lovely line the melody traces out ! Like the line of those hills against the sky.' She pointed.

On the further side of the valley to westward of the promontory of hill on which the palace stood, projected a longer and higher headland. From the terrace one looked up at its huge impending mass. . . . It was at this that Miss Thriplow now pointed. With her forefinger she followed the scalloped and undulating outline of its silhouette.

' Even Nature, in Italy, is like a work of art,' she added.

Mrs. Aldwinkle was mollified. ' That's very true,' she said ; and stepping out, she began the evening's promenading along the terrace. The train of her velvet robe rustled after her over the dusty flagstones. Mrs. Aldwinkle didn't mind in the least if it got dirty. It was the general effect that mattered ; stains, dust, clinging twigs and millepedes—those were mere details. She treated her clothes, in consequence, with a fine aristocratic carelessness. The little troop followed her.

There was no moon ; only stars in a dark blue firmament. Black and flat against the sky, the Herculeses and the bowed Atlases, the kilted Dianas and the Venuses who concealed their charms with a two-handed gesture of alluring modesty, stood, like as many petrified dancers, on the piers of the balustrade. The stars looked between them. Below, in the blackness of the plain, burned constellations of yellow lights. Unremittingly, the croaking of frogs came up, thin, remote, but very clear, from invisible waters.

'Nights like this,' said Mrs. Aldwinkle, halting and addressing herself with intensity to Calamy, ' make one understand the passion of the South.' She had an alarming habit, when she spoke to any one at all intimately or seriously, of approaching her face very close to that of her interlocutor, opening her eyes to their fullest extent and staring for a moment with the fixed penetrating stare of an oculist examining his patient.

Like trucks at the tail of a suddenly braked locomotive, Mrs. Aldwinkle's guests came joltingly to a stop when she stopped.

Calamy nodded. ' Quite,' he said, ' quite.' Even in this faint starlight, he noticed, Mrs. Aldwinkle's eyes glittered alarmingly as she approached her face to his.

' In this horrible bourgeois age ' — Mrs. Aldwinkle's vocabulary (like Mr. Falx's, though for different reasons) contained no word of bitterer disparagement than ' bourgeois '—' it 's only Southern people who still understand or even, I believe, feel passion.' Mrs. Aldwinkle believed in passion, passionately.

From behind the glowing red end of his cigar Mr. Cardan began to speak. In the darkness his voice sounded more than ever ripe and fruity. ' You 're quite right,' he assured Mrs. Aldwinkle, ' quite right. It 's the climate, of course. The warmth has a double effect on the inhabitants, direct and indirect. The direct effect needs no explaining ; warmth calls to warmth. It 's obvious. But the indirect is fully as important. In a hot country one doesn't care to work too hard. One works enough to keep oneself alive (and it 's tolerably easy to keep alive under these stars), and one cultivates long leisures. Now it 's sufficiently obvious that practically the only thing that anybody who is not a philosopher can do in his leisure is to make love. No serious-minded, hard-working man has the time, the spare energy or the inclination to abandon himself to passion. Passion can only flourish among the well-fed unemployed. Consequently, except among women and men of the leisured class, passion in all its luxuriant intricacy hardly exists in the hard-working North. It is only among those whose desires and whose native idleness are fostered by the cherishing Southern heat that it has flourished and continues to flourish, as you rightly point out, my dear Lilian, even in this burgess age.'

Mr. Cardan had hardly begun to speak before Mrs. Aldwinkle indignantly moved on again. He outraged all her feelings.

Mr. Cardan talking all the way, they passed the silhouettes of modest Venus, of Diana and her attendant dog, of Hercules leaning on his club and Atlas bending under the weight of his globe, of Bacchus lifting to heaven the stump of a broken arm whose hand had once held the wine cup. Arrived at the end of the terrace, they turned and walked back again past the same row of symbols.

' It's easy to talk like that,' said Mrs. Aldwinkle, when he had finished. ' But it doesn't make any difference to the grandeur of passion, to its purity and beauty and . . .' She faded out breathlessly.

' Wasn't it Bossuet,' asked Irene timidly, but with determination, for she felt that she owed it to Aunt Lilian to intervene ; and besides, Aunt Lilian liked her to take part in the conversation, ' wasn't it Bossuet who said that there was something of the Infinite in passion ? '

' Splendid, Irene,' Mr. Cardan cried encouragingly.

Irene blushed in the concealing darkness. 'But I think Bossuet's quite right,' she declared. She could become a lioness, in spite of her blushes, when it was a question of supporting Aunt Lilian. ' I think he's absolutely right,' she confirmed, after a moment of recollection, out of her own experience. She herself had felt most infinitely, more than once—for Irene had run through a surprising number of passions in her time. ' I can't think,' her Aunt Lilian used to say to her, when Irene came in the evenings to brush her hair before she went to bed, ' I can't think how it is that

45

you 're not wildly in love with Peter—or Jacques—or Mario.'
(The name might change as Mrs. Aldwinkle and her niece moved
in their seasonal wanderings, backwards and forwards across the
map of Europe ; but, after all, what 's in a name ?) ' If I were
your age I should be quite bowled over by him.' And thinking
more seriously now of Peter, or Jacques, or Mario, Irene would
discover that Aunt Lilian was quite right ; the young man was
indeed a very remarkable young man. And for the remainder of
their stay at the Continental, the Bristol, the Savoia, she would be
in love—passionately. What she had felt on these occasions was
decidedly infinite. Bossuet, there was no doubt of it, knew what
he was talking about.

' Well, if *you* think he 's right, Irene,' said Mr. Cardan, ' why
then, there 's nothing for me to do but retire from the argument.
I bow before superior authority.' He took the cigar out of his
mouth and bowed.

Irene felt herself blushing once more. ' Now you 're making
fun of me,' she said.

Mrs. Aldwinkle put her arm protectively round the young girl's
shoulders. ' I won't let you tease her, Cardan,' she said. ' She 's
the only one of you all who has a real feeling for what is noble
and fine and grand.' She drew Irene closer to her, pressed her
in a sidelong and peripatetic embrace. Happily, devotedly, Irene
abandoned herself. Aunt Lilian was wonderful !

' Oh, I know,' said Mr. Cardan apologetically, ' that I 'm nothing
but an old capripede.'

Meanwhile Lord Hovenden, humming loudly and walking a little
apart from the rest of the company, was making it clear, he hoped,
to every one that he was occupied with his own thoughts and had
not heard anything that had been said for the last five minutes.
What had been said disturbed him none the less. How did Irene
know so much about passion, he wondered ? Had there been,
could there still be . . . other people ? Painfully and persistently

the question asked itself. With the idea of dissociating himself
still more completely from all that had been said, he addressed
himself to Mr. Falx.

'Tell me, Mr. Falx,' he said in a pensive voice, as though he
had been thinking about the subject for some time before he spoke,
'what do you think of the Fascist Trades Unions?'

Mr. Falx told him.

Passion, Calamy was thinking, passion. . . . One could have
enough of it, good Lord! He sighed. If one could say: Never
again, and be sure of meaning what one said, it would be a great
comfort. Still, he reflected, there was something rather perversely
attractive about this Thriplow woman.

Miss Thriplow meanwhile would have liked to say something
showing that she too believed in passion—but in a passion of a
rather different brand from Mrs. Aldwinkle's; in a natural,
spontaneous and almost childish kind of passion, not the hot-house
growth that flourishes in drawing-rooms. Cardan was right in
not thinking very seriously of that. But he could hardly be
expected to know much about the simple and dewy loves that she
had in mind. Nor Mrs. Aldwinkle, for that matter. She herself
understood them perfectly. On second thoughts, however,
Miss Thriplow decided that they were too tenuous and delicate
—these gossamer passions of hers—to be talked of here, in the
midst of unsympathetic listeners.

Casually, as she passed, she plucked a leaf from one of the overhanging trees. Absent-mindedly she crushed it between her
fingers. From the bruised leaf a fragrance mounted to her nostrils
She lifted her hand towards her face, she sniffed, once, again.
And suddenly she was back in the barber's shop at Weltringham,
waiting there while her cousin Jim had his hair cut. Mr. Chigwell,
the barber, had just finished with the revolving brush. The shaft
of the machine was still turning, the elastic driving band went
round and round over the wheel, writhing from side to side as it

47

went round, like a dying snake suspended, dangerously, above Jim's cropped head.

'A little brilliantine, Mr. Thriplow ? Hair's rather dry, you know, rather dry, I'm afraid. Or the usual bay rum ? '

'Bay rum,' said Jim in the gruffest, most grown-up voice he could get out of his chest.

And Mr. Chigwell would pick up a vaporizer and squirt Jim's hair with clouds made out of a clear brown liquid. And the air in the shop was filled with a fragrance which was the fragrance of this leaf, this leaf from Apollo's tree, that she held in her hand. It all happened years ago and Jim was dead. They had loved one another childishly, with that profound and delicate passion of which she could not speak—not here, not now.

The others went on talking. Miss Thriplow sniffed at her crushed bay leaf and thought of her girlhood, of the cousin who had died. Darling, darling Jim, she said to herself; darling Jim ! Again and again. How much she had loved him, how terribly unhappy she had been when he died. And she still suffered ; still, after all these years. Miss Thriplow sighed. She was proud of being able to suffer so much ; she encouraged her suffering. This sudden recollection of Jim, when he was a little boy, in the barber's shop, this vivid remembrance conjured up by the smell of a crushed leaf, was a sign of her exquisite sensibility. Mingled with her grief there was a certain sense of satisfaction. After all, this had happened quite by itself, of its own accord, and spontaneously. She had always told people that she was sensitive, had a deep and quivering heart. This was a proof. Nobody knew how much she suffered, underneath. How could people guess what lay behind her gaiety ? 'The more sensitive one is,' she used to tell herself, ' the more timid and spiritually chaste, the more necessary it is for one to wear a mask.' Her laughter, her little railleries were the mask that hid from the outside world what was in her soul ; they were her armour against a probing and wounding curiosity. How could they guess, for example, what Jim had meant to her, what he still meant—after all these years ? How could they imagine that there was a little holy of holies in her heart where she still held communion with him ? Darling Jim, she said to herself, darling, darling Jim. The tears came into her eyes. With a finger that still smelt of crushed bay leaves she brushed them away.

It suddenly occurred to her that this would make a splendid short story. There would be a young man and a young girl walking like this under the stars—the huge Italian stars, tremoloing away like tenors (she would remember to bring that into the description) overhead in the velvet sky. Their conversation edges nearer and nearer to the theme of love. He's rather a timid young man. (His name, Miss Thriplow decided, would be Belamy.) One of those charming young men who adore at long range, feel that the girl's too good for them, daren't hope that she might stoop from her divinity, and all that. He's afraid of saying definitely that he loves her for fear of being ignominiously rejected. She, of course, likes him most awfully and her name is Edna. Such a delicate, sensitive creature ; his gentleness and diffidence are the qualities in him that particularly charm her.

The conversation gets nearer and nearer to love ; the stars palpitate more and more ecstatically. Edna picks a leaf from the fragrant laurel as she passes. ' What must be so wonderful about love,' the young man is just saying (it's a set speech and he's been screwing up his courage to get it out for the last half-hour), ' about real love, I mean, is the complete understanding, the fusion of spirits, the ceasing to be oneself and the becoming some one else, the . . .' But sniffing at the crushed leaf, she suddenly cries out, uncontrollably (impulsiveness is one of Edna's charms), ' Why, it's the barber's shop at Weltringham ! Funny little Mr. Chigwell with the squint ! And the rubber band still going round and round over the wheel, wriggling like a snake.' But the poor young man, poor Belamy, is most dreadfully upset. If that's the way she's going to respond when he talks about love, he may as well be silent.

There's a long pause; then he begins talking about Karl Marx. And of course she somehow can't explain—it's a psychological impossibility—that the barber's shop at Weltringham is a symbol of her childhood and that the smell of the crushed laurel leaf brought back her dead brother—in the story it would be a brother—to her. She simply can't explain that her apparently heartless interruption was prompted by a sudden anguish of recollection. She longs to, but somehow she can't bring herself to begin. It's too difficult and too elusive to be talked about, and when one's heart is so sensitive, how can one uncover it, how can one probe the wound? And besides, he ought somehow to have guessed, he ought to have loved her enough to understand; she has her pride too. Every second she delays, the explanation becomes more impossible. In a flat, miserable voice he goes on talking about Karl Marx. And suddenly, unrestrainedly, she begins sobbing and laughing at the same time.

CHAPTER V

THE black silhouette that on the terrace had so perfunctorily symbolized Mr. Cardan transformed itself as he entered the lamp-lit saloon into the complete and genial man. His red face twinkled in the light; he was smiling.

'I know Lilian,' he was saying. 'She'll sit out there under the stars, feeling romantic and getting colder and colder, for hours. There's nothing to be done, I assure you. To-morrow she'll have rheumatism. We can only resign ourselves and try to bear her sufferings in patience.' He sat down in an arm-chair in front of the enormous empty hearth. 'That's better,' he said, sighing. Calamy and Miss Thriplow followed his example.

'But don't you think I'd better bring her a shawl?' suggested Miss Thriplow after a pause.

'She'd only be annoyed,' Mr. Cardan answered. 'If Lilian has said that it's warm enough to sit out of doors, then it *is* warm enough. We've already proved ourselves fools by wanting to go indoors; if we brought her a shawl, we should become something worse than fools: we should be rude and impertinent, we should be giving her the lie. "My dear Lilian," we'd be as good as saying, "it isn't warm. And when you say that it is, you're talking nonsense. So we have brought you your shawl." No, no, Miss Mary. You must surely see yourself that it wouldn't do.'

Miss Thriplow nodded. 'How diplomatic!' she said. 'You're obviously right. We're all children compared to you, Mr. Cardan. Only so high,' she added irrelevantly—but it was all in the childish part—reaching down her hand to within a foot or two of the floor. Childishly she smiled at him.

'Only *so*,' said Mr. Cardan ironically; and lifting his right hand to the level of his eyes, he measured between his thumb and forefinger a space of perhaps half an inch. With his winking eye he peeped at her through the gap. 'I've seen children,' he went on, 'com-

51

pared to whom Miss Mary Thriplow would be . . .' He threw up his hands and let them fall with a clap on to his thighs, leaving the sentence to conclude itself in the pregnant silence.

Miss Thriplow resented this denial of her child-like simplicity. Of such is the Kingdom of Heaven. But circumstances did not permit her to insist on the fact too categorically in Mr. Cardan's presence. The history of their friendship was a little unfortunate. At their first meeting, Mr. Cardan, summing her up at a glance (wrongly, Miss Thriplow insisted), had taken her into a kind of cynical and diabolic confidence, treating her as though she were a wholly ' modern ' and unprejudiced young woman, one of those young women who not only *do* what they like (which is nothing ; for the demurest and the most ' old-fashioned ' can and do act), but who also airily and openly talk of their diversions. Inspired by her desire to please, and carried away by her facility for adapting herself to her spiritual environment, Miss Thriplow had gaily entered into the part assigned to her. How brilliant she had been, how charmingly and wickedly daring ! until finally, twinkling benevolently all the time, Mr. Cardan had led the conversation along such strange and such outrageous paths that Miss Thriplow began to fear that she had put herself in a false position. Goodness only knew what mightn't, with such a man, happen next. By imperceptible degrees Miss Thriplow transformed herself from a salamander, sporting gaily among the flames, into a primrose by the river's brim. Henceforward, whenever she talked to Mr. Cardan, the serious young female novelist—so cultured and intelligent, but so unspoiled—put in an appearance. For his part, with that tact which distinguished him in all his social negotiations, Mr. Cardan accepted the female novelist without showing the least astonishment at the change. At most, he permitted himself from time to time to look at her through his winking eye and smile significantly. Miss Thriplow on these occasions pretended not to notice. In the circumstances, it was the best thing she could do.

'People always seem to imagine,' said Miss Thriplow with a martyr's sigh, 'that being educated means being sophisticated. And what's more, they never seem to be able to give one credit for having a good heart as well as a good head.'

And she had *such* a good heart. Any one can be clever, she used to say. But what matters is being kind and good, and having nice feelings. She felt more than ever pleased about that bay-leaf incident. That was having nice feelings.

'They always seem entirely to misunderstand what one writes,' Miss Thriplow went on. 'They like my books because they're smart and unexpected and rather paradoxical and cynical and elegantly brutal. They don't see how serious it all is. They don't see the tragedy and the tenderness underneath. You see,' she explained, 'I'm trying to do something new—a chemical compound of all the categories. Lightness and tragedy and loveliness and wit and fantasy and realism and irony and sentiment all combined. People seem to find it merely amusing, that's all.' She threw out her hands despairingly.

'It's only to be expected,' said Mr. Cardan comfortingly. 'Any one who has anything to say can't fail to be misunderstood. The public only understands the things with which it is perfectly familiar. Something new makes it lose its orientation. And then think of the misunderstandings between even intelligent people, people who know one another personally. Have you ever corresponded with a distant lover?' Miss Thriplow slightly nodded; she was familiar, professionally, with every painful experience. 'Then you must know how easy it is for your correspondent to take the expression of one of your passing moods—forgotten long before the arrival of the letter at its destination—as your permanent spiritual condition. Haven't you been shocked to receive, by the returning post, a letter rejoicing with you in your gaiety, when in fact, at the moment, you are plunged in gloom; or astonished, when you come whistling down to breakfast, to find beside your plate sixteen pages of sympathy and consolation ? And have you ever had the misfortune to be loved by somebody you do not love ? Then you know very well how expressions of affection which must have been written with tears in the eyes and from the depth of the heart seem to you not merely silly and irritating, but in the worst possible bad taste. Positively vulgar, like those deplorable letters that are read in the divorce courts. And yet these are precisely the expressions that you habitually use when writing to the person you yourself are in love with. In the same way, the reader of a book who happens to be out of tune with the author's prevailing mood will be bored to death by the things that were written with the greatest enthusiasm. Or else, like the far-away correspondent, he may seize on something which for you was not essential, to make of it the core and kernel of the whole book. And then, you admitted it yourself, you make it very hard for your readers. You write sentimental tragedies in terms of satire and they see only the satire. Isn't it to be expected ? '

' There 's something in that, of course,' said Miss Thriplow. But not everything, she added to herself.

' And then you must remember,' Mr. Cardan went on, ' that most readers don't really read. When you reflect that the pages which cost a week of unremitting and agonizing labour to write are casually read through—or, more likely, skipped through—in a few minutes, you cannot be surprised if little misunderstandings between author and reader should happen from time to time. We all read too much nowadays to be able to read properly. We read with the eyes alone, not with the imagination ; we don't take the trouble to reconvert the printed word into a living image. And we do this, I may say, in sheer self-defence. For though we read an enormous number of words, nine hundred and ninety out of every thousand of them are not worth reading properly, are not even susceptible of being read except superficially, with the eye alone. Our perfunctory reading of nonsense habituates us to be careless and remiss with all our reading, even of good books. You may take endless pains with your writing, my dear Miss Mary ; but out of every hundred of your readers, how many, do you suppose, ever take the pains to read what you write—and when I say read,' Mr. Cardan added, ' I mean really *read*—how many, I repeat ? '

' Who knows ? ' said Miss Thriplow. But even if they did read properly, she was thinking, would they really unearth that Heart ? That was the vital question.

' It 's this mania for keeping up to date,' said Mr. Cardan, ' that has killed the art of reading. Most of the people I know read three or four daily newspapers, look at half a dozen weeklies between Saturday and Monday, and a dozen reviews at the end of every month. And the rest of the time, as the Bible with justifiable vigour would put it, the rest of the time they are whoring after new fiction, new plays and verses and biographies. They 've no time to do anything but skim along uncomprehendingly. If you must complicate the matter by writing tragedy in terms of farce you can only expect confusion. Books have their destinies like men. And their fates, as made by generations of readers, are very different from the destinies foreseen for them by their authors. *Gulliver's Travels*, with a minimum of expurgation, has become a children's book ; a new illustrated edition is produced every Christmas. That 's what comes of saying profound things about humanity in terms of a fairy story. The publications of the Purity League figure invariably under the heading " Curious " in the booksellers' catalogues. The theological and, to Milton himself, the fundamental and essential part of *Paradise Lost* is now so ludicrous that we ignore it altogether. When somebody speaks of Milton, what do we call to mind ? A great religious poet ? No. Milton means for us a collection of isolated passages, full of bright light, colour and thunderous harmony, hanging like musical stars in the lap of nothing. Sometimes the adult masterpieces of one generation become the reading of schoolboys in the next. Does any one over sixteen now read the poems of Sir Walter Scott ? or his novels, for that matter ? How many books of piety and morality survive only for their fine writing ! and how our interest in the merely aesthetic qualities of these books would have scandalized their authors ! No, at the end of the account it is the readers who make the book what it ultimately is. The writer proposes, the readers dispose. It 's inevitable, Miss Mary. You must reconcile yourself to fate.'

' I suppose I must,' said Miss Thriplow.

Calamy broke silence for the first time since they had entered the room. ' But I don't know why you complain of being mis-understood,' he said, smiling. ' I should have thought that it was much more disagreeable to be understood. One can get annoyed with imbeciles for failing to understand what seems obvious to one-self ; one's vanity may be hurt by their interpretation of you—they make you out to be as vulgar as themselves. Or you may feel that you have failed as an artist, in so far as you haven't managed to make yourself transparently plain. But what are all these compared to the horrors of being understood—completely understood? You 've given yourself away, you 're known, you 're at the mercy of the creatures into whose keeping you have committed your soul—why, the thought 's terrifying. If I were you,' he went on, ' I 'd con-gratulate myself. You have a public which likes your books, but for the wrong reasons. And meanwhile you 're safe, you 're out of their reach, you possess yourself intact.'

' Perhaps you 're right,' said Miss Thriplow. Mr. Cardan understood her, she reflected, or at least understood part of her— an unreal, superficial part, it was true ; but still, she had to admit, a part. And it certainly wasn't agreeable.

CHAPTER VI

To be torn between divided allegiances is the painful fate of almost every human being. Pull devil, pull baker; pull flesh, pull spirit; pull love, pull duty; pull reason and pull hallowed prejudice. The conflict, in its various forms, is the theme of every drama. For though we have learnt to feel disgust at the spectacle of a bull-fight, an execution or a gladiatorial show, we still look on with pleasure at the contortions of those who suffer spiritual anguish. At some distant future date, when society is organized in a rational manner so that every individual occupies the position and does the work for which his capacities really fit him, when education has ceased to instil into the minds of the young fantastic prejudices instead of truths, when the endocrine glands have been taught to function in perfect harmony and diseases have been suppressed, all our literature of conflict and unhappiness will seem strangely incomprehensible; and our taste for the spectacle of mental torture will be regarded as an obscene perversion of which decent men should feel ashamed. Joy will take the place of suffering as the principal theme of art; in the process, it may be, art will cease to exist. A happy people, we now say, has no history; and we might add that happy individuals have no literature. The novelist dismisses in a paragraph his hero's twenty years of happiness; over a week of misery and spiritual debate he will linger through twenty chapters. When there is no more misery, he will have nothing to write about. Perhaps it will be all for the best.

The conflict which had raged during the last few months within Irene's spirit, though not so serious as some of the inward battles that have distracted strong men in their search for the salvation of integrity, was still for her a painful one. Put baldly in its most concrete form, the question at issue was this: should she paint pictures and write? or should she make her own underclothing?

But for Aunt Lilian the conflict would never have become

serious; indeed, it would never, in all probability, have begun at all. For if it had not been for Aunt Lilian, the Natural Woman in Irene would have remained undisputed mistress of the field, and she would have passed her days in a placid contentment over the lacy intricacies of her undergarments. Aunt Lilian, however, was on the side of the Unnatural Woman; it was she who had practically called the writer and the painter of pictures into existence, had invented Irene's higher talents and ranged them against the homelier.

Mrs. Aldwinkle's enthusiasm for the arts was such that she wanted every one to practise one or other of them. It was her own greatest regret that she herself had no aptitude for any of them. Nature had endowed her with no power of self-expression; even in ordinary conversation she found it difficult to give utterance to what she wanted to say. Her letters were made up of the fragments of sentences; it was as though her thoughts had been blown to ungrammatical pieces by a bomb and scattered themselves on the page. A curious clumsiness of hand united with her native impatience to prevent her from drawing correctly or even doing plain sewing. And though she listened to music with an expression of rapture, she had an ear that could not distinguish a major from a minor third. ' I'm one of those unfortunate people,' she used to say, ' who have an artistic temperament without an artist's powers.' She had to content herself with cultivating her own temperament and developing other people's capacities. She never met a young person of either sex without encouraging him or her to become a painter, a novelist, a poet or a musician. It was she who had persuaded Irene that her little dexterity with camel's-hair brushes was a talent and that she ought on the strength of her amusing letters to write lyrics. ' How can you spend your time so stupidly and frivolously ? ' she used to ask, whenever she found Irene busy at her underlinen. And Irene, who adored her Aunt Lilian with the dog-like devotion that is only possible when one is eighteen, and rather young for one's age at that, put her sewing away and devoted all her energy to portraying in water-colours and describing in rhyme the landscape and the flowers of the garden. But the underclothing remained, none the less, a permanent temptation. She found herself wondering whether her chain-stitch wasn't better than her painting, her button-holing superior to her verse. She asked herself whether nightdresses weren't more useful than water-colours. More useful —and besides she was so awfully particular about what she wore next her skin ; and she adored pretty things. So did Aunt Lilian, who used to laugh at her when she wore ugly, dowdy ones. At the same time Aunt Lilian didn't give her much of an allowance. For thirty shillings Irene could make a garment that it would have cost her five or six guineas to buy in a shop. . . .

Underclothing became for Irene the flesh, became illicit love and rebellious reason ; poetry and water-colour painting, invested by her adoration of Aunt Lilian with a quality of sacredness, became spirit, duty and religion. The struggle between her inclination and what Aunt Lilian considered good was prolonged and distressing.

On nights like this, however, the Natural Woman faded completely out. Under the stars, in the solemn darkness, how could one think of underclothing ? And Aunt Lilian was being so affectionate. Still, it certainly *was* rather cool.

' Art 's the great thing,' Mrs. Ardwinkle was saying earnestly, ' the thing that really makes life worth living and justifies one's existence.' When Mr. Cardan was away she let herself go more confidently on her favourite themes.

And Irene, sitting at her feet, leaning against her knee, couldn't help agreeing. Mrs. Aldwinkle stroked the girl's soft hair, or with combing fingers disordered its sleek surface. Irene shut her eyes ; happily, drowsily, she listened. Mrs. Aldwinkle's talk came to her in gusts—here a phrase, there a phrase.

' Disinterested,' she was saying, ' disinterested . . .' Mrs. Aldwinkle had a way, when she wanted to insist on an idea, of repeating the same word several times. 'Disinterested . . .' It saved her the trouble of looking for phrases which she could never find, of making explanations which always turned out, at the best, rather incoherent. 'Joy in the work for its own sake. . . . Flaubert spent days over a single sentence. . . . Wonderful. . . .'

'Wonderful!' Irene echoed.

A little breeze stirred among the bay trees. Their stiff leaves rattled dryly together, like scales of metal. Irene shivered a little; it was downright cold.

'It's the only really creative . . .' Mrs. Aldwinkle couldn't think of the word 'activity' and had to content herself with making a gesture with her free hand. 'Through art man comes nearest to being a god . . . a god. . . .'

The night wind rattled more loudly among the bay leaves. Irene crossed her arms over her chest, hugging herself to keep warm. Unfortunately, this boa of flesh and blood was itself sensitive. Her frock was sleeveless. The warmth of her bare arms drifted off along the wind; the temperature of the surrounding atmosphere rose by a hundred-billionth of a degree.

'It's the highest life,' said Mrs. Aldwinkle. 'It's the only life.' Tenderly she rumpled Irene's hair. And at this very moment, Mr. Falx was meditating, at this very moment, on tram-cars in the Argentine, among Peruvian guano-beds, in humming power-stations at the foot of African waterfalls, in Australian refrigerators packed with slaughtered mutton, in the heat and darkness of Yorkshire coal-mines, in tea-plantations on the slopes of the Himalaya, in Japanese banks, at the mouth of Mexican oil-wells, in steamers walloping along across the China Sea—at this very moment, men and women of every race and colour were doing their bit to supply Mrs. Aldwinkle with her income. On the two hundred and seventy thousand pounds of Mrs. Aldwinkle's capital the sun never set. People worked; Mrs. Aldwinkle led the higher life. She for art only, they—albeit unconscious of the privilege—for art in her.

Young Lord Hovenden sighed. If only it were he whose fingers were playing in the smooth thick tresses of Irene's hair! It seemed an awful waste that she should be so fond of her Aunt Lilian. Somehow, the more he liked Irene the less he liked Aunt Lilian.

'Haven't you sometimes longed to be an artist yourself, Hovenden?' Mrs. Aldwinkle suddenly asked. She leaned forward, her eyes glittering with the reflected light of two or three hundred million remote suns. She was going to suggest that he might try his hand at poetical rhapsodies about political injustice and the condition of the lower classes. Something half-way between Shelley and Walt Whitman.

'Me!' said Hovenden in astonishment. Then he laughed aloud: Ha, ha, ha! It was a jarring note.

Mrs. Aldwinkle drew back, pained. 'I don't know why you should think the idea so impossibly comic,' she said.

'Perhaps he has other work to do,' said Mr. Falx out of the darkness. 'More important work.' And at the sound of that thrilling, deep, prophetical voice Lord Hovenden felt that, indeed, he had.

'More important?' queried Mrs. Aldwinkle. 'But can anything be more important? When one thinks of Flaubert . . .' One thought of Flaubert—working through all a fifty-four hour week at a relative clause. But Mrs. Aldwinkle was too enthusiastic to be able to say what followed when one had thought of Flaubert.

'Think of coal-miners for a change,' said Mr. Falx in answer. 'That's what I suggest.'

'Yes,' Lord Hovenden agreed, gravely nodding. A lot of his money came from coal. He felt particularly responsible for miners when he had time to think of them.

'Think,' said Mr. Falx in his deep voice; and he relapsed into a silence more eloquently prophetical than any speech.

For a long time nobody spoke. The wind came draughtily and in ever chillier gusts. Irene clasped her arms still tightlier over her breast; she shivered, she yawned with cold. Mrs. Aldwinkle felt the shaking of the young body that leaned against her knees. She herself was cold too; but after what she had said to Cardan and the others it was impossible for her to go indoors yet awhile. She felt, in consequence, annoyed with Irene for shivering. 'Do stop,' she said crossly. 'It's only a stupid habit. Like a little dog that shivers even in front of the fire.'

'All ve same,' said Lord Hovenden, coming to Irene's defence, 'it is getting raver cold.'

'Well, if you find it so,' retorted Mrs. Aldwinkle, with overwhelming sarcasm, 'you'd better go in and ask them to light a fire.'

It was nearly midnight before Mrs. Aldwinkle finally gave the word to go indoors.

CHAPTER VII

To say good-night definitely and for the last time was a thing which Mrs. Aldwinkle found most horribly difficult. With those two fatal words she pronounced sentence of death on yet another day (on yet another, and the days were so few now, so agonizingly brief); she pronounced it also, temporarily at least, on herself. For, the formula once finally uttered, there was nothing for her to do but creep away out of the light and bury herself in the black unconsciousness of sleep. Six hours, eight hours would be stolen from her and never given back. And what marvellous things might not be happening while she was lying dead between the sheets! Extraordinary happinesses might present themselves and, finding her asleep and deaf to their calling, pass on. Or some one, perhaps, would be saying the one supremely important, revealing, apocalyptic thing that she had been waiting all her life to hear. 'There!' she could imagine somebody winding up, 'that's the secret of the Universe. What a pity poor Lilian should have gone to bed. She would have loved to hear it.' Good-night—it was like parting with a shy lover who had not yet ventured to declare himself. A minute more and he would speak, would reveal himself the unique soul-mate. Good-night, and he would remain for ever merely diffident little Mr. Jones. Must she part with this day too, before it was transfigured?

Good-night. Every evening she put off the saying of it as long as she possibly could. It was generally half-past one or two before she could bring herself to leave the drawing-room. And even then the words were not finally spoken. For on the threshold of her bed-chamber she would halt, desperately renewing the conversation with whichever of her guests had happened to light her upstairs. Who knew? Perhaps in these last five minutes, in the intimacy, in the nocturnal silence, the important thing really would be said. The five minutes often lengthened themselves out to forty, and still

Mrs. Aldwinkle stood there, desperately putting off and putting off the moment when she would have to pronounce the sentence of death.

When there was nobody else to talk to, she had to be content with the company of Irene, who always, when she herself had undressed, came back in her dressing-gown to help Mrs. Aldwinkle —since it would have been unfair to keep a maid up to such late hours—make ready for the night. Not that little Irene was particularly likely to utter the significant word or think the one apocalyptic thought. Though of course one never knew : out of the mouths of babes and sucklings . . . And in any case, talking with Irene, who was a dear child and so devoted, was better than definitely condemning oneself to bed.

To-night, it was one o'clock before Mrs. Aldwinkle made a move towards the door. Miss Thriplow and Mr. Falx, protesting that they too were sleepy, accompanied her. And like an attendant shadow, Irene silently rose when her aunt rose and silently walked after her. Half-way across the room Mrs. Aldwinkle halted and turned round. Formidable she was, a tragedy queen in coral-red velvet. Her little white muslin mirage halted too. Less patient, Mr. Falx and Miss Thriplow moved on towards the door.

' You must all come to bed soon, you know,' she said, addressing herself to the three men who remained at the further end of the room in a tone at once imperious and cajoling. ' I simply won't allow you, Cardan, to keep those poor young men out of their beds to all hours of the night. Poor Calamy has been travelling all day. And Hovenden needs all the sleep, at his age, that he can get.' Mrs. Aldwinkle took it hardly that any of her guests should be awake and talking while she was lying dead in the tomb of sleep. ' *Poor* Calamy ! ' she pathetically exclaimed, as though it were a case of cruelty to animals. She felt herself filled, all at once, with an enormous and maternal solicitude for this young man.

' Yes, poor Calamy ! ' Mr. Cardan repeated, twinkling. ' Out of pure sympathy I was suggesting that we should drink a pint or two of red wine before going to bed. There's nothing like it for making one sleep.'

Mrs. Aldwinkle turned her bright blue eyes on Calamy, smiled her sweetest and most piercing smile. 'Do come,' she said. 'Do.' She extended her hand in a clumsy and inexpressive gesture. 'And you, Hovenden,' she added, almost despairingly.

Hovenden looked uncomfortably from Mr. Cardan to Calamy, hoping that one or other of them would answer for him.

'We shan't be long,' said Calamy. 'The time to drink a glass of wine, that's all. I'm not a bit tired, you know. And Cardan's suggestion of Chianti is very tempting.'

'Ah well,' said Mrs. Aldwinkle, 'if you prefer a glass of wine . . .' She turned away with a sad indignation and rustled off towards the door, sweeping the tiled floor with the train of her velvet dress. Mr. Falx and Miss Thriplow, who had been linger-ing impatiently near the door, drew back in order that she might make her exit in full majesty. With a face that looked very gravely out of the little window in her bell of copper hair, Irene followed. The door closed behind them.

Calamy turned to Mr. Cardan. 'If I prefer a glass of wine?' he repeated on a note of interrogation. 'But prefer it to what? She made it sound as if I had had to make a momentous and eternal choice between her and a pint of Chianti—and had chosen the Chianti. It passes my understanding.'

'Ah, but then you don't know Lilian as well as I do,' said Mr. Cardan. 'And now, let's go and hunt out that flask and some glasses in the dining-room.'

Half-way up the stairs—they were a grand and solemn flight sloping gradually upwards under a slanting tunnel of barrel vaulting —Mrs. Aldwinkle paused. 'I always think of them,' she said ecstatically, 'going up, coming down. Such a spectacle!'

'Who?' asked Mr. Falx.

' Those grand old people.'

' Oh, the tyrants.'

Mrs. Aldwinkle smiled pityingly. ' And the poets, the scholars, the philosophers, the painters, the musicians, the beautiful women. You forget those, Mr. Falx.' She raised her hand, as though summoning their spirits from the abyss. Psychical eyes might have seen a jewelled prince with a nose like an ant-eater's slowly descending between obsequious human hedges. Behind him a company of buffoons and little hunch-backed dwarfs, stepping cautiously, sidelong, from stair to stair. . . .

' I forget nothing,' said Mr. Falx. ' But I think tyrants are too high a price to pay.'

Mrs. Aldwinkle sighed and resumed her climbing. ' What a queer fellow Calamy is, don't you think ? ' she said, addressing herself to Miss Thriplow. Mrs. Aldwinkle, who liked discussing other people's characters and who prided herself on her perspicacity and her psychological intuition, found almost everybody ' queer,' even, when she thought it worth while discussing her, little Irene. She liked to think that every one she knew was tremendously complicated ; had strange and improbable motives for his simplest actions, was moved by huge, dark passions ; cultivated secret vices ; in a word, was larger than life and a good deal more interesting. ' What did you think of him, Mary ? '

' Very intelligent,' thought Miss Thriplow.

' Oh, of course, of course,' Mrs. Aldwinkle agreed almost impatiently ; that wasn't anything much to talk about. ' But one hears odd stories of his amorous tastes, you know.' The party halted at the door of Mrs. Aldwinkle's room. ' Perhaps that was one of the reasons,' she went on mysteriously, ' why he went travelling all that time—right away from civilization. . . .' On such a theme a conversation might surely be almost indefinitely protracted ; the moment for uttering the final, fatal good-night had not yet come.

Downstairs in the great saloon the three men were sitting over their red wine. Mr. Cardan had already twice refilled his glass. Calamy was within sight of the bottom of his first tumbler; young Lord Hovenden's was still more than half full. He was not a very accomplished drinker and was afraid of being sick if he swallowed too much of this young and generous brew.

'Bored, you're just bored. That's all it is,' Mr. Cardan was saying. He looked at Calamy over the top of his glass and took another sip, as though to his health. 'You haven't met any one of late who took your fancy; that's all. Unless, of course, it's a case of catarrh in the bile ducts.'

'It's neither,' said Calamy, smiling.

'Or perhaps it's the first great climacteric. You don't happen to be thirty-five, I suppose? Five times seven—a most formidable age. Though not quite so serious as sixty-three. That's the grand climacteric.' Mr. Cardan shook his head. 'Thank the Lord, I got past it without dying, or joining the Church of Rome, or getting married. Thank the Lord; but you?'

'I'm thirty-three,' said Calamy.

'A most harmless time of life. Then it's just boredom. You'll meet some little ravishment and all the zest will return.'

Young Lord Hovenden laughed in a very ventriloquial, man-of-the-worldly fashion.

Calamy shook his head. 'But I don't really want it to return,' he said. 'I don't want to succumb to any more little ravishments. It's too stupid; it's too childish. I used to think that there was something rather admirable and enviable about being an *homme à bonnes fortunes*. Don Juan has an honoured place in literature; it's thought only natural that a Casanova should complacently boast of his successes. I accepted the current view, and when I was lucky in love—and I've always been only too deplorably fortunate—I used to think the more highly of myself.'

'We have all thought the same,' said Mr. Cardan. 'The weakness is a pardonable one.'

Lord Hovenden nodded and took a sip of wine to show that he entirely agreed with the last speaker.

' Pardonable, no doubt,' said Calamy. ' But when one comes to think it over, not very reasonable. For, after all, there 's nothing really to be very proud of, there 's nothing very much to boast about. Consider first of all the other heroes who have had the same sort of successes—more notable, very probably, and more numerous than one 's own. Consider them. What do you see ? Rows of insolent grooms and pugilists ; leather-faced ruffians and disgusting old satyrs ; louts with curly hair and no brains, and cunning little pimps like weasels ; soft-palmed young epicenes and hairy gladiators —a vast army composed of the most odious specimens of humanity. Is one to be proud of belonging to their numbers ? '

' Why not ? ' asked Mr. Cardan. ' One should always thank God for whatever native talents one possesses. If your talent happens to lie in the direction of higher mathematics, praise God ; and if in the direction of seduction, praise God just the same. And thanking God, when one comes to examine the process a little closely, is very much the same as boasting or being proud. I see no harm in boasting a little of one's Casanovesque capacities. You young men are always so damned intolerant. You won't allow any one to go to heaven, or hell, or nowhere, whichever the case may be, by any road except the one you happen to approve of. . . . You should take a leaf out of the Indians' book. The Indians calculate that there are eighty-four thousand different types of human beings, each with its own way of getting through life. They probably underestimate.'

Calamy laughed. ' I only speak for my type,' he said.

' And Hovenden and I for ours,' said Mr. Cardan. ' Don't we, Hovenden ? '

' Oh yes. Yes, of course,' Lord Hovenden answered ; and for some reason he blushed.

' Proceed,' said Mr. Cardan, refilling his glass.

'Well then,' Calamy went on, 'belonging to the species I do belong to, I can't take much satisfaction in these successes. The more so when I consider their nature. For either you 're in love with the woman or you aren't ; either you 're carried away by your inflamed imagination (for, after all, the person you 're really violently in love with is always your own invention and the wildest of fancies) or by your senses and your intellectual curiosity. If you aren't in love, it 's a mere experiment in applied physiology, with a few psychological investigations thrown in to make it a little more interesting. But if you are, it means that you become enslaved, involved, dependent on another human being in a way that 's positively disgraceful, and the more disgraceful the more there is in you to be enslaved and involved.'

'It wasn't Browning's opinion,' said Mr. Cardan.

> 'The woman yonder, there 's no use in life
> But just to obtain her.'

'Browning was a fool,' said Calamy.

But Lord Hovenden was silently of opinion that Browning was quite right. He thought of Irene's face, looking out of the little window in the copper bell.

'Browning belonged to another species,' Mr. Cardan corrected.

'A foolish species, I insist,' said Calamy.

'Well, to tell the truth,' Mr. Cardan admitted, closing his winking eye a little further, 'I secretly agree with you about that. I 'm not really as entirely tolerant as I should like to be.'

Calamy was frowning pensively over his own affairs, and without discussing the greater or less degree of Mr. Cardan's tolerance he went on. 'The question is, at the end of it all : what 's the way out ? what 's to be done about it ? For it 's obvious, as you say, that the little ravishments will turn up again. And appetite grows with fasting. And philosophy, which knows very well how to deal with past and future temptations, always seems to break down before the present, the immediate ones.'

'Happily,' said Mr. Cardan. 'For, when all is said, is there a better indoor sport ? Be frank with me ; *is* there ? '

'Possibly not,' said Calamy, while young Lord Hovenden smiled at Mr. Cardan's last remark, but unenthusiastically, in a rather painful indecision between amusement and horror. 'But the point is, aren't there better occupations for a man of sense than indoor sports, even the best of indoor sports ? '

'No,' said Mr. Cardan, with decision.

'For you, perhaps, there mayn't be. But it seems to me,' Calamy went on, 'that I'm beginning to have had enough of sports, whether indoor or out-of-door. I'd like to find some more serious occupation.'

'But that's easier said than done.' Mr. Cardan shook his head. 'For members of our species it's precious hard to find any occupation that seems entirely serious. Eh ? '

Calamy laughed, rather mournfully. 'That's true,' he said. 'But at the same time the sports begin to seem rather an outrage on one's human dignity. Rather immoral, I would say, if the word weren't so absurd.'

'Not at all absurd, I assure you, when used as you use it.' Mr. Cardan twinkled more and more genially over the top of his glass. 'As long as you don't talk about moral laws and all that sort of thing there's no absurdity. For, it's obvious, there are no moral laws. There are social customs on the one hand, and there are individuals with their individual feelings and moral reactions on the other. What's immoral in one man may not matter in another. Almost nothing, for example, is immoral for me. Positively, you know, I can do anything and yet remain respectable in my own eyes, and in the eyes of others not merely wonderfully decent, but even noble.

> Ah, what avail the loaded dice ?
> Ah, what the tubs of wine ?
> What every weakness, every vice ?
> Tom Cardan, all were thine.

I won't bore you with the rest of this epitaph which I composed for myself some little time ago. Suffice to say that I point out in the two subsequent stanzas that these things availed absolutely nothing and that, *malgré tout*, I remained the honest, sober, pure and high-minded man that every one always instinctively recognizes me to be.' Mr. Cardan emptied his glass and reached out once more for the fiasco.

' You 're fortunate,' said Calamy. ' It 's not all of us whose personalities have such a natural odour of sanctity that they can disinfect our septic actions and render them morally harmless. When I do something stupid or dirty I can't help feeling that it is stupid or dirty. My soul lacks virtues to make it wise or clean. And I can't dissociate myself from what I do. I wish I could. One does such a devilish number of stupid things. Things one doesn't want to do. If only one could be a hedonist and only do what was pleasant ! But to be a hedonist one must be wholly rational ; there 's no such thing as a genuine hedonist, there never has been. Instead of doing what one wants to do or what would give one pleasure, one drifts through existence doing exactly the opposite, most of the time—doing what one has no desire to do, following insane promptings that lead one, fully conscious, into every sort of discomfort, misery, boredom and remorse. Some-times,' Calamy went on, sighing, ' I positively regret the time I spent in the army during the war. Then, at any rate, there was no question of doing what one liked ; there was no liberty, no choice. One did what one was told and that was all. Now I 'm free ; I have every opportunity for doing exactly what I like—and I consistently do what I don't like.'

' But do you know exactly what you do like ? ' asked Mr. Cardan.

Calamy shrugged his shoulders. ' Not exactly,' he said. ' I suppose I should say reading, and satisfying my curiosity about things, and thinking. But about what, I don't feel perfectly certain. I don't like running after women, I don't like wasting my time in futile social intercourse, or in the pursuit of what is technically known as pleasure. And yet for some reason and quite against my will I find myself passing the greater part of my time immersed in precisely these occupations. It's an obscure kind of insanity.'

Young Lord Hovenden, who knew that he liked dancing and desired Irene Aldwinkle more than anything in the world, found all this a little incomprehensible. 'I can't see what vere is to prevent a man from doing what he wants to do. Except,' he qualified, remembering the teaching of Mr. Falx, 'economic necessity.'

'And himself,' added Mr. Cardan.

'And what's the most depressing of all,' Calamy went on, without paying attention to the interruption, 'is the feeling that one will go on like this for ever, in the teeth of every effort to stop. I sometimes wish I weren't externally free. For then at any rate I should have something to curse at, for getting in my way, other than my own self. Yes, positively, I sometimes wish I were a navvy.'

'You wouldn't if you had ever been one,' said Lord Hovenden, gravely and with a knowing air of speaking from personal experience.

Calamy laughed. 'You're perfectly right,' he said, and drained his glass. 'Shouldn't we think of going to bed?'

CHAPTER VIII

To Irene fell the privilege every evening of brushing her aunt's hair. For her these midnight moments were the most precious in the day. True, it was sometimes an agony for her to keep awake and the suppression of yawns was always painful; three years of incessant practice had not yet accustomed her to her Aunt Lilian's late hours. Aunt Lilian used to twit her sometimes on her childish longing for sleep; at other times she used to insist, very solicitously, that Irene should rest after lunch and go to bed at ten. The teasing made Irene feel ashamed of her babyishness; the solicitude made her protest that she wasn't a baby, that she was never tired and could easily do with five or six hours' sleep a night. The important thing, she had found, was not to be seen yawning by Aunt Lilian and always to look fresh and lively. If Aunt Lilian noticed nothing there was neither teasing nor solicitude.

But in any case, every inconvenience was paid for a thousand times by the delights of these confidential conversations in front of the dressing-table mirror. While the young girl brushed and brushed away at the long tresses of pale golden-brown hair, Mrs. Aldwinkle, her eyes shut, and with an expression of beatitude on her face—for she took a cat's pleasure in the brushing—would talk, spasmodically, in broken sentences, of the events of the day, of her guests, of the people they had met; or of her own past, of plans for the future—hers or Irene's—of love. On all these subjects Mrs. Aldwinkle spoke intimately, confidentially, without reserve. Feeling that she was being treated by her Aunt Lilian as entirely grown-up and almost as an equal, Irene was proud and grateful. Without deliberately setting out to complete the subjugation of her niece, Mrs. Aldwinkle had discovered, in those midnight conversations, the most perfect means for achieving this end. If she talked like this to Irene, it was merely because she felt the need of talking intimately to some one, and because there

73

was nobody else to talk to. Incidentally, however, she had contrived in the process to make the girl her slave. Made her Aunt Lilian's confidante, invested, so to speak, with a title of honour, Irene felt a gratitude which strengthened her original childish attachment to her aunt.

Meanwhile, she had learned to talk with an airy familiarity of many things concerning which young girls are supposed to be ignorant, and of which, indeed, she herself knew, except intellectually and at second hand, nothing. She had learned to be knowing and worldly wise, in the void, so to speak, and with no personal knowledge of the world. Gravely, ingenuously, she would say things that could only be uttered out of the depths of the profoundest innocence, amplifying and making embarrassingly explicit in public things that Mrs. Aldwinkle had only fragmentarily hinted at in the confidential small hours. She regarded herself as immensely mature.

To-night Mrs. Aldwinkle was in a rather gloomy, complaining mood.

' I 'm getting old,' she said, sighing, and opening her eyes for a moment to look at her image in the glass that confronted her. The image did not deny the statement. ' And yet I always feel so young.'

' That 's what really matters,' Irene declared. ' And besides, it 's nonsense ; you 're not old ; you don't look old.' In Irene's eyes, moreover, she really didn't look old.

' People don't like one any more when one gets old,' Mrs. Aldwinkle continued. ' Friends are terribly faithless. They fall away.' She sighed. ' When I think of all the friends . . .' She left the sentence unfinished.

All her life long Mrs. Aldwinkle had had a peculiar genius for breaking with her friends and lovers. Mr. Cardan was almost the sole survivor from an earlier generation of friends. From all the rest she had parted, and she had parted with a light heart. It

74

had seemed easy to her, when she was younger, to make new friends in place of the old. Potential friends, she thought, were to be found everywhere, every day. But now she was beginning to doubt whether the supply was, after all, so inexhaustible as she had once supposed. People of her own age, she found, were already set fast in the little social worlds they had made for themselves. And people of the younger generation seemed to find it hard to believe that she felt, in her heart, just as young as they did. They mostly treated her with the rather distant politeness which one accords to a stranger and an elder person.

' I think people are horrid,' said Irene, giving a particularly violent sweep with the hair-brush to emphasize her indignation.

' You won't be faithless ? ' asked Mrs. Aldwinkle.

Irene bent over and, for all answer, kissed her on the forehead. Mrs. Aldwinkle opened her glittering blue eyes and looked up at her, smiling, as she did so, that siren smile that, for Irene, was still as fascinating as it had ever been.

' If only everybody were like my little Irene ! ' Mrs. Aldwinkle let her head fall forward and once more closed her eyes. There was a silence. ' What are you sighing about in that heart-breaking way ? ' she suddenly asked.

Irene's blush ran tingling up into her temples and disappeared under the copper-coloured fringe. ' Oh, nothing,' she said, with an off-handedness that expressed the depth of her guilty embarrassment. That deep intake of breath, that brief and passionate expiry were not the components of a sigh. She had been yawning with her mouth shut.

But Mrs. Aldwinkle, with her bias towards the romantic, did not suspect the truth. ' Nothing, indeed ! ' she echoed incredulously. ' Why, it was the noise of the wind blowing through the cracks of a broken heart. I never heard such a sigh.' She looked at the reflection of Irene's face in the mirror. ' And you 're blushing like a peony. What is it ? '

'But it's nothing, I tell you,' Irene declared, speaking almost in a tone of irritation. She was annoyed with herself for having yawned so ineptly and blushed so pointlessly, rather than with her aunt. She immersed herself more than ever deeply in her brushing, hoping and praying that Mrs. Aldwinkle would drop the subject.

But Mrs. Aldwinkle was implacable in her tactlessness. 'I never heard anything that sounded so love-sick,' she said, smiling archly into the looking-glass. Mrs. Aldwinkle's humorous sallies had a way of falling ponderously, like bludgeon strokes, on the objects of her raillery. One never knew, when she was being sprightly, whether to feel sorrier for the victim or for Mrs. Aldwinkle herself. For though the victim might get hard knocks, the spectacle of Mrs. Aldwinkle laboriously exerting herself to deliver them was sadly ludicrous; one wished, for her sake, for the sake of the whole human race, that she would desist. But she never did. Mrs. Aldwinkle always carried all her jokes to the foreseen end, and generally far further than was foreseeable by any one less ponderously minded than herself. 'It was like a whale sighing!' she went on with a frightful playfulness. 'It must be a grand passion of the largest size. Who is it? Who is it?' She raised her eyebrows, she smiled with what seemed to her, as she studied it in the glass, a most wickedly sly but charming smile—like a smile in a comedy by Congreve, it occurred to her.

'But, Aunt Lilian,' protested Irene, almost in despair, almost in tears, 'it was nothing, I tell you.' At moments like this she could almost find it in her to hate Aunt Lilian. 'As a matter of fact, I was only . . .' She was going to blurt it out courageously; she was just going to tell Aunt Lilian—at the risk of a teasing or an almost equally unwelcome solicitude: either were better than this—that she had been merely yawning. But Mrs. Aldwinkle, still relentlessly pursuing her fun, interrupted her.

'But I guess who it is,' she said, wagging a forefinger at the glass. ' I guess. I 'm not such a blind stupid old auntie as you think. You imagine I haven't noticed. Silly child ! Did she think I didn't see that he was very assiduous and that she rather liked it ? Did she think her stupid old auntie was blind ? '

Irene blushed again ; the tears came into her eyes. ' But who are you talking about ? ' she said in a voice that she had to make a great effort to keep from breaking and trembling out of control.

' What an innocent ! ' mocked Mrs. Aldwinkle, still very Congreve. And at this point—earlier than was usual with her on these occasions—she had mercy and consented to put poor Irene out of her agony. ' Why, Hovenden,' she said. ' Who else should it be ? '

' Hovenden ? ' Irene repeated with genuine surprise.

' Injured innocence ! ' Mrs. Aldwinkle momentarily renewed her trampling fun. ' But it 's sufficiently obvious,' she went on in a more natural voice. ' The poor boy follows you like a dog.'

' Me ? ' Irene had been too much preoccupied in following her Aunt Lilian to notice that she in her turn was being followed.

' Now don't pretend,' said Mrs. Aldwinkle. ' It 's so stupid pretending. Much better to be frank and straightforward. Admit, now, that you like him.'

Irene admitted. ' Yes, of course I like him. But not . . . not in any special way. I 'd really not thought of him like that.'

A shade contemptuously, benevolently amused, Mrs. Aldwinkle smiled. She forgot her depression, forgot her causes of personal complaint against the universal order of things. Absorbed in the uniquely interesting subject, in the sole and proper study of mankind, she was once more happy. Love—it was the only thing. Even Art, compared with it, hardly existed. Mrs. Aldwinkle was almost as much interested in other people's love as in her own. She wanted every one to love, constantly and complicatedly. She liked to bring people together, to foster tender feelings, to watch the development of passion, to assist—when it happened ; and Mrs. Aldwinkle was always rather disappointed when it did not—

at the tragic catastrophe. And then, when the first love, growing old, had lingeringly or violently died, there was the new love to think of, to arrange, to foster, to watch ; and then the third, the fourth. . . . One must always follow the spontaneous motions of the heart ; it is the divine within us that stirs in the heart. And one must worship Eros so reverently that one can never be content with anything but the most poignant, most passionate manifestations of his power. To be content with a love that has turned in the course of time to mere affection, kindliness and quiet comprehension is almost to blaspheme against the name of Eros. Your true lover, thought Mrs. Aldwinkle, leaves the old, paralytic love and turns whole-heartedly to the young passion.

'What a goose you are !' said Mrs. Aldwinkle. 'I sometimes wonder,' she went on, 'whether you 're capable of being in love at all, you 're so uncomprehending, so cold.'

Irene protested with all the energy of which she was capable. One could not have lived as long as she had in Mrs. Aldwinkle's company without regarding the imputation of coldness, of insensitiveness to passion, as the most damning of all possible impeachments. It was better to be accused of being a murderess —particularly if it were a case of *crime passionnel*. 'I don't know how you say that,' she said indignantly. 'I 'm always in love.' Had there not been Peter, and Jacques, and Mario ?

'You may think you have,' said Mrs. Aldwinkle contemptuously, forgetting that it was she herself who had persuaded Irene that she was in love. 'But it was more imagination than the real thing. Some women are born like that.' She shook her head. 'And they die like that.' One might have inferred from Mrs. Aldwinkle's words and the tone of her voice that Irene was a superannuated spinster of forty, proved conclusively, after twenty years of accumulated evidence, to be incapable of anything remotely resembling an amorous passion.

Irene made no answer, but went on brushing her aunt's hair.

Mrs. Aldwinkle's aspersions were particularly wounding to her. She wished that she could do something startling to prove their baselessness. Something spectacular.

'And I've always thought Hovenden an extremely nice boy,' Mrs. Aldwinkle continued, with the air of pursuing an argument. She talked on. Irene listened and went on brushing.

CHAPTER IX

IN the silence and solitude of her room, Miss Thriplow sat up for a long time, pen in hand, in front of an open note-book. 'Darling Jim,' she wrote, 'darling Jim. To-day you came back to me so suddenly and unexpectedly that I could almost have cried aloud in front of all those people. Was it an accident that I picked that stiff leaf from Apollo's tree and crushed it to fragrance between my fingers? Or were you there? was it you who secretly whispered to the unconscious part of me, telling me to pick that leaf? I wonder; oh, I wonder and wonder. Sometimes I believe that there are no accidents, that we do nothing by chance. To-night I felt sure of it.

'But I wonder what made you want to remind me of Mr. Chigwell's little shop at Weltringham. Why did you want to make me see you sitting in the barber's chair, so stiff and grown-up, with the wheel of the mechanical brush still turning overhead and Mr. Chigwell saying, "Hair's very dry, Mr. Thriplow"? And the rubber driving band used always to remind me . . .' Miss Thriplow recorded the simile of the wounded snake which had first occurred to her this evening. There was no particular reason why she should have antedated the conceit and attributed its invention to her childhood. It was just a question of literary tact; it seemed more interesting if one said that it had been made up when one was a child; that was all. 'I ask myself whether there is any particular significance in this reminder. Or perhaps it's just that you find me neglectful and unremembering—poor darling, darling Jim—and take whatever opportunity offers of reminding me that you existed, that you still exist. Forgive me, Jim. Everybody forgets. We should all be kind and good and unselfish if we always remembered—remembered that other people are just as much alive and individual and complicated as we are, remembered that everybody can be just as easily hurt, that everybody needs love just as much, that the only visible reason why we exist in the world is to love and be loved. But that's no excuse for me. It's no excuse for any one to say that other people are just as bad. I ought to remember more. I oughtn't to let my mind be choked with weeds. It's not only the memory of you that the weeds choke; it's everything that's best and most delicate and finest. Perhaps you reminded me of Mr. Chigwell and the bay rum in order to remind me at the same time to love more, and admire more, and sympathize more, and be more aware. Darling Jim.'

She put down her pen, and looking out through the open window at the starry sky she tried to think of him, tried to think of death. But it was difficult to think of death. It was difficult, she found, to keep the mind uninterruptedly on the idea of extinction, of non-life instead of life, of nothingness. In books one reads about sages meditating. She herself had often tried to meditate. But somehow it never seemed to come to much. All sorts of little irrelevant thoughts kept coming into her head. There was no focussing death, no keeping it steadily under the mind's eye. In the end she found herself reading through what she had written putting in a stop here and there, correcting slips in the style, where it seemed to be too formal, too made-up, insufficiently spontaneous and unsuitable to the secret diary.

At the end of the last paragraph she added another 'darling Jim,' and she repeated the words to herself, aloud, again and again. The exercise produced its usual effect; she felt the tears coming into her eyes.

The Quakers pray as the spirit moves them; but to let oneself be moved by the spirit is an arduous business. Kindlier and more worldly churches, with a feeling for human weakness, provide their worshippers with rituals, litanies, beads and prayer wheels.

'Darling Jim, darling Jim.' Miss Thriplow had found the form of words for her worship. 'Darling Jim.' The tears did her good; she felt better, kinder, softer. And then, suddenly, she seemed to be listening to herself from outside. 'Darling Jim.' But did she really care at all ? Wasn't it all a comedy, all a pretence ? He had died so long ago; he had nothing to do with her now. Why should she care or remember ? And all this systematic thinking about him, this writing of things in a secret diary devoted to his memory—wasn't all that merely for the sake of keeping her emotions in training ? Wasn't she deliberately scratching her heart to make it bleed, and then writing stories with the red fluid ?

Miss Thriplow put away the thoughts as soon as they occurred to her : put them aside indignantly. They were monstrous thoughts, lying thoughts.

She picked up her pen again and wrote, very quickly, as though she were writing an exorcizing spell and the sooner it had been put on paper the sooner the evil thoughts would vanish.

'Do you remember, Jim, that time we went out in the canoe together and nearly got drowned ? . . .'

PART II

FRAGMENTS *from the* AUTOBIOGRAPHY
of FRANCIS CHELIFER

Chapter I

OLD gentlemen in clubs were not more luxuriously cradled than I along the warm Tyrrhenian. Arms outstretched, like a live cross, I floated face upwards on that blue and tepid sea. The sun beat down on me, turning the drops on my face and chest to salt. My head was pillowed in the unruffled water; my limbs and body dimpled the surface of a pellucid mattress thirty feet thick and cherishingly resilient through all its thickness, down to the sandy bed on which it was spread. One might lie paralysed here for a life-time and never get a bedsore.

The sky above me was filmy with the noonday heat. The mountains, when I turned towards the land to look for them, had almost vanished behind a veil of gauze. But the Grand Hotel, on the other hand, though not perhaps quite so grand as it appeared in its illustrated prospectus—for there the front door was forty feet high and four tall acrobats standing on one another's shoulders could not have reached to the sills of the ground-floor windows—the Grand Hotel made no attempt to conceal itself; the white villas glared out unashamedly from their groves of pines; and in front of them, along the tawny beach, I could see the bathing huts, the striped umbrellas, the digging children, the bathers splashing and wallowing in the hot shallows—half-naked men like statues of copper, girls in bright tunics, little boiled shrimps instead of little boys, and sleek ponderous walruses with red heads, who were the matrons in their rubber caps and their wet black bathing garments. Here and there over the surface of the sea moved what the natives called *patini*—catamarans made of a pair of boxed-in pontoons joined together near the ends and with a high seat for the rower in the middle. Slowly, trailing behind them as they went loud wafts of Italian gallantry, giggles and song, they crawled across the flat blueness. Sometimes, at the head of its white wake, its noise and its stink, a motor boat would pass, and suddenly my transparent mattress would rock beneath me, as the waves of its passage lifted me and let me drop and lifted me up again, more and ever more languidly, till all was once more smooth.

So much for that. The description, as I see now that I come to re-read it, is not inelegant. For though I may not have played a hand of Bridge since I was eight and have never learned Mah Jong, I can claim at least to have studied the rules of style. I have learned the art of writing well, which is the art of saying nothing elaborately. I have acquired all the literary accomplishments. But then, if I may say so without fatuity, I also have a talent. ' Nothing profits more than self-esteem founded on just and right.' I have Milton on my side to justify me in my assertion. When I write well, it is not merely another way of writing badly about nothing. In this respect my effusions differ a little from those of my cultured colleagues. I occasionally have something to say, and I find that the elegant but florid saying of it is as easy to me as walking. Not, of course, that I attach the slightest importance to that. I might have as much to say as La Rochefoucauld and as much facility for saying it as Shelley. But what of that ? It would be great art, you say. No doubt ; but what of *that* ? It 's a queer prejudice, this one of ours in favour of art. Religion, patriotism, the moral order, humanitarianism, social reform—we have all of us, I imagine, dropped all those overboard long ago. But we still cling pathetically to art. Quite unreasonably ; for the thing has far less reason for existence than most of the objects of worship we have got rid of, is utterly senseless, indeed, without their support and justification. Art for art's sake—halma for halma's sake. It is time to smash the last and silliest of the idols. My friends, I adjure you, put away the ultimate and sweetest of the inebriants and wake up at last completely sober—among the dustbins at the bottom of the area steps.

This little digression will suffice, I hope, to show that I labour, while writing, under no illusions. I do not suppose that anything I do has the slightest importance, and if I take so much pains in imparting beauty and elegance to these autobiographical fragments, it is chiefly from force of habit. I have practised the art of literature so long that it comes natural to me to take the pains I have always taken. You may ask why I write at all, if I regard the process as being without importance ? It is a pertinent question. Why do you do this inconsistent thing ? I can only plead weakness in justification. On principle I disapprove of writing ; on principle I desire to live brutishly like any other ordinary human being. The flesh is willing, but the spirit is weak. I confess I grow bored. I pine for amusements other than those legitimate distractions offered by the cinema and the Palais de Danse. I struggle, I try to resist the temptation ; but in the end I succumb. I read a page of Wittgenstein, I play a little Bach ; I write a poem, a few aphorisms, a fable, a fragment of auto-biography. I write with care, earnestly, with passion even, just as if there were some point in what I were doing, just as if it were important for the world to know my thoughts, just as if I had a soul to save by giving expression to them. But I am well aware, of course, that all these delightful hypotheses are inadmissible. In reality I write as I do merely to kill time and amuse a mind that is still, in spite of all my efforts, a prey to intellectual self-indulgence. I look forward to a placid middle age when, having finally over-come the old Adam in me, finally quenched all the extravagant spiritual cravings, I shall be able to settle down in tranquillity to that life of the flesh, that natural human existence which still, I fear, seems to me so forbidding, so austerely monotonous, so tedious. I have not yet attained to that blessed state. Hence these divagations into art ; let me beg forgiveness for them. And above all, let me implore you once more not to imagine that I attach the slightest importance to them. My vanity would be hurt if I thought you did.

Poor Mrs. Aldwinkle, for example—there was some one who could never believe that I was not an art-for-arter. ' But Chelifer,' she used to say to me in her aimed, intent, breathless way, ' how *can* you blaspheme like that against your own talent ? ' And I would put on my most Egyptian air—I have always been accused of looking like an Egyptian sculpture—my most Sphingine smile, and say : ' But I am a democrat ; how can I allow my talent to blaspheme against my humanity ? '—or something enigmatic of that kind. Poor Mrs. Aldwinkle ! But I run on too fast. I have begun to talk of Mrs. Aldwinkle and you do not know who Mrs. Aldwinkle is. Nor did I, for that matter, as I reclined that morning along the soft resilient water—I knew no more, then, than her name ; who does not ? Mrs. Aldwinkle the salonnière, the hostess, the giver of literary parties and agapes of lions—is she not classical ? a household word ? a familiar quotation ? Of course. But in the flesh, till that moment, I had never seen her. Not through any lack of exertions on her part. For only a few months before, a telegram had arrived for me at my publisher's :

PRINCE PAPADIAMANTOPOULOS JUST ARRIVED MOST ANXIOUS TO KNOW BEST LITERARY ARTISTIC INTELLECTUAL SOCIETY IN LONDON COULD YOU DINE MEET HIM THURSDAY EIGHT FIFTEEN 112 BERKELEY SQUARE LILIAN ALDWINKLE.' In this telegraphic form, and couched in those terms, the invitation had certainly seemed alluring. But a little judicious inquiry showed me that the prospect was not really quite so attractive as it appeared. For Prince Papadia-mantopoulos turned out, in spite of his wonderfully promising title and name, to be a perfectly serious intellectual like the rest of us. More serious indeed ; for I discovered, to my horror, that he was a first-class geologist and could understand the differential calculus. Among the other guests were to be at least three decent writers and one painter. And Mrs. Aldwinkle herself was rumoured to be quite well educated and not entirely a fool. I filled up the reply-paid form and took it to the nearest post office. ' MUCH REGRET NEVER DINE OUT EXCEPT IN LENT FRANCIS CHELIFER.' During Lent I confidently expected to receive another invitation. I was relieved, however, and a little disappointed, to hear no more from Mrs. Aldwinkle. I should have liked her to make, in vain, a further effort to lure me from my allegiance to Lady Giblet.

Ah, those evenings at Lady Giblet's—I never miss a single one if I can help it. The vulgarity, ignorance and stupidity of the hostess, the incredible second-rateness of her mangy lions— these are surely unique. And then those camp-followers of the arts, those delicious Bohemians who regard their ability to appreciate the paintings of the cubists and the music of Stravinsky as a sufficient justification for helping themselves freely to one another's wives —nowhere can you see such brilliant specimens of the type as at Lady Giblet's. And the conversations one hears within those marble halls—nowhere, surely, are pretensions separated from justifying facts by a vaster gulf. Nowhere can you hear the ignorant, the illogical, the incapable of thought talking so glibly about things of which they have not the slightest understanding. And then you should hear them boasting parenthetically, as they express an imbecile's incoherent opinion, of their own clear-headed-ness, their modern outlook, their ruthless scientific intelligence. Surely you can find nothing so perfect in its kind as at Lady Giblet's —I at least know of nothing more complete. At Mrs. Aldwinkle's one might very likely hear a serious conversation ; never by any chance in the salon of *my* choice.

But that morning in the blue Tyrrhenian was the last of my life to be passed beyond the pale of Mrs. Aldwinkle's acquaintance-ship ; it was also as nearly as possible the first of my future life. Fate seemed that morning to be in doubt whether to extinguish me completely or merely to make me acquainted with Mrs. Ald-

winkle. Fortunately, as I like to think, it chose the latter alternative. But I anticipate.

I first saw Mrs. Aldwinkle on this particular morning without
knowing who she was. From where I was lying on my mattress
of blue brine I noticed a heavily laden *patino* bearing slowly down
upon me from the shore. Perched high on the rower's bench a
tall young man was toiling languidly at the oars. His back against
the bench, his hairy legs stretched out along the prow of one of the
pontoons, sat a thick-set oldish man with a red face and short
white hair. The bow of the other pontoon accommodated two
women. The elder and larger of them sat in front, trailing her
legs in the water ; she was dressed in a kilted bathing costume of
flame-coloured silk and her hair was tied up in a pink bandana
handkerchief. Immediately behind her there squatted, her knees
drawn up to her chin, a very youthful slender little creature in a
black maillot. In one of her hands she held a green parasol with
which she kept off the sunlight from her elder companion. Within
the cylinder of greenish shadow the pink and flame-coloured lady,
whom I afterwards learnt to be Mrs. Aldwinkle herself, looked
like a Chinese lantern lighted in a conservatory ; and when an
accidental movement of the young girl's umbrella allowed the
sunlight for a moment to touch her face, one could imagine that
the miracle of the raising of Lazarus was being performed before
one's eyes—for the green and corpse-like hue suddenly left the
features, the colours of health, a little inflamed by the reflections
from the bathing dress, seemed to rush back. The dead lived.
But only for an instant ; for the solicitous care of the young girl
soon reversed the miracle. The sunshade swung back into position, the penumbra of the greenhouse enveloped the glowing
lamp and the living face once more became ghastly, as though it
belonged to some one who had lain for three days in the tomb.

At the stern, seen clearly only when the ponderous boat was
already beginning to pass me, sat another young woman with a pale

face and large dark eyes. A tendril of almost black hair escaped from under her bathing cap and fell, like a curling whisker, down her cheek. A handsome young man with a brown face and brown muscular arms and legs sprawled along the stern of the other pontoon, smoking a cigarette.

The voices that faintly came to me from the approaching boat sounded, somehow, more familiar than those I had heard from other *vatini*. I became aware, all at once, that they were speaking English.

'The clouds,' I heard the old red-faced gentleman saying (he had just turned round, in obedience to a gesture from the Chinese lantern in the conservatory, to look at the piled-up masses of vapour that hung like another fantastic range above the real mountains), ' the clouds you so much admire are only made possible by the earth's excrementitious dust hanging in the air. There are thousands of particles to every cubic centimetre. The water vapour condenses round them in droplets sufficiently large to be visible. Hence the clouds—marvellous and celestial shapes, but with a core of dust. What a symbol of human idealism!' The melodious voice grew louder and louder as the young man dipped and dipped his oars. ' Earthy particles transfigured into heavenly forms. The heavenly forms are not self-existent, not absolute. Dust writes these vast characters across the sky.'

Preserve me, I thought. Did I come to Marina di Vezza to listen to this sort of thing ?

In a voice loud but indistinct, and strangely unmusical, the Chinese lantern lady began to quote Shelley, incorrectly. ' " From peak to peak in a bridge-like . . ." ' she began, and relapsed into silence, clawing the air in search of the synonym for shape which ought to rhyme with peak. ' " Over a something sea." I think *The Cloud* is almost the loveliest of all. It 's wonderful to think that Shelley sailed in this sea. And that he was burnt only a little way off, down there.' She pointed down the coast to where, behind the haze, the interminable sea-front of Viareggio stretched away mile after mile. Faintly now one might discern the ghost of its nearest outskirts. But at evening it would emerge; clear and sharp in the sloping light, as though they had been cut from gems, Palace and Grande Bretagne, Europe (*già* Aquila Nera) and Savoia would twinkle there, majestic toys, among the innumerable lesser inns and boarding-houses, reduced at this distance to an exquisite loveliness and so pathetically small and delicate that one could almost have wept over them. At this very moment, on the other side of the curtain of haze, a hundred thousand bathers were thronging the empty beaches where Shelley's body had been committed to the fire. The pinewoods in which, riding out from Pisa, he hunted lovely thoughts through the silence and the fragrant shadows teemed now with life. Unnumbered country copulatives roamed at this moment through those glades. . . . And so forth. Style pours out of my fountain pen. In every drachm of blue-black ink a thousand *mots iustes* are implicit, like the future characteristics of a man in a piece of chromosome. I apologize.

Youth, then, at the prow and pleasure at the helm—and the flesh was so glossy under the noonday sun, the colours so blazingly bright, that I was really reminded of Etty's little ravishment—the laden boat passed slowly within a few yards of me. Stretched like a live cross on my mattress of brine I looked at them languidly through half-closed eyes. They looked at me; a blank incuriosity was on their faces—for a glimpse only, then they averted their eyes as though I had been one of those exhausted frogs one sees, after the breeding season, floating belly upwards on the surface of a pond. And yet I was what is technically known as an immortal soul. It struck me that it would have been more reasonable if they had stopped their boat and hailed me across the water. ' Good morning, stranger. How goes your soul? And what shall we do to be saved?' But on the other hand, our habit of regarding strangers as being nothing more to us than exhausted frogs probably saves a good deal of trouble.

'From cape to cape,' emended the red-faced gentleman, as they receded from me.

And very diffidently, in a soft shy voice, the solicitous young creature suggested that the something sea was a torrent sea.

'Whatever vat may be,' said the young rower, whose exertions under the broiling sun entitled him to take the professionally nautical, commonsense view about the matter.

'But it's obvious what it is,' said the Chinese lantern lady, rather contemptuously. The young man at the stern threw away his cigarette and started meditatively whistling the tune of ' *Deh, vieni alla finestra* ' from *Don Giovanni*.

There was a silence; the boat receded, stroke after stroke. The last words I heard were uttered, drawlingly and in a rather childish voice, by the young woman in the stern. 'I wish I could get brown more quickly,' she said, lifting one foot out of the water and looking at the white bare leg. 'One might have been living in a cellar. Such a dreadfully unwholesome look of blanched asparagus. Or even mushrooms,' she added pensively.

The Chinese lantern lady said something, then the red-faced man. But the conversation had ceased to be articulately audible. Soon I could hear no more; they had gone, leaving behind them, however, the name of Shelley. It was here, along these waters, that he had sailed his flimsy boat. In one hand he held his Sophocles, with the other the tiller. His eyes looked now at the small Greek letters, now to the horizon, or landwards towards the mountains and clouds. 'Port your helm, Shelley,' Captain Williams would shout. And the helm went hard over to starboard; the ship staggered, almost capsized. Then, one day, flash! the black opaque sky split right across; crash and rumble! the thunder exploded overhead and with the noise of boulders being trundled over the surface of the metal clouds, the echoes rolled about the heavens and among the mountains—'from peak to peak,' it occurred to me, adopting the Chinese lantern lady's emendation, ' from peak to peak with a gong-like squeak.' (What an infamy !) And then, with a hiss and a roar, the whirl-blast was upon them. It was all over.

Even without the Chinese lantern lady's hint I should probably have started thinking of Shelley. For to live on this coast, between the sea and the mountains, among alternate flawless calms and shattering sudden storms, is like living inside one of Shelley's poems. One walks through a transparent and phantasmagorical beauty. But for the hundred thousand bathers, the jazz band in the Grand Hotel, the unbroken front which civilization, in the form of boarding-houses, presents for miles at a time to the alien and empty sea, but for all these, one might seriously lose one's sense of reality and imagine that fancy had managed to transform itself into fact. In Shelley's days, when the coast was all but uninhabited, a man might have had some excuse for forgetting the real nature of things. Living here in an actual world practically indistinguishable from one of imagination, a man might almost be justified for indulging his fancy to the extravagant lengths to which Shelley permitted his to go.

But a man of the present generation, brought up in typical contemporary surroundings, has no justifications of this sort. A modern poet cannot permit himself the mental luxuries in which his predecessors so freely wallowed. Lying there on the water, I repeated to myself some verses, inspired by reflections like these, which I had written some few months before.

> The Holy Ghost comes sliding down
> On Ilford, Golders Green and Penge.
> His hosts infect him as they rot ;
> The victims take their just revenge.
>
> For if of old the sons of squires
> And livery stable keepers turned
> To flowers and hope, to Greece and God,
> We in our later age have learned

That we are native where we walk
Through the dim streets of Camden Town.
But hopeful still through twice-breathed air
The Holy Ghost comes shining down.

I wrote these lines, I remember, one dark afternoon in my office in Gog's Court, Fetter Lane. It is in the same office, on an almost perfectly similar afternoon, that I am writing now. The reflector outside my window reflects a faint and muddy light that has to be supplemented by electricity from within. An inveterate smell of printer's ink haunts the air. From the basement comes up the thudding and clanking of presses; they are turning out the weekly two hundred thousand copies of the 'Woman's Fiction Budget.' We are at the heart, here, of our human universe. Come, then, let us frankly admit that we are citizens of this mean city, make the worst of it resolutely and not try to escape.

To escape, whether in space or in time, you must run a great deal further now than there was any need to do a hundred years ago when Shelley boated on the Tyrrhenian and conjured up millennial visions. You must go further in space, because there are more people, more and faster vehicles. The Grand Hotel, the hundred thousand bathers, the jazz bands have introduced themselves into that Shelleian poem which is the landscape of Versilia. And the millennium which seemed in the days of Godwin not so very remote has receded further and further from us, as each Reform Bill, each victory over entrenched capitalism dashed yet another illusion to the ground. To escape, in 1924, one must go to Tibet, one must look forward to at least the year 3000; and who knows? they are probably listening-in in the Dalai Lama's palace; and it is probable that the millennial state of a thousand years hence will be millennial only because it has contrived to make slavery, for the first time, really scientific and efficient.

An escape in space, even if one contrives successfully to make one, is no real escape at all. A man may live in Tibet or among the Andes; but he cannot therefore deny that London and Paris actually exist, he cannot forget that there are such places as New York and Berlin. For the majority of contemporary human beings, London and Manchester are the rule; you may have fled to the eternal spring of Arequipa, but you are not living in what is, for the mass of human consciousness, reality.

An escape in time is no more satisfactory. You live in the radiant future, live for the future. You console yourself for the spectacle of things as they are by the thought of what they will be. And you work, perhaps, to make them be what you think they ought to be. I know all about it, I assure you. I have done it all myself—lived in a state of permanent intoxication at the thought of what was to come, working happily for a gorgeous ideal of happiness. But a little reflection suffices to show how absurd these forward lookings, these labours for the sake of what is to be, really are. For, to begin with, we have no reason to suppose that there is going to be a future at all, at any rate for human beings. In the second place we do not know whether the ideal of happiness towards which we are striving may not turn out either to be totally unrealizable or, if realizable, utterly repellent to humanity. Do people want to be happy? If there were a real prospect of achieving a permanent and unvarying happiness, wouldn't they shrink in horror from the boring consummation? And finally, the contemplation of the future, the busy working for it, does not prevent the present from existing. It merely partially blinds us to the present.

The same objections apply with equal force to the escapes which do not launch out into space or time, but into Platonic eternity, into the ideal. An escape into mere fancy does not prevent facts from going on; it is a disregarding of the facts.

Finally there are those people, more courageous than the escapers, who actually plunge into the real contemporary life around them, and are consoled by finding in the midst of its squalor, its repulsiveness and stupidity, evidences of a widespread kindliness, of charity, pity and the like. True, these qualities exist and the spectacle of them is decidedly cheering; in spite of civilization, men have not fallen below the brutes. Parents, even in human society, are devoted to their offspring; even in human society the weak and the afflicted are sometimes assisted. It would be surprising, considering the origins and affinities of man, if this were not the case. Have you ever read an obituary notice of which the subject did not possess, under his rough exterior and formidable manner, a heart of gold? And the obituarists, however cloying their literary productions, are perfectly right. We all have hearts of gold, though we are sometimes, it is true, too much preoccupied with our own affairs to remember the fact. The really cruel, the fundamentally evil man is as rare as the man of genius or the total idiot. I have never met a man with a really bad heart. And the fact is not surprising; for a man with a really bad heart is a man with certain instincts developed to an abnormal degree and certain others more or less completely atrophied. I have never met a man like Mozart for that matter.

Charles Dickens, it is true, managed to feel elated and chronically tearful over the existence of virtues among the squalor. 'He shows,' as one of his American admirers so fruitily puts it, 'that life in its rudest forms may wear a tragic grandeur; that amidst follies and excesses the moral feelings do not wholly die, and that the haunts of the blackest crime are sometimes lighted up by the presence of the noblest souls.' And very nice too. But is there any great reason to feel elated by the emergence of virtues in human society? We are not specially elated by the fact that men have livers and pancreases. Virtues are as natural to man as his digestive organs; any sober biologist, taking into consideration his gregarious instincts, would naturally expect to find them.

This being the case, there is nothing in these virtues *à la* Dickens to ' write home about '—as we used to say at a time when we were remarkably rich in such virtues. There is no reason to be particularly proud of qualities which we inherit from our animal forefathers and share with our household pets. The gratifying thing would be if we could find in contemporary society evidences of peculiarly human virtues—the conscious rational virtues that ought to belong by definition to a being calling himself Homo Sapiens. Open-mindedness, for example, absence of irrational prejudice, complete tolerance and a steady, reasonable pursuit of social goods. But these, alas, are precisely what we fail to discover. For to what, after all, are all this squalor, this confusion and ugliness due but to the lack of the human virtues ? The fact is that—except for an occasional sport of Nature, born now here, now there, and always out of time—we sapient men have practically no human virtues at all. Spend a week in any great town, and the fact is obvious. So complete is this lack of truly human qualities that we are reduced, if we condescend to look at reality at all, to act like Charles Dickens and congratulate the race on its merely animal virtues. The jolly, optimistic fellows who assure us that humanity is all right, because mothers love their children, poor folk pity and help one another, and soldiers die for a flag, are comforting us on the grounds that we resemble the whales, the elephants and the bees. But when we ask them to adduce evidence of human sapience, to give us a few specimens of conscious and reasonable well-doing, they rebuke us for our intellectual coldness and our general ' inhumanity '—which means our refusal to be content with the standards of the animals. However grateful we may feel for the existence in civilized society of these homely jungle virtues, we cannot justifiably set them off against the horrors and squalors of civilized life. The horrors

and squalors arise from men's lack of reason—from their failure
to be completely and sapiently human. The jungle virtues are
merely the obverse of this animalism, whose Heads is instinctive
kindliness and whose Tails is stupidity and instinctive cruelty.

So much for the last consolation of philosophy. We are left
with reality. My office in Gog's Court is situated, I repeat, at
the very heart of it, the palpitating heart.

CHAPTER II

GOG'S COURT, the navel of reality! Repeating those verses of mine in the silence, I intimately felt the truth of it.

> For if of old the sons of squires
> And livery stable keepers turned
> To flowers and hope, to Greece and God,
> We in our later age have learned
> That we are native where we walk.

My voice boomed out oracularly across the flat sea. Nothing so richly increases the significance of a statement as to hear it uttered by one's own voice, in solitude. 'Resolved, so help me God, never to touch another drop!' Those solemn words, breathed out in a mist of whiskey—how often, in dark nights, on icy mornings, how often have they been uttered! And the portentous imprecation seems to engage the whole universe to do battle on behalf of the Better Self against its besetting vice. Thrilling and awful moment! Merely for the sake of living through it again, for the sake of once more breaking the empty silence with the reverberating Stygian oath, it is well worth neglecting the good resolution. I say nothing of the pleasures of inebriation.

My own brief recital served to confirm for me the truth of my speculations. For not only was I uttering the substance of my thoughts aloud; I was voicing it in terms of a formula that had an element, I flatter myself, of magic about it. What is the secret of these verbal felicities? How does it come about that a commonplace thought embodied by a poet in some abracadabrical form seems bottomlessly profound, while a positively false and stupid notion may be made by its expression to seem true? Frankly, I don't know. And what is more, I have never found any one who could give an answer to the riddle. What is it that makes the two words 'defunctive music' as moving as the dead march out of the *Eroica* and the close of *Coriolan* ? Why should it be somehow more profoundly comic to ' call Tullia's ape a marmosite ' than to write a whole play of Congreve ? And the line, ' Thoughts that do often lie too deep for tears '—why should it in effect lie where it does ? Mystery. This game of art strangely resembles conjuring. The quickness of the tongue deceives the brain. It has happened, after all, often enough. Old Shakespeare, for example. How many critical brains have been deceived by the quickness of *his* tongue ! Because he can say ' Shoughs, water-rugs and demi-wolves,' and ' defunctive music,' and ' the expense of spirit in a waste of shame ' and all the rest of it, we credit him with philosophy, a moral purpose and the most penetrating psychology. Whereas his thoughts are incredibly confused, his only purpose is to entertain and he has created only three characters. One, Cleopatra, is an excellent copy from the life, like a character out of a good realistic novel, say one of Tolstoy's. The other two—Macbeth and Falstaff—are fabulous imaginary figures, consistent with themselves but not real in the sense that Cleopatra is real. My poor friend Calamy would call them more real, would say that they belong to the realm of Absolute Art. And so forth. I cannot go into poor Calamy's opinions, at any rate in this context ; later on, perhaps. For me, in any case, Macbeth and Falstaff are perfectly genuine and complete mythological characters, like Jupiter or Gargantua, Medea or Mr. Winkle. They are the only two well-invented mythological monsters in the whole of Shakespeare's collection ; just as Cleopatra is the only well-copied reality. His boundless capacity for abracadabra has deceived innumerable people into imagining that all the other characters are as good.

But the Bard, heaven help me, is not my theme. Let me return to my recitation on the face of the waters. As I have said, my conviction ' that we are native where we walk ' was decidedly strengthened by the sound of my own voice pronouncing the elegant formula in which the notion was embalmed. Repeating the words, I thought of Gog's Court, of my little room with the reflector at the window, of the light that burns in winter even at noon, of the smell of printer's ink and the noise of the presses. I was back there, out of this irrelevant poem of a sunshiny landscape, back in the palpitating heart of things. On the table before me lay a sheaf of long galleys ; it was Wednesday ; I should have been correcting proofs, but I was idle that afternoon ! On the blank six inches at the bottom of a galley I had been writing those lines : ' For if of old the sons of squires . . .' Pensively, a halma player contemplating his next move, I hung over them. What were the possible improvements ? There was a knock at the door. I drew a sheet of blotting paper across the bottom of the galley—' Come in '—and went on with my interrupted reading of the print. ' . . . Since Himalayas were made to breed true to colour, no event has aroused greater enthusiasm in the fancier's world than the fixation of the new Flemish-Angora type. Mr. Spargle's achievement is indeed a nepoch-making one. . . .' I restored the n of nepoch to its widowed a, and looked up. Mr. Bosk, the sub-editor, was standing over me.

' Proof of the leader, sir,' he said, bowing with that exquisitely contemptuous politeness which characterized all his dealings with me, and handed me another galley.

' Thank you, Mr. Bosk,' I said.

But Mr. Bosk did not retire. Standing there in his favourite and habitual attitude, the attitude assumed by our ancestors (of whom, indeed, old Mr. Bosk was one) in front of the half-draped marble column of the photographer's studio, he looked at me, faintly smiling through his thin white beard. The third button of his waistcoat was undone and his right hand, like a half-posted letter, was inserted in the orifice. He rested his weight on a rigid right leg. The other leg was slightly bent, and the heel of one touching the toe of the other, his left foot made with his right a perfect right angle. I could see that I was in for a reproof.

' What is it, Mr. Bosk ? ' I asked.

Among the sparse hairs Mr. Bosk's smile became piercingly sweet. He put his head archly on one side. His voice when he spoke was mellifluous. On these occasions when I was to be dressed down and put in my place his courtesy degenerated into a kind of affected girlish coquetry. ' If you don't mind my saying so, Mr. Chelifer,' he said mincingly, ' I think you 'll find that *rabear* in Spanish does not mean " to wag the tail," as you say in your leader on the derivation of the word " rabbit," so much as " to wag the hind quarters." '

' Wag the hind quarters, Mr. Bosk ? ' I said. ' But that sounds to me a very difficult feat.'

' Not in Spain, apparently,' said Mr. Bosk, almost giggling.

' But this is England, Mr. Bosk.'

' Nevertheless, my authority is no less than Skeat himself.' And triumphantly, with the air of one who, at a critical moment of the game, produces a fifth ace, Mr. Bosk brought forward his left hand, which he had been keeping mysteriously behind his back. It held a dictionary ; a strip of paper marked the page. Mr. Bosk laid it, opened, on the table before me ; with a thick nail he pointed ' " . . . or possibly," I read aloud, " from Spanish *rabear*, to wag the hind quarters." Right as usual, Mr. Bosk. I 'll alter it in the proof.'

' Thank you, sir,' said Mr. Bosk with a mock humility. Inwardly he was exulting in his triumph. He picked up his dictionary, repeated his contemptuously courteous bow and walked with a gliding noiseless motion towards the door. On the threshold he paused. ' I remember that the question arose once before, sir,' he said ; his voice was poisonously honeyed. ' In Mr. Parfitt's time,' and he slipped out, closing the door quietly behind him.

It was a Parthian shot. The name of Mr. Parfitt was meant to wound me to the quick, to bring the blush of shame to my cheek. For had not Mr. Parfitt been the perfect, complete and infallible editor ? Whereas I . . . Mr. Bosk left it to my own conscience to decide what I was.

And indeed I was well aware of my short-comings. 'The Rabbit Fanciers' Gazette,' with which, as every schoolboy knows, is incorporated 'The Mouse Breeders' Record,' could hardly have had a more unsuitable editor than I. To this day, I confess, I hardly know the right end of a rabbit from the wrong. Mr. Bosk was a survivor from the grand old days of Mr. Parfitt, the founder and for thirty years the editor of the Gazette.

'Mr. Parfitt, sir,' he used to tell me every now and then, ' was a *real* fancier.' His successor, by implication, was not.

It was at the end of the war. I was looking for a job—a job at the heart of reality. The illusory nature of the position had made me decline my old college's offer of a fellowship. I wanted something—how shall I put it ?—more palpitating. And then in *The Times* I found what I had been looking for. 'Wanted Editor of proved literary ability for livestock trade paper. Apply Box 92.' I applied, was interviewed, and conquered. The directors couldn't finally resist my testimonial from the Bishop of Bosham. 'A life-long acquaintance with Mr. Chelifer and his family permits me confidently to assert that he is a young man of great ability and high moral purpose. (signed) Hartley Bosh.' I was appointed for a probationary period of six months.

Old Mr. Parfitt, the retiring editor, stayed on a few days at the office to initiate me into the secrets of the work. He was a benevolent old gentleman, short, thick and with a very large head. His square face was made to seem even broader than it was by the grey whiskers which ran down his cheeks to merge imperceptibly into the ends of his moustache. He knew more about mice and rabbits than any man in the country ; but what he prided himself on was his literary gift. He explained to me the principles on which he wrote his weekly leaders.

'In the fable,' he told me, smiling already in anticipation of the end of this joke which he had been elaborating and polishing since 1892, 'in the fable it is the mountain which, after a long and, if I may say so, geological labour, gives birth to the mouse. My principle, on the contrary, has always been, wherever possible, to make my mice parturate mountains.' He paused expectantly. When I had laughed, he went on. 'It's astonishing what reflections on life and art and politics and philosophy and what not you can get out of a mouse or a rabbit. Quite astonishing!'

The most notable of Mr. Parfitt's mountain thoughts still hangs, under glass and in an Oxford frame, on the wall above the editorial desk. It was printed in the Rabbit Fancier for August 8, 1914.

'It is not the readers of the Rabbit Fanciers' Gazette,' Mr. Parfitt had written on that cardinal date, 'who have made this war. No Mouse Breeder, I emphatically proclaim, has desired it. No! Absorbed in their harmless and indeed beneficent occupations, they have had neither the wish nor the leisure to disturb the world's peace. If all men whole-heartedly devoted themselves to avocations like ours, there would be no war. The world would be filled with the innocent creators and fosterers of life, not, as at present, with its tigerish destroyers. Had Kaiser William the Second been a breeder of rabbits or mice, we should not find ourselves to-day in a world whose very existence is threatened by the unimaginable horrors of modern warfare.'

Noble words! Mr. Parfitt's righteous indignation was strengthened by his fears for the future of his paper. The war, he gloomily foreboded, would mean the end of rabbit breeding. But he was wrong. Mice, it is true, went rather out of fashion between 1914 and 1918. But in the lean years of rationing, rabbits took on a new importance. In 1917 there were ten fanciers of Flemish Giants to every one there had been before the war. Subscriptions rose, advertisements were multiplied.

'Rabbits,' Mr. Parfitt assured me, 'did a great deal to help us win the war.'

And conversely, the war did so much to help rabbits that Mr. Parfitt was able to retire in 1919 with a modest but adequate fortune. It was then that I took over control. And in spite of Mr. Bosk's contempt for my ignorance and incompetence, I must in justice congratulate myself on the way in which I piloted the concern through the evil times which followed. Peace found the English people at once less prosperous and less hungry than they had been during the war. The time had passed when it was necessary for them to breed rabbits; and they could not afford the luxury of breeding them for pleasure. Subscriptions declined, advertisements fell off. I averted an impending catastrophe by adding to the paper a new section dealing with goats. Biologically, no doubt, as I pointed out to the directors in my communication on the subject, this mingling of ruminants with rodents was decidedly unsound. But commercially, I felt sure, the innovation would be justified. It was. The goats brought half a dozen pages of advertisements in their train and several hundred new subscribers. Mr. Bosk was furious at my success; but the directors thought very highly of my capacities.

They did not, it is true, always approve of my leading articles. 'Couldn't you try to make them a little more popular,' suggested the managing director, 'a little more practical too, Mr. Chelifer? For instance,' and clearing his throat, he unfolded the typewritten sheet of complaints which he had had prepared and had brought with him to the board meeting, 'for instance, what's the practical value of this stuff about the use of the word " cony " as a term of endearment in the Elizabethan dramatists? And this article on the derivation of " rabbit " '—he looked at his paper again and coughed. 'Who wants to know that there's a Walloon word " robett " ? Or that our word may have something to do with the Spanish *rabear*, to wag the hind quarters? And who, by the way,' he added, looking up at me over his pince-nez with an air—prematurely put on—of triumph, ' who ever heard of an animal wagging its hind quarters ? ' 'Nevertheless,' I said, apologetically, but firmly, as befits a man who knows that he is right, ' my authority is no less than Skeat himself.'

The managing director, who had hoped to score a point, went on, defeated, to the next count in the indictment. ' And then, Mr. Chelifer,' he said, ' we don't very much like, my fellow directors and I, we don't much like what you say in your article on " Rabbit Fancying and its Lesson to Humanity." It may be true that breeders have succeeded in producing domesticated rabbits that are four times the weight of wild rabbits and possess only half the quantity of brains—it may be true. Indeed, it is true. And a very remarkable achievement it is, Mr. Chelifer, very remarkable indeed. But that is no reason for upholding, as you do, Mr. Chelifer, that the ideal working man, at whose production the eugenist should aim, is a man eight times as strong as the present-day workman, with only a sixteenth of his mental capacity. Not that my fellow directors and I entirely disagree with what you say, Mr. Chelifer ; far from it. All right-thinking men must agree that the modern workman is too well educated. But we have to remember, Mr. Chelifer, that many of our readers actually belong to that class.'

' Quite.' I acquiesced in the reproof.

' And finally, Mr. Chelifer, there is your article on the " Symbology of the Goat." We feel that the facts you have there collected, however interesting to the anthropologist and the student of folk-lore, are hardly of a kind to be set before a mixed public like ours.'

The other directors murmured their assent. There was a prolonged silence.

CHAPTER III

I REMEMBER an advertisement—for some sort of cough drops I think it was—which used to figure very largely in my boyhood on the back covers of the illustrated weeklies. Over the legend, ' A Pine Forest in every Home,' appeared a picture of three or four magnificent Norway spruces growing out of the drawing-room carpet, while the lady of the house, her children and guests took tea, with a remarkable air of unconcern and as though it was quite natural to have a sequoia sprouting out of the hearth-rug, under their sanitary and aromatic shade. A Pine Forest in every Home. . . . But I have thought of something even better. A Luna Park in every Office. A British Empire Exhibition Fun Fair in every Bank. An Earl's Court in every Factory. True, I cannot claim to bring every attraction of the Fun Fair into your place of labour—only the switchback, the water-shoot and the mountain railway. Merry-go-round, wiggle-woggle, flip-flap and the like are beyond the power of my magic to conjure up. Horizontal motion and a rotary giddiness I cannot claim to reproduce; my speciality is headlong descents, breathlessness and that delicious sickening feeling that your entrails have been left behind on an upper storey. Those who chafe at the tameness and sameness of office life, who pine for a little excitement to diversify the quotidian routine, should experiment with this little recipe of mine and bring the water-shoot into the counting-house. It is quite simple. All you have got to do is to pause for a moment in your work and ask yourself: Why am I doing this ? What is it all for ? Did I come into the world, supplied with a soul which may very likely be immortal, for the sole purpose of sitting every day at this desk ? Ask yourself these questions thoughtfully, seriously. Reflect even for a moment on their significance—and I can guarantee that, firmly seated though you may be in your hard or your padded chair, you will feel all at once that the void has opened beneath you, that you are sliding headlong, fast and faster, into nothingness.

For those who cannot dispense with formularies and fixed prayers, I recommend this little catechism, to be read through in office hours whenever time hangs a little heavy.

Q. Why am I working here ?

A. In order that Jewish stockbrokers may exchange their Rovers for Armstrong-Siddeleys, buy the latest jazz records and spend the week-end at Brighton.

Q. Why do I go on working here ?

A. In the hope that I too may some day be able to spend the week-end at Brighton.

Q. What is progress ?

A. Progress is stockbrokers, more stockbrokers and still more stockbrokers.

Q. What is the aim of social reformers ?

A. The aim of social reformers is to create a state in which every individual enjoys the greatest possible amount of freedom and leisure.

Q. What will the citizens of this reformed state do with their freedom and leisure ?

A. They will do, presumably, what the stockbrokers do with these things to-day, *e.g.* spend the week-end at Brighton, ride rapidly in motor vehicles and go to the theatre.

Q. On what condition can I live a life of contentment ?

A. On the condition that you do not think.

Q. What is the function of newspapers, cinemas, radios, motor-bikes, jazz bands, etc ?

A. The function of these things is the prevention of thought and the killing of time.   They are the most powerful instruments of human happiness.

Q. What did Buddha consider the most deadly of the deadly sins ?

A. Unawareness, stupidity.

Q. And what will happen if I make myself aware, if I actually begin to think ?

A. Your swivel chair will turn into a trolley on the mountain railway, the office floor will gracefully slide away from beneath you and you will find yourself launched into the abyss.

Down, down, down ! The sensation, though sickening, is really delightful. Most people, I know, find it a little too much for them and consequently cease to think, in which case the trolley reconverts itself into the swivel chair, the floor closes up and the hours at the desk seem once more to be hours passed in a perfectly reasonable manner ; or else, more rarely, flee in panic horror from the office to bury their heads like ostriches in religion or what not. For a strong-minded and intelligent person both courses are inadmissible ; the first because it is stupid and the second because it is cowardly. No self-respecting man can either accept unreflectingly or, having reflected upon it, irresponsibly run away from the reality of human life. The proper course, I flatter myself, is that which I have adopted. Having sought out the heart of reality—Gog's Court, to be explicit—I have taken up my position there ; and though fully aware of the nature of the reality by which I am surrounded, though deliberately keeping myself reminded of the complete imbecility of what I am doing, I yet remain heroically at my post. My whole time is passed on the switchback ; all my life is one unceasing slide through nothing.

All my life, I insist ; for it is not merely into Gog's Court that I magically introduce the fun of the fair. I so arrange my private life that I am sliding even out of office hours. My heart, to borrow the poetess's words, is like a singing bird whose nest is permanently in a water-shoot. Miss Carruthers's boarding-house in Chelsea is, I assure you, as suitable a place to slither in as any east of Temple Bar. I have lived there now for four years. I am a pillar of the establishment and every evening, when I sit down to dinner with my fellow guests, I feel as though I were taking my place in a specially capacious family trolley on the switchback railway. All aboard! and away we go. With gathering momentum the trolley plunges down into vacancy.

Let me describe an evening on the Domestic water-shoot. At the head of the table sits Miss Carruthers herself; thirty-seven, plump though unmarried, with a face broadening towards the base and very flabby about the cheeks and chin—bull-doggy, in a word; and the snub nose, staring at you out of its upward-tilted nostrils, the small brown eyes do not belie the comparison. And what activity! never walks, but runs about her establishment like a demoniac, never speaks but shrilly shouts, carves the roast beef with scientific fury, laughs like a giant woodpecker. She belongs to a distinguished family which would never, in its days of glory, have dreamed of allowing one of its daughters to become what Miss Carruthers calls, applying to herself the most humiliating of titles and laughing as she does so, to emphasize the picturesque contrast between what she is by birth and what circumstance has reduced her to becoming, ' a common lodging-house keeper.' She is a firm believer in her class, and to her more distinguished guests deplores the necessity under which she labours to admit into her establishment persons not really, really . . . She is careful not to mix people of different sorts together. Her most genteel guests sit the closest to her at table; it is implied that, in the neighbourhood of Miss Carruthers, they will feel at home. For years I have had the honour of sitting at her left hand; for if less prosperous than Mrs. Cloudesley Shove, the broker's widow (who sits in glory on the right), I have at least attended in my youth an ancient seat of learning.

The gong reverberates; punctually I hurry down to the dining-room. With fury and precision, like a conductor immersed in a Wagner overture, Miss Carruthers is carving the beef.

' Evening, Mr. Chelifer,' she loudly calls, without interrupting her labours. 'What news have you brought back with you from the city to-day ? '

Affably I smile, professionally I rub the hands. 'Well, I don't know that I can think of any.'

'Evening, Mrs. Fox. Evening, Mr. Fox.' The two old people take their places near the further end of the table. They are not quite, quite . . . 'Evening, Miss Monad.' Miss Monad does responsible secretarial work and sits next to the Fox's. 'Evening, Mr. Quinn. Evening, Miss Webber. Evening, Mrs. Crotch.' But the tone in which she responds to Mr. Dutt's courteous greeting is much less affable. Mr. Dutt is an Indian—a black man, Miss Carruthers calls him. Her 'Evening, Mr. Dutt' shows that she knows her place and hopes that the man of the inferior race knows his. The servant comes in with a steaming dish of greens. *Crambe ripetita*—inspiring perfume ! Mentally I burst into song.

> These like remorse inveterate memories,
> Being of cabbage, are prophetic too
> Of future feasts, when Mrs. Cloudesley Shove
> Will still recall lamented Cloudesley.
> Still
> Among the moonlit cedars Philomel
> Calls back to mind, again, again,
> The ancient pain, the everlasting pain ;
> And still inveterately the haunted air
> Remembers and foretells that roses were
> Red and to-morrow will again be red,
> But, 'Cloudesley, Cloudesley !' Philomel in vain
> Sobs on the night ; for Cloudesley Shove is dead. . . .

And in the flesh, as though irresistibly summoned by my incantation, Mrs. Cloudesley Shove blackens the doorway with her widowhood.

'Not a very naice day,' says Mrs. Cloudesley, as she sits down.

'Not at all,' Miss Carruthers heartily agrees. And then, without turning from the beef, without abating for an instant the celerity of her carving, ' Fluffy ! ' she shouts through the increasing din, ' don't giggle like that.'

Politely Mr. Chelifer half raises himself from his chair as Miss Fluffy comes tumbling, on the tail end of her giggle, into the chair next to his. Always the perfect gent.

' I wasn't giggling, Miss Carruthers,' Fluffy protests. Her smile reveals above the roots of her teeth a line of almost blood-less gums.

' Quite true,' says young Mr. Brimstone, following her less tumultuously from the door and establishing himself in the seat opposite, next to Mrs. Cloudesley. ' She wasn't giggling. She was merely cachinnating.'

Everybody laughs uproariously, even Miss Carruthers, though she does not cease to carve. Mr. Brimstone remains perfectly grave. Behind his rimless pince-nez there is hardly so much as a twinkle. As for Miss Fluffy, she fairly collapses.

' What a horrible man ! ' she screams through her laughter, as soon as she has breath enough to be articulate. And picking up her bread, she makes as though she were going to throw it across the table in Mr. Brimstone's face.

Mr. Brimstone holds up a finger. ' Now you be careful,' he admonishes. ' If you don't behave, you 'll be put in the corner and sent to bed without your supper.'

There is a renewal of laughter.

Miss Carruthers intervenes. ' Now don't tease her, Mr. Brimstone.'

' Tease ? ' says Mr. Brimstone, in the tone of one who has been misjudged. ' But I was only applying moral suasion, Miss Carruthers.'

Inimitable Brimstone ! He is the life and soul of Miss Car-ruthers's establishment. So serious, so clever, such an alert young city man—but withal so exquisitely waggish, so gallant ! To see him with Fluffy—it 's as good as a play.

'There!' says Miss Carruthers, putting down her carving tools with a clatter. Loudly, energetically, she addresses herself to her duties as a hostess. 'I went to Buszard's this afternoon,' she proclaims, not without pride. We old county families have always bought our chocolate at the best shops. 'But it isn't what it used to be.' She shakes her head; the high old feudal times are past. 'It isn't the same. Not since the A B C took it over.'

'Do you see,' asks Mr. Brimstone, becoming once more his serious self, 'that the new Lyons Corner House in Piccadilly Circus will be able to serve fourteen million meals a year?' Mr. Brimstone is always a mine of interesting statistics.

'No, really?' Mrs. Cloudesley is astonished.

But old Mr. Fox, who happens to have read the same evening paper as Mr. Brimstone, takes almost the whole credit of Mr. Brimstone's erudition to himself by adding, before the other has time to say it: 'Yes, and that's just twice as many meals as any American restaurant can serve.'

'Good old England!' cried Miss Carruthers patriotically. 'These Yanks haven't got us beaten in everything yet.'

'So naice, I always think, these Corner Houses,' says Mrs. Cloudesley. 'And the music they play is really quite classical, you know, sometimes.'

'Quite,' says Mr. Chelifer, savouring voluptuously the pleasure of dropping steeply from the edge of the convivial board into interstellar space.

'And so sumptuously decorated,' Mrs. Cloudesley continues.

But Mr. Brimstone knowingly lets her know that the marble on the walls is less than a quarter of an inch thick.

And the conversation proceeds. 'The Huns,' says Miss Carruthers, 'are only shamming dead.' Mr. Fox is in favour of a business government. Mr. Brimstone would like to see a few strikers shot, to encourage the rest; Miss Carruthers agrees.

From below the salt Miss Monad puts in a word for the working classes, but her remark is treated with the contempt it deserves. Mrs. Cloudesley finds Charlie Chaplin so vulgar, but likes Mary Pickford. Miss Fluffy thinks that the Prince of Wales ought to marry a nice simple English girl. Mr. Brimstone says something rather cutting about Mrs. Asquith and Lady Diana Manners. Mrs. Cloudesley, who has a profound knowledge of the Royal Family, mentions the Princess Alice. Contrapuntally to this, Miss Webber and Mr. Quinn have been discussing the latest plays and Mr. Chelifer has engaged Miss Fluffy in a conversation which soon occupies the attention of all the persons sitting at the upper end of the table—a conversation about flappers. Mrs. Cloudesley, Miss Carruthers and Mr. Brimstone agree that the modern girl is too laxly brought up. Miss Fluffy adheres in piercing tones to the opposite opinion. Mr. Brimstone makes some splendid jokes at the expense of co-education, and all concur in deploring cranks of every variety. Miss Carruthers, who has a short way with dissenters, would like to see them tarred and feathered—all except pacifists, who, like strikers, could do with a little shooting. Lymphatic Mrs. Cloudesley, with sudden and surprising ferocity, wants to treat the Irish in the same way. (Lamented Cloudesley had connections with Belfast.) But at this moment a deplorable incident occurs. Mr. Dutt, the Indian, who ought never, from his lower sphere, even to have listened to the conversation going on in the higher, leans forward and speaking loudly across the intervening gulf ardently espouses the Irish cause. His eloquence rolls up the table between two hedges of horrified silence. For a moment nothing can be heard but ardent nationalistic sentiments and the polite regurgitation of prune stones. In the presence of this shocking and unfamiliar phenomenon nobody knows exactly what to do. But Miss Carruthers rises, after the first moment, to the occasion.

'Ah, but then, Mr. Dutt,' she says, interrupting his tirade

about oppressed nationalities, 'you must remember that Mrs. Cloudesley Shove is English. *You* can hardly expect to understand what *she* feels. Can you ? '

We all feel inclined to clap. Without waiting to hear Mr. Dutt's reply, and leaving three prunes uneaten on her plate, Miss Carruthers gets up and sweeps with dignity towards the door. Loudly, in the corridor, she comments on the insolence of black men. And what ingratitude, too !

' After I had made a special exception in his case to my rule against taking coloured people ! '

We all sympathize. In the drawing-room the conversation proceeds. Headlong the trolley plunges.

A home away from home—that was how Miss Carruthers described her establishment in the prospectus. It was the awayness of it that first attracted me to the place. The vast awayness from what I had called home up till the time I first stayed there—that was what made me decide to settle for good at Miss Carruthers's. From the house where I was born Miss Carruthers's seemed about as remote as any place one could conveniently find.

' I remember, I remember . . .' It is a pointless and futile occupation, difficult none the less not to indulge in. I remember. Our house at Oxford was dark, spiky and tall. Ruskin himself, it was said, had planned it. The front windows looked out on to the Banbury Road. On rainy days, when I was a child, I used to spend whole mornings staring down into the thoroughfare. Every twenty minutes a tram-car drawn by two old horses, trotting in their sleep, passed with an undulating motion more slowly than a man could walk. The little garden at the back once seemed enormous and romantic, the rocking-horse in the nursery a beast like an elephant. The house is sold now and I am glad of it. They are dangerous, these things and places inhabited by memory. It is as though, by a process of metempsychosis, the soul of dead events goes out and lodges itself in a house, a flower, a landscape, in a group of trees seen from the train against the sky-line, an old snapshot, a broken pen-knife, a book, a perfume. In these memory-charged places, among these things haunted by the ghosts of dead days, one is tempted to brood too lovingly over the past, to live it again, more elaborately, more consciously, more beautifully and harmoniously, almost as though it were an imagined life in the future. Surrounded by these ghosts one can neglect the present in which one bodily lives. I am glad the place is sold; it was dangerous. *Evviva* Miss Carruthers!

Nevertheless my thoughts, as I lay on the water that morning, reverted from the Home Away to the other home from which it was so distant. I recalled the last visit I had paid to the old house, a month or two since, just before my mother finally decided herself to move out. Mounting the steps that led up to the ogival porch I had felt like an excavator on the threshold of a tomb. I tugged at the wrought-iron bell pull; joints creaked, wires wheezily rattled, and far off, as though accidentally, by an afterthought, tinkled the cracked bell. In a moment the door would open, I should walk in, and there, there in the unrifled chamber the royal mummy would be lying—my own.

Nothing within those Gothic walls ever changed. Impercept-ibly the furniture grew older; the wall-papers and the upholstery recalled with their non-committal russets and sage-greens the refinements of another epoch. And my mother herself, pale and grey-haired, draped in the dateless dove-grey dresses she had always worn, my mother was still the same. Her smile was the same dim gentle smile; her voice still softly modulated, like a studied and cultured music, from key to key. Her hair was hardly greyer—for it had whitened early and I was a late-born child—than I always remember it to have been. Her face was hardly more deeply wrinkled. She walked erect, seemed still as active as ever, she had grown no thinner and no stouter.

And she was still surrounded by those troops of derelict dogs, so dreadfully profuse, poor beasts! in their smelly gratitude. There were still the same moth-eaten cats picked up starving at a street corner to be harboured in luxury—albeit on a diet that was, on principle, strictly vegetarian—in the best rooms of the house. Poor children still came for buns and tea and traditional games in the garden—so traditional, very often, that nobody but my mother had ever heard of them; still came, when the season happened to be winter, for gloves and woolly stockings and traditional games indoors. And the writing-table in the drawing-room was piled high, as it had always been piled, with printed appeals for some deserving charity. And still in her beautiful calligraphy my mother addressed the envelopes that were to contain them, slowly, one after another—and each a little work of art, like a page from a mediaeval missal, and each destined, without reprieve, to the waste-paper basket.

All was just as it had always been. Ah, but not quite, all the same! For though the summer term was in full swing and the afternoon bright, the little garden behind the house was deserted and unmelodious. Where were the morris dancers, where the mixolydian strains? And remembering that music, those dances, those distant afternoons, I could have wept.

In one corner of the lawn my mother used to sit at the little harmonium; I sat beside her to turn the pages of the music. In the opposite corner were grouped the dancers. My mother looked up over the top of the instrument; melodiously she inquired:

' Which dance shall we have next, Mr. Toft? "Trenchmore"? Or "Omnium Gatherum"? Or "John come kiss me now"? Or what do you say to "Up tails all"? Or "Rub her down with straw"? Or "An old man's a bed full of bones"? Such an *embarras de richesse*, isn't there?'

And Mr. Toft would break away from his little company of dancers and come across the lawn wiping his face—for ' Hoite-cum-Toite' a moment before had been a most furious affair. It was a grey face with vague indeterminate features and a bright almost clerical smile in the middle of it. When he spoke it was in a very rich voice.

'Suppose we try "Fading," Mrs. Chelifer,' he suggested. '"Fading is a fine dance"—you remember the immortal words of the Citizen's Wife in the *Knight of the Burning Pestle* ? Ha ha !' And he gave utterance to a little laugh, applausive of his own wit. For to Mr. Toft every literary allusion was a joke, and the obscurer the allusion the more exquisite the waggery. It was rarely, alas, that he found any one to share his merriment. My mother was one of the few people who always made a point of smiling whenever Mr. Toft laughed at himself. She smiled even when she could not track the allusion to its source. Sometimes she even went so far as to laugh. But my mother had no facility for laughter ; by nature she was a grave and gentle smiler.

And so 'Fading' it would be. My mother touched the keys and the gay, sad mixolydian air came snoring out of the harmonium like a strangely dissipated hymn tune. 'One, two, three . . .' called Mr. Toft richly. And then in unison all five—the don, the two undergraduates, the two young ladies from North Oxford —would beat the ground with their feet, would prance and stamp till the garters of little bells round the gentlemen's grey flannel trousers (it went without saying, for some reason, that the ladies should not wear them) jingled like the bells of a runaway hansom-cab horse. One, two, three. . . . The Citizen's Wife (ha ha !) was right. Fading is a fine dance indeed. Everybody dances Fading. Poor Mr. Toft had faded out of Oxford, had danced completely out of life, like Lycidas (tee-hee !) before his prime. Influenza had faded him. And of the undergraduates who had danced here, first and last, with Mr. Toft—how many of them had danced Fading under the German barrage ? Young Flint, the one who used always to address his tutor as ' Mr. Toft—oh, I mean Clarence ' (for Mr. Toft was one of those genial boyish dons who insisted on being called by their Christian names), young Flint was dead for certain. And Ramsden too, I had a notion that Ramsden too was dead.

And then there were the young women from North Oxford. What, for example, of Miss Dewball's cheeks ? How had those cabbage roses weathered the passage of the years ? But for Miss Higlett, of course, there could be no more fading, no further desiccation. She was already a harebell baked in sand. Un-withering Higlett, blowsy Dewball. . . .

And I myself, I too had faded. The Francis Chelifer who, standing by the dissipated harmonium, had turned the pages of his mother's music, was as wholly extinct as Mr. Toft. Within this Gothic tomb reposed his mummy. My week-end visits were archaeological expeditions.

'Now that poor Mr. Toft's dead,' I asked as we walked, my mother and I, that afternoon, up and down the little garden behind the house, ' isn't there any one else here who's keen on morris dancing ? ' Or were those folky days, I wondered, for ever past ?

My mother shook her head. ' The enthusiasm for it is gone,' she said sadly. ' This generation of undergraduates doesn't seem to take much interest in that kind of thing. I don't really know,' she added, ' what it *is* interested in.'

What indeed, I reflected. In my young days it had been Social Service and Fabianism ; it had been long hearty walks in the country at four and a half miles an hour, with draughts of Five X beer at the end of them, and Rabelaisian song and conversations with yokels in incredibly picturesque little wayside inns ; it had been reading parties in the Lakes and climbing in the Jura ; it had been singing in the Bach Choir and even—though somehow I had never been able quite to rise to that—even morris dancing with Mr. Toft. . . . But Fading is a fine dance, and all these occupations seemed now a little queer. Still, I caught myself envying the being who had lived within my skin and joined in these activities.

'Poor Toft!' I meditated. 'Do you remember the way he had of calling great men by little pet names of his own? Just to show that he was on terms of familiarity with them, I suppose. Shakespeare was always Shake-bake, which was short, in its turn, for Shake-Bacon. And Oven, *tout court*, was Beethoven.'

'And always J. S. B. for Bach,' my mother continued, smiling elegiacally.

'Yes, and Pee Em for Philipp Emanuel Bach. And Madame Dudevant for George Sand, or, alternatively, I remember, "The Queen's Monthly Nurse"—because Dickens thought she looked like that the only time he saw her.' I recalled the long-drawn and delighted laughter which used to follow that allusion.

'You were never much of a dancer, dear boy.' My mother sadly shook her head over the past.

'Ah, but at any rate,' I answered, 'at any rate I was a Fabian. And I went for hearty long walks in the country. I drank my pint of Five X at the Red Lion.'

'I wish you could have gone without the beer,' said my mother. That I had not chosen to be a total abstainer had always a little distressed her. Moreover, I had a taste for beefsteaks.

'It was my substitute for morris dancing, if you follow me.'

But I don't think she did follow me. We took two or three turns up and down the lawn in silence.

'How is your paper doing?' she asked at last.

I told her with a great show of enthusiasm about the cross between Angoras and Himalayans which we had just announced.

'I often wish,' she said after a pause, 'that you had accepted the college's offer. It would have been so good to have you here, filling the place your dear father occupied.'

She looked at me sadly. I smiled back at her as though from across a gulf. The child, I thought, grows up to forget that he is of the same flesh with his parents; but they do not forget. I wished, for her sake, that I were only five years old.

CHAPTER IV

AT five years old, among other things, I used to write poems which my mother thoroughly and whole-heartedly enjoyed. There was one about larks which she still preserves, along with the locks of my pale childish hair, the faded photographs, the precocious drawings of railway trains and all the other relics of the period.

> Oh lark, how you do fly
> Right up into the sky.
> How loud he sings
> And quickly wags his wings.
> The sun does shine,
> The weather is fine.
> Father says, Hark,
> Do you hear the lark ?

My mother likes that poem better, I believe, than anything I have written since. And I dare say that my father, if he had lived, would have shared her opinion. But then he was an ardent Wordsworthian. He knew most of the *Prelude* by heart. Sometimes, unexpectedly breaking that profound and god-like silence with which he always enveloped himself, he would quote a line or two. The effect was always portentous ; it was as though an oracle had spoken.

I remember with particular vividness one occasion when Wordsworth broke my father's prodigious silence. It was one Easter time, when I was about twelve. We had gone to North Wales for the holidays ; my father liked walking among hills and even amused himself occasionally with a little mild rock climbing. Easter was early that year, the season backward and inclement ; there was snow on all the hills. On Easter Sunday my father, who considered a walk among the mountains as the equivalent of church-going, suggested that we should climb to the top of Snowdon. We started early ; it was cold ; white misty clouds shut off the distant prospects. Silently we trudged upwards through the snow. Like the page of King Wenceslas I followed in my father's footsteps, treading in the holes he had kicked in the snow. Every now and then he would look round to see how I was getting on. Icy dewdrops hung in his brown beard. Gravely he smiled down on me as I came panting up, planting my small feet in his large tracks. He was a huge man, tall and broad-shouldered, with a face that might have been the curly-bearded original of one of those Greek busts of middle-aged statesmen or philosophers. Standing beside him, I always felt particularly small and insignificant. When I had come up with him, he would pat me affectionately on the shoulder with his large heavy hand, then turning his face towards the heights he addressed himself once more to the climb. Not a word was spoken.

As the sun mounted higher, the clouds dispersed. Through the rifted mist we saw the sky. Great beams of yellow light went stalking across the slopes of snow. By the time we reached the summit the sky was completely clear ; the landscape opened out beneath us. The sun was shining brightly, but without heat ; the sky was pale blue, remote and icy. Every northern slope of the glittering hills was shadowed with transparent blues or purples. Far down, to the westward, was the scalloped and indented coast, and seeming in its remoteness utterly calm, the grey sea stretched upwards and away towards the horizon. We stood there for a long time in silence, gazing at the astonishing landscape. Sometimes, I remember, I stole an anxious look at my father. What was he thinking about ? I wondered. Huge and formidable he stood there, leaning on his ice-axe, turning his dark bright eyes slowly and meditatively this way and that. He spoke no word. I did not dare to break the silence. In the end he straightened himself up. He raised his ice-axe and with an emphatic gesture dug the pointed ferrule into the snow. ' Bloody fine ! ' he said slowly in his deep, cavernous voice. He said no more. In silence we retraced our steps towards the Pen-y-pass Hotel.

But my father had not, as I supposed, spoken his last word. When we were about half-way down I was startled and a little alarmed to hear him suddenly begin to speak. ' For I have learned,' he began abruptly (and he seemed to be speaking less for my benefit than to himself), ' to look on nature, not as in the hour of thoughtless youth ; but hearing oftentimes the still sad music of humanity, not harsh, nor grating, but of ample power to chasten and subdue. And I have felt a presence that disturbs me with the joy of elevated thoughts ; a sense sublime of something far more deeply inter-fused, whose dwelling is the light of setting suns and the round ocean and the living air, and the blue sky, and in the minds of men.' I listened to him with a kind of terror. The strange words (I had no idea at that time whence they came) reverberated mysteriously in my mind. It seemed an oracle, a divine revelation. My father ceased speaking as abruptly as he had begun. The words hung, as it were, isolated in the midst of his portentous silence. We walked on. My father spoke no more till on the threshold of the inn, sniffing the frozen air, he remarked with a profound satisfaction : ' Onions ! ' And then, after a second sniff : ' Fried.'

' A sense of something far more deeply interfused.' Ever since that day those words, pronounced in my father's cavernous voice, have rumbled through my mind. It took me a long time to dis-cover that they were as meaningless as so many hiccoughs. Such is the nefarious influence of early training.

My father, however, who never contrived to rid himself of the prejudices instilled into him in childhood, went on believing in his Wordsworthian formulas till the end. Yes, he too, I am afraid, would have preferred the precocious larks to my maturer lucubra-tions. And yet, how competently I have learned to write ! In mere justice to myself I must insist on it. Not, of course, that it matters in the least. The larks might be my masterpiece ; it would not matter a pin. Still, I insist. I insist. . . .

CHAPTER V

'QUITE the little poet'—how bitterly poor Keats resented the remark! Perhaps because he secretly knew that it was just. For Keats, after all, was that strange, unhappy chimaera—a little artist and a large man. Between the writer of the Odes and the writer of the letters there is all the gulf that separates a halma player from a hero.

Personally, I do not go in for heroic letters. I only modestly lay claim to being a competent second-class halma player—but a good deal more competent, I insist (though of course it doesn't matter), than when I wrote about the larks. 'Quite the little poet'—always and, alas, incorrigibly I am that.

Let me offer you a specimen of my matured competence. I select it at random, as the reviewers say, from my long-projected and never-to-be-concluded series of poems on the first six Caesars. My father, I flatter myself, would have liked the title. That, at any rate, is thoroughly Wordsworthian ; it is in the great tradition of that immortal ' Needle Case in the form of a Harp.' ' Caligula crossing the bridge of boats between Baiae and Puteoli. By Peter Paul Rubens (b. 1577 : d. 1640).' The poem itself, however, is not very reminiscent of the Lake District.

> Prow after prow the floating ships
> Bridge the blue gulph ; the road is laid.
> And Caesar on a piebald horse
> Prances with all his cavalcade.
>
> Drunk with their own quick blood they go.
> The waves flash as with seeing eyes ;
> The tumbling cliffs mimic their speed,
> And they have filled the vacant skies
>
> With waltzing Gods and Virtues, set
> The Sea Winds singing with their shout,
> Made Vesta's temple on the headland
> Spin like a twinkling roundabout.

The twined caduceus in his hand,
And having golden wings for spurs,
Young Caesar dressed as God looks on
And cheers his jolly mariners ;

Cheers as they heave from off the bridge
The trippers from the seaside town ;
Laughs as they bang the bobbing heads
And shove them bubbling down to drown.

There sweeps a spiral whirl of gesture
From the allegoric sky :
Beauty, like conscious lightning, runs
Through Jove's ribbed trunk and Juno's thigh,

Slides down the flank of Mars and takes
From Virtue's rump a dizzier twist,
Licks round a cloud and whirling stoops
Earthwards to Caesar's lifted fist.

A burgess tumbles from the bridge
Headlong, and hurrying Beauty slips
From Caesar through the plunging legs
To the blue sea between the ships.

Reading it through, I flatter myself that this is very nearly up to international halma form. A little more, and I shall be playing in critical test-matches against Monsieur Cocteau and Miss Amy Lowell. Enormous honour ! I shrink from beneath its impendence.

But ah ! those Caesars. They have haunted me for years. I have had such schemes for putting half the universe into two or three dozen poems about those monsters. All the sins, to begin with, and complementarily all the virtues. . . . Art, science, history, religion—they too were to have found their place. And God knows what besides. But they never came to much, these Caesars. The notion, I soon came to see, was too large and pretentious ever to be realized. I began (deep calls to deep) with

Nero, the artist.   ' Nero and Sporus walking in the gardens of the
Golden House.'

> Dark stirrings in the perfumed air
> Touch your cheeks, lift your hair.
> With softer fingers I caress,
> Sporus, all your loveliness.
> Round as a fruit, tree-tangled, shines
> The moon ; and fire-flies in the vines,
> Like stars in a delirious sky,
> Gleam and go out.   Unceasingly
> The fountains fall, the nightingales
> Sing.   But time flows and love avails
> Nothing.   The Christians smoulder red ;
> Their brave blue-hearted flames are dead.
> And you, sweet Sporus, you and I,
> We too must die, we too must die.

But the soliloquy which followed was couched in a more philosophic
key.   I set forth in it all the reasons for halma's existence—reasons
which, at the time when I composed the piece, I almost believed
in still.   One lives and learns.   Meanwhile, here it is.

> The Christians by whose muddy light
> Dimly, dimly I divine
> Your eyes and see your pallid beauty
> Like a pale night-primrose shine
>
> Colourless in the dark, revere
> A God who slowly died that they
> Might suffer the less ; who bore the pain
> Of all time in a single day,
>
> The pain of all men in a single
> Wounded body and sad heart.
>
> The yellow marble smooth as water
> Builds me a Golden House ; and there
> The marble gods sleep in their strength
> And the white Parian girls are fair.

Roses and waxen oleanders,
Green grape bunches and the flushed peach,—
All beautiful things I taste, touch, see,
Knowing, loving, becoming each.

The ship went down, my mother swam;
I wedded and myself was wed;
Old Claudius died of emperor-bane:
Old Seneca too slowly bled.

The wild beast and the victim both,
The ravisher and the wincing bride;
King of the world and a slave's slave,
Terror-haunted, deified—

An artist, O sweet Sporus, an artist,
All these I am and needs must be.
Is the tune Lydian?   I have loved you.
And you have heard my symphony

Of wailing voices and clashed brass,
With long shrill flutings that suspend
Pain o'er a muttering gulf of terrors,
And piercing breathless joys that end

In agony—could I have made
My song of Furies were the bane
Still sap within the hemlock stalk,
The red swords virgin bright again?

Or take a child's love that is all
Worship, all tenderness and trust,
A dawn-web, dewy and fragile—take
And with the violence of lust

Tear and defile it.   You shall hear
The breaking dumbness and the thin
Harsh crying that is the very music
Of shame and the remorse of sin.

Christ died; the artist lives for all;
Loves, and his naked marbles stand
Pure as a column on the sky,
Whose lips, whose breast and thighs demand

> Not our humiliation, not
> The shuddering of an after shame ;
> And of his agonies men know
> Only the beauty born of them.
>
> Christ died, but living Nero turns
> Your mute remorse to song ; he gives
> To idiot fate eyes like a lover's,
> And while his music plays, God lives.

Romantic and noble sentiments ! I protest, they do me credit.

And then there are the fragments about Tiberius ; Tiberius, need I add, the representative in my symbolic scheme of love. Here is one. 'In the gardens at Capri.' (All my scenes are laid in gardens, I notice, at night, under the moon. Perhaps the fact is significant. Who knows ?)

> Hour after hour the stars
> Move, and the moon towards remoter night
> Averts her cheek.
> Blind now, these gardens yet remember
> That there were crimson petals glossy with light,
> And their remembrance is this scent of roses.
> Hour after hour the stars march slowly on,
> And year by year mysteriously the flowers
> Unfold the same bright pattern towards the sky.
>
> Incurious under the streaming stars,
> Breathing this new yet immemorial perfume
> Unmoved, I lie along the tumbled bed ;
> And the two women who are my bedfellows,
> Whose breath is sour with wine and their soft bodies
> Still hot and rank, sleep drunkenly at my side.

Commendable, I should now think, this fixture of the attention upon the relevant, the human reality in the centre of the pointless landscape. It was just at the time I wrote this fragment that I was learning the difficult art of this exclusive concentration on the relevant. They were painful lessons. War had prepared me to receive them ; Love was the lecturer.

Her name was Barbara Waters. I saw her first when I was about fourteen. She was a month or two older than I. It was at one of those enormous water picnics on the Cherwell that were organized from time to time during the summer vacation by certain fiery and energetic spirits among the dons' wives. We would start out at seven, half a dozen punt-loads of us, from the most northerly of the Oxford boat-houses and make our way up-stream for an hour or so until night had fairly set in. Then, disembarking in some solitary meadow, we would spread cloths, unpack hampers, eat hilariously. And there were so many midges that even the schoolboys were allowed to smoke cigarettes to keep them off— even the schoolgirls. And how knowingly and with what a relish we, the boys, puffed away, blowing the smoke through our noses, opening our mouths like frogs to make rings! But the girls always managed to make their cigarettes come to pieces, got the tobacco into their mouths and, making faces, had to pick the bitter-tasting threads of it from between their lips. In the end, after much giggling, they always threw their cigarettes away, not half smoked; the boys laughed, contemptuously and patronizingly. And finally we packed ourselves into the punts again and floated home, singing; our voices across the water sounded praeter-naturally sweet. A yellow moon as large as a pumpkin shone overhead; there were gleamings on the crests of the ripples and in the troughs of the tiny waves, left in the wake of the punts, shadows of almost absolute blackness. The leaves of the willow trees shone like metal. A white mist lay along the meadows. Corncrakes incessantly ran their thumbs along the teeth of combs. A faint weedy smell came up from the river; the aroma of tobacco cut violently across it in pungent gusts; sometimes the sweet animal smell of cows insinuated itself into the watery atmosphere, and looking between the willows, we would see a company of the large and gentle beasts kneeling in the grass, their heads and backs projecting like the crests of mountains above the mist, still hard at work, though the laborious day was long since over, chewing and chewing away at a green breakfast that had merged into luncheon, at the tea that had become in due course a long-drawn-out vegetarian dinner. Munchily, squelchily, they moved their indefatigable jaws. The sound came faintly to us through the silence. Then a small clear voice would begin singing ' Drink to me only with thine eyes ' or ' Greensleeves.'

Sometimes, for the fun of the thing, though it was quite un-necessary, and if the weather happened to be really warm, positively disagreeable, we would light a fire, so that we might have the pleasure of eating our cold chicken and salmon mayonnaise with potatoes baked—or generally either half baked or burnt—in their jackets among the glowing cinders. It was by the light of one of these fires that I first saw Barbara. The punt in which I came had started some little time after the others ; we had had to wait for a late arrival. By the time we reached the appointed supping place the others had disembarked and made all ready for the meal. The younger members of the party had collected materials for a fire, which they were just lighting as we approached. A group of figures, pale and colourless in the moonlight, were standing or sitting round the white cloth. In the black shadow of a huge elm tree a few yards further off moved featureless silhouettes. Suddenly a small flame spurted from a match and was shielded between a pair of hands that were transformed at once into hands of transparent coral. The silhouettes began to live a fragmentary life. The fire-bearing hands moved round the pyre ; two or three new little flames were born. Then, to the sound of a great hurrah, the bonfire flared up. In the heart of the black shadow of the elm tree a new small universe, far vivider than the ghostly world of moonlight beyond, was suddenly created. By the light of the bright flames I saw half a dozen familiar faces belonging to the boys and girls I knew. But I hardly noticed them ; I heeded only one face, a face I did not know. The leaping flame revealed it apocalyptically. Flushed, bright and with an air of being almost supernaturally alive in the quivering, changing light of the flames, it detached itself with an incredible clarity and precision from against a background of darkness which the fire had made to seem yet darker. It was the face of a young girl. She had dark hair with ruddy golden lights in it. The nose was faintly aquiline. The openings of the eyes were narrow, long and rather slanting, and the dark eyes looked out through them as though through mysterious loopholes, brilliant, between the fringed eyelids, with an intense and secret and unutterable happiness.

The mouth seemed to share in the same exquisite secret. Not full, but delicately shaped, the unparted lips were curved into a smile that seemed to express a delight more piercing than any laughter, any outburst of joy could give utterance to. The corners of the mouth were drawn upwards so that the line of the meeting of the lips was parallel with her tilted eyes. And this slanting close-lipped smile seemed as though suspended on two little folds that wrinkled the cheeks at the corners of the mouth. The face, which was rather broad across the cheek-bones, tapered away to a pointed chin, small and firm. Her neck was round and slender ; her arms, which were bare in her muslin dress, very thin.

The punt moved slowly against the current. I gazed and gazed at the face revealed by the flickering light of the fire. It seemed to me that I had never seen anything so beautiful and wonderful. What was the secret of that inexpressible joy ? What nameless happiness dwelt behind those dark-fringed eyes, that silent, un-emphatic, close-lipped smile ? Breathlessly I gazed. I felt the tears coming into my eyes—she was so beautiful. And I was almost awed, I felt something that was almost fear, as though I had suddenly come into the presence of more than a mere mortal being, into the presence of life itself. The flame leapt up. Over the silent, secret-smiling face the tawny reflections came and went, as though wild blood were fluttering deliriously beneath the skin.

The others were shouting, laughing, waving their arms. She remained perfectly still, close-lipped and narrow-eyed, smiling. Yes, life itself was standing there.

The punt bumped against the bank. 'Catch hold,' somebody shouted, 'catch hold, Francis.'

Reluctantly I did as I was told; I felt as though something precious were being killed within me.

In the years that followed I saw her once or twice. She was an orphan, I learned, and had relations in Oxford with whom she came occasionally to stay. When I tried to speak to her, I always found myself too shy to do more than stammer or say something trivial or stupid. Serenely, looking at me steadily between her eyelids, she answered. I remember not so much what she said as the tone in which she spoke—cool, calm, assured, as befitted the embodiment of life itself.

'Do you play tennis?' I would ask in desperation—and I could have wept at my own stupidity and lack of courage. Why are you so beautiful? What do you think about behind your secret eyes? Why are you so inexplicably happy? Those were the questions I wanted to ask her.

'Yes, I love tennis,' she gravely answered.

Once, I remember, I managed to advance so far along the road of coherent and intelligent conversation as to ask her what books she liked best. She looked at me unwaveringly while I spoke. It was I who reddened and turned away. She had an unfair advantage over me—the advantage of being able to look out from between her narrowed eyelids as though from an ambush. I was in the open and utterly without protection.

'I don't read much,' she said at last, when I had finished. 'I don't really very much like reading.'

My attempt to approach, to make contact, was baffled. At the same time I felt that I ought to have known that she wouldn't like reading. After all, what need was there for her to read?

When one is life itself, one has no use for mere books. Years later she admitted that she had always made an exception for the novels of Gene Stratton-Porter. When I was seventeen she went to live with another set of relations in South Africa.

Time passed. I thought of her constantly. All that I read of love in the poets arranged itself significantly round the memory of that lovely and secretly smiling face. My friends would boast about their little adventures. I smiled unenviously, knowing not merely in theory but by actual experience that that sort of thing was not love. Once, when I was a freshman at the university, I myself, at the end of a tipsy evening in a night club, lapsed from the purity in which I had lived up till then. Afterwards, I was horribly ashamed. And I felt that I had made myself unworthy of love. In consequence—the link of cause and effect seems to me now somewhat difficult to discover, but at the time, I know, I found my action logical enough—in consequence I overworked myself, won two university prizes, became an ardent revolutionary and devoted many hours of my leisure to ' social service ' in the college Mission. I was not a good social servant, got on only indifferently well with fierce young adolescents from the slums and thoroughly disliked every moment I spent in the Mission. But it was precisely for that reason that I stuck to the job. Once or twice, even, I consented to join in the morris dancing in my mother's garden. I was making myself worthy—for what ? I hardly know. The possibility of marriage seemed almost infinitely remote ; and somehow I hardly desired it. I was fitting myself to go on loving and loving, and incidentally to do great things.

Then came the war. From France I wrote her a letter, in which I told her all the things I had lacked the power to say in her presence. I sent the letter to the only address I knew—she had left it years before—not expecting, not even hoping very much, that she would receive it. I wrote it for my own satisfaction, in order to make explicit all that I felt. I had no doubt that I should soon be dead. It was a letter addressed not so much to a woman as to God, a letter of explanation and apology posted to the universe.

In the winter of 1916 I was wounded. At the end of my spell in hospital I was reported unfit for further active service and appointed to a post in the contracts department of the Air Board. I was put in charge of chemicals, celluloid, rubber tubing, castor oil, linen and balloon fabrics. I spent my time haggling with German Jews over the price of chemicals and celluloid, with Greek brokers over the castor oil, with Ulstermen over the linen. Spectacled Japanese came to visit me with samples of crêpe de Chine which they tried to persuade me—and they offered choice cigars— would be both better and cheaper than cotton for the manufacture of balloons. Of every one of the letters I dictated first eleven, then seventeen, and finally, when the department had flowered to the height of its prosperity, twenty-two copies were made, to be noted and filed by the various sub-sections of the ministry concerned. The Hotel Cecil was filled with clerks. In basements two stories down beneath the surface of the ground, in attics above the level of the surrounding chimney-pots, hundreds of young women tapped away at typewriters. In a subterranean ball-room, that looked like the setting for Belshazzar's feast, a thousand cheap lunches were daily consumed. In the hotel's best bedrooms overlooking the Thames sat the professional civil servants of long standing with letters after their names, the big business men who were helping to win the war, the staff officers. A fleet of very large motor cars waited for them in the courtyard. Sometimes, when I entered the office of a morning, I used to imagine myself a visitor from Mars. . . .

One morning—it was after I had been at the Air Board for several months—I found myself faced with a problem which could only be solved after consultation with an expert in the Naval Department. The naval people lived in the range of buildings on the opposite side of the courtyard from that in which our offices were housed. It was only after ten minutes of labyrinthine wanderings that I at last managed to find the man I was looking for. He was a genial fellow, I remember; asked me how I liked Bolo House (which was the nickname among the knowing of our precious Air Board office), gave me an East Indian cheroot and even offered whiskey and soda. After that we settled down to a technical chat about non-inflammable celluloid. I left him at last, much enlightened.

' So long,' he called after me. ' And if ever you want to know any mortal thing about acetone or any other kind of bloody dope, come to me and I 'll tell you.'

' Thanks,' I said. ' And if by any chance you should happen to want to know about Apollonius Rhodius, shall we say, or Chaucer, or the history of the three-pronged fork . . .'

He roared very heartily. ' I 'll come to you,' he concluded.

Still laughing, I shut the door behind me and stepped out into the corridor. A young woman was hurrying past with a thick bundle of papers in her hand, humming softly as she went. Startled by my sudden emergence, she turned and looked at me. As though with fear, my heart gave a sudden thump, then seemed to stop for a moment altogether, seemed to drop down within me.

' Barbara ! '

At the sound of the name she halted and looked at me with that steady unwavering gaze between the narrowed eyelids that I knew so well. A little frown appeared on her forehead; puzzled, she pursed her lips. Then all at once her face brightened, she laughed; the light in the dark eyes joyously quivered and danced.

' Why, it 's Francis Chelifer,' she exclaimed. ' I didn't know you for the first minute. You 've changed.'

' You haven't,' I said. ' You 're just the same.'

She said nothing, but smiled, close-lipped, and from between her lashes looked at me as though from an ambush. In her young maturity she was more beautiful than ever. Whether I was glad or sorry to see her again, I hardly know. But I do know that I was moved, profoundly ; I was shaken and troubled out of whatever equanimity I possessed. That memory of a kind of symbolic loveliness for which and by which I had been living all these years was now reincarnated and stood before me, no longer a symbol, but an individual ; it was enough to make one feel afraid.

' I thought you were in South Africa,' I went on. ' Which is almost the same as saying I thought you didn't exist.'

' I came home a year ago.'

' And you 've been working here ever since ? '

Barbara nodded.

' And you 're working in Bolo House too ? ' she asked.

' For the last six months.'

' Well I never ! And to think we never met before ! But how small the world is—how absurdly small.'

We met for luncheon.

' Did you get my letter ? ' I summoned up courage to ask her over the coffee.

Barbara nodded. ' It was months and months on its way,' she said ; and I did not know whether she made the remark deliberately, in order to stave off for a moment the inevitable discussion of the letter, or if she made it quite spontaneously and without afterthought, because she found it interesting that the letter should have been so long on its way. ' It went to South Africa and back again,' she explained.

' Did you read it ? '

' Of course.'

' Did you understand what I meant ? ' As I asked the question I wished that I had kept silence. I was afraid of what the answer might be.

She nodded and said nothing, looking at me mysteriously, as though she had a secret and profound comprehension of everything.

' It was something almost inexpressible,' I said. Her look encouraged me to go on. ' Something so deep and so vast that there were no words to describe it. You understood? You really understood?'

Barbara was silent for some time. Then with a little sigh she said : ' Men are always silly about me. I don't know why.'

I looked at her. Could she really have uttered those words? She was still smiling as life itself might smile. And at that moment I had a horrible premonition of what I was going to suffer. Nevertheless I asked how soon I might see her again. To-night? Could she dine with me to-night? Barbara shook her head ; this evening she was engaged. What about lunch to-morrow? ' I must think.' And she frowned, she pursed her lips. No, she remembered in the end, to-morrow was no good. Her first moment of liberty was at dinner-time two days later.

I returned to my work that afternoon feeling particularly Martian. Eight thick files relating to the Imperial Cellulose Company lay on my desk. My secretary showed me the experts' report on proprietary brands of castor oil, which had just come in. A rubber tubing man was particularly anxious to see me. And did I still want her to get a trunk call through to Belfast about that linen business? Pensively I listened to what she was saying. What was it all for?

' Are men often silly about you, Miss Masson?' it suddenly occurred to me to ask. I looked up at my secretary, who was waiting for me to answer her questions and tell her what to do.

Miss Masson became surprisingly red and laughed in an embarrassed, unnatural way. ' Why, no,' she said. ' I suppose I'm an ugly duckling.' And she added : ' It's rather a relief. But what makes you ask?'

She had reddish hair, bobbed and curly, a very white skin and brown eyes. About twenty-three, I supposed ; and she wasn't an ugly duckling at all. I had never talked to her except about business, and seldom looked at her closely, contenting myself with being merely aware that she was there—a secretary, most efficient.

'What makes you ask?' A strange expression that was like a look of terror came into Miss Masson's eyes.

'Oh, I don't know. Curiosity. Perhaps you'll see if you can get me through to Belfast some time in the afternoon. And tell the rubber tubing man that I can't possibly see him.'

Miss Masson's manner changed. She smiled at me efficiently, secretarially. Her eyes became quite impassive. 'You can't possibly see him,' she repeated. She had a habit of repeating what other people had just said, even reproducing like an echo opinions or jokes uttered an instant before as though they were her own. She turned away and walked towards the door. I was left alone with the secret history of the Imperial Cellulose Company, the experts' report on proprietary brands of castor oil, and my own thoughts.

Two days later Barbara and I were dining very expensively at a restaurant where the diners were able very successfully to forget that the submarine campaign was in full swing and that food was being rationed.

'I think the decorations are so pretty,' she said, looking round her. 'And the music.' (Mrs. Cloudesley Shove thought the same of the Corner Houses.)

While she looked round at the architecture, I looked at her. She was wearing a rose-coloured evening dress, cut low and without sleeves. The skin of her neck and shoulders was very white. There was a bright rose in the opening of her corsage. Her arms without being bony were still very slender, like the arms of a little girl; her whole figure was slim and adolescent.

'Why do you stare at me like that?' she asked, when the fascination of the architecture was exhausted. She had heightened the colour of her cheeks and faintly smiling lips. Between the darkened eyelids her eyes looked brighter than usual.

'I was wondering why you were so happy. Secretly happy, inside, all by yourself. What's the secret? That's what I was wondering.'

'Why shouldn't I be happy?' she asked. 'But, as a matter of fact,' she added an instant later, 'I'm not happy. How can one be happy when thousands of people are being killed every minute and millions more are suffering?' She tried to look grave, as though she were in church. But the secret joy glittered irrepressibly through the slanting narrow openings of her eyes. Within its ambush her soul kept incessant holiday.

I could not help laughing. 'Luckily,' I said, 'our sympathy for suffering is rarely strong enough to prevent us from eating dinner. Do you prefer lobster or salmon?'

'Lobster,' said Barbara. 'But how stupidly cynical you are! You don't believe what I say. But I do assure you, there's not a moment when I don't remember all those killed and wounded. And poor people too: the way they live—in the slums. One can't be happy. Not really.' She shook her head.

I saw that if I pursued this subject of conversation, thus forcing her to continue her pretence of being in church, I should ruin her evening and make her thoroughly dislike me. The waiter with the wine list made a timely diversion. I skimmed the pages. 'What do you say to a quart of champagne cup?' I suggested.

'That would be delicious,' she said, and was silent, looking at me meanwhile with a questioning, undecided face that did not know how to adjust itself—whether to continued gravity or to a more natural cheerfulness.

I put an end to her indecision by pointing to a diner at a neighbouring table and whispering: 'Have you ever seen anything so like a tapir?'

She burst into a peal of delighted laughter; not so much because what I had said was particularly funny, but because it was such a tremendous relief to be allowed to laugh again with a good conscience.

'Or wouldn't you have said an ant-eater?' she suggested,

looking in the direction I had indicated and then leaning across
the table to speak the words softly and intimately into my ear.
Her face approached, dazzlingly beautiful. I could have cried
aloud. The secret happiness in her eyes was youth, was health,
was uncontrollable life. The close lips smiled with a joyful sense
of power. A rosy perfume surrounded her. The red rose between her breasts was brilliant against the white skin. I was
aware suddenly that under the glossy silk of her dress was a young
body, naked. Was it for this discovery that I had been preparing
myself all these years?

After dinner we went to a music hall, and when the show was
over to a night club where we danced. She told me that she went
dancing almost every night. I did not ask with whom. She
looked appraisingly at all the women who came in, asked me if I
didn't think this one very pretty, that most awfully attractive; and
when, on the contrary, I found them rather repulsive, she was
annoyed with me for being insufficiently appreciative of her sex.
She pointed out a red-haired woman at another table and asked me
if I liked women with red hair. When I said that I preferred
Buckle's *History of Civilization*, she laughed as though I had said
something quite absurdly paradoxical. It was better when she
kept silence; and fortunately she had a great capacity for silence,
could use it even as a defensive weapon, as when, to questions that
at all embarrassed or nonplussed her, she simply returned no
answer, however often they were repeated, smiling all the time
mysteriously and as though from out of another universe.

We had been at the night club about an hour, when a stoutish
and flabby young man, very black-haired, very dark-skinned, with
a large fleshy nose and a nostril curved in an opulent oriental
volute, came sauntering in with a lordly air of possession. He
wore a silver monocle in his left eye, and among the irrepressible
black stubbles of his chin the grains of poudre de riz glittered
like little snowflakes. Catching sight of Barbara he smiled,

lavishly, came up to our table and spoke to her. Barbara seemed very glad to see him.

'Such a clever man,' she explained, when he had moved away to another table with the red-haired lady to whom I preferred the *History of Civilization*. 'He's a Syrian. You ought to get to know him. He writes poetry too, you know.'

I was unhappy the whole evening; but at the same time I wished it would never end. I should have liked to go on for ever sitting in that stuffy cellar, where the jazz band sounded so loud that it seemed to be playing inside one's head. I would have breathed the stale air and wearily danced for ever, I would even have listened for ever to Barbara's conversation—for ever, so that I might have been allowed to be near her, to look at her, to speculate, until she next spoke, on the profound and lovely mysteries behind her eyes, on the ineffable sources of that secret joy which kept her faintly and yet how intently and how rapturously smiling.

The weeks passed. I saw her almost every day. And every day I loved her more violently and painfully, with a love that less and less resembled the religious passion of my boyhood. But it was the persistent memory of that passion which made my present desire so parching and tormenting, that filled me with a thirst that no possible possession could assuage. No possible possession, since whatever I might possess, as I realized more and more clearly each time I saw her, would be utterly different from what I had desired all these years to possess. I had desired all beauty, all that exists of goodness and truth, symbolized and incarnate in one face. And now the face drew near, the lips touched mine; and what I had got was simply a young woman with a 'temperament,' as the euphemists who deplore the word admiringly and lovingly qualify the lascivious thing. And yet, against all reason, in spite of all the evidence, I could not help believing that she was somehow and secretly what I had imagined her. My love for her as a symbol strengthened my desire for her as an individual woman.

All this, were it to happen to me now, would seem perfectly natural and normal. If I were to make love to a young woman, I should know precisely what I was making love to. But that, in those days, was something I still had to learn. In Barbara's company I was learning it with a vengeance. I was learning that it is possible to be profoundly and slavishly in love with some one for whom one has no esteem, whom one does not like, whom one regards as a bad character and who, finally, not only makes one unhappy but bores one. And why not, I might now ask, why not? That things should be like this is probably the most natural thing in the world. But in those days I imagined that love ought always to be mixed up with affection and admiration, with worship and an intellectual rapture, as unflagging as that which one experiences during the playing of a symphony. Sometimes, no doubt, love does get involved with some or all of these things; sometimes these things exist by themselves, apart from love. But one must be prepared to swallow one's love completely neat and unadulterated. It is a fiery, crude and somewhat poisonous draught.

Every hour I spent with Barbara brought fresh evidence of her inability to play the ideal part my imagination had all these years been assigning to her. She was selfish, thirsty for pleasures of the most vulgar sort, liked to bask in an atmosphere of erotic admiration, amused herself by collecting adorers and treating them badly, was stupid and a liar—in other words, was one of the normal types of healthy young womanhood. I should have been less disturbed by these discoveries if only her face had been different. Unfortunately, however, the healthy young woman who now revealed herself had the same features as that symbolic child on the memory of whose face I had brooded through all an ardent adolescence. And the contrast between what she was and what—with that dazzling and mysteriously lovely face—she ought to have been, what in my imagination she indeed had been, was a perpetual source of surprise and pain. And at the same time the nature of my passion for her had changed—changed inevitably and profoundly, the moment she ceased to be a symbol and became an individual. Now, I desired her; before, I had loved her for God's sake and almost as though she were herself divine. And con-trasting this new love with the love I had felt before, I was ashamed, I fancied myself unworthy, base, an animal. And I tried to persuade myself that if she seemed different it was because I felt differently and less nobly towards her. And sometimes, when we sat silent through long summer twilights under the trees in the Park, or at my Chelsea rooms, looking out on to the river, I could persuade myself for a precarious moment that Barbara was what she had been in my imagination and that I felt towards her now what I had felt towards the memory of her. In the end, however, Barbara would break the magic silence and with it the illusion.

'It's such a pity,' she would say pensively, 'that July hasn't got an r in it. Otherwise we might have had supper in an oyster bar.'

Or else, remembering that I was a literary man, she would look at the gaudy remains of the sunset and sigh. 'I wish *I* were a poet,' she would say.

And I was back again among the facts, and Barbara was once more a tangible young woman who bored me, but whom I desired —with what a definite and localized longing!—to kiss, to hold fast and caress.

It was a longing which, for some time, I rigorously suppressed. I fought against it as against an evil thing, too horribly unlike my previous love, too outrageously incompatible with my conception of Barbara's higher nature. I had not yet learned to reconcile myself to the fact that Barbara's higher nature was an invention of my own, a figment of my proper imagination.

One very hot evening in July I drove her to the door of the house in Regent Square, Bloomsbury, in which she occupied a little flat under the roof. We had been dancing and it was late; a hunch-backed moon had climbed a third of the way up the sky and was shining down into the square over the shoulder of the church that stands on its eastern side. I paid off the cabman and we were left alone on the pavement. I had been bored and irritated the whole evening; but at the thought that I should have to bid her good-night and walk off by myself I was filled with such an anguish that the tears came into my eyes. I stood there in silent irresolution, looking into her face. It was calmly and mysteriously smiling as though to itself and for some secret reason; her eyes were very bright. She too was silent, not restlessly, not irresolutely as I was silent, but easily, with a kind of majesty. She could live in silence, when she so desired, like a being in its proper element.

' Well,' I brought myself to say at last, ' I must go.'

' Why not come in for a final cup of tea ? ' she suggested.

Actuated by that spirit of perversity which makes us do what we do not want to do, what we know will make us suffer as much as it is possible in the given circumstance to suffer, I shook my head. ' No,' I said. ' I must get back.'

I had never longed for anything more passionately than I longed to accept Barbara's invitation.

She repeated it. ' Do come in,' she said. ' It won't take a minute to make tea on the gas ring.'

Again I shook my head, in too much anguish, this time, to be able to speak. My trembling voice, I was afraid, would have betrayed me. Instinctively I knew that if I went into the house with her we should become lovers. My old determination to resist what had seemed the baser desires strengthened my resolution not to go in.

' Well, if you won't,' she shrugged her shoulders, ' then good-night.' Her voice had a note of annoyance in it.

I shook her hand and walked dumbly away. When I had gone ten yards my resolution abjectly broke down. I turned. Barbara was still standing on the doorstep, trying to fit the latchkey into the lock.

'Barbara,' I called in a voice that sounded horribly unnatural in my own ears. I hurried back. She turned to look at me. 'Do you mind if I change my mind and accept your invitation after all? I find I really am rather thirsty.' What a humiliation, I thought.

She laughed. 'What a goose you are, Francis.' And she added in a bantering tone: 'If you weren't such a silly old dear I'd tell you to go to the nearest horse-trough and drink there.'

'I'm sorry,' I said. Standing once more close to her, breathing once again her rosy perfume, I felt as I had felt when, a child, I had run down from my terrifying night nursery to find my mother sitting in the dining-room—reassured, relieved of a hideous burden, incredibly happy, but at the same time profoundly miserable in the consciousness that what I was doing was against all the rules, was a sin, the enormity of which I could judge from the very mournful tenderness of my mother's eyes and the severe, portentous silence out of which, as though from a thundercloud, my huge and bearded father looked at me like an outraged god. I was happy, being with Barbara; I was utterly miserable because I was not with her, so to speak, in the right way: I was not I; she, for all that the features were the same, was no longer herself. I was happy at the thought that I should soon be kissing her; miserable because that was not how I wanted to love my imaginary Barbara; miserable too, when I secretly admitted to myself the existence of the real Barbara, because I felt it an indignity to be the slave of such a mistress.

'Of course, if you want me to go,' I said, reacting feebly again towards revolt, 'I'll go.' And desperately trying to be facetious, 'I'm not sure that it wouldn't be best if I drowned myself in that horse-trough,' I added.

'As you like,' she said lightly. The door was open now; she walked into the darkness. I followed her, closing the door behind me carefully. We groped our way up steep dark stairs. She unlocked another door, turned a switch. The sudden light was dazzling.

'All's well that ends well,' she said, smiling at me, and she slipped the cloak from off her bare shoulders.

On the contrary, I thought, it was the tragedy of errors. I stepped towards her, I stretched out my hands and gripped her by her two thin arms a little below the shoulder. I bent down and kissed her averted cheek; she turned her face towards me, and it was her mouth.

> There is no future, there is no more past ;
> No roots nor fruits, but momentary flowers,
> Lie still, only lie still and night will last
> Silent and dark, not for a space of hours,
> But everlastingly. Let me forget
> All but your perfume, every night but this,
> The shame, the fruitless weeping, the regret.
> Only lie still : this faint and quiet bliss
> Shall flower upon the brink of sleep and spread
> Till there is nothing else but you and I
> Clasped in a timeless silence. But like one
> Who, doomed to die, at morning will be dead,
> I know, though night seem dateless, that the sky
> Must brighten soon before to-morrow's sun.

It was then that I learned to live only in the moment—to ignore causes, motives, antecedents, to refuse responsibility for what should follow. It was then that I learned, since the future was always bound to be a painful repetition of what had happened before, never to look forward for comfort or justification, but to live now and here in the heart of human reality, in the very centre of the hot dark hive. But there is a spontaneous thoughtlessness which no thoughtful pains can imitate. Being what I am, I shall never rival with those little boys who throw their baby sisters over the cliff for the sake of seeing the delightful splash ; never put a pistol to my head and for the mere fun of the thing pull the trigger; never, looking down from the gallery at Covent Garden at the thronged Wagnerites or Saint-Saënsians in the stalls below, lightly toss down that little hand-grenade (however piercingly amusing the jest might be), which I still preserve, charged with its pound of high explosive, in my hat-box, ready for all emergencies. Such gorgeous carelessness of all but the immediate sensation I can only remotely imitate. But I do my best, and I did it always conscientiously with Barbara. Still, the nights always did come to an end. And even during them, lapped in the temperament, I could never, even for an instant, be quite unaware of who she was, who I was and had been and would be to-morrow. The recollection of these things deprived every rapture of its passionate integrity and beneath the surface of every calm and silent trance spread out a profound uneasiness. Kissing her I wished that I were not kissing her, holding her in my arms I wished that it were somebody else I was holding. And sometimes in the dark quiet silences I thought that it would be better if I were dead.

Did she love me? At any rate she often said so, even in writing. I have all her letters still—a score of scribbled notes sent up by messenger from one wing of the Hotel Cecil to the other and a few longer letters written when she was on her holiday or week-ending somewhere apart from me. Here, I spread out the sheets. It is a competent, well-educated writing; the pen rarely leaves the paper, running on from letter to letter, from word to word. A rapid writing, flowing, clear and legible. Only here and there, generally towards the ends of her brief notes, is the clarity troubled; there are scrawled words made up of formless letters. I pore over them in an attempt to interpret their meaning. 'I adore you, my beloved . . . kiss you a thousand times . . . long for it to be night . . . love you madly.' These are the fragmentary meanings I contrive to disengage from the scribbles. We write such things illegibly for the same reason as we clothe our bodies.

Modesty does not permit us to walk naked, and the expression of our most intimate thoughts, our most urgent desires and secret memories, must not—even when we have so far done violence to ourselves as to commit the words to paper—be too easily read and understood. Pepys, when he recorded the most scabrous details of his loves, is not content with writing in cipher; he breaks into bad French as well. And I remember, now that I mention Pepys, having done the same sort of thing in my own letters to Barbara; winding up with a ' Bellissima, ti voglio un bene enorme,' or a ' Je t'embrasse un peu partout.'

But did she love me? In a kind of way I think she did. I gratified her vanity. Her successes so far had mostly been with genial young soldiers. She had counted few literary men among her slaves. And being infected with the queer snobbery of those who regard an artist, or any one calling himself by that name, as somehow superior to other beings—she was more impressed by a Café Royal loafer than by an efficient officer, and considered that it was a more arduous and finer thing to be able to paint, or even appreciate, a cubist picture or play a piece by Bartok on the piano than to run a business or plead in a court of law—being therefore deeply convinced of my mysterious importance and significance —she was flattered to have me abjectly gambolling around her. There is a German engraving of the sixteenth century, made at the time of the reaction against scholasticism, which represents a naked Teutonic beauty riding on the back of a bald and bearded man, whom she directs with a bridle and urges on with a switch. The old man is labelled Aristotle. After two thousand years of slavery to the infallible sage it was a good revenge. To Barbara, no doubt, I appeared as a kind of minor Aristotle. But what made the comparison somewhat less flattering to me was the fact that she was equally gratified by the attentions of another literary man, the swarthy Syrian with the blue jowl and the silver monocle. Even more gratified, I think; for he wrote poems which were frequently published in the monthly magazines (mine, alas, were not) and, what was more, he never lost an opportunity of telling people that he was a poet; he was for ever discussing the inconveniences and compensating advantages of possessing an artistic temperament. That, for a time at any rate, she preferred me to the Syrian was due to the fact that I was quite unattached and far more hopelessly in love with Barbara than he. The red-haired and, to me, inferior substitute for Buckle's *History* engrossed the greater part of his heart at this time. Moreover, he was a calm and experienced lover who did not lose his head about trifles. From me Barbara got passion of a kind she could not have hoped for from the Syrian —a passion which, in spite of my reluctance, in spite of my efforts to resist it, reduced me to a state of abjection at her feet. It is pleasant to be worshipped, to command and inflict pain; Barbara enjoyed these things as much as any one.

It was the Syrian who in the end displaced me. I had noticed in October that friends from South Africa, with whom it was necessary for Barbara to lunch and dine, kept arriving in ever increasing quantities. And when it wasn't friends from South Africa it was Aunt Phoebe, who had become suddenly importunate. Or old Mr. Goble, the one who had known her grandfather so well.

When I asked her to describe these festivities, she either said: 'Oh, it was dreadfully dull. We talked about the family,' or merely smiled, shrugged her shoulders and retired into her impregnable silence.

'Why do you lie to me?' I asked.

She preserved her silence and her secret smile.

There were evenings when I insisted that she should throw over the friends from South Africa and dine with me. Reluctantly she would consent; but she took her revenge on these occasions by talking about all the jolly men she had known.

One evening, when, in spite of all my entreaties, my threats and commands, she had gone to dine with Aunt Phoebe in Golders

Green and stay the night, I kept watch in Regent Square. It was a damp, cold night. From nine o'clock till past midnight I remained at my post, marching up and down opposite the house where she lived. As I walked I ran the point of my stick with a rattling noise along the railings which surrounded the gardens in the middle of the square ; that rattling accompanied my thoughts. From the dank black trees overhead an occasional heavy drop would fall. I must have walked twelve miles that evening.

In those three hours I thought of many things. I thought of the suddenly leaping bonfire and the young face shining in the darkness. I thought of my boyish love, and then how I had seen that face again and the different love it had inspired in the man. I thought of kisses, caresses, whispers in the darkness. I thought of the Syrian with his black eyebrows and his silver monocle, his buttery dark skin damply shining through the face-powder, and the powder snowy white among the black stubbles of his jowl. She was probably with him at this moment. Monna Vanna, Monna Bice—' Love 's not so pure and abstract as they use to say, who have no mistress but their Muse.' Reality gives imagination the lie direct. Barbara is the truth, I thought, and that she likes the man with the silver monocle is the truth, and that I have slept with her is the truth, and that he has too is quite probably the truth.

And it is the truth that men are cruel and stupid and that they suffer themselves to be driven even to destruction by shepherds as stupid as themselves. I thought of my passion for universal justice, of my desire that all men should be free, leisured, educated, of my imaginations of a future earth peopled by human beings who should live according to reason. But of what use is leisure, when leisure is occupied with listening-in and going to football matches ? freedom, when men voluntarily enslave themselves to politicians like those who now rule the world ? education, when the literate read the evening papers and the fiction magazines ? And the future, the radiant future—supposing that it should differ from the past in anything but the spread of material comfort and spiritual uniformity, suppose it conceivably were to be in some way superior, what has that to do with me ? Nothing whatever. Nothing, nothing, nothing.

I was interrupted in my meditations by a policeman who came up to me, politely touched his helmet and asked me what I was doing. ' I seen you walking up and down here for the last hour,' he said. I gave him half a crown and told him I was waiting for a lady. The policeman laughed discreetly. I laughed too. Indeed, the joke was a marvellously good one. When he was gone, I went on with my walking.

And this war, I thought. Was there the slightest prospect that any good would come of it ? The war to end war ! The argument was forcible enough this time ; it was backed up with a kick in the breech, the most terrific kick ever administered. But would it convince humanity more effectively than any other argument had ever done ?

Still, men are courageous, I thought, are patient, kind, self-sacrificing. But they are all the contradictory things, as well— and both, good and bad, because they can't help it. Forgive them, for they know not what they do. Everything arises from a great primeval animal stupidity. That is the deepest of all realities— stupidity, the being unaware.

And the aware, the not stupid—they are the odd exceptions, they are irrelevant to the great reality, they are lies like the ideal of love, like dreams of the future, like belief in justice. To live among their works is to live in a world of bright falsehoods, apart from the real world ; it is to escape. Escape is cowardly ; to be comforted by what is untrue or what is irrelevant to the world in which we live is stupid.

And my own talents, such as they are, are irrelevant. So is the art to whose service I devote them, a lying consolation. A Martian would find the writing of phrases containing words of similar sound at fixed recurrent intervals as queer as buying castor oil for the lubrification of machines of destruction. I remembered the lines I had written for Barbara—the cheerful comic-amorous lines—at the time of the last epidemic of air raids. The octosyllables jingled in my head.

> But when the next full moon invites
> New bugaboos and fly-by-nights,
> Let us seek out some deep alcove,
> Some immemorial haunt of love.
> There we 'll retire with cakes and wine
> And dare the imbecile to shine. . . .

I was just repeating them to myself, when a taxi turned into the quiet square, rolled slowly along the curb and came to a halt in front of the house where Barbara lived. By the dim light of a muffled street lamp I saw two people stepping out of it, a man and a woman. The masculine silhouette moved forward and, bending over his hand, began to count money by the light of the little lamp at the recording clock-face. In the narrow beam I saw the glitter of a monocle. Money clinked, the taxi drove away. The two figures mounted the steps ; the door opened before them, they passed into the house.

I walked away, repeating to myself every injurious and abusive word that can be applied to a woman. I felt, if anything, rather relieved. It pleased me to think that all was over, all was now definitely and for ever done with.

' 'Night, sir.'

It was the friendly policeman ; I thought I heard an almost imperceptible note of amusement in his voice.

For the next four days I made no sign of life. Every day I hoped that she would write or telephone to ask what had become of me. She did nothing of the kind. My sense of relief had turned into a feeling of misery. On the fifth day, as I was going out to lunch, I met her in the courtyard. She made no reference to the unprecedented length of my silence. I said none of the bitter things that I had planned to say in the event of just such an accidental meeting as this. Instead, I asked her, I implored her even, to come to lunch. Barbara declined the invitation; she had a South African engagement.

' Come to dinner, then,' I abjectly begged. Humiliation, I felt, could go no further. I would give anything to be received back into grace.

Barbara shook her head. ' I wish I could,' she said. ' But that tiresome old Mr. Goble . . .'

CHAPTER VI

SUCH, then, were the phantoms that my recitation called up to dance on the surface of the Tyrrhenian. Salutarily they reminded me that I was only on my holiday, that the landscape in the midst of which I was now floating was hardly better than an illusion and that life was only real and earnest during the eleven months of each year which I spent between Gog's Court and Miss Carruthers's. I was a democratic Englishman and a Londoner at that, living in an age when the *Daily Mail* sells two million copies every morning; I had no right to so much sunlight, so tepid and clear a sea, such spiky mountains, such clouds, such blue expanses of sky; I had no right to Shelley; and if I were a true democrat, then I ought not even to think. But again I must plead my congenital weakness.

Couched on the water, I was dreaming of the ideal democratic state where no irrelevant Holy Ghost-possessed exception should trouble the flat serenity of the rule—the rule of Cloudesley and Carruthers, Fluffy and the alert, inimitable Brimstone—when all at once I became aware that a sailing-boat was coming up behind me, was right on top of me, in fact. The white sail towered over me; with a little sizzling ripple at the prow, with a clop clop of tiny waves against its flanks, the brown varnished boat bore quickly down on me. It is a horrible thing to be afraid, to be shaken by that sudden spasm of fear which cannot be controlled because it comes so quickly that the controlling forces of the mind are taken unaware. Every cell in the body, it seems, feels terror; from a man one is humiliated for a moment into a congeries of shrinking amoebae. One descends the scale of being; one drops down the evolutionary gamut to become for a second no more than a startled and terrified beast. One moment I had been dozing on my translucent mattress, like a philosopher; the next I was inarticulately shouting, frantically moving my limbs to escape from the approaching and now inevitable peril.

F

'Hi!' I was yelling, and then something caught me a fearful crack on the side of the head and pushed me down into the water. I was conscious of swallowing a vast quantity of brine, of breathing water into my lungs and violently choking. Then for a time I knew nothing; the blow must momentarily have stunned me. I became more or less conscious again, to find myself just coming to the surface, my face half in, half out of water. I was coughing and gasping—coughing to get rid of the water that was in my lungs, gasping for air. Both processes, I now perceive, achieved exactly the contrary of what they were intended to achieve. For I coughed up all the stationary air that was in my lungs and, my mouth being under water, I drew in fresh gulps of brine. Meanwhile my blood, loaded with carbonic acid gas, kept rushing to my lungs in the hope of exchanging the deadly stuff for oxygen. In vain; there was no oxygen to exchange it for.

I felt an extraordinary pain in the back of my neck—not excruciating, but dull; dull and far-reaching and profound, and at the same time strangely disgusting—a sickening, revolting sort of pain. The nerves controlling my respiratory system were giving up in despair; that disgusting pain in my neck was their gesture of farewell, their last spasm of agony. Slowly I ceased to be conscious; I faded gradually out of life like the Cheshire Cat in *Alice in Wonderland*. The last thing that was left of me, that continued to hang in my consciousness when everything else had vanished, was the pain.

In the circumstances, I know, it would have been the classical thing if all my past life had unwound itself in a flash before the mind's eye. Whiz—an uninteresting drama in thirty-two reels ought duly to have run its course and I should have remembered everything, from the taste of the baby food in my bottle to the taste of yesterday's marsala at the Grand Hotel, from my first caning to my last kiss. In point of fact, however, none of the correct things happened. The last thoughts I remember thinking as I went down were about the Rabbit Fanciers' Gazette and my mother. In a final access of that conscientiousness which has haunted and handicapped me all my life long, I reflected that I ought to have another leading article ready by next Friday. And it struck me very forcibly that my mother would be most seriously inconvenienced when she arrived in a few days' time to find that I was no longer in a position to accompany her on her journey to Rome.

When I next came to my senses I was lying face downwards on the beach with somebody sitting astride of my back, as though we were playing horses, using Professor Schaefer's method of producing artificial respiration. ' Uno, due, tre, quattro '—and at every ' quattro ' the man on my back threw his weight forward on to his hands, which were resting, one on either side of the spine, on my lower ribs. The contents of my lungs were violently expelled. Then my rescuer straightened himself up again, the pressure was relaxed and my lungs replenished themselves with air. ' Uno, due, tre, quattro '—the process began again.

' He 's breathing ! He 's all right. He 's opening his eyes ! '

Carefully, as though I were a crate of very valuable china, they turned me right way up. I was aware of the strong sunshine, of a throbbing headache centred somewhere above the left temple, of a crowd of people standing round. With deliberation and consciously I breathed the air; loud voices shouted instructions. Two people began to rub the soles of my feet. A third ran up with a child's bucket full of sun-scorched sand and poured it on the pit of my stomach. This happy thought immediately had an immense success. All the curious and sympathetic spectators who had been standing round my corpse, looking on while Professor Schaefer was being applied to me and wishing that they could do something to help, now discovered that there was actually something helpful that they could do. They could help to restore my circulation by sprinkling hot sand on me. In a moment I had a dozen sympathizers busy around me, skimming the cream off the hot tideless beach in little buckets, with spades or in the palms of their scooping hands, to pour it over me. In a few seconds I was almost buried under a mound of burning grey sand. On the faces of all my good Samaritans I noticed an expression of child-like earnestness. They rushed backwards and forwards with their little buckets as though there were nothing more serious in life than building sand castles on the stomachs of drowned men. And the children themselves joined in. Horrified at first by the spectacle of my limp and livid corpse, they had clung to paternal hands, shrunk away behind protecting skirts, looking on while Professor Schaefer was being practised on me, with a reluctant and disgusted curiosity. But when I had come alive again, when they saw their elders burying me with sand and understood that it was really only a tremendously good game, then how violent was their reaction! Shrilly laughing, whooping with excitement and delight, they rushed on me with their little implements. It was only with difficulty that they could be prevented from throwing handfuls of sand in my face, from pouring it into my ears, from making me eat it. And one small boy, ambitious to do something that nobody else had done, rushed down to the sea, filled his bucket with water and stale foam, ran back and emptied its contents, with what a shout of triumph! plop, from a height on to my solar plexus.

That was too much for my gravity. I began to laugh. But I did not get very far with my laughter. For after the first outburst of it, when I wanted to take breath for the next, I found that I had forgotten how to breathe, and it was only after a long choking struggle that I managed to reacquire the art. The children were frightened ; this was no part of the delightful game. The grown-ups stopped being helpful and allowed themselves to be driven away from my corpse by the competent authorities. An umbrella was planted in the sand behind me. Within its rosy shadow I was left in peace to make secure my precarious footing on existence. For a long time I lay with my eyes shut. An immensely long way off, it seemed, somebody was still rubbing my feet. Periodically, somebody else pushed a spoon with brandy and milk in it into my mouth. I felt very tired, but wonderfully comfortable. And it seemed to me at that moment that there could be nothing more exquisitely pleasurable than merely breathing.

After a while, I felt sufficiently strong and sufficiently safe in my strength to open my eyes again and look about me. How novel, how wonderfully charming everything seemed! The first thing I saw was a half-naked young giant crouching obsequiously at my feet, rubbing my bloodless soles and ankles. Under his shining copper skin there was a sliding of muscles. His face was like a Roman's, his hair jet black and curly. When he noticed that I had opened my eyes and was looking at him he smiled, and his teeth were brilliantly white, his brown eyes flashed from a setting of shiny bluish enamel.

A voice asked me in Italian how I was feeling. I looked round. A stout man with a large red, rubbery face and a black moustache was sitting beside me. In one hand he held a teacup, in the other a spoon. He was dressed in white duck. The sweat was pouring off his face; he looked as though he had been buttered. From all round his very bright black eyes little wrinkles spread out like rays from a gloria. He proffered the spoon. I swallowed. The backs of his large brown hands were covered with fine hairs.

' I am the doctor,' he explained, and smiled.

I nodded and smiled back. It seemed to me that I had never seen such a lovely doctor before.

And then, when I looked up, there was the blue sky, beautifully scalloped by the edge of the pink umbrella. And lowering my eyes I saw people standing round looking at me—all smiling. Between them I caught glimpses of the blue sea.

' Belli sono,' I said to the doctor, and shut my eyes again.

And many men so beautiful. . . . In the blood-red darkness

behind my eyelids I listened to their voices. Slowly, voluptuously, I breathed the salty air. The young giant went on rubbing my feet. With an effort I lifted one of my hands and laid it on my chest. Lightly, like a blind man feeling for the sense of a page of Braille, I ran my fingers over the smooth skin. I felt the ribs and the little depressions between them. And all at once, under my finger tips, I was aware of a hardly perceptible throbbing—pulse, pulse, pulse—it was that I had been searching for. The blind fingers creeping across the page had spelled out a strange word. I did not try to interpret it. It was enough to be glad that the word was there. For a long time I lay quite still, feeling my beating heart.

'Si sente meglio?' asked the doctor.

I opened my eyes. 'Mi sento felice.' He smiled at me. The rays round the twin bright glories of his eyes emphasized themselves. It was as though the holy symbol had somehow suddenly become more holy.

'It is good not to be dead,' he said.

'It is very good.'

And I looked once more at the sky and the pink umbrella overhead. I looked at the young giant, so strong and yet so docile at my feet. I turned my eyes to right and left. The circle of curious spectators had dissolved. Out of danger, I had ceased to be an object of sympathy or curiosity. The holiday-makers were going about their business as usual. I watched them, happily.

A young couple in bathing dresses walked slowly past me towards the sea. Their faces, their necks and shoulders, their bare arms and legs were burned to a soft transparent brown. They walked slowly, holding hands, walked with such a grace, such an easy majesty that I felt like weeping. They were very young, they were tall, slender and strong. They were beautiful as a couple of young thoroughbred horses; gracefully, idly, majestically they seemed to be walking in a world that was beyond good and evil. It did not matter what they might do or say; they were justified by the mere fact that they existed. They paused, looked at me for a moment, one with brown eyes, one with grey, flashed at me with their white teeth, asked how I was, and when I told them that I was better, smiled again and passed on.

A little girl dressed in a primrose-coloured garment that was paler in tone than her dark face and limbs came running up, halted two or three yards away and began to look at me earnestly. Her eyes were very large and fringed by absurdly long black lashes. Above them there expanded an immense domed forehead that would have done credit to a philosopher. Her snub nose was so small that you hardly noticed it was there at all. Black and frizzy, her hair stood out, in a state of permanent explosion, round her head. For a long time she stared at me. I stared back.

'What do you want?' I asked at last.

And suddenly, at the sound of my voice, the child was overwhelmed by shyness. She covered her face with her forearm as though she were warding off a blow. Then, after a second or two, she peeped out at me cautiously from under her elbow. Her face had become quite red. I called again. It was once too often. She turned and ran away, ran back to her family, who were sitting, twenty yards down the beach, in the precarious and shifting oasis of shadow cast by a large striped umbrella. I saw her hurl herself into the arms of a large placid mother in white muslin. Then, having successfully abolished my existence by burying her face in the comfortable bosom, she slid down again from her mother's knee and went on playing with her little sister, serenely, as though the untoward incident had never occurred.

Mournfully, from somewhere in the distance, came the long, suspended cry of the vendor of doughnuts. 'Bomboloni.' Two young American marchesas in purple bathing gowns went past, talking together on one note, in indefatigable even voices. ' . . . and he has such a lovely mentality,' I heard one of them saying.

'But what I like,' said the other, who seemed to have acquired more completely the Latin habit of mind, 'what I like is his teeth.' A middle-aged man, with the large stomach that comes of too much *pasta*, and a very thin little boy of twelve now entered my field of vision, all wet and shiny from the sea. The hot sand burned their feet and they went hopping across the scorching beach with an agility which it was good to see. But the soles of mad Concetta's feet were made of hornier stuff. Barefooted, she walked down every morning from the mountains, carrying her basket of fruit over one arm and holding in the other hand a long staff. She hawked her wares along the beach, she went the round of the villas until her basket was empty. Then she walked back again, across the plain and up into the hills. Turning from the fat man and the little thin boy I saw her standing before me. She was dressed in a stained and tattered old dress. Her grey hair escaped in wisps from under a wide straw hat. Her old face was eager, thin and sharp; the wrinkled skin was like brown parchment stretched over the bones. Leaning on her staff, she looked at me for a little in silence.

'So you 're the drowned foreigner,' she said at last.

'If he were drowned, how could he be alive ? ' asked the doctor. The young giant found this exquisitely witty; he laughed profoundly, out of the depths of his huge chest. 'Go away now, Concetta,' the doctor went on. 'He must be kept quiet. We can't have you treating him to one of your discourses.'

Concetta paid no attention to him. She was used to this sort of thing.

'The mercy of God,' she began, shaking her head, 'where should we be without it ? You are young, signorino. You still have time to do much. God has preserved you. I am old. But I lean on the cross.' And straightening herself up, she lifted her staff. A cross-piece of wood had been nailed near the top of it. Affectionately she kissed it. 'I love the cross,' she said. 'The

cross is beautiful, the cross is . . .' But she was interrupted by
a young nurserymaid who came running up to ask for half a kilo
of the best grapes. Theology could not be allowed to interfere
with business. Concetta took out her little steelyard, put a bunch
of grapes in the pan and moved the weight back and forth along
the bar in search of equilibrium. The nurserymaid stood by.
She had a round face, red cheeks, dimples, black hair and eyes
like black buttons. She was as plump as a fruit. The young
giant looked up at her in frank admiration. She rolled the buttons
towards him—for an instant, then utterly ignored him, and humming
nonchalantly to herself as though she were alone on a desert island
and wanted to keep her spirits up, she gazed pensively away at the
picturesque beauties of nature.

'Six hundred grammes,' said Concetta.

The nurserymaid paid for them, and still humming, still on
her desert island, she walked off, taking very small steps, undulating
rotundly, like a moon among wind-driven clouds. The young
giant stopped rubbing my feet and stared after her. With the
moon's beauty and the moon's soft pace the nurserymaid tottered
along, undulating unsteadily on her high heels across the sand.

Rabear, I thought: old Skeat was perfectly right to translate
the word as he did.

'Bella grassa,' said the doctor, voicing what were obviously
the young giant's sentiments. Mine too; for after all, she was
alive, obeyed the laws of her nature, walked in the sun, ate grapes
and *rabear'd*. I shut my eyes again. Pulse, pulse, pulse; the
heart beat steadily under my fingers. I felt like Adam, newly
created and weak like a butterfly fresh from its chrysalis—the
red clay still too wet and limp to allow of my standing upright.
But soon, when it had dried to firmness, I should arise and scamper
joyously about this span new world, and be myself a young giant, a
graceful and majestic thoroughbred, a child, a wondering Bedlamite.

There are some people who contrive to pass their lives in a

state of permanent convalescence. They behave at every moment as though they had been miraculously preserved from death the moment before; they live exhilaratedly for the mere sake of living and can be intoxicated with happiness just because they happen not to be dead. For those not born convalescent it may be that the secret of happiness consists in being half-drowned regularly three times a day before meals. I recommend it as a more drastic alternative to my 'water-shoot-in-every-office' remedy for ennui.

'You 're alone here?' asked the doctor.

I nodded.

'No relations?'

'Not at present.'

'No friends of any kind?'

I shook my head.

'H 'm,' he said.

He had a wart growing on one side of his nose where it joined the cheek. I found myself studying it intently; it was a most interesting wart, whitish, but a little flushed on its upper surface. It looked like a small unripe cherry. 'Do you like cherries?' I asked.

The doctor seemed rather surprised. 'Yes,' he said, after a moment's silence and with great deliberation, as though he had been carefully weighing the matter in his mind.

'So do I.' And I burst out laughing. This time, however, my breathing triumphantly stood the strain. 'So do I. But not unripe ones,' I added, gasping with mirth. It seemed to me that nothing funnier had ever been said.

And then Mrs. Aldwinkle stepped definitely into my life. For, looking round, still heaving with the after-swell of my storm of laughter, I suddenly saw the Chinese lantern lady of the *patino* standing before me. Her flame-coloured costume, a little less radiant now that it was wet, still shone among the aquarium shadows of her green parasol, and her face looked as though it were she who had been drowned, not I.

'They tell me that you're an Englishman,' she said in the same ill-controlled, unmusical voice I had heard, not long since, misquoting Shelley.

Still tipsy, still light-headed with convalescence, I laughingly admitted it.

'I hear you were nearly drowned.'

'Quite right,' I said, still laughing; it was such a marvellous joke.

'I'm most sorry to hear . . .' She had a way of leaving her sentences unfinished. The words would tail off into a dim inarticulate blur of sound.

'Don't mention it,' I begged her. 'It isn't at all disagreeable, you know. Afterwards, at any rate . . .' I stared at her affectionately and with my convalescent's boundless curiosity. She stared back at me. Her eyes, I thought, must have the same bulge as those little red lenses one screws to the rear forks of bicycles; they collected all the light diffused around them and reflected it again with a concentrated glitter.

'I came to ask whether I could be of any assistance,' said the Chinese lantern lady.

'Most kind.'

'You're alone here?'

'Quite, for the present.'

'Then perhaps you might care to come and stay a night or two at my house, until you're entirely . . .' She mumbled, made a gesture that implied the missing word and went on. 'I have a house over there.' She waved her hand in the direction of the mountainous section of the Shelleian landscape.

Gleefully, in my tipsy mood, I accepted her invitation. 'Too delightful,' I said. Everything, this morning, was too delightful. I should have accepted with genuine, unmixed pleasure an invitation to stay with Miss Carruthers or Mr. Brimstone.

'And your name?' she asked. 'I don't know that yet.'

' Chelifer.'

' Chelifer ?   Not Francis Chelifer ? '

' Francis Chelifer,' I affirmed.

' Francis Chelifer ! '   Positively, her soul was in my name.
But how *won*derful !   I 've wanted to meet you for years.'

For the first time since I had risen intoxicated from the dead
I had an awful premonition of to-morrow's sobriety.   I remembered
for the first time that round the corner, only just round the corner,
lay the real world.

' And what 's your name ? ' I asked apprehensively.

' Lilian Aldwinkle,' said the Chinese lantern lady ; and she
shaped her lips into a smile that was positively piercing in its
sweetness.   The blue lamps that were her eyes glittered with such
a focussed intensity that even the colour-blind chauffeurs who see
green omnibuses rolling down Piccadilly and in the Green Park
blood-coloured grass and vermilion trees would have known them
for the danger signals they were.

An hour later I was reclining on cushions in Mrs. Aldwinkle's
Rolls-Royce.   There was no escape.

CHAPTER VII

No escape. . . . But I was still tipsy enough not seriously to desire escape. My premonition of sobriety had been no more than a momentary flash. It came and it passed again, almost immediately, as I became once more absorbed in what seemed to me the endless and lovely comedy that was being acted all around me. It was enough for me that I existed and that things were happening to me. I was carried by two or three young giants to the hotel, I was dressed, my clothes were packed for me. In the entrance hall, while I was waiting for Mrs. Aldwinkle to come and fetch me, I made some essays at walking; the feebleness of my legs was a source to me of delighted laughter.

Dressed in pale yellow tussore with a large straw hat on her head, Mrs. Aldwinkle finally appeared. Her guests, she explained, had gone home in another machine; I should be able to lie flat, or very nearly, in her empty car. And in case I felt bad—she shook a silver brandy flask at me. Escape ? I did not so much as think of it, I was enchanted.

Luxuriously I reclined among the cushions. Mrs. Aldwinkle tapped the forward-looking window. The chauffeur languidly moved his hand and the machine rolled forward, nosing its way through the crowd of admiring car-fanciers which, in Italy, collects as though by magic round every stationary automobile. And Mrs. Aldwinkle's was a particularly attractive specimen. Young men called to their friends : ' *Venite. È una Ro-Ro.*' And in awed voices little boys whispered to one another : ' *Una Ro-Ro.*' The crowd reluctantly dispersed before our advance ; we glided away from before the Grand Hotel, turned into the main street, crossed the piazza, in the centre of which, stranded high and dry by the receding sea, stood the little pink fort which had been built by the Princes of Massa Carrara to keep watch on a Mediterranean made dangerous by Barbary pirates, and rolled out of the village by the road leading across the plain towards the mountains.

Shuffling along in a slowly moving cloud of dust, a train of white oxen advanced, shambling and zig-zagging along the road to meet us. Eight yoke of them there were, a long procession, with half a dozen drivers shouting and tugging at the leading ropes and cracking their whips. They were dragging a low truck, clamped to which was a huge monolith of flawless white marble. Uneasily, as we crawled past them, the animals shook their heads, turning this way and that, as though desperately seeking some way of escape. Their long curving horns clashed together; their soft white dewlaps shook; and into their blank brown eyes there came a look of fear, an entreaty that we should take pity on their invincible stupidity and remember that they simply could not, however hard they tried, get used to motor cars.

Mrs. Aldwinkle pointed at the monolith. 'Imagine what Michelangelo could have made out of that,' she said. Then, noticing that her pointing hand still grasped the silver flask, she became very solicitous. 'You 're sure you wouldn't like a sip of this ?' she asked, leaning forward. The twin blue danger signals glittered in my face. Her garments exhaled a scent in which there was ambergris. Her breath smelt of heliotrope cachous. But even now I did not take fright; I made no effort to escape. Guided by their invincible stupidity, the white oxen had behaved more sensibly than I.

We rolled on. The hills came nearer. The far-away peaks of bare limestone were hidden by the glowing mass of the tilled and wooded foot-hills. Happily I looked at those huge hilly forms. 'How beautiful !' I said. Mrs. Aldwinkle seemed to take my words as a personal compliment.

' I 'm so glad you think so. So awfully . . .' she replied in the tone of an author to whom you have just said that you enjoyed his last book so much.

We drew nearer; the hills towered up, they opposed themselves like a huge wall. But the barrier parted before us; we
passed through the gates of a valley that wound up into the mountain. Our road now ran parallel with the bed of a torrent. In
the flanks of the hill to our right a marble quarry made a huge
bare scar, hundreds of feet long. The crest of the hill was fringed
with a growth of umbrella pines. The straight slender tree trunks
jetted up thirty feet without a branch; their wide-spreading
flattened domes of foliage formed a thin continuous silhouette,
between which and the dark mass of the hill one could see a band
of sky, thinly barred by the bare stems. It was as though, to
emphasize the outlines of his hills, an artist had drawn a fine and
supple brush stroke parallel with the edge of the silhouette and
a little apart from it.

We rolled on. The high road narrowed into the squalid street
of a little town. The car crept along, hooting as it went.

'Vezza,' Mrs. Aldwinkle explained. 'Michelangelo used to
come here for his marbles.'

'Indeed?' I was charmed to hear it.

Over the windows of a large shop filled with white crosses,
broken columns and statues, I read the legend: 'Anglo-American
Tombstone Company.' We emerged from the narrow street
on to an embankment running along the edge of a river. From
the opposite bank the ground rose steeply.

'There,' said Mrs. Aldwinkle on a note of triumph as we crossed
the bridge, 'that's my house.' She pointed up. From the
hill-top a long façade stared down through twenty windows; a
tall tower pricked the sky. 'The palace was built in 1630,' she
began. I even enjoyed the history lesson.

We had crossed the bridge, we were climbing by a steep and
winding road through what was almost a forest of olive trees. The
abrupt grassy slope had been built up into innumerable little
terraces on which the trees were planted. Here and there, in

167

the grey luminous shadow beneath the trees, little flocks of sheep were grazing. The barefooted children who attended them came running to the side of the road to watch us passing.

'I like to think of these old princely courts,' Mrs. Aldwinkle was saying. 'Like abbeys of . . . abbeys of . . .' She shook her brandy flask impatiently. 'You know . . . in Thingumy.'

'Abbeys of Thelema,' I suggested.

'That's it,' said Mrs. Aldwinkle. 'Sort of retiring-places where people were free to live intelligently. That's what I want to make this house. I'm so delighted to have met you like this. You're exactly the sort of person I want.' She leaned forward, smiling and glittering. But even at the prospect of entering the Abbey of Thelema I did not blench.

At this moment the car passed through a huge gateway. I caught a glimpse of a great flight of steps, set between cypresses, mounting up past a series of terraced landings to a carved doorway in the centre of the long façade. The road turned, the car swung round and the vista was closed. By an ilex avenue that wound round the flank of the hill we climbed more gradually towards the house, which we approached from the side. The road landed us finally in a large square court opposite a shorter reproduction of the great façade. At the head of a double flight of steps, curving horse-shoe fashion from the landing at its threshold, a tall pompous doorway surmounted by a coat of arms cavernously invited. The car drew up.

And about time too, as I notice on re-reading what I have written. Few things are more profoundly boring and unprofitable than literary descriptions. For the writer, it is true, there is a certain amusement to be derived from the hunt for apt expressive words. Carried away by the excitement of the chase he dashes on, regardless of the poor readers who follow toilsomely through his stiff and clayey pages like the runners at the tail of a hunt, seeing nothing of the fun. All writers are also readers—though perhaps I should make exceptions in favour of a few of my colleagues who make a speciality of native wood-notes—and must therefore know how dreary description is. But that does not prevent them from inflicting upon others all that they themselves have suffered. Indeed I sometimes think that some authors must write as they do purely out of a desire for revenge.

Mrs. Aldwinkle's other guests had arrived and were waiting for us. I was introduced and found them all equally charming. The little niece rushed to Mrs. Aldwinkle's assistance ; the young man who had rowed the *patino* rushed in his turn to the little niece's and insisted on carrying all the things of which she had relieved her aunt. The old man with the red face, who had talked about the clouds, looked on benevolently at this little scene. But another elderly gentleman with a white beard, whom I had not seen before, seemed to view it with a certain disapproval. The young lady who had talked about the whiteness of her legs and who turned out to be my distinguished colleague, Miss Mary Thriplow, was now dressed in a little green frock with a white turned-down collar, white cuffs and buttons, which made her look like a schoolgirl in a comic opera by Offenbach. The brown young man stood near her.

I got out of the car, refused all proffered assistance and contrived, a little wamblingly, it is true, to mount the steps.

' You must be very careful for a little,' said Mrs. Aldwinkle with a maternal solicitude. ' These,' she added, waving her hand in the direction of a vista of empty saloons, the entrance to which we were just then passing, ' these are the apartments of the Princesses.'

We walked right through the house into a great quadrangle surrounded on three sides by buildings and on the fourth, towards the rising hill, by an arcade. On a pedestal in the centre of the court stood a more than life-sized marble statue, representing, my hostess informed me, the penultimate Prince of Massa Carrara, wearing a very curly full-bottomed wig, Roman kilts, buskins, and one of those handsome classical breastplates which have the head of a Gorgon embossed in the middle of the chest and a little dimple to indicate the position of the navel in the middle of the round and polished belly. With the expression of one who is about to reveal a delightful secret and who can hardly wait until the moment of revelation comes to give vent to his pleasure, Mrs. Aldwinkle, smiling as it were below the surface of her face, led me to the foot of the statue. 'Look!' she said. It was one of those pretty peep-shows on which, for the sake of five minutes' amusement and titillation of the eye, Grand Monarchs used to spend the value of a rich province. From the central arch of the arcade a flight of marble steps climbed up to where, set against a semi-circle of cypresses, at the crest of the hill, a little round temple played gracefully at paganism, just as the buskined and corseleted statue in the court below played heroically at Plutarch.

'And now look here!' said Mrs. Aldwinkle; and taking me round to the other side of the statue, she led me towards a great door in the centre of the long range of buildings opposite the arcade. It was open; a vaulted corridor, like a tunnel, led clean through the house. Through it I could see the blue sky and the remote horizon of the sea. We walked along it; from the further threshold I found myself looking down the flight of steps which I had seen from below, at the entrance gate. It was a stage scene, but made of solid marble and with growing trees.

'What do you think of that?' asked Mrs. Aldwinkle.

'Magnificent,' I answered, with an enthusiasm that was beginning to be tempered by a growing physical weariness.

'Such a view,' said Mrs. Aldwinkle, poking at it with the tip of her sunshade. 'The contrast between the cypresses and the olive trees . . .'

'But the view's still lovelier from the temple,' said the little

170

niece, who was evidently very anxious to make me realize the full pricelessness of her Aunt Lilian's possessions.

Mrs. Aldwinkle turned on her. ' How utterly thoughtless you are ! ' she said severely. ' Do try to remember that poor Mr. Chelifer is still suffering from the effects of his accident. And you expect him to go climbing up to the temple ! '

The little niece blushed and drooped beneath the reproach. We sat down.

' How are you feeling now ? ' asked Mrs. Aldwinkle, remembering once more to be solicitous. . . . ' Too appalling to think,' she added, ' how nearly . . . And I 've always so enormously admired your work.'

' So have I,' declared my colleague in the green frock. ' Most awfully. Still, I confess, I find some of your things a little, how shall I say, a little alembicated. I like my poetry to be rather straightforwarder.'

' A very sophisticated desire,' said the red-faced gentleman. ' Really simple, primitive people like their poetry to be as complicated, conventional, artificial and remote from the language of everyday affairs as possible. We reproach the eighteenth century with its artificiality. But the fact is that *Beowulf* is couched in a diction fifty times more complicated and unnatural than that of the *Essay on Man*. And when you compare the Icelandic Sagas with Dr. Johnson, you find that it 's the Doctor who lisps and prattles. Only the most complicated people, living in the midst of the most artificial surroundings, desire their poetry to be simple and straightforward.'

I shut my eyes and allowed the waves of conversation to roll over me. And what a classy conversation ! Prince Papadia-mantopoulos could hardly have kept the ball rolling on a higher level. Fatigue was sobering me.

Fatigue, the body's weariness—some industrious little scientific emmet ought to catalogue and measure all its various effects. All

—for it isn't enough to show that when wage-slaves have worked too long they tend to fall into the machines and get pulped. The fact is interesting, no doubt; but there are other facts of no less significance. There is the fact, for example, that slight fatigue increases our capacity for sentiment. Those compromising love letters are always written in the small hours; it is at night, not when we are fresh and reposed, that we talk about ideal love and indulge our griefs. Under the influence of slight fatigue we feel more ready than at other times to discuss the problems of the universe, to make confidences, to dogmatize about the nature of God and to draw up plans for the future. We are also inclined to be more languidly voluptuous. When, however, the fatigue is increased beyond a certain point, we cease entirely to be sentimental, voluptuous, metaphysical or confiding. We cease to be aware of anything but the decrepitude of our being. We take no further interest in other people or the outside world—no further interest unless they will not leave us in peace, when we come to hate them with a deep but ineffectual loathing, mingled with disgust.

With me, fatigue had almost suddenly passed the critical point. My convalescent's delight in the world evaporated. My fellow beings no longer seemed to me beautiful, strange and amiable. Mrs. Aldwinkle's attempts to bring me into the conversation exasperated me; when I looked at her, I thought her a monster. I realized, too late (which made the realization the more vexatious), what I had let myself in for when I accepted Mrs. Aldwinkle's invitation. Fantastic surroundings, art, classy chats about the cosmos, the intelligentsia, love. . . . It was too much, even on a holiday.

I shut my eyes. Sometimes, when Mrs. Aldwinkle interpellated me, I said yes or no, without much regard to the sense of her remark. Discussion raged around me. From the alembication of my poetry they had gone on to art in general. Crikey, I said to myself, crikey. . . . I did my best to close the ears of my mind;

and for some little time I did, indeed, contrive to understand nothing of what was said. I thought of Miss Carruthers, of Fluffy and Mr. Brimstone, of Gog's Court and Mr. Bosk.

Mrs. Aldwinkle's voice, raised by irritation to a peculiar loudness, made itself audible to my muffled mind. 'How often have I told you, Cardan,' it said, 'that you understand nothing of modern art?'

'At least a thousand times,' Mr. Cardan replied cheerfully. 'But bless your heart,' he added (and I opened my eyes in time to see his benevolent smile), 'I never mind at all.'

The smile was evidently too much for Mrs. Aldwinkle's patience. With the gesture of a queen who implies that the audience is at an end she rose from her seat. 'Just time,' she said, looking at her watch, 'there's just time. I really must give Mr. Chelifer some idea of the inside of the palace before lunch. You'd like to come?' She smiled at me like a siren.

Too polite to remind her of her recent outburst against the little niece, I declared myself delighted by the idea. Wamblingly I followed her into the house. Behind me I heard the young rower exclaiming on a note of mingled astonishment and indignation: 'But a moment ago she was saying that Mr. Chelifer was too ill to . . .'

'Ah, but that was different,' said the voice of the red-faced man.

'Why was it different?'

'Because, my young friend, the other fellow is in all cases the rule; but *I* am invariably the exception. Shall we follow?'

Mrs. Aldwinkle made me look at painted ceilings till I almost fell down from giddiness. She dragged me through room after baroque room; then drove me up dark stairs into the Middle Ages. By the time we were back in the *trecento* I was so much exhausted that I could hardly stand. My knees trembled, I felt sick.

'This is the old armoury,' said Mrs. Aldwinkle with mounting enthusiasm. 'And there are the stairs leading up to the tower.'

She pointed to a low archway, through which, in a dusty twilight, the bottom of a steep stair could be seen corkscrewing up to unknown heights. 'There are two hundred and thirty-two steps,' she added.

At this moment the gong for luncheon rumbled remotely from the other end of the huge empty house.

'Thank God!' said the red-faced man devoutly.

But our hostess, it was evident, had no feeling for punctuality. 'What a bore!' she exclaimed. 'But never mind. We can make time. I wanted just to run up the tower before lunch. There's such a wonderful bird's-eye . . .' She looked inquiringly round. 'What do you think, all of you? Shouldn't we just dash up? It won't take a minute.' She repeated the siren smile. 'Do let's. Do!' And without waiting for the result of her plebiscite she walked rapidly towards the stairs.

I followed her. But before I had taken five steps, the floor, the walls of the room seemed to fade into the distance. There was a roaring in my ears. It grew suddenly dark. I felt myself falling. For the second time since breakfast I lost consciousness.

When I came to, I was lying on the floor, with my head on Mrs. Aldwinkle's knees; and she was dabbing my forehead with a wet sponge. The first objects of which I was aware were her bright blue eyes hanging over me, very close, very bright and alarming. 'Poor fellow,' she was saying, 'poor fellow.' Then, looking up, she shouted angrily to the owners of the various legs and skirts which I distinguished mistily to right and left of me: 'Stand back, you must stand back! Do you want to suffocate the poor fellow?'

PART III

THE LOVES OF THE PARALLELS

Chapter I

Do all he could, Lord Hovenden had somehow found it impossible, these last few days, to get Irene for a moment to himself. The change had come about almost suddenly, just after that fellow Chelifer had made his appearance. Before he came, there had been a time—beginning, strangely enough, almost as suddenly as it had ended—a time of blissful happiness. Whenever during those days an opportunity for a *tête-à-tête* presented itself Irene had been always at hand and, what was more, always delighted to seize the opportunity. They had been for long walks together, they had swum together far out into the sea, sat together in the gardens, sometimes talking, sometimes silent; but very happy, whether they spoke or not. He had talked to her about motoring and dancing and shooting, and occasionally, feeling rather shamefaced and embarrassed by the disquieting gravity of the subject, about the working classes. And Irene had listened with pleasure to everything he said and had talked too. They found that they had many tastes in common. It had been an enchantment while it lasted. And then, all at once, with the coming of that creature Chelifer, it all came to an end. Irene was never on the spot when opportunities offered, she never suggested spontaneously, as once or twice, during the heavenly time, she had actually done, that they should go for a walk together. She had no time to talk to him; her thoughts, it seemed, were elsewhere, as with grave and preoccupied face she hurried mysteriously about the palace and the gardens. With an extreme anguish of spirit Lord Hovenden observed that it was always in the direction of Chelifer that Irene seemed to be hurrying. Did he slip out unobtrusively into the garden after lunch, Irene was sure, a moment later, to slip out after him. When he proposed a stroll with Calamy or Mr. Cardan,

Irene always asked, shyly but with the pallid resolution of one who by an effort of will overcomes a natural weakness for the sake of some all-important cause, to be allowed to join the party. And if ever Chelifer and Miss Thriplow happened to find themselves for a moment together, Irene was always certain to come gliding silently after them.

For all this Lord Hovenden could find only one explanation. She was in love with the man. True, she never made any effort to talk to him when she was in his company; she seemed even rather intimidated by his polished silences, his pointedly insincere formulas of courtesy and compliment. And for his part Chelifer, as far as his rival could see, behaved with a perfect correctitude. Too correctly, indeed, in Hovenden's opinion. He couldn't tolerate the fellow's sarcastic politeness; the man ought to be more human with little Irene. Lord Hovenden would have liked to wring his neck; wring it for two mutually exclusive offences— luring the girl on and being too damned stand-offish. And she looked so wretched. Looking out of its square window in the thick bright bell of copper hair, the little face, so childish in the largeness and limpidity of the eyes, in the shortness of the upper lip, had been, these last days, the face of a pathetic, not a merry child. Lord Hovenden could only suppose that she was pining with love for that creature—though what the devil she contrived to see in him he, for one, couldn't imagine. And it was so obvious, too, that old Lilian was also quite gone on the fellow and making a fool of herself about him. Did she want to compete with her Aunt Lilian? There'd be the devil and all to pay if Mrs. Aldwinkle discovered that Irene was trying to cut her out. The more he thought of the wretched business, the wretcheder it seemed. Lord Hovenden was thoroughly miserable.

So too was Irene. But not for the reasons Lord Hovenden supposed. It was true that she had spent most of her days since Chelifer's arrival in following the new guest like an unhappy shadow.

But it had not been on her own account, not at her own desire. Chelifer did indeed intimidate her; so far Lord Hovenden had guessed aright. He had been hopelessly at fault in imagining that Irene adored the man in spite of her fear of him. If she followed him about, it was because Mrs. Aldwinkle had asked her to. And if she looked unhappy, it was because Aunt Lilian was unhappy—and a little, too, because the task which Aunt Lilian had set her was a disagreeable one; disagreeable not only in itself, but because it prevented her from continuing those pleasant talks with Hovenden. Ever since that evening when Aunt Lilian twitted her on her coldness and her blindness, Irene had made a point of seeing Hovenden as much as she could. She wanted to prove that Aunt Lilian had been wrong. She wasn't cold, she wasn't blind; she could see as clearly as any one when people liked her, and she could be as warmly appreciative. And really, after the episodes with Jacques, Mario and Peter, it wasn't fair of Aunt Lilian to tease her like that. It simply wasn't. Moved by an indignant desire to confute Aunt Lilian as quickly as possible, she had positively made advances to Hovenden; he was so shy that, if she hadn't, it would have been months before she could have offered her aunt anything like convincing rebuttal of her imputation. She had talked with him, gone for walks with him, quite prepared to feel at any moment the infinitude of passion. But the affair passed off, somehow, very differently from the others. She began to feel something indeed, but something quite unlike that which she had felt for Peter and Jacques. For them it had been a fizzy, exciting, restless feeling, intimately connected with large hotels, jazz bands, coloured lights and Aunt Lilian's indefatigable desire to get everything out of life, her haunting fear that she was missing something, even in the heart of the fun. ' Enjoy yourself, let yourself go,' Aunt Lilian was always telling her. And ' How handsome he is ! what a lovely fellow ! ' she would say as one of the young men passed. Irene had done her best to take Aunt

Lilian's advice. And it had seemed to her, sometimes, when she was dancing and the lights, the music, the moving crowd had blended together into a single throbbing whole, it had seemed to her that she had indeed climbed to the peak of happiness. And the young man, the Peter or Jacques whom Aunt Lilian had hypnotized her into thinking a marvel among young men, was regarded as the source of this bliss. Between the dances, under the palm trees in the garden, she had even suffered herself to be kissed; and the experience had been rather momentous. But when the time came for them to move on, Irene departed without regret. The fizzy feeling had gone flat. But with Hovenden it was different. She just liked him quietly, more and more. He was so nice and simple and eager and young. So young—she liked that particularly. Irene felt that he was really younger, in spite of his age, than she. The other ones had all been older, more knowing and accomplished; all rather bold and insolent. But Hovenden wasn't in the least like that. One felt very secure with him, Irene thought. And there was somehow no question of love when one was with him—at any rate the question wasn't at all pressing or urgent. Aunt Lilian used to ask her every evening how they were getting on and if it were getting exciting. And Irene never quite knew what to answer. She found very soon that she didn't want to talk about Hovenden; he was so different from the others, and their friendship had nothing infinite about it. It was just a sensible friendship. She dreaded Aunt Lilian's questions; and she found herself almost disliking Aunt Lilian when, in that dreadful bantering way of hers, she ruthlessly insisted on putting them. In some ways, indeed, the coming of Chelifer had been a relief; for Aunt Lilian became at once so profoundly absorbed in her own emotions that she had no time or inclination to think of any one else's. Yes, that had been a great relief. But on the other hand, the work of supervision and espionage to which Aunt Lilian had set her made it all but impossible for Irene ever to talk to Hovenden. She might as well not be there, Irene sadly reflected. Still, poor Aunt Lilian was so dreadfully unhappy. One must do all one could for her. Poor Aunt Lilian!

'I want to know what he thinks of me,' Aunt Lilian had said to her in the secret hours of the night. 'What does he say about me to other people?' Irene answered that she had never heard him say anything about her. 'Then you must listen, you must keep your ears open.'

But however much she listened, Irene never had anything to report. Chelifer never mentioned Aunt Lilian. For Mrs. Aldwinkle that was almost worse than if he had spoken badly of her. To be ignored was terrible. 'Perhaps he likes Mary,' she had suggested. 'I thought I saw him looking at her to-day in a strange, intent sort of way.' And Irene had been ordered to watch them. But for all she could discover, Mrs. Aldwinkle's jealousies were utterly unfounded. Between Chelifer and Mary Thriplow there passed no word or look that the most suspicious imagination could interpret in terms of amorous intimacy. 'He's queer, he's an extraordinary creature.' That was the refrain of Mrs. Aldwinkle's talk about him. 'He seems to care for nothing. So cold, such a fixed, frigid mask. And yet one has only to look at him—his eyes, his mouth—to see that underneath . . .' And Mrs. Aldwinkle would shake her head and sigh. And her speculations about him would go rambling on and on, round and round, treading the same ground again and again, arriving nowhere. Poor Aunt Lilian! She was dreadfully unhappy.

In her own mind Mrs. Aldwinkle had begun by saving Chelifer's life. She saw herself standing there on the beach between sea and sky, and with the mountains in the middle distance, looking like one of those wonderfully romantic figures who, in the paintings of Augustus John, stand poised in a meditative and passionate ecstasy against a cosmic background. She *saw* herself—a John down even to her flame-coloured tunic and her emerald-green parasol.

And at her feet, like Shelley, like Leander washed up on the sands of Abydos, lay the young poet, pale, naked and dead. And she had bent over him, had called him back to life, had raised him up and, figuratively speaking, had carried him off in maternal arms to a haven of peace where he should gather new strength and, for his poetry, new inspiration.

Such were the facts as they appeared to Mrs. Aldwinkle, after passing through the dense refractive medium of her imagination. Given these facts, given the resultant situation, given her character, it was almost necessary and inevitable that Mrs. Aldwinkle should feel romantically towards her latest guest. The mere fact that he was a new arrival, hitherto unknown, and a poet at that, would have been enough in any circumstances to make Mrs. Aldwinkle take a lively interest in the young man. But seeing that she had saved him from a watery grave and was now engaged in supplying him with inspiration, she felt something more than interest. She would have been disobeying the laws of her being if she had not fallen in love with him. Moreover, he made it easier for her by being so darkly and poetically handsome. And then he was queer —queer to the point of mysteriousness. His very coldness attracted while it filled her with despair.

' He can't really be so utterly indifferent to everything and everybody as he makes out,' she kept insisting to Irene.

The desire to break down his barriers, enter into his intimacy and master his secret quickened her love.

From the moment of her discovery of him, in those romantic circumstances which her imagination had made so much more romantic, Mrs. Aldwinkle had tried to take possession of Chelifer ; she had tried to make him as much her property as the view, or Italian art. He became at once the best living poet ; but it followed as a corollary that she was his only interpreter. In haste she had telegraphed to London for copies of all his books.

' When I think,' she would say, leaning forward embarrassingly close and staring into his face with those bright, dangerous eyes of hers, ' when I think how nearly you were drowned. Like Shelley . . .' She shuddered. ' It 's too appalling.'

And Chelifer would bend his full Egyptian lips into a smile and answer : ' They 'd have been inconsolable on the staff of the Rabbit Fancier,' or something of the sort. Oh, queer, queer, queer !

' He slides away from one,' Mrs. Aldwinkle complained to her young confidante of the small hours.

She might try to take his barriers by storm, might try to creep subtly into his confidence from the flank, so to speak ; but Chelifer was never to be caught napping. He evaded her. There was no taking possession of him. It was for nothing, so far as Mrs. Aldwinkle was concerned, that he was the best living poet and she his prophetess.

He evaded her—evaded her not merely mentally and spiritually, but even in the flesh. For after a day or two in the Cybo Malaspina palace he developed an almost magical faculty for disappearing. One moment he 'd be there, walking about in the garden or sitting in one of the saloons ; something would distract Mrs. Aldwinkle's attention, and the next moment, when she turned back towards the place where he had been, he was gone, he was utterly vanished. Mrs. Aldwinkle would search ; there was no trace of him to be found. But at the next meal he 'd walk in, punctual as ever ; he would ask his hostess politely if she had had an agreeable morning or afternoon, whichever the case might be, and when she asked him where he had been, would answer vaguely that he 'd gone for a little walk, or that he 'd been writing letters.

After one of these disappearances Irene, who had been set by her aunt to hunt for him, finally ran him to earth on the top of the tower. She had climbed the two hundred and thirty-two steps for the sake of the commanding view of the whole garden and hill-side to be obtained from the summit. If he was anywhere above ground, she ought to see him from the tower. But when at last, panting, she emerged on to the little square platform from which the ancient marquesses had dropped small rocks and molten lead on their enemies in the court below, she got a fright that nearly made her fall backwards down the steps. For as she came up through the trap-door into the sunlight, she suddenly became aware of what seemed, to eyes that looked up from the level of the floor, a gigantic figure advancing, toweringly, towards her.

Irene uttered a little scream; her heart jumped violently and seemed to stop beating.

'Allow me,' said a very polite voice. The giant bent down and took her by the hand. It was Chelifer. 'So you 've climbed up for a bird's-eye view of the picturesque beauties of nature ? ' he went on, when he had helped her up through the hatchway. 'I 'm very partial to bird's-eye views myself.'

'You gave me such a start,' was all that Irene could say. Her face was quite pale.

'I 'm exceedingly sorry,' said Chelifer. There was a long and, for Irene, embarrassing silence.

After a minute she went down again.

'Did you find him ? ' asked Mrs. Aldwinkle, when her niece emerged a little while later on to the terrace.

Irene shook her head. Somehow she lacked the courage to tell Aunt Lilian the story of her adventure. It would make her too unhappy to think that Chelifer was prepared to climb two hundred and thirty-two steps for the sake of getting out of her way.

Mrs. Aldwinkle tried to guard against his habit of vanishing by never, so far as it was practicable, letting him out of her sight. She arranged that he should always sit next to her at table. She took him for walks and drives in the motor car, she made him sit with her in the garden. It was with difficulty and only by the employment of stratagems that Chelifer managed to procure a moment of liberty and solitude. For the first few days of his stay Chelifer found that 'I must go and write' was a good excuse to get away. Mrs. Aldwinkle professed such admiration for him in his poetical capacity that she could not decently refuse to let him go. But she soon found a way of controlling such liberty as he could get in this way by insisting that he should write under the ilex trees, or in one of the mouldering sponge-stone grottoes hollowed in the walls of the lower terrace. Vainly Chelifer protested that he loathed writing or reading out of doors.

'These lovely surroundings,' Mrs. Aldwinkle insisted, 'will inspire you.'

'But the only surroundings that really inspire me,' said Chelifer, 'are the lower middle class quarters of London, north of the Harrow Road, for example.'

'How can you say such things?' said Mrs. Aldwinkle.

'But I assure you,' he protested, 'it's quite true.'

None the less, he had to go and write under the ilexes or in the grotto. Mrs. Aldwinkle, at a moderate distance, kept him well in sight. Every ten minutes or so she would come tip-toeing into his retreat, smiling, as she imagined, like a sibyl, her finger on her lips, to lay beside his permanently virgin sheet of paper a bunch of late-flowering roses, a dahlia, some Michaelmas daisies or a few pink berries from the spindle tree. Courteously, in some charming and frankly insincere formula, Chelifer would thank her for the gift, and with a final smile, less sibylline, but sweeter, tenderer, Mrs. Aldwinkle would tip-toe away again, like Egeria bidding farewell to King Numa, leaving her inspiration to do its work. It didn't seem to do its work very well, however. For whenever she asked him how much he had written, he regularly answered 'Nothing,' smiling at her meanwhile that courteous and Sphingine smile which Mrs. Aldwinkle always found so baffling, so pre-eminently 'queer.'

Often Mrs. Aldwinkle would try to lead the conversation upwards on to those high spiritual planes from which the most satisfactory and romantic approach to love is to be made. Two souls that have acclimatized themselves to the thin air of religion, art, ethics or metaphysics have no difficulty in breathing the similar atmosphere of ideal love, whose territory lies contiguous to those of the other inhabitants of high mental altitudes. Mrs. Aldwinkle liked to approach love from the heights. One landed, so to speak, by aeroplane on the snowy summit of Popocatepetl, to descend by easy stages into the tropical *tierra caliente* in the plains below. But with Chelifer it was impossible to gain a footing on any height at all. When, for example, Mrs. Aldwinkle started rapturously on art and the delights of being an artist, Chelifer would modestly admit to being a tolerable second-rate halma player.

'But how can you speak like that?' cried Mrs. Aldwinkle. 'How can you blaspheme so against art and your own talent? What's your talent for?'

'For editing the Rabbit Fanciers' Gazette, it appears,' Chelifer answered, courteously smiling.

Sometimes she started on the theme of love itself; but with no greater success. Chelifer just politely agreed with everything she said, and when she pressed him for a definite opinion of his own replied, 'I don't know.'

'But you must know,' Mrs. Aldwinkle insisted, 'you must have some opinion. You have had experience.'

Chelifer shook his head. 'Alas,' he deplored, 'never.'

It was hopeless.

'What am I to do?' asked Mrs. Aldwinkle despairingly in the small hours.

Wise in the experience of eighteen years, Irene suggested that the best thing to do would be to think no more about him—in that way.

Mrs. Aldwinkle only sighed and shook her head. She had started loving because she believed in love, because she wanted to love and because a romantic opportunity had presented itself. She had rescued a Poet from death. How could she help loving him ? The circumstances, the person were her invention; she had fallen in love, deliberately almost, with the figments of her own imagination. But there was no deliberately falling out again. The romantic yearnings had aroused those profounder instincts of which they were but the polite and literary emanation. The man was young, was beautiful—these were facts, not imaginings. These deep desires once started by the conscious mind from their sleep, once made aware of their quarry, how could they be held back ? ' He is a poet. For the love of poetry, for the love of passion and because I saved him from death, I love him.' If that had been all, it might have been possible for Mrs. Aldwinkle to take Irene's advice. But from the obscure caves of her being another voice was speaking. ' He is young, he is beautiful. The days are so few and short. I am growing old. My body is thirsty.' How could she cease to think of him ?

' And suppose he did come to love me a little,' Mrs. Aldwinkle went on, taking a perverse delight in tormenting herself in every possible way, ' suppose he should come to love me just a little for what I am and think and do—should come to love me because, to begin with, I love him and admire his work, and because I understand what an artist feels and can sympathize with him—suppose all that, wouldn't he be repelled at the same time by the fact that I'm old ? ' She peered into the mirror. ' My face looks terribly old,' she said.

' No, no,' protested Irene encouragingly.

' He 'd be disgusted,' Mrs. Aldwinkle went on. ' It would be enough to drive him away even if he were attracted in some other way.' She sighed profoundly. The tears trickled slowly down her sagging cheeks.

' Don't talk like that, Aunt Lilian,' Irene implored her. ' Don't talk like that.' She felt the tears coming into her own eyes. At that moment she would have done anything, given anything to make Aunt Lilian happy. She threw her arms round Mrs. Ald' winkle's neck and kissed her. 'Don't be unhappy,' she whispered. 'Don't think any more about it. What does it matter about that man? What does it matter? You must think only of the people who *do* love you. I love you, Aunt Lilian. So much, so much.'

Mrs. Aldwinkle suffered herself to be a little comforted. She dried her eyes. 'I shall make myself look still uglier,' she said, 'if I go on crying.' There was a silence. Irene went on brushing her aunt's hair; she hoped that Aunt Lilian had turned her thoughts elsewhere.

'At any rate,' said Mrs. Aldwinkle at last, breaking the long silence, 'my body is still young.'

Irene was distressed. Why couldn't Aunt Lilian think of something else? But her distress turned into an uneasy sense of embarrassment and shame as Mrs. Aldwinkle pursued the subject started by her last words into more and more intimate detail. In spite of her five years' training in Aunt Lilian's school, Irene felt profoundly shocked.

CHAPTER II

'WE two,' said Mr. Cardan one late afternoon some fortnight after Chelifer's arrival, 'we two seem to be rather left out of it.'

' Left out of what ? ' asked Mr. Falx.

' Out of love,' said Mr. Cardan. He looked down over the balustrade. On the next terrace below, Chelifer and Mrs. Aldwinkle were walking slowly up and down. On the terrace below that strolled the diminished and foreshortened figures of Calamy and Miss Thriplow. ' And the other two,' said Mr. Cardan, as if continuing aloud the enumeration which he and his companion had made in silence, with the eye alone, ' your young pupil and the little niece, have gone for a walk in the hills. Can you ask what we 're left out of ? '

Mr. Falx nodded. ' To tell you the truth,' he said, ' I don't much like the atmosphere of this house. Mrs. Aldwinkle's an excellent woman, of course, in many respects. But . . .' he hesitated.

' Yes ; but . . .' Mr. Cardan nodded. ' I see your point.'

' I shall be rather glad when I have got young Hovenden away from here,' said Mr. Falx.

' If you get him alone I shall be surprised.'

Mr. Falx went on, shaking his head : ' There 's a certain moral laxity, a certain self-indulgence. . . . I confess I don't like this way of life. I may be prejudiced ; but I don't like it.'

' Every one has his favourite vice,' said Mr. Cardan. ' You forget, Mr. Falx, that we probably don't like *your* way of life.'

' I protest,' said Mr. Falx hotly. ' Is it possible to compare my way of life with the way of life in this house ? Here am I, working incessantly for a noble cause, devoting myself to the public good . . .'

' Still,' said Mr. Cardan, ' they do say that there 's nothing more intoxicating than talking to a crowd of people and moving them the way you want them to go ; they do say, too, that it 's piercingly delicious to listen to applause. And people who have tried both have told me that the joys of power are far preferable, if only because they are a good deal more enduring, to those one can derive from wine or love. No, no, Mr. Falx; if we chose to climb on to our high horses we should be as amply justified in disapproving of your laxity and self-indulgence as you are in disapproving of ours. I always notice that the most grave and awful denunciations of obscenity in literature are to be found precisely in those periodicals whose directors are most notoriously alcoholic. And the preachers and politicians with the greatest vanity, the most inordinate itch for power and notoriety, are always those who denounce most fiercely the corruptions of the age. One of the greatest triumphs of the nineteenth century was to limit the connotation of the word " immoral " in such a way that, for practical purposes, only those were immoral who drank too much or made too copious love. Those who indulged in any or all of the other deadly sins could look down in righteous indignation on the lascivious and the gluttonous. And not only could but can—even now. This exaltation of two out of the seven deadly sins is most unfair. In the name of all lechers and boozers I most solemnly protest against the invidious distinction made to our prejudice. Believe me, Mr. Falx, we are no more reprehensible than the rest of you. Indeed, compared with some of your political friends, I feel I have a right to consider myself almost a saint.'

' Still,' said Mr. Falx, whose face, where it was not covered by his prophetical white beard, had become very red with ill-suppressed indignation, ' you won't persuade me out of my conviction that these are not the most healthy surroundings for a young fellow like Hovenden at the most impressionable period of his life. Be as paradoxical and ingenious as you like : you will not persuade me, I repeat.'

' No need to repeat, I assure you,' said Mr. Cardan, shaking his head. ' Did you think I ever supposed I could persuade you ?

You don't imagine I'd waste my time trying to persuade a full-grown man with fixed opinions of the truth of something he doesn't already believe? If you were twelve years old, even if you were twenty, I might try. But at your age—no, no.'

'Then why do you argue, if you don't want to persuade?' asked Mr. Falx.

'For the sake of argument,' Mr. Cardan replied, 'and because one must murder the time somehow.

> Come ingannar questi noiosi e lenti
> Giorni di vita cui si lungo tedio
> E fastidio insoffribile accompagna
> Or io t'insegnero.

I could write a better handbook of the art than old Parini.'

'I'm sorry,' said Mr. Falx, 'but I don't know Italian.'

'Nor should I,' said Mr. Cardan, 'if I had your unbounded resources for killing time. Unhappily, I was born without much zeal for the welfare of the working classes.'

'Working classes . . .' Mr. Falx swooped down on the words. Passionately he began to talk. What was that text, thought Mr. Cardan, about the measure with which ye mete? How fearfully applicable it was! For the last ten minutes he'd been boring poor old Mr. Falx. And now Mr. Falx had turned round and was paying him back with his own measure—but, oh Lord, pressed down and, heaven help us! running over. He looked down over the balustrade. On the lower terraces the couples were still parading up and down. He wondered what they were saying; he wished he were down there to listen. Boomingly, Mr. Falx played his prophetic part.

CHAPTER III

IT was a pity that Mr. Cardan could not hear what his hostess was saying. He would have been delighted; she was talking about herself. It was a subject on which he specially loved to hear her. There were few people, he used to say, whose Authorized Version of themselves differed so strikingly from that Revised, formed of them by others. It was not often, however, that she gave him a chance to compare them. With Mr. Cardan she was always a little shy; he had known her so long.

'Sometimes,' Mrs. Aldwinkle was saying, as she walked with Chelifer on the second of the three terraces, 'sometimes I wish I were less sensitive. I feel everything so acutely—every slightest thing. It's like being . . . like being . . .' she fumbled in the air with groping fingers, feeling for the right word, 'like being flayed,' she concluded triumphantly, and looked at her companion.

Chelifer nodded sympathetically.

'I'm so fearfully aware,' Mrs. Aldwinkle went on, 'of other people's thoughts and feelings. They don't have to speak to make me know what they've got in their minds. I know it, I *feel* it just by seeing them.'

Chelifer wondered whether she felt what was going on in his mind. He ventured to doubt it. 'A wonderful gift,' he said.

'But it has its disadvantages,' insisted Mrs. Aldwinkle. 'For example, you can't imagine how much I suffer when people round me are suffering, particularly if I feel myself in any way to blame. When I'm ill, it makes me miserable to think of servants and nurses and people having to sit up without sleep and run up and down stairs, all because of me. I know it's rather stupid; but, do you know, my sympathy for them is so . . . so . . . profound, that it actually prevents me from getting well as quickly as I should. . . .'

'Dreadful,' said Chelifer in his polite, precise voice.

'You 've no idea how deeply all suffering affects me.' She looked at him tenderly. 'That day, that *first* day, when you fainted—you can't imagine . . .'

'I 'm sorry it should have had such a disagreeable effect on you,' said Chelifer.

'You would have felt the same yourself—in the circumstances,' said Mrs. Aldwinkle, uttering the last words in a significant tone.

Chelifer shook his head modestly. 'I 'm afraid,' he answered, 'I 'm singularly stoical about other people's sufferings.'

'Why do you always speak against yourself ? ' asked Mrs. Aldwinkle earnestly. 'Why do you malign your own character ? You know you 're not what you pretend to be. You pretend to be so much harder and dryer than you really are. Why do you ? '

Chelifer smiled. 'Perhaps,' he said, 'it 's to re-establish the universal average. So many people, you see, try to make themselves out softer and damper than they are. Don't they ? '

Mrs. Aldwinkle ignored his question. 'But you,' she insisted, 'I want to know about you.' She stared into his face. Chelifer smiled and said nothing. 'You won't tell me ? ' she went on. 'But it doesn't matter. I know already. I have an intuition about people. It 's because I 'm so sensitive. I *feel* their character. I 'm never wrong.'

'You 're to be envied,' said Chelifer.

'It 's no good thinking you can deceive me,' she went on. 'You can't. I understand you.' Chelifer sighed, inwardly ; she had said that before, more than once. 'Shall I tell you what you are really like ? '

'Do.'

'Well, to begin with,' she said, 'you 're sensitive, just as sensitive as I am. I can see that in your face, in your actions. I can hear it when you speak. You can pretend to be hard and . . . and . . . armour-plated, but I . . .'

Wearily, but with patience, Chelifer listened. Mrs. Aldwinkle's hesitating voice, moving up and down from note to unrelated note, sounded in his ears. The words became blurred and vague. They lost their articulateness and sense. They were no more than the noise of the wind, a sound that accompanied, but did not interrupt his thoughts. Chelifer's thoughts, at the moment, were poetical. He was engaged in putting the finishing touches to a little ' Mythological Incident,' the idea of which had recently occurred to him and to which, during the last two days, he had been giving its definite form. Now it was finished ; a little polishing, that was all it needed now.

> Through the pale skeleton of woods
> Orion walks. The north wind lays
> Its cold lips to the twin steel flutes
> That are his gun and plays.
>
> Knee-deep he goes where, penny-wiser
> Than all his kind who steal and hoard,
> Year after year, some sylvan miser
> His copper wealth has stored.
>
> The Queen of Love and Beauty lays
> In neighbouring beechen aisles her baits—
> Bread-crumbs and the golden maize.
> Patiently she waits.
>
> And when the unwary pheasant comes
> To fill his painted maw with crumbs,
> Accurately the sporting Queen
> Takes aim. The bird has been.
>
> Secure, Orion walks her way.
> The Cyprian loads, presents, makes fire.
> He falls. 'Tis Venus all entire
> Attached to her recumbent prey.

Chelifer repeated the verses to himself and was not displeased. The second stanza was a little too ' quaint,' perhaps ; a little too— how should he put it ?—too Walter-Crane's-picture-book. One might omit it altogether, perhaps ; or substitute, if one could think of it, something more perfectly in harmony with the silver-age, allusive elegance of the rest. As for the last verse, that was really masterly. It gave Racine his *raison d'être*; if Racine had never existed, it would have been necessary to invent him, merely for the sake of those last lines.

> He falls. 'Tis Venus all entire
> Attached to her recumbent prey.

Chelifer lingered over them in ecstasy. He became aware, all at once, that Mrs. Aldwinkle was addressing herself to him more directly. From inharmoniously Aeolian, her voice became once more articulate.

'That's what you're like,' she was saying. 'Tell me I'm right. Say I understand you.'

'Perhaps,' said Chelifer, smiling.

Meanwhile, on the terrace below, Calamy and Miss Thriplow strolled at leisure. They were discussing a subject about which Miss Thriplow professed a special competence; it was—to speak in the language of the examination room—her Special Subject. They were discussing Life. 'Life's so wonderful,' Miss Thriplow was saying. 'Always. So rich, so gay. This morning, for instance, I woke up and the first thing I saw was a pigeon sitting on the window sill—a big fat grey pigeon with a captive rainbow pinned to his stomach.' (That phrase, peculiarly charming and felicitous, Miss Thriplow thought, had already been recorded for future reference in her note-books.) 'And then high up on the wall above the washstand there was a little black scorpion standing tail-upwards, looking quite unreal, like something out of the signs of the Zodiac. And then Eugenia came in to call me—think of having one's hot water brought by a maid called Eugenia to begin with!—and spent a quarter of an hour telling me about her fiancé. It seems that he's so dreadfully jealous. So should I be, if I were engaged to a pair of such rolling eyes. But think of all that happening before breakfast, just casually ! What extravagance ! But Life's so generous, so copious.' She turned a shining face to her companion.

Calamy looked down at her, through half-closed eyes, smiling, with that air of sleepy insolence, of indolent power, characteristic of him, especially in his relations with women. ' Generous ! ' he repeated. ' Yes, I should think it was. Pigeons before breakfast. And at breakfast it offers you.'

' As if I were a broiled kipper,' said Miss Thriplow, laughing.

But Calamy was not disturbed by her laughter. He continued to look at her between his puckered eyelids with the same steady insolence, the same certainty of power—a certainty so complete that he could afford to make no exertions ; placidly, drowsily, he could await the inevitable triumph. He disquieted Miss Thriplow. That was why she liked him.

They strolled on. Fifteen days ago they could never have walked like this, two on a terrace, talking at leisure of Miss Thriplow's Special Subject. Their hostess would have put an end to any such rebellious attempt at independence in the most prompt and ruthless fashion. But since the arrival of Chelifer Mrs. Aldwinkle had been too much preoccupied with the affairs of her own heart to be able to take the slightest interest in the doings, the sayings, the comings and goings of her guests. Her gaoler's vigilance was relaxed. Her guests might talk together, might wander off alone or in couples, might say good-night when they pleased ; Mrs. Aldwinkle did not care. So long as they did not interfere with Chelifer, they might do what they liked. *Fay ce que vouldras* had become the rule in Cybo Malaspina's palace.

' I can never understand,' Miss Thriplow went on, meditatively pursuing her Special Subject, ' I can never understand how it is that everybody isn't happy—I mean fundamentally happy, underneath ; for of course there's suffering, there's pain, there are a thousand reasons why one can't always be consciously happy, on the top, if you see what I mean. But fundamentally happy, under-neath—how can any one help being that ? Life 's so extraordinary, so rich and beautiful—there 's no excuse for not loving it always, even when one 's consciously miserable. Don't you think so ? ' She was fairly carried away by her love of Life. She was young, she was ardent ; she saw herself as a child who goes and turns head over heels, out of pure joy, in the perfumed haycocks. One could be as clever as one liked, but if one had that genuine love of Life it didn't matter ; one was saved.

' I agree,' said Calamy. ' It 's always worth living, even at the worst of times. And if one happens to be in love, it 's really intoxicating.'

Miss Thriplow glanced at him. Calamy was walking with bent head, his eyes fixed on the ground. There was a faint smile on his lips ; his eyelids were almost closed, as though he were too drowsy to keep them apart. Miss Thriplow felt annoyed. He made a remark like that and then didn't even take the trouble to look at her.

' I don't believe you 've ever been in love,' she said.

' I can't remember ever having been out of it,' Calamy answered.

' Which is the same thing as saying that you 've never really been in. Not really,' Miss Thriplow repeated. She knew what the real thing was like.

' And you ? ' asked Calamy.

Mary Thriplow did not answer. They took two or three turns in silence. It was a folly, Calamy was thinking. He wasn't really in love with the woman. It was a waste of time and there were other things far more important to be done, to be thought about. Other things. They loomed up enormously behind the distracting bustle of life, silently on the further side of the noise and chatter. But what were they ? What was their form, their name, their meaning ? Through the fluttering veil of movement it was impossible to do more than dimly guess ; one might as well try to look at the stars through the London smoke. If one could stop the movement, or get away from it, then surely one would be able to see clearly the large and silent things beyond. But there was no stopping the movement and there was, somehow, no escaping from it. To check it was impossible ; and the gesture of escape was ludicrous. The only sensible thing to do was to go on in the usual way and ignore the things outside the world of noise. That was what Calamy tried to do. But he was conscious, none the less, that the things were still there. They were still calmly and immutably there, however much he might agitate himself and distractedly pretend to ignore them. Mutely they claimed attention. They had claimed it, of late, with a most irritating persistence. Calamy's response had been to make love to Mary Thriplow. That was something which ought to keep him well occupied. And up to a point it did. Up to a point. The best indoor sport, old Cardan had called it ; but one demanded something better. Could he go on like this ? Or if not, what should he do ? The questions exasperated him. It was because the things were there, outside the tumult, that he had to ask them. They forced themselves on him, those questions. But it was intolerable to be bullied. He refused to let himself be bullied. He 'd do what he damned well liked. But then, did he really like philandering with Mary Thriplow ? In a way, no doubt, up to a point. But the real answer was no ; frankly, no. But yes, yes, he insisted with another part of his mind. He did like it. And even if he didn't, he 'd damned well say that he did. And if necessary he 'd damned well do what he didn't like—just because he chose to. He 'd do what he didn't like ; and that was the end of it. He worked himself up into a kind of fury.

' What are you thinking about ? ' Miss Thriplow suddenly asked.

' You,' he said ; and there was a savage exasperation in his voice, as though he passionately resented the fact that he was thinking about Mary Thriplow.

' *Tiens!* ' she said on a note of polite curiosity.

' What would you say if I told you I was in love with you ? ' he asked.

' I should say that I didn't believe you.'

' Do you want me to compel you to believe ? '

' I 'd be most interested to know, at any rate, how you proposed to set about it.'

Calamy halted, put his hand on Mary Thriplow's shoulder and turned her round towards him. ' By force, if necessary,' he said, looking into her face.

Miss Thriplow returned his stare. He looked insolent still, still arrogantly conscious of power ; but all the drowsiness and indolence that had veiled his look were now fallen away, leaving his face bare, as it were, and burning with a formidable and satanic beauty. At the sight of this strange and sudden transformation Miss Thriplow felt at once exhilarated and rather frightened. She had never seen that expression on a man's face before. She had aroused passions, but never a passion so violent, so dangerous as this seemed to be.

' By force ? ' By the tone of her voice, by the mockery of her smile she tried to exasperate him into yet fiercer passion.

Calamy tightened his grip on her shoulder. Under his hand the bones felt small and fragile. When he spoke, he found that he had been clenching his teeth. ' By force,' he said. ' Like this.' And taking her head between his two hands he bent down and kissed her, angrily, again and again. Why do I do this ? he was thinking. This is a folly. There are other things, important things. ' Do you believe me now ? ' he asked.

Mary Thriplow's face was flushed. ' You 're insufferable,' she said. But she was not really angry with him.

CHAPTER IV

'WHY have you been so funny all vese days?' Lord Hovenden had at last brought himself to put the long-premeditated question.

'Funny?' Irene echoed on another note, trying to make a joke of it, as though she didn't understand what he meant. But of course she did understand, perfectly well.

They were sitting in the thin luminous shadow of the olive trees. The bright sky looked down at them between the sparse twi-coloured leaves. On the parched grass about the roots of the trees the sunlight scattered an innumerable golden mintage. They were sitting at the edge of a little terrace scooped out of the steep slope, their legs dangling, their backs propped against the trunk of a hoary tree.

'You know,' said Hovenden. 'Why did you suddenly avoid me?'

'Did I?'

'You know you did.'

Irene was silent for a moment before she admitted: 'Yes, perhaps I did.'

'But why,' he insisted, 'why?'

'I don't know,' she answered unhappily. She couldn't tell him about Aunt Lilian.

Her tone emboldened Lord Hovenden to become more insistent. 'You don't know?' he repeated sarcastically, as though he were a lawyer carrying out a cross-examination. 'Perhaps you were walking in your sleep all ve time.'

'Don't be stupid,' she said in a weary little voice.

'At any rate, I'm not too stupid to see vat you were running after vat fellow Chelifer.' Lord Hovenden became quite red in the face as he spoke. For the sake of his manly dignity, it was a pity that his th's should sound quite so childish.

Irene said nothing, but sat quite still, her head bent, looking

down at the slanting grove of olives.   Framed within the square-
cut hair, her face was sad.

' If you were so much interested in him, why did you suggest
vat we should go for a walk vis afternoon ? ' he asked.   ' Perhaps
you fought I was Chelifer.'   He was possessed by an urgent
desire to say disagreeable and hurting things.   And yet he was
perfectly aware, all the time, that he was making a fool of himself
and being unfair to her.   But the desire was irresistible.

' Why do you try to spoil everything ? ' she asked with an
exasperating sadness and patience.

' I don't try to spoil anyfing,' Hovenden answered irritably.
' I merely ask a simple question.'

' You know I don't take the slightest interest in Chelifer,' she said.

' Ven why do you trot after him all day long, like a little dog ? '

The boy's stupidity and insistence began to annoy her.   ' I
don't,' she said angrily.   ' And in any case it 's no business of yours.'

' Oh, it 's no business of mine, is it ? ' said Hovenden in a
provocative voice.   ' Fanks for ve information.'   And he was
pointedly silent.

For a long time neither of them spoke.   Some dark brown sheep
with bells round their necks came straying between the trees a little
way down the slope.   With set, sad faces the two young people
looked at them.   The bells made a tinkling as the creatures moved.
The sweet thin noise sounded, for some reason, extremely sad in
their ears.   Sad, too, was the bright sky between the leaves ; profoundly melancholy the redder, richer light of the declining sun,
colouring the silver leaves, the grey trunks, the parched thin grass.
It was Hovenden who at last broke silence.   His anger, his desire
to say hurting, disagreeable things had utterly evaporated ; there
remained only the conviction that he had made a fool of himself
and been unfair—only that and the profound aching love which
had given his anger, his foolish cruel desire such force.   ' You know
I don't take the slightest interest in Chelifer.'   He hadn't known

but now that she had said so, and in that tone of voice, now he knew. One couldn't doubt ; and even if one could, was it worth doubting ?

' Look here,' he said at last, in a muffled voice, ' I made a fool of myself, I'm afraid. I've said stupid things. I'm sorry, Irene. Will you forgive me ? '

Irene turned towards him the little square window in her hair. Her face looked out of it smiling. She gave him her hand. ' One day I'll tell you,' she said.

They sat there hand in hand for what seemed to them at once a very long time and a timeless instant. They said nothing, but they were very happy. The sun set. A grey half-night came creeping in under the trees. Between the black silhouetted leaves the sky looked exceedingly pale. Irene sighed.

' I think we ought to be getting back,' she said reluctantly.

Hovenden was the first to scramble to his feet. He offered Irene his hand. She took it and raised herself lightly up, coming forward as she rose towards him. They stood for a moment very close together. Lord Hovenden suddenly took her in his arms and kissed her again and again. Irene uttered a cry. She struggled, she pushed him away.

' No, no,' she entreated, averting her face, leaning back, away from his kisses. ' Please.' And when he let her go, she covered her face with her hands and began to cry. ' Why did you spoil it again ?' she asked through her tears. Lord Hovenden was overwhelmed with remorse. ' We'd been so happy, such friends.' Irene dabbed her eyes with her handkerchief ; but her voice still came sobbingly.

' I'm a brute,' said Hovenden ; and he spoke with such a passion of self-condemnation that Irene couldn't help laughing. There was something positively comic about a repentance so sudden and whole-hearted.

' No, you're not a brute,' she said. Her sobs and her laughter were getting curiously mixed up together. ' You're a dear and I like you. So much, so much. But you mustn't do that, I don't know why. It spoils everything. I was a goose to cry. But somehow . . .' She shook her head. ' I like you so much,' she repeated. ' But not like that. Not now. Some day, perhaps. Not now. You won't spoil it again ? Promise.'

Lord Hovenden promised devoutly. They walked home through the grey night of the olive orchard.

That evening at dinner the conversation turned on feminism. Under pressure from Mr. Cardan, Mrs. Aldwinkle reluctantly admitted that there *was* a considerable difference between Maud Valerie White and Beethoven and that Angelica Kauffmann compared unfavourably with Giotto. But she protested, on the other hand, that in matters of love women were, definitely, treated unfairly.

' We claim *all* your freedom,' she said dramatically.

Knowing that Aunt Lilian liked her to take part in the conversation, and remembering—for she had a good memory—a phrase that her aunt used at one time to employ frequently, but which had recently faded out of the catalogue of her favourite locutions, Irene gravely brought it out. ' Contraception,' she pronounced, ' has rendered chastity superfluous.'

Mr. Cardan leaned back in his chair and roared with laughter.

But across the prophetical face of Mr. Falx there passed a pained expression. He looked anxiously at his pupil, hoping that he had not heard, or at least had not understood what had just been said. He caught Mr. Cardan's winking eye and frowned. Could corruption and moral laxity go further ? his glance seemed to inquire. He looked at Irene ; that such a youthful, innocent appearance should be wedded to so corrupt a mind appalled him. He felt glad, for Hovenden's sake, that their stay in this bad house was not to last much longer. If it were not for the necessity of behaving politely, he would have left the place at once ; like Lot, he would have shaken the dust of it from his feet.

CHAPTER V

WHEN the butcher's boy tells you in confidence, and with an eye to a tip, that the grocer's brother has a very fine piece of very old sculpture which he is prepared to part with for a moderate consideration, what do you suppose he means ? ' Walking slowly up-hill among the olive trees, Mr. Cardan meditatively put the question.

' I suppose he means what he says,' said Miss Thriplow.

' No doubt,' said Mr. Cardan, halting for a moment to wipe his face, which shone, even though the sun came only slantingly through the thin foliage of the olive trees, with an excess of heat. Miss Thriplow in the green uniform of the musical comedy schoolgirl looked wonderfully cool and neat beside her unbuttoned companion. ' But the point is this : what exactly is it that he says ? What is a butcher's boy likely to mean when he says that a piece of sculpture is very beautiful and very old ? ' They resumed their climbing. Below them, through a gap in the trees, they could see the roofs and the slender tower of the Cybo Malaspina palace, and below these again the dolls' village of Vezza, the map-like plain, the sea.

' I should ask him, if you want to know.' Miss Thriplow spoke rather tartly ; it was not to talk of butchers' boys that she had accepted Mr. Cardan's invitation to go for a walk with him. She wanted to hear Mr. Cardan's views on life, literature and herself. He knew a thing or two, it seemed to her, about all these subjects. Too many things, and not exactly the right ones at that, about the last. Too many—it was precisely for that reason that Miss Thriplow liked to talk with him. Horrors always exercise a fascination. And now, after the prolonged silence, he was starting on butchers' boys.

' I have asked him,' said Mr. Cardan. ' But do you suppose there 's anything intelligible to be got out of him ? All I can gather is that the sculpture represents a man—not a whole man, part

of a man, and that it's made of marble. Beyond that I can
discover nothing.'

' Why do you want to discover ? ' asked Miss Thriplow.

Mr. Cardan shook his head. ' Alas,' he said, ' for sordid reasons.
You remember what the poet wrote ?

> I have been in love, in debt and in drink
> This many and many a year ;
> And these are three evils too great, one would think,
> For one poor mortal to bear.
> 'Twas love that first drove me to drinking,
> And drinking first drove me to debt,
> And though I have struggled and struggled and strove,
> I cannot get out of them yet.
> There's nothing but money can cure me
> And ease me of all my pain ;
> 'Twill pay all my debts and remove all my lets,
> And my mistress who cannot endure me
> Will turn to and love me again,
> Will turn to and love me again.

There's a summary of a lifetime for you. One has no regrets,
of course. But still, one does need cash—needs it the more, alas,
the older one grows, and has less of it. What other reason, do
you think, would send me sweating up this hill to talk with the
village grocer about his brother's statuary ? '

' You mean that you'd buy it if it were worth anything ? '

' At the lowest possible price,' confirmed Mr. Cardan. ' And
sell it at the highest. If I had ever adopted a profession,' he
continued, ' I think it would have been art dealing. It has the
charm of being more dishonest than almost any other form of
licensed brigandage in existence. And dishonest, moreover, in a
much more amusing way. Financiers, it is true, can swindle on a
larger scale ; but their swindling is mostly impersonal. You may
ruin thousands of trusting investors ; but you haven't the pleasure
of knowing your victims. Whereas if you're an art dealer, your

swindling, though less extensive, is most amusingly personal You meet your victims face to face and do them down. You take advantage of the ignorance or urgent poverty of the vendor to get the work for nothing. You then exploit the snobbery and the almost equally profound ignorance of the rich buyer to make him take the stuff off your hands at some fantastic price. What huge elation one must feel when one has succeeded in bringing off some splendid *coup*! bought a blackened panel from some decayed gentleman in need of a new suit, cleaned it up and sold it again to a rich snob who thinks that a collection and the reputation of being a patron of the ancient arts will give him a leg up in society—what vast Rabelaisian mirth! No, decidedly, if I were not Diogenes and idle, I would be Alexander, critic and dealer. A really gentlemanly profession.'

' Can you never be serious ? ' asked Miss Thriplow, who would have preferred the conversation to turn on something more nearly related to her own problems.

Mr. Cardan smiled at her. ' Can anybody fail to be serious when it 's a question of making money ? '

' I give you up,' said Miss Thriplow.

' I 'm sorry,' Mr. Cardan protested. ' But perhaps it 's all for the best. Meanwhile, what about that butcher's boy ? What *does* he mean by a bit of very old sculpture ? Is it the head of some rich Etruscan cheese-monger of Lunae that they 've dug up ? Some long-nosed primitive oriental with a smile of imbecile rapture on his face ? Or a fragment of one of his Hellenized posterity, reclining on the lid of his sarcophagus as though along his prandial couch and staring blankly out of a head that might, if Praxiteles had carved it, have been Apollo's, but which the Etruscan mason has fattened into an all too human grossness ? Or perhaps it 's a Roman bust, so thoroughly real, life-like and up-to-date that, but for the toga, we might almost take it for our old friend Sir William Midrash, the eminent civil servant. Or perhaps—and I should like that better—perhaps it dates from that strange, grey Christian dawn that followed the savage night into which the empire went down. I can imagine some fragment from Modena or Toscanella —some odd, unpredictable figure bent by excess of faith into the most profoundly expressive and symbolic of attitudes : a monster physically, a barbarism, a little mumbo-jumbo, but glowing so passionately with inward life—it may be lovely, it may be malignant —that it is impossible to look at it with indifference or merely as a shape, ugly or beautiful. Yes. I should like the thing to be a piece of Romanesque carving. I'd give the butcher's boy an extra five francs if it were. But if it turned out to be one of those suave Italian Gothic saints elegantly draped and leaning a little sideways, like saplings in the mystical breeze—and it might be, you never can tell—I'd deduct five francs. Not but what it mightn't fetch just as much in the American market. But how they bore me, those accomplished Gothicisms, how they bore me !'

They were at the top of the hill. Emerging from the sloping forest of olive trees, the road now ran along a bare and almost level ridge. Some little way off, where the ground began to rise once more towards further heights, one could see a cluster of houses and a church tower. Mr. Cardan pointed.

'There,' he said, ' we shall find out what the butcher's boy really did mean. But in the meantime it's amusing to go on speculating. For example, suppose it were a chunk of a bas-relief designed by Giotto. Eh ? Something so grand, so spiritually and materially beautiful that you could fall down and worship it. But I'd be very well pleased, I assure you, with a bit of a sarcophagus from the earliest renaissance. Some figure marvellously bright, ethereal and pure, like an angel, but an angel, not of the kingdom of heaven ; an angel of some splendid and, alas, imaginary kingdom of earth. Ah,' pursued Mr. Cardan, shaking his head, ' that's the kingdom one would like to live in—the kingdom of ancient Greece, purged of every historical Greek that ever existed, and colonized out of the imaginations of modern artists, scholars and philosophers. In such a world one might live positively, so to speak—live with the stream, in the direction of the main current—not negatively, as one has to now, in reaction against the general trend of existence.'

Positive and negative living. Miss Thriplow made a mental note of the notions. It might be an idea to work up in an article. It might even throw light on her own problems. Perhaps what one suffered from was the sense of being negative and in reaction. More positiveness—that was what one needed. The conversation, she thought, seemed to be growing more serious. They walked on for a moment in silence. Mr. Cardan broke it at last.

' Or can it possibly be,' he said, ' that the grocer's brother has lighted on some fragmentary rough-hewing by Michelangelo, begun in a frenzy while he was living among these mountains and abandoned when he left them ? Some tormented Slave, struggling to free himself more of his inward than his outward chains ; straining with more than human violence, but at the same time pensively, with a passion concentrated upon itself instead of explosively dissipated, as in the baroque, which all too fatally and easily developed out of him ? And after all our hopes and speculations, that's what my treasure will probably resolve itself into—a bit of seventeenth-century baroque. I picture the torso of a waltzing angel in the middle of a whirlwind of draperies turning up to heaven the ecstatic eye of the clergyman in a Lyceum melodrama ; or perhaps a Bacchus, dancing by a miracle of virtuosity on one marble leg, his mouth open in a tipsy laugh and the fingers of both hands splayed out to their fullest extent, just to show what can be done by a sculptor who knows his business ; or the bust of a prince, prodigiously alive and characteristic, wearing a collar of Brussels lace imitated in stone down to the finest thread. The butcher's boy kept on insisting that the thing was very beautiful as well as very old. And it's obvious, now I come to think of it, that he'd really and sincerely like baroque and baroque only, just because it

would be so familiar to him, because it would be just like everything
he had been brought up to admire. For by some strange and
malignant fate the Italians, once arrived at baroque, seem to have
got stuck there. They are still up to the eyes in it. Consider
their literature, their modern painting and architecture, their
music—it's all baroque. It gesticulates rhetorically, it struts
across stages, it sobs and bawls in its efforts to show you how
passionate it is. In the midst, like a huge great Jesuit church,
stands d'Annunzio.'

'I should have thought,' said Miss Thriplow with barbed
ingenuousness, ' that you 'd have liked that sort of elaboration and
virtuosity. It 's " amusing "—isn't that the word ? '

'True,' answered Mr. Cardan, 'I like being amused. But I
demand from my art the added luxury of being moved. And,
somehow, one can't feel emotion about anything so furiously and
consciously emotional as these baroque things. It 's not by making
wild and passionate gestures that an artist can awake emotion in
the spectator. It isn't done that way. These seventeenth-century
Italians tried to express passion by making use of passionate gestures.
They only succeeded in producing something that either leaves us
cold—though it may, as you say, amuse us—or which actually
makes us laugh. Art which is to move its contemplator must
itself be still ; it is almost an aesthetic law. Passion must never
be allowed to dissipate itself in wild splashings and boilings over.
It must be shut up, so to speak, and compressed and moulded by
the intellect. Concentrated within a calm, untroubled form, its
strength will irresistibly move. Styles that protest too much are not
fit for serious, tragical use. They are by nature suited to comedy,
whose essence is exaggeration. That is why good romantic art
is so rare. Romanticism, of which the seventeenth-century baroque
style is a queer sub-species, makes violent gestures ; it relies on
violent contrasts of light and shade, on stage effects ; it is ambitious
to present you with emotion in the raw and palpitating form.

That is to say, the romantic style is in essence a comic style. And, except in the hands of a few colossal geniuses, romantic art is, in point of historical fact, almost always comic. Think of all the hair-raising romances written during the later eighteenth and earlier nineteenth centuries; now that the novelty has worn off them, we perceive them for what they are—the broadest comedies. Even writers of a great and genuine talent were betrayed by the essentially comic nature of the style into being farcical when they meant to be romantically tragical. Balzac, for example, in a hundred serious passages; George Sand in all her earlier novels; Beddoes, when he tries to make his *Death's Jest Book* particularly blood-curdling; Byron in *Cain*; de Musset in *Rolla*. And what prevents Herman Melville's *Moby Dick* from being a really great book is precisely the pseudo-Shakespearean idiom in which what are meant to be the most tragical passages are couched—an idiom to whose essential suitability to comedy the exceptional tragic successes of Shakespeare himself, of Marlowe and a few others has unfortunately blinded all their imitators. Moreover, if the romantic style is essentially fitted to comedy, it is also true, conversely, that the greatest comic works have been written in a romantic style. *Pantagruel* and the *Contes Drolatiques*; the conversation of Falstaff and Wilkins Micawber; Aristophanes' *Frogs*; *Tristram Shandy*. And who will deny that the finest passages in Milton's reverberating prose are precisely those where he is writing satirically and comically? A comic writer is a very large and copious man with a zest for all that is earthy, who unbuttons himself and lets himself freely go, following wherever his indefatigably romping spirit leads him. The unrestrained, exaggerated, wildly gesticulating manner which is the romantic manner exactly fulfils his need.'

Miss Thriplow listened with growing attention. This was serious; moreover, it seemed really to touch her own problems. In her new novel she had done her best to throw off the light satiric vestments in which, in the past, she had clothed her tender-nesses; this time, she had decided to give the public her naked heart. Mr. Cardan was making her wonder whether she wasn't exposing it in too palpitating a manner.

'When you come to pictorial art,' Mr. Cardan went on, 'you find that seriousness and romanticism are even less frequently combined than in literature. The greatest triumphs of the nine-teenth-century romantic style are to be found precisely among the comedians and the makers of grotesques. Daumier, for example, produced at once the most comic and the most violently romantic pictures ever made. And Doré, when he ceased from trying to paint serious pictures in the romantic style—with what involun-tarily ludicrous results I leave you to recall to mind—and applied himself to illustrating *Don Quixote* and the *Contes Drolatiques* in the same romantic terms, Doré produced masterpieces. Indeed, the case of Doré quite clinches my argument. Here was a man who did precisely the same romantic things in both his serious and his comic works, and who succeeded in making what was meant to be sublime ludicrous and what was meant to be ludicrous sublime in its rich, extravagant, romantic grotesqueness.'

They had passed the outlying houses of the village and were walking slowly up its single, steep street.

'That's very true,' said Miss Thriplow pensively. She was wondering whether she oughtn't to tone down a little that descrip-tion in her new novel of the agonies of the young wife when she discovers that her husband had been unfaithful to her. A dramatic moment, that. The young wife has just had her first baby—with infinite suffering—and now, still very frail, but infinitely happy, lies convalescent. The handsome young husband, whom she adores and who, she supposes, adores her, comes in with the after-noon post. He sits down by her bed, and putting the bunch of letters on the counterpane begins opening his correspondence. She opens hers too. Two boring notes. She tosses them aside.

Without looking at the address, she opens another envelope, unfolds the sheet within and reads : ' Doodlums darling, I shall be waiting for you to-morrow evening in our love-nest. . . .' She looks at the envelope ; it is addressed to her husband. Her feelings . . . Miss Thriplow wondered ; yes, perhaps, in the light of what Mr. Cardan had been saying, the passage was a little too palpitating. Particularly that bit where the baby is brought in to be suckled. Miss Thriplow sighed ; she 'd read through the chapter critically when she got home.

' Well,' said Mr. Cardan, interrupting the course of her thoughts, ' here we are. It only remains to find out where the grocer lives, and to find out from the grocer where his brother lives, and to find out from the brother what his treasure is and how much he wants for it, and then to find some one to buy it for fifty thousand pounds—and we 'll live happily ever after. What ? '

He stopped a passing child and put his question. The child pointed up the street. They walked on.

At the door of his little shop sat the grocer, unoccupied at the moment, taking the sun and air and looking on at such stray drops from the flux of life as trickled occasionally along the village street. He was a stout man with a large fleshy face that looked as though it had been squeezed perpendicularly, so broadly it bulged, so close to one another the horizontal lines of eyes, nose and mouth. His cheeks and chin were black with five days' beard—for to-day was Thursday and shaving-time only came round on Saturday evening. Small, sly, black eyes looked out from between pouchy lids. He had thick lips, and his teeth when he smiled were yellow. A long white apron, unexpectedly clean, was tied at neck and waist and fell down over his knees. It was the apron that struck Miss Thriplow's imagination—the apron and the thought that this man wore it, draped round him like an ephod, when he was cutting up ham and sausages, when he was serving out sugar with a little shovel. . . .

'How extraordinarily nice and jolly he looks!' she said enthusiastically, as they approached.

'Does he?' asked Mr. Cardan in some surprise. To his eyes the man looked like a hardly mitigated ruffian.

'So simple and happy and contented!' Miss Thriplow went on. 'One envies them their lives.' She could almost have wept over the little shovel—momentarily the masonic emblem of prelapsarian ingenuousness. 'We make everything so unnecessarily complicated for ourselves, don't we?'

'Do we?' said Mr. Cardan.

'These people have no doubts, or after-thoughts,' pursued Miss Thriplow, 'or — what's worse than after-thoughts— simultaneous-thoughts. They know what they want and what's right; they feel just what they ought to feel by nature— like the heroes in the *Iliad*—and act accordingly. And the result is, I believe, that they're much better than we are, much gooder, we used to say when we were children; the word's more expressive. Yes, much gooder. Now you're laughing at me!'

Mr. Cardan twinkled at her with benevolent irony. 'I assure you I'm not,' he declared.

'But I shouldn't mind if you were,' said Miss Thriplow. 'For after all, in spite of all that you people may say or think, it's the only thing that matters—being good.'

'I entirely agree,' said Mr. Cardan.

'And it's easier if you're like that.' She nodded in the direction of the white apron.

Mr. Cardan nodded, a little dubiously.

'Sometimes,' Miss Thriplow continued, with a gush of confidence that made her words come more rapidly, 'sometimes, when I get on a bus and take my ticket from the conductor, I suddenly feel the tears come into my eyes at the thought of this life, so simple and straightforward, so easy to live well, even if it is a hard one—and perhaps, too, just because it is a hard one. Ours is so difficult.' She shook her head.

By this time they were within a few yards of the shopkeeper, who, seeing that they were proposing to enter his shop, rose from his seat at the door and darted in to take up his stand, professionally, behind the counter.

They followed him into the shop. It was dark within and filled with a violent smell of goat's milk cheese, pickled tunny, tomato preserve and highly flavoured sausage.

' Whee-ew ! ' said Miss Thriplow, and pulling out a small handkerchief, she took refuge with the ghost of Parma violets. It was a pity that these simple lives in white aprons had to be passed amid such surroundings.

' Rather deafening, eh ? ' said Mr. Cardan, twinkling. ' Puzza,' he added, turning to the shopkeeper. ' It stinks.'

The man looked at Miss Thriplow, who stood there, her nose in the oasis of her handkerchief, and smiled indulgently. ' I forestieri sono troppo delicati. Troppo delicati,' he repeated.

' He 's quite right,' said Mr. Cardan. ' We are. In the end, I believe, we shall come to sacrifice everything to comfort and cleanliness. Personally, I always have the greatest suspicion of your perfectly hygienic and well-padded Utopias. As for this particular stink,' he sniffed the air, positively with relish, ' I don't really know what you have to object to it. It 's wholesome, it 's natural, it 's tremendously historical. The shops of the Etruscan grocers, you may be sure, smelt just as this does. No, on the whole, I entirely agree with our friend here.'

' Still,' said Miss Thriplow, speaking in a muffled voice through the folds of her handkerchief, ' I shall stick to my violets. However synthetic.'

Having ordered a couple of glasses of wine, one of which he offered to the grocer, Mr. Cardan embarked on a diplomatic conversation about the object of his visit. At the mention of his brother and the sculpture, the grocer's face took on an expression of altogether excessive amiability. He bent his thick lips into smiles ; deep folds in the shape of arcs of circles appeared in his fat cheeks. He kept bowing again and again. Every now and then he joyously laughed, emitting a blast of garlicky breath that smelt so powerfully like acetylene that one was tempted to put a match to his mouth in the hope that he would immediately break out into a bright white flame. He confirmed all that the butcher's boy had said. It was all quite true ; he had a brother ; and his brother had a piece of marble statuary that was beautiful and old, old, old. Unfortunately, however, his brother had removed from this village and had gone down to live in the plain, near the lake of Massaciuccoli, and the sculpture had gone with him. Mr. Cardan tried to find out from him what the work of art looked like ; but he could gather nothing beyond the fact that it was beautiful and old and represented a man.

' It isn't like this, I suppose ? ' asked Mr. Cardan, bending himself into the attitude of a Romanesque demon and making a demoniac grimace.

The grocer thought not. Two peasant women who had come in for cheese and oil looked on with a mild astonishment. These foreigners . . .

' Or like this ? ' He propped his elbow on the counter and, half reclining, conjured up, by his attitude and his fixed smile of imbecile ecstasy, visions of Etruscan revelry.

Again the grocer shook his head.

' Or like this ? ' He rolled his eyes towards heaven, like a baroque saint.

But the grocer seemed doubtful even of this.

Mr. Cardan wiped his forehead. ' If I could make myself look like a Roman bust,' he said to Miss Thriplow, ' or a bas-relief of Giotto, or a renaissance sarcophagus, or an unfinished group by

Michelangelo, I would. But it's beyond my powers.' He shook his head. ' For the moment I give it up.'

He took out his pocket-book and asked for the brother's address. The grocer gave directions ; Mr. Cardan carefully took them down. Smiling and bowing, the grocer ushered them out into the street, Miss Thriplow vailed her handkerchief and drew a breath of air—redolent, however, even here, of organic chemistry.

' Patience,' said Mr. Cardan, ' tenacity of purpose. One needs them here.'

They walked slowly down the street. They had only gone a few yards when the noise of a violent altercation made them turn round. At the door of the shop the grocer and his two customers were furiously disputing. Voices were raised, the grocer's deep and harsh, the women's shrill ; hands moved in violent and menacing gestures, yet gracefully withal, as was natural in the hands of those whose ancestors had taught the old masters of painting all they ever knew of expressive and harmonious movement.

' What is it ? ' asked Miss Thriplow. ' It looks like the preliminaries of a murder.'

Mr. Cardan smiled and shrugged his shoulders. ' It 's nothing,' he said. ' They 're just calling him a robber ; that 's all.' He listened for a moment more to the shouting. ' A little question of short weight, it seems.' He smiled at Miss Thriplow. ' Should we go on ? '

They turned away ; the sound of the dispute followed them down the street. Miss Thriplow did not know whether to be grateful to Mr. Cardan for saying nothing more about her friend in the white apron. These simple folk . . . the little shovel for the sugar . . . so much better, so much *gooder* than we. . . . In the end she almost wished that he would say something about it. Mr. Cardan's silence seemed more ironic than any words.

CHAPTER VI

THE sun had set. Against a pale green sky the blue and purple mountains lifted a jagged silhouette. Mr. Cardan found himself alone in the middle of the flat plain at their feet. He was standing on the bank of a broad ditch, brimming with gleaming water, that stretched away in a straight line apparently for miles across the land, to be lost in the vague twilight distance. Here and there a line of tall thin poplars marked the position of other dykes, intersecting the plain in all directions. There was not a house in sight, not a human being, not even a cow or a grazing donkey. Far away on the slopes of the mountains, whose blue and purple were rapidly darkening to a uniform deep indigo, little yellow lights began to appear, singly or in clusters, attesting the presence of a village or a solitary farm. Mr. Cardan looked at them with irritation ; very pretty, no doubt, but he had seen it done better on many musical comedy stages. And in any case, what was the good of a light six or seven miles away, on the hills, when he was standing in the middle of the plain, with nobody in sight, night coming on, and these horrible ditches to prevent one from taking the obvious bee-line towards civilization ? He had been a fool, he reflected, three or four times over : a fool to refuse Lilian's offer of the car and go on foot (this fetish of exercise ! still, he would certainly have to cut down his drinking if he didn't take it) ; a fool to have started so late in the afternoon ; a fool to have accepted Italian estimates of distance ; and a fool to have followed directions for finding the way given by people who mixed up left and right and, when you insisted on knowing which they meant, told you that either would bring you where you wanted to go. The path which Mr. Cardan had been following seemed to have come to a sudden end in the waters of this ditch ; perhaps it was a suicides' path. The lake of Massaciuccoli should be somewhere on the further side of the ditch ; but where ? and how to get across ? The twilight rapidly deepened. In a few minutes the sun would have gone down its full eighteen degrees below the horizon and it would be wholly dark. Mr. Cardan swore; but that got him no further. In the end he decided that the best thing to do would be to walk slowly and cautiously along this ditch, in the hope that in time one might arrive, at any rate somewhere. Meanwhile, it would be well to fortify oneself with a bite and a sup. He sat down on the grass and opening his jacket, dipped into the capacious poacher's pockets excavated in its lining, producing first a loaf, then a few inches of a long polony, then a bottle of red wine; Mr. Cardan was always prepared against emergencies.

The bread was stale, the sausage rather horsey and spiced with garlic; but Mr. Cardan, who had had no tea, ate with a relish. Still more appreciatively he drank. In a little while he felt a little more cheerful. Such are the little crosses, he reflected philosophically, the little crosses one has to bear when one sets out to earn money. If he got through the evening without falling into a ditch, he'd feel that he had paid lightly for his treasure. The greatest bore was these mosquitoes; he lighted a cigar and tried to fumigate them to a respectful distance. Without much success, however. Perhaps the brutes were malarial, too. There might be a little of the disease still hanging about in these marshes; one never knew. It would be tiresome to end one's days with recurrent fever and an enlarged spleen. It would be tiresome, for that matter, to end one's days anyhow, in one's bed or out, naturally or un-naturally, by the act of God or of the King's enemies. Mr. Cardan's thoughts took on, all at once, a dismal complexion. Old age, sickness, decrepitude; the bath-chair, the doctor, the bright efficient nurse; and the long agony, the struggle for breath, the thickening darkness, the end, and then—how did that merry little song go?

> More work for the undertaker,
> 'Nother little job for the coffin-maker.

> At the local cemetery they are
> Very very busy with a brand new grave.
> He'll keep warm next winter.

Mr. Cardan hummed the tune to himself cheerfully enough. But his tough, knobbly face became so hard, so strangely still, an expression of such bitterness, such a profound melancholy, appeared in his winking and his supercilious eye, that it would have startled and frightened a man to look at him. But there was nobody in that deepening twilight to see him. He sat there alone.

> At the local cemetery they are
> Very very busy with a brand new grave . .

He went on humming. 'If I were to fall sick,' he was thinking, 'who would look after me? Suppose one were to have a stroke. Hemorrhage on the brain; partial paralysis; mumbling speech; the tongue couldn't utter what the brain thought; one was fed like a baby; clysters; such a bright doctor, rubbing his hands and smelling of disinfectant and eau-de-Cologne; saw nobody but the nurse; no friends; or once a week, perhaps, for an hour, out of charity; 'Poor old Cardan, done for, I'm afraid; must send the old chap a fiver—hasn't a penny, you know; get up a subscription; what a bore; astonishing that he can last so long. . . .'

> He'll keep warm next winter.

The tune ended on a kind of trumpet call, rising from the dominant to the tonic—one dominant, three repeated tonics, drop down again to the dominant and then on the final syllable of 'winter' the last tonic. Finis, and no *da capo*, no second movement.

Mr. Cardan took another swig from his bottle; it was nearly empty now.

Perhaps one ought to have married. Kitty, for example. She would be old now and fat; or old and thin, like a skeleton very imperfectly disguised. Still, he had been very much in love with Kitty. Perhaps it would have been a good thing if he had married her. Pooh! with a burst of mocking laughter Mr. Cardan laughed aloud savagely. Marry indeed ! She looked very coy, no doubt ; but you bet, she was a little tart underneath, and lascivious as you make them. He remembered her with hatred and contempt. Portentous obscenities reverberated through the chambers of his mind.

He thought of arthritis, he thought of gout, of cataract, of deafness. . . . And in any case, how many years were left him ? Ten, fifteen, twenty if he were exceptional. And what years, what years !

Mr. Cardan emptied the bottle and replacing the cork threw it into the black water beneath him. The wine had done nothing to improve his mood. He wished to God he were back at the palace, with people round him to talk to. Alone, he was without defence. He tried to think of something lively and amusing ; indoor sports, for example. But instead of indoor sports he found himself contemplating visions of disease, decrepitude, death. And it was the same when he tried to think of reasonable, serious things : what is art, for example ? and what was the survival value to a species of eyes or wings or protective colouring in their rudimentary state, before they were developed far enough to see, fly or protect ? Why should the individuals having the first and still quite useless variation in the direction of something useful have survived more effectively than those who were handicapped by no eccentricity ? Absorbing themes. But Mr. Cardan couldn't keep his attention fixed on them. General paralysis of the insane, he reflected, was luckily an ailment for which he had not qualified in the past ; luckily ! miraculously, even ! But stone, but neuritis, but fatty degeneration, but diabetes. . . . Lord, how he wished he had somebody to talk to !

And all at once, as though in immediate answer to his prayer, he heard the sound of voices approaching through the now complete darkness. ' Thank the Lord !' said Mr. Cardan, and scrambling to his feet he walked in the direction from which the voices came. Two black silhouettes, one tall and masculine, the other, very small, belonging to a woman, loomed up out of the dark. Mr. Cardan removed the cigar from his mouth, took off his hat and bowed in their direction.

'*Nel mezzo del cammin di nostra vita,*' he began,
  '*mi ritrovai per una selva oscura,*
    che la diritta via era smarrita.'

How lucky that Dante should also have lost his way, six hundred
and twenty-four years ago ! 'In a word,' Mr. Cardan went on,
'*ho perso la mia strada*—though I have my doubts whether that's
very idiomatic. *Forse potrebbero darmi qualche indicazione.*' In
the presence of the strangers and at the sound of his own voice
conversing, all Mr. Cardan's depression had vanished. He was
delighted by the fantastic turn he had managed to give the conversation at its inception. Perhaps with a little ingenuity he would be
able to find an excuse for treating them to a little Leopardi. It
was so amusing to astonish the natives.

The two silhouettes, meanwhile, had halted at a little distance.
When Mr. Cardan had finished his macaronic self-introduction,
the taller of them answered in a harsh and, for a man's, a shrill
voice : 'There's no need to talk Italian. We're English.'

'I'm enchanted to hear it,' Mr. Cardan protested. And he
explained at length and in his mother tongue what had happened
to him. It occurred to him, at the same time, that this was a very
odd place to find a couple of English tourists.

The harsh voice spoke again. 'There's a path to Massarosa
through the fields,' it said. 'And there's another, in the opposite
direction, that joins the Viareggio road. But they're not very
easy to find in the dark, and there are a lot of ditches.'

'One can but perish in the attempt,' said Mr. Cardan gallantly.

This time it was the woman who spoke. 'I think it would be
better,' she said, 'if you slept at our house for the night. You'll
never find the way. I almost tumbled into the ditch myself just
now.' She laughed shrilly and more loudly, Mr. Cardan thought,
at greater length, than was necessary.

'But have we room ?' asked the man in a tone which showed
that he was very reluctant to receive a guest.

'But you know we 've got room,' the feminine voice answered in a tone of child-like astonishment. 'It 's rough, though.'

'That doesn't matter in the least,' Mr. Cardan assured her. 'I 'm most grateful to you for your offer,' he added, making haste to accept the invitation before the man could take it back. He had no desire to go wandering at night among these ditches. Moreover, the prospect of having company, and odd company, he guessed, was alluring. 'Most grateful,' he repeated.

'Well, if you think there 's room,' said the man grudgingly.

'Of course there is,' the feminine voice replied, and laughed again. 'Isn't it six spare rooms that we 've got ? or is it seven ? Come with us, Mr. . . . Mr. . . .'

'Cardan.'

'. . . Mr. Cardan. We 're going straight home. Such fun,' she added, and repeated her excessive laughter.

Mr. Cardan accompanied them, talking as agreeably as he could all the time. The man listened in a gloomy silence. But his sister —Mr. Cardan had discovered that they were brother and sister and that their name was Elver—laughed heartily at the end of each of Mr. Cardan's sentences, as though everything he said were a glorious joke ; laughed extravagantly and then made some remark which showed that she could have had no idea what Mr. Cardan had meant. Mr. Cardan found himself making his conversation more and more elementary, until as they approached their destination it was frankly addressed to a child of ten.

'Here we are at last,' she said, as they emerged from the denser night of a little wood of poplar trees. In front of them rose the large square mass of a house, utterly black but for a single lighted window.

To the door, when they knocked, came an old woman with a candle. By its light Mr. Cardan saw his hosts for the first time. That the man was tall and thin he had seen even without the light ; he revealed himself now as a stooping, hollow-chested creature of about forty, with long spidery legs and arms and a narrow yellow face, long-nosed, not too powerfully chinned, and lit by small and furtive grey eyes that looked mostly on the ground and seemed afraid of encountering other eyes. Mr. Cardan fancied there was something faintly clerical about his appearance. The man might be a broken-down clergyman—broken-down and possibly, when one considered the furtive eyes, unfrocked as well. He was dressed in a black suit, well cut and not old, but baggy at the knees and bulgy about the pockets of the coat. The nails of his long bony hands were rather dirty and his dark brown hair was too long above the ears and at the back of his neck.

Miss Elver was nearly a foot shorter than her brother; but she looked as though Nature had originally intended to make her nearly as tall. For her head was too large for her body and her legs too short. One shoulder was higher than the other. In face she somewhat resembled her brother. One saw in it the same long nose, but better shaped, the same weakness of chin; compensated for, however, by an amiable, ever-smiling mouth and large hazel eyes, not at all furtive or mistrustful, but on the contrary exceedingly confiding in their glance, albeit blank and watery in their brightness and not more expressive than the eyes of a young child. Her age, Mr. Cardan surmised, was twenty-eight or thirty. She wore a queer little shapeless dress, like a sack with holes in it for the head and arms to go through, made of some white material with a large design, that looked like an inferior version of the willow pattern, printed on it in bright red. Round her neck she wore two or three sets of gaudy beads. There were bangles on her wrists, and she carried a little reticule made of woven gold chains.

Using gesture to supplement his scanty vocabulary, Mr. Elver gave instructions to the old woman. She left him the candle and went out. Holding the light high, he led the way from the hall into a large room. They sat down on hard uncomfortable chairs round the empty hearth.

'Such an uncomfy house!' said Miss Elver. 'You know I don't like Italy much.'

'Dear, dear,' said Mr. Cardan. 'That's bad. Don't you even like Venice? All the boats and gondolas?' And meeting those blank infantile eyes, he felt that he might almost go on about there being no gee-gees. The cat is on the mat; the pig in the gig is a big pig; the lass on the ass a crass lass. And so on.

'Venice?' said Miss Elver. 'I've not been there.'

'Florence, then. Don't you like Florence?'

'Nor there, either.'

'Rome? Naples?'

Miss Elver shook her head.

'We've only been here,' she said. 'All the time.'

Her brother, who had been sitting, bent forward, his elbows on his knees, his hands clasped in front of him, looking down at the floor, broke silence. 'The fact is,' he said in his harsh high voice, 'my sister has to keep quiet; she's doing a rest cure.'

'Here?' asked Mr. Cardan. 'Doesn't she find it a bit hot? Rather relaxing?'

'Yes, it's awfully hot, isn't it?' said Miss Elver. 'I'm always telling Philip that.'

'I should have thought you'd have been better at the sea, or in the mountains,' said Mr. Cardan.

Mr. Elver shook his head. 'The doctors,' he said mysteriously, and did not go on.

'And the risk of malaria?'

'That's all rot,' said Mr. Elver, with so much violence, such indignation, that Mr. Cardan could only imagine that he was a landed proprietor in these parts and meant to develop his estate as a health resort.

'Oh, of course it's mostly been got rid of,' he said mollifyingly. 'The Maremma isn't what it was.'

Mr. Elver said nothing, but scowled at the floor.

CHAPTER VII

THE dining-room was also large and bare. Four candles burned on the long narrow table; their golden brightness faded in the remoter corners to faint twilight; the shadows were huge and black. Entering, Mr. Cardan could fancy himself Don Juan walking down to supper in the Commander's vault.

Supper was at once dismal and exceedingly lively. While his sister chattered and laughed unceasingly with her guest, Mr. Elver preserved throughout the meal an unbroken silence. Gloomily he ate his way through the mixed and fragmentary meal which the old woman kept bringing in, relay after unexpected relay, on little dishes from the kitchen. Gloomily too, with the air of a weak man who drinks to give himself courage and the illusion of strength, he drank glass after glass of the strong red wine. He kept his eyes fixed most of the time on the table-cloth in front of his plate; but every now and then he would look up for a second to dart a glance at the other two—for a moment only, then, fearful of being caught in the act and looked at straight in the face, he turned away again.

Mr. Cardan enjoyed his supper. Not that the food was particularly good; it was not. The old woman was one of those inept practitioners of Italian cookery who disguise their short-comings under floods of tomato sauce, with a pinch of garlic thrown in to make the disguise impenetrable. No, what Mr. Cardan enjoyed was the company. It was a long time since he had sat down with such interesting specimens. One's range, he reflected, is altogether too narrowly limited. One doesn't know enough people; one's acquaintanceship isn't sufficiently diversified. Burglars, for example, millionaires, imbeciles, clergymen, Hottentots, sea captains —one's personal knowledge of these most interesting human species is quite absurdly small. To-night, it seemed to him, he was doing something to widen his range.

'I'm so glad we met you,' Miss Elver was saying. 'In the

dark—such a start you gave me too ! ' She shrieked with laughter. ' We were getting so dull here. Weren't we, Phil ? ' She appealed to her brother ; but Mr. Elver said nothing, did not even look up. ' So dull. I 'm awfully glad you were there.'

' Not so glad as I am, I assure you,' said Mr. Cardan gallantly.

Miss Elver looked at him for a moment, coyly and confidentially ; then putting up her hand to her face, as though she were screening herself from Mr. Cardan's gaze, she turned away, tittering. Her face became quite red. She peeped at him between her fingers and tittered again.

It occurred to Mr. Cardan that he 'd be in for a breach of promise case very soon if he weren't careful. Tactfully he changed the subject ; asked her what sort of food she liked best and learned that her favourites were strawberries, cream ice and mixed chocolates.

The dessert had been eaten. Mr. Elver suddenly looked up and said : ' Grace, I think you ought to go to bed.'

Miss Elver's face, from having been bright with laughter, became at once quite overcast. A film of tears floated up into her eyes, making them seem more lustrous ; she looked at her brother appealingly. ' Must I go ? ' she said. ' Just this once ! ' She tried to coax him. ' This once ! '

But Mr. Elver was not to be moved. ' No, no,' he said sternly. ' You must go.'

His sister sighed and made a little whimpering sound. But she got up, all the same, and walked obediently towards the door. She was almost on the threshold, when she halted, turned and ran back to say good-night to Mr. Cardan. ' I 'm so glad,' she said, ' that we found you. Such fun. Good-night. But you mustn't look at me like that.' She put up her hand again to her face. ' Oh, not like that.' And still giggling, she ran out of the room.

There was a long silence.

' Have some wine,' said Mr. Elver at last, and pushed the flask in Mr. Cardan's direction.

Mr. Cardan replenished his glass and then, politely, did the same for his host. Wine—it was the only thing that was likely to make this dismal devil talk. With his practised and professional eye, Mr. Cardan thought he could detect in his host's expression certain hardly perceptible symptoms of incipient tipsiness. A spidery creature like that, thought Mr. Cardan contemptuously, couldn't be expected to hold his liquor well; and he had been putting it down pretty steadily all through supper. A little more and, Mr. Cardan was confident, he'd be as clay in the hands of a sober interrogator (and Mr. Cardan could count on being sober for at least three bottles longer than a poor feeble creature like this); he'd talk, he'd talk; the only difficulty would be to get him to stop talking.

'Thanks,' said Mr. Elver, and gloomily gulped down the replenished glass.

That's the style, thought Mr. Cardan; and in his liveliest manner he began to tell the story of the grocer's brother's statue and of his pursuit of it, ending up with an account, already more florid than the previous version, of how he lost himself.

'I console myself superstitiously,' he concluded, ' by the reflection that fate wouldn't have put me to these little troubles and inconveniences if it weren't intending to do something handsome by me in the end. I'm paying in advance; but I trust I'm paying for something round and tidy. All the same, what a curse this hunt for money is!'

Mr. Elver nodded. 'It's the root of all evil,' he said, and emptied his glass. Unobtrusively Mr. Cardan replenished it.

'Quite right,' he confirmed. 'And it's twice cursed, if you'll allow me to play Portia for a moment: it curses him that hath— can you think of a single really rich person of your acquaintance who wouldn't be less avaricious, less tyrannous, self-indulgent and generally porkish if he didn't pay super-tax? And it also curses him that hath not, making him do all manner of absurd, humiliating, discreditable things which he 'd never think of doing if the hedge-rows grew breadfruit and bananas and grapes enough to keep one in free food and liquor.'

' It curses him that hath not the most,' said Mr. Elver with a sudden savage animation. This was a subject, evidently, on which he felt deeply. He looked sharply at Mr. Cardan for a moment, then turned away to dip his long nose once more in his tumbler.

' Perhaps,' said Mr. Cardan judicially. ' At any rate there are more complaints about this curse than about the other. Those that have not complain about their own fate. Those that have do not, it is only those in contact with them—and since the havers are few these too are few—who complain of the curse of having. In my time I have belonged to both categories. Once I had ; and I can see that to my fellow men I must then have been intolerable. Now '—Mr. Cardan drew a deep breath and blew it out between trumpeting lips, to indicate the way in which the money had gone—' now I have not. The curse of insolence and avarice has been removed from me. But what low shifts, what abjections this not-having has, by compensation, reduced me to ! Swindling peasants out of their artistic property, for example ! '

' Ah, but that 's not so bad,' cried Mr. Elver excitedly, ' as what I 've had to do. That 's nothing at all. You 've never been an advertisement canvasser.'

' No,' Mr. Cardan admitted, ' I 've never been an advertisement canvasser.'

' Then you can't know what the curse of not-having really is. You can't have an idea. You 've no right to talk about the curse.' Mr. Elver's harsh, unsteady voice rose and fell excitedly as he talked. ' No right,' he repeated.

' Perhaps I haven't,' said Mr. Cardan mollifyingly. He took the opportunity to pour out some more wine for his host. Nobody has a right, he reflected, to be more miserable than we are. Each one of us is the most unhappily circumstanced creature in the world.

Hence it 's enormously to our credit that we bear up and get on as well as we do.

' Look here,' Mr. Elver went on confidentially, and he tried to look Mr. Cardan squarely in the face as he spoke ; but the effort was too great and he had to avert his eyes ; ' look here, let me tell you.' He leaned forward eagerly and slapped the table in front of where Mr. Cardan was sitting to emphasize what he was saying and to call his guest's attention to it. ' My father was a country parson,' he began, talking rapidly and excitedly. ' We were very poor—horribly. Not that he minded much : he used to read Dante all the time. That annoyed my mother—I don't know why. You know the smell of very plain cooking ? Steamed puddings—the very thought of them makes me sick now.' He shuddered. ' There were four of us then. But my brother was killed in the war and my elder sister died of influenza. So now there 's only me and the one you saw to-night.' He tapped his forehead. ' She never grew up, but got stuck somehow. A moron.' He laughed compassionlessly. ' Though I don't know why I need tell you that. For it 's obvious enough, isn't it ? '

Mr. Cardan said nothing. His host flinched away from his half-winking, half-supercilious gaze, and fortifying himself with another gulp of wine, which Mr. Cardan a moment later unobtrusively made good from the flask, went on :

' Four of us,' he repeated. ' You can imagine it wasn't easy for my father. And my mother died when we were still children. Still, he managed to send us to a rather shabby specimen of the right sort of school, and we 'd have gone on to the university if we could have got scholarships. But we didn't.' At this Mr. Elver, on whom the wine seemed quite suddenly to be making its effect, laughed loudly, as though he had made a very good joke. ' So my brother went into an engineering firm, and it was just being arranged, at goodness knows what sort of a sacrifice, that I should be turned into a solicitor, when pop ! my father falls down dead with heart failure. Well, he was all right rambling about the *Paradiso*. But I had to scramble into the nearest job available. That was how I came to be an advertisement canvasser. Oh Lord!' He put his hand over his eyes, as though to shut out some disgusting vision. 'Talk of the curse of not-having! For a monthly magazine it was—the sort of one with masses of little ads for indigestion cures; and electric belts to make you strong; and art by correspondence; and Why Wear a Truss? and superfluous hair-killers; and pills to enlarge the female figure; and labour-saving washing machines on the instalment system; and Learn to Play the Piano without Practising; and thirty-six reproductions of nudes from the Paris Salon for five bob; and drink cures in plain wrapper, strictly confidential, and all the rest. There were hundreds and hundreds of small advertisers. I used to spend all my days running round to shops and offices, cajoling old advertisers to renew or fishing for new ones. And, God! how horrible it was! Worming one's way in to see people who didn't want to see one and to whom one was only a nuisance, a sort of tiresome beggar on the hunt for money. How polite one had to be to insolent underlings, strong in their office and only too delighted to have an opportunity to play the bully in their turn! And then there was that terrible cheerful, frank, manly manner one had to keep up all the time. The " I put it to you, sir," straight from the shoulder business; the persuasive honesty, the earnestness and the frightful pretence one had to keep up so strenuously and continuously that one believed in what one was talking about, thought the old magazine a splendid proposition and regarded the inventor of advertisements as the greatest benefactor the human race has ever known. And what a presence one had to have! I could never achieve a presence, somehow. I could never even look neat. And you had to try and impress the devils as a keen, competent salesman. God, it was awful! And the way some of them would treat you. As the damnedest bore in the world—that was the best you could hope. But sometimes they treated you as a robber and a swindler. It was your fault if an insufficient number of imbeciles hadn't bought galvanic belly bands or learned to play like Busoni without practising. It was your fault; and they 'd fly in a rage and curse at you, and you had to be courteous and cheery and tactful and always enthusiastic in the face of it. Good Lord, is there anything more horrible than having to face an angry man? I don't know why, but it 's somehow so profoundly humiliating to take part in a squabble, even when one 's the aggressor. One feels afterwards that one 's no better than a dog. But when one 's the victim of somebody else's anger—that 's awful. That 's simply awful,' he repeated, and brought his hand with a clap on to the table to emphasize his words. ' I 'm not built for that sort of thing. I 'm not a bully or a fighter. They used to make me almost ill, those scenes. I couldn't sleep, thinking of them—remembering those that were past and looking forward with terror to the ones that were coming. People talk about Dostoievsky's feelings when he was marched out into the barrack square, tied to a post with the firing party lined up in front of him, and then, at the very last second, when his eyes were already bandaged, reprieved. But I tell you I used to go through his experiences half a dozen times a day, nerving myself to face some inevitable interview, the very thought of which made me sick with apprehension. And for me there was no reprieve. The execution was gone through with, to the very end. Good Lord, how often I 've hesitated at the door of some old bully's office, all in a bloody sweat, hesitating to cross the threshold. How often I 've turned back at the last moment and turned into a pub for a nip of brandy to steady my nerves, or gone to a chemist for a pick-me-up! You can't imagine what I suffered then!' He emptied his glass, as though to drown the rising horror. ' Nobody can imagine,' he repeated, and his voice quivered with the anguish of his self-pity. ' And then how little one got in return! One suffered daily torture for the privilege of being hardly able to live. And all the things one might have done, if one had had capital! To know for an absolute certainty that — given ten thousand—one could turn them into a hundred thousand in two years; to have the whole plan worked out down to its smallest details, to have thought out exactly how one would live when one was rich, and meanwhile to go on living in poverty and squalor and slavery—that's the curse of not-having. That's what *I* suffered.' Overcome by wine and emotion, Mr. Elver burst into tears.

Mr. Cardan patted him on the shoulder. He was too tactful to offer the philosophical consolation that such suffering is the lot of nine-tenths of the human race. Mr. Elver, he could see, would never have forgiven such a denial of his dolorous uniqueness. 'You must have courage,' said Mr. Cardan, and pressing the glass into Mr. Elver's hand he added : ' Drink some of this. It 'll do you good.'

Mr. Elver drank and wiped his eyes. 'But I 'll make them smart for it one day,' he said, banging the table with his fist. The violent self-pity of a moment ago transformed itself into an equally violent anger. ' I 'll make them all pay for what I suffered. When I 'm rich.'

' That 's the spirit,' said Mr. Cardan encouragingly.

' Thirteen years of it I had,' Mr. Elver went on. ' And two and a half years during the war, dressed in uniform and filling up forms in a wooden hut at Leeds ; but that was better than touting for advertisements. Thirteen years. Penal servitude with torture. But I 'll pay them, I 'll pay them.' He banged the table again.

' Still,' said Mr. Cardan, ' you seem to have got out of it now all right. Living here in Italy is a sign of freedom ; at least I hope so.'

At these words Mr. Elver's anger against ' them ' suddenly dropped. His face took on a mysterious and knowing expression. He smiled to himself what was meant to be a dark, secret and satanic smile, a smile that should be all but imperceptible to the acutest eye. But he found, in his tipsiness, that the smile was growing uncontrollably broader and broader; he wanted to grin, to laugh aloud. Not that what he was secretly thinking about was at all funny; it was not, at any rate when he was sober. But now the whole world seemed to swim in a bubbly sea of hilarity. Moreover, the muscles of his face, when he started to smile satanically, had all at once got out of hand and were insisting on expanding what should have been the expression of Lucifer's darkest and most fearful thoughts into a bumpkin's grin. Hastily Mr. Elver extinguished his face in his glass, in the hope of concealing from his guest that rebellious smile. He emerged again choking. Mr. Cardan had to pat him on the back. When it was all over, Mr. Elver reassumed his mysterious expression and nodded significantly. 'Perhaps,' he said darkly, not so much in response to anything Mr. Cardan had said as on general principles, so to speak, and to indicate that the whole situation was in the last degree dubious, dark and contingent—contingent on a whole chain of further contingencies.

Mr. Cardan's curiosity was roused by the spectacle of this queer pantomime; he refilled his host's glass. 'Still,' he insisted, 'if you hadn't freed yourself, how would you be staying here—' in this horrible marsh, he had almost added; but he checked himself and said 'in Italy' instead.

The other shook his head. 'I can't tell you,' he said darkly, and again the satanic smile threatened to enlarge itself to imbecility.

Mr. Cardan relapsed into silence, content to wait. From the expression on Mr. Elver's face he could see that the effort of keeping a secret would be, for his host, intolerably great. The fruit must be left to ripen of itself. He said nothing and looked pensively into one of the dark corners of the tomb-like chamber as though occupied with his own thoughts.

Mr. Elver sat hunched up in his chair, frowning at the table in front of him. Every now and then he took a sip of wine. Tipsily mutable, his mood changed all at once from hilarious to profoundly gloomy. The silence, the darkness funereally tempered by the four unwavering candles, worked on his mind. What a moment since had seemed an uproarious joke now presented itself to his thoughts as appalling. He felt a great need to unburden himself, to transfer responsibilities on to other shoulders, to get advice that should confirm him in his course. Furtively, for a glimpse only, he looked at his guest. How abstractedly and regardlessly he was staring into vacancy! Not a thought, no sympathy for poor Philip Elver. Ah, if he only knew. . . .

He broke silence at last. 'Tell me,' he said abruptly, and it seemed to his drunken mind that he was displaying an incredible subtlety in his method of approaching the subject; 'do you believe in vivisection?'

Mr. Cardan was surprised by the question. 'Believe in it?' he echoed. 'I don't quite know how one can *believe* in vivisection. I think it useful, if that's what you mean.'

'You don't think it's wrong?'

'No,' said Mr. Cardan.

'You think it doesn't matter cutting up animals?'

'Not if the cutting serves some useful human purpose.'

'You don't think animals have got rights?' pursued Mr. Elver with a clarity and tenacity that, in a drunken man, surprised Mr. Cardan. This was a subject, it was clear, on which Mr. Elver must long have meditated. 'Just like human beings?'

'No,' said Mr. Cardan. 'I'm not one of those fools who think that one life is as good as another, simply because it *is* a life; that a grasshopper is as good as a dog and a dog as good as a man. You must recognize a hierarchy of existences.'

'A hierarchy,' exclaimed Mr. Elver, delighted with the word, 'a hierarchy—that's it. That's exactly it. A hierarchy. And among human beings too?' he added.

'Yes, of course,' Mr. Cardan affirmed. 'The life of the soldier who killed Archimedes isn't worth the life of Archimedes. It's the fundamental fallacy of democracy and humanitarian Christianity to suppose that it is. Though of course,' Mr. Cardan added pensively, 'one has no justifying reason for saying so, but only one's instinctive taste. For the soldier, after all, may have been a good husband and father, may have spent the non-professional, unsoldierly portions of his life in turning the left cheek and making two blades of grass grow where only one grew before. If, like Tolstoy, your tastes run to good fatherhood, left cheeks and agriculture, then you'll say that the life of the soldier is worth just as much as the life of Archimedes—much more, indeed; for Archimedes was a mere geometrician, who occupied himself with lines and angles, curves and surfaces, instead of with good and evil, husbandry and religion. But if, on the contrary, one's tastes are of a more intellectual cast, then one will think as I think—that the life of Archimedes is worth the lives of several billion of even the most amiable soldiers. But as for saying which point of view is right—' Mr. Cardan shrugged his shoulders. 'Partner, I leave it to you.'

Mr. Elver seemed rather disappointed by the inconclusive turn that his guest's discourse had taken. 'But still,' he insisted, 'it's obvious that a wise man's better than a fool. There *is* a hierarchy.'

'Well, I personally should say there was,' said Mr. Cardan. 'But I can't speak for others.' He saw that he had been carried away by the pleasures of speculation into saying things his host did not want to hear. To almost all men, even when they are sober, a suspense of judgment is extraordinarily distasteful. And Mr. Elver was far from sober; moreover, Mr. Cardan began to suspect, this philosophic conversation was a tortuous introduction to personal confidences. If one wanted the confidences one must agree with the would-be confider's opinion. That was obvious.

'Good,' said Mr. Elver. 'Then you'll admit that an intelligent

233

man is worth more than an imbecile, a moron; ha ha, a moron. . . .' And at this word he burst into violent and savage laughter, which, becoming more and more extravagant as it prolonged itself, turned at last into an uncontrollable screaming and sobbing.

His chair turned sideways to the table, his legs crossed, the fingers of one hand playing caressingly with his wine glass, the other manipulating his cigar, Mr. Cardan looked on, while his host, the tears streaming down his cheeks, his narrow face distorted almost out of recognition, laughed and sobbed, now throwing himself back in his chair, now covering his face with his hands, now bending forward over the table to rest his forehead on his arms, while his whole body shook and shook with the repeated and uncontrollable spasms. A disgusting sight, thought Mr. Cardan; and a disgusting specimen too. He began to have an inkling of what the fellow was up to. Translate 'intelligent man' and 'moron' into 'me' and 'my sister'—for the general, the philosophical in any man's conversation must always be converted into the particular and personal if you want to understand him—interpret in personal terms what he had said about vivisection, animal rights and the human hierarchy, and there appeared, as the plain transliteration of the cipher—what? Something that looked exceedingly villainous, thought Mr. Cardan.

'Then I suppose,' he said in a very cool and level voice, when the other had begun to recover from his fit, 'I suppose it's your sister who has the liberating cash.'

Mr. Elver glanced at him, with an expression of surprise, almost of alarm, on his face. His eyes wavered away from Mr. Cardan's steady, genial gaze. He took refuge in his tumbler. 'Yes,' he said, when he had taken a gulp. 'How did you guess?'

Mr. Cardan shrugged his shoulders. 'Purely at random,' he said.

'After my father died,' Mr. Elver explained, 'she went to live with her godmother, who was the old lady at the big house in our parish. A nasty old woman she was. But she took to Grace, she kind of adopted her. When the old bird died at the beginning of this year, Grace found she 'd been left twenty-five thousand.'

For all comment, Mr. Cardan clicked his tongue against his palate and slightly raised his eyebrows.

' Twenty-five thousand,' the other repeated. ' A half-wit, a moron ! What can she do with it ? '

' She can take you to Italy,' Mr. Cardan suggested.

' Oh, of course we can live on the interest all right,' said Mr. Elver contemptuously. ' But when I think how I could multiply it.' He leaned forward eagerly, looking into Mr. Cardan's face for a second, then the shifty grey eyes moved away and fixed themselves on one of the buttons of Mr. Cardan's coat, from which they would occasionally dart upwards again to reconnoitre and return. ' I 've worked it out, you see,' he began, talking so quickly that the words tumbled over one another and became almost incoherent. ' The Trade Cycle. . . . I can prophesy exactly what 'll happen at any given moment. For instance . . .' He rambled on in a series of complicated explanations.

' Well, if you 're as certain as all that,' said Mr. Cardan when he had finished, ' why don't you get your sister to lend you the money ? '

' Why not ? ' Mr. Elver repeated gloomily and leaned back again in his chair. ' Because that blasted old hag had the capital tied up. It can't be touched.'

' Perhaps she lacked faith in the Trade Cycle,' Mr. Cardan suggested.

' God rot her ! ' said the other fervently. ' And when I think of what I 'd do with the money when I 'd made really a lot. Science, art . . .'

' Not to mention revenge on your old acquaintances,' said Mr. Cardan, cutting him short. ' You 've worked out the whole programme ? '

'Everything,' said Mr. Elver. 'There'd never have been anything like it. And now this damned fool of an old woman goes and gives the money to her pet moron and makes it impossible for me to touch it.' He ground his teeth with rage and disgust.

'But if your sister were to die unmarried,' said Mr. Cardan, 'the money, I suppose, would be yours.'

The other nodded.

'It's a very hierarchical question, certainly,' said Mr. Cardan. In the vault-like room there was a prolonged silence.

Mr. Elver had reached the final stage of intoxication. Almost suddenly he began to feel weak, profoundly weary and rather ill. Anger, hilarity, the sense of satanic power—all had left him. He desired only to go to bed as soon as possible; at the same time he doubted his capacity to get there. He shut his eyes.

Mr. Cardan looked at the limp and sodden figure with an expert's eye, scientifically observing it. It was clear to him that the creature would volunteer no more; that it had come to a state when it could hardly think of anything but the gradually mounting nausea within it. It was time to change tactics. He leaned forward, and tapping his host's arm launched a direct attack.

'So you brought the poor girl here to get rid of her,' he said.

Mr. Elver opened his eyes and flashed at his tormentor a hunted and terrified look. His face became very pale. He turned away. 'No, no, not that.' His voice had sunk to an unsteady whisper.

'Not that?' Mr. Cardan echoed scornfully. 'But it's obvious. And you've as good as been telling me so for the last half-hour.'

Mr. Elver could only go on whispering : 'No.'

Mr. Cardan ignored the denial. 'How did you propose to do it?' he asked. 'It's always risky, whatever way you choose, and I shouldn't put you down as being particularly courageous. How, how?'

The other shook his head.

Mr. Cardan insisted, ruthlessly. 'Ratsbane?' he queried.

236

'Steel ?—no, you wouldn't have the guts for that. Or did you mean that she should tumble by accident into one of those convenient ditches ? '

' No, no. No.'

' But I insist on being told,' said Mr. Cardan truculently, and he thumped the table till the reflections of the candles in the brimming glasses quivered and rocked.

Mr. Elver put his face in his hands and burst into tears. ' You 're a bully,' he sobbed, ' a dirty bully, like all the rest.'

' Come, come,' Mr. Cardan protested encouragingly. ' Don't take it so hardly. I 'm sorry I upset you. You mustn't think,' he added, ' that I have any of the vulgar prejudices about this affair. I 'm not condemning you. Far from it. I don't want to use your answers against you. I merely ask out of curiosity—pure curiosity. Cheer up, cheer up. Try a little more wine.'

But Mr. Elver was feeling too deplorably sick to be able to think of wine without horror. He refused it, shuddering. ' I didn't mean to do anything,' he whispered. ' I meant it just to happen.'

' Just to happen ? Yours must be a very hopeful nature,' said Mr. Cardan.

' It 's in Dante, you know. My father brought us up on Dante ; I loathed the stuff,' he added, as though it had been castor oil. ' But things stuck in my mind. Do you remember the woman who tells how she died : " *Siena mi fe', disfecemi Maremma* " ? Her husband shut her up in a castle in the Maremma and she died of fever. Do you remember ? '

Mr. Cardan nodded.

' That was the idea. I had the quinine : I 've been taking ten grains a day ever since I arrived—for safety's sake. But there doesn't seem to be any fever here nowadays,' Mr. Elver added. ' We 've been here nine weeks. . . .'

' And nothing 's happened ! ' Mr. Cardan leaned back in his chair and roared with laughter. ' Well, the moral of that,' he added, when he had breath enough to begin talking again, 'the moral of that is : See that your authorities are up to date.'

But Mr. Elver was past seeing a joke. He got up from his chair and stood unsteadily, supporting himself with a hand on the table. 'Would you mind helping me to my room?' he faintly begged. 'I don't feel very well.'

Mr. Cardan helped him first into the garden. 'You ought to learn to carry your liquor more securely,' he said, when the worst was over. 'That's another of the evening's morals.'

When he had lighted his host to bed, Mr. Cardan went to his appointed room and undressed. It was a long time before he fell asleep. The mosquitoes, partly, and partly his own busy thoughts, were responsible for his wakefulness.

CHAPTER VIII

NEXT morning Mr. Cardan was down early. The first thing he saw in the desolate garden before the house was Miss Elver. She was dressed in a frock cut on the same sack-like lines as her last night's dress, but made of a gaudy, large-patterned material that looked as though it had been designed for the upholstery of chairs and sofas, not of the human figure. Her beads were more numerous and more brilliant than before. She carried a parasol of brightly flowered silk.

Emerging from the house, Mr. Cardan found her in the act of tying a bunch of Michaelmas daisies to the tail of a large white maremman dog that stood, its mouth open, its pink tongue lolling out and its large brown eyes fixed, so it seemed, meditatively on the further horizon, waiting for Miss Elver to have finished the operation. But Miss Elver was very slow and clumsy. The fingers of her stubby little hands seemed to find the process of tying a bow in a piece of ribbon extraordinarily difficult. Once or twice the dog looked round with a mild curiosity to see what was happening at the far end of its anatomy. It did not seem in the least to resent the liberties Miss Elver was taking with its tail, but stood quite still, resigned and waiting. Mr. Cardan was reminded of that enormous tolerance displayed by dogs and cats of even the most fiendish children. Perhaps, in a flash of Bergsonian intuition, the beast had realized the childish essence of Miss Elver's character, had recognized the infant under the disguise of the full-grown woman. Dogs are good Bergsonians, thought Mr. Cardan. Men, on the other hand, are better Kantians. He approached softly.

Miss Elver had at last succeeded in tying the bow to her satisfaction; the dog's white tail was tipped with a rosette of purple flowers. She straightened herself up and looked admiringly at her handiwork. 'There!' she said at last, addressing herself to the dog. 'Now you can run away. Now you look lovely.'

The dog took the hint and trotted off, waving his flower-tipped tail.

Mr. Cardan stepped forward. ' " Neat but not gaudy," ' he quoted, ' " genteel but not expensive, like the gardener's dog with a primrose tied to his tail." Good-morning.' He took off his hat.

But Miss Elver did not return his salutation. Taken by surprise, she had stood, as though petrified, staring at him with stretched eyes and open mouth while he spoke. At Mr. Cardan's ' good-morning,' which was the first word of his that she had understood, the enchantment of stillness seemed to be lifted from her. She burst into a nervous laugh, covered her blushing face with her hands —for a moment only—then turned and ran down the path, un-gainly as an animal moving in an element not its own, to take refuge behind a clump of rank bushes at the end of the garden. Seeing her run, the big dog came bounding after her, joyously barking. One Michaelmas daisy dropped to the ground, then another. In a moment they were all gone and the ribbon with them.

Slowly, cautiously, as though he were stalking a shy bird, and with a reassuring air of being absorbed in anything rather than the pursuit of a runaway, Mr. Cardan walked after Miss Elver down the path. Between the leaves of the bushes he caught glimpses of her bright frock ; sometimes, with infinite circum-spection, and certain, it was clear, that she was escaping all notice, she peeped at Mr. Cardan round the edge of the bush. Gambol-ling round her, the dog continued to bark.

Arrived within five or six yards of Miss Elver's hiding-place, Mr. Cardan halted. ' Come now,' he said cajolingly, ' what 's there so frightening about me ? Take a good look at me. I don't bite. I 'm quite tame.'

The leaves of the bushes shook ; from behind them came a peal of shrill laughter.

' I don't even bark, like your stupid dog,' Mr. Cardan went on. ' And if you tied a bunch of flowers on to my tail I should never have the bad manners to get rid of them in the first two minutes like that rude animal.'

There was more laughter.

' Won't you come out ? '

There was no answer.

' Oh, very well then,' said Mr. Cardan, in the tone of one who is deeply offended, ' I shall go away. Good-bye.' He retraced his steps for a few yards, then turned off to the right along a little path that led to the garden gate. When he was about three-quarters of the way along it, he heard the sound of hurrying footsteps coming up behind him. He walked on, pretending to notice nothing. There was a touch on his arm.

' Don't go. Please.' Miss Elver's voice spoke imploringly. He looked round, as though startled. ' I won't run away again. But you mustn't look at me like that.'

' Like what ? ' asked Mr. Cardan.

Miss Elver put up a screening hand and turned away. ' Like I don't know what,' she said.

Mr. Cardan thought he perfectly understood ; he pursued the subject no further. ' Well, if you promise not to run away,' he said, ' I won't go.'

Miss Elver's face shone with pleasure and gratitude. ' Thank you,' she said. ' Should we go and look at the chickens ? They 're round at the back.'

They went round to the back. Mr. Cardan admired the chickens. ' You like animals ? ' he asked.

' I should think so,' said Miss Elver rapturously, and nodded.

' Have you ever had a parrot of your own ? '

' No.'

' Or a monkey ? '

She shook her head.

' Not even a Shetland pony ? ' asked Mr. Cardan on a note of astonishment.

Miss Elver's voice trembled as she again had to answer 'No.' At the thought of all these enchanting things she had never possessed, the tears came into her eyes.

'In my house,' said Mr. Cardan, conjuring up fairy palaces as easily as Aladdin, 'there are hundreds of them. I'll give you some when you come to stay with me.'

Miss Elver's face became bright again. 'Will you?' she said. 'Oh, that would be nice, that would be nice. And do you keep bears?'

'One or two,' said Mr. Cardan modestly.

'Well . . .' Miss Elver looked up at him, her blank bright eyes opened to their fullest extent. She paused, drew a deep breath and let it slowly out again. 'It must be a nice house,' she added at last, turning away and nodding slowly at every word, 'a nice house. That's all I can say.'

'You'd like to come and stay?' asked Mr. Cardan.

'I should think I would,' Miss Elver replied decidedly, looking up at him again. Then suddenly she blushed, she put up her hands. 'No, no, no,' she protested.

'Why not?' asked Mr. Cardan.

She shook her head. 'I don't know.' And she began to laugh.

'Remember the bears,' said Mr. Cardan.

'Yes. But . . .' She left the sentence unfinished. The old woman came to the back door and rang the bell for breakfast. Ungainly as a diving-bird on land, Miss Elver scuttled into the house. Her companion followed more slowly. In the dining-room, less tomb-like in the bright morning light, breakfast was waiting. Mr. Cardan found his hostess already eating with passion, as though her life depended on it.

'I'm so hungry,' she explained with her mouth full. 'Phil's late,' she added.

'Well, I'm not surprised,' said Mr. Cardan, as he sat down and unfolded his napkin.

When he came down at last, it was in the guise of a cleric so obviously unfrocked, so deplorably seedy and broken-down that Mr. Cardan felt almost sorry for him.

'Nothing like good strong coffee,' he said cheerfully, as he filled his host's cup. Mr. Elver looked on, feeling too melancholy and too ill to speak. For a long time he sat motionless in his chair, without moving, lacking the strength to stretch out his hand to his cup.

'Why don't you eat, Phil?' asked his sister, as she decapitated her second egg. 'You generally eat such a lot.'

Goaded, as though by a taunt, Philip Elver reached for his coffee and swallowed down a gulp. He even took some toast and buttered it; but he could not bring himself to eat.

At half-past ten Mr. Cardan left the house. He told his host that he was going in search of his sculpture; and he comforted Miss Elver, who, seeing him put on his hat and take his walking stick, had begun to whimper, by assuring her that he would be back to luncheon. Following the old woman's directions, Mr. Cardan soon found himself on the shores of the shallow lake of Massaciuccoli. A mile away, on the further shore, he could see the clustering pink and whitewashed houses of the village in which, he knew, the grocer's brother lived and kept his treasure. But instead of proceeding directly to the goal of his pilgrimage, Mr. Cardan lighted a cigar and lay down on the grass at the side of the path. It was a bright clear day. Over the mountains floated great clouds, hard-edged against the sky, firm and massive as though carved from marble and seeming more solid than the marble mountains beneath. A breeze stirred the blue water of the lake into innumerable dazzling ripples. It rustled among the leaves of the poplars and the sound was like that of the sea heard from far off. In the midst of the landscape lay Mr. Cardan, pensively smoking his cigar; the smoke of it drifted away along the wind.

Twenty-five thousand pounds, Mr. Cardan was thinking. If

one were to invest them in the seven per cent. Hungarian Loan, they would bring in seventeen hundred and fifty a year. And if one lived in Italy that went a long way; one could consider oneself rich on that. A nice house in Siena, or Perugia, or Bologna— Bologna he decided would be the best; there was nothing to compare with Bolognese cooking. A car—one could afford to keep something handsome. Plenty of nice books, nice people to stay with one all the time, jaunts in comfort through Europe. A secure old age; the horrors of decrepitude in poverty for ever averted. The only disadvantage—one's wife happened to be a harmless idiot. Still, she'd obviously be most devoted; she'd do her best. And one would make her happy, one would even allow her a domesticated bear. In fact, Mr. Cardan assured himself, it was the poor creature's only chance of happiness. If she stayed with her brother, he'd find some substitute for the inefficient anopheles sooner or later. If she fell into the hands of an adventurer in need of her money, the chances were that he'd be a great deal more of a scoundrel than Tom Cardan. In fact, Mr. Cardan saw, he could easily make out a case for its being his bounden duty, for the poor girl's sake, to marry her. That would do very nicely for romantic spirits like Lilian Aldwinkle. For them, he'd be the gallant rescuer, the Perseus, the chivalrous St. George. Less enthusiastic souls might look at the twenty-five thousand and smile. But let them smile. After all, Mr. Cardan asked himself, a grin more or less—what does it matter? No, the real problem, the real difficulty was himself. Could he do it? Wasn't it, somehow, a bit thick—an idiot? Wasn't it too—too Russian? Too Stavroginesque?

True, his motive would be different from the Russian's. He would marry his idiot for comfort and a placid old age—not for the sake of strengthening his moral fibres by hard exercise, not in the voluptuous hope of calling new scruples and finer remorses into existence, or in the religious hope of developing the higher consciousness by leading a low life. But on the other hand, nothing could prevent the life from being, in point of fact, thoroughly low; and he couldn't guarantee his conscience against the coming of strange qualms. Would seventeen hundred and fifty per annum be a sufficient compensation?

For more than an hour Mr. Cardan lay there, smoking, looking at the bright lake, at the ethereal fantastic mountains and the marbly clouds, listening to the wind among the leaves and the occasional far-away sounds of life, and pondering all the time. In the end he decided that seventeen hundred and fifty, or even the smaller income that would result from investment in something a little safer than seven per cent. Hungarian Loan, was a sufficient compensation. He'd do it. Mr. Cardan got up, threw away the stump of his second cigar and walked slowly back towards the house. As he approached it through the little plantation of poplar trees Miss Elver, who had been on the look-out for his return, came running out of the gate to meet him. The gaudy upholstery material blazed up as she passed out of the shade of the house into the sunlight, her coloured beads flashed. Uttering shrill little cries and laughing, she ran towards him. Mr. Cardan watched her as she came on. He had seen frightened cormorants bobbing their heads in a ludicrous anxiety from side to side. He had seen penguins waving their little flappers, scuttling along, undignified, on their short legs. He had seen vultures with trailing wings hobbling and hopping, ungainly, over the ground. Memories of all these sights appeared before his mind's eye as he watched Miss Elver's approach. He sighed profoundly.

'I'm so glad you've come back,' Miss Elver cried breathlessly, as she approached, 'I was really afraid you were going right away.' She shook his hand earnestly and looked up into his face. 'You've not forgotten about the monkeys and the Shetland ponies, have you?' she added, rather anxiously.

Mr. Cardan smiled. 'Of course not,' he answered; and he

added gallantly : 'How could I forget anything that gives you pleasure ?' He squeezed her hand and, bending down, kissed it.

Miss Elver's face flushed very red, then, the moment after, became exceedingly pale. Her breath came quickly and unsteadily. She shut her eyes. A shuddering ran through her ; she wavered on her feet, she seemed on the point of falling. Mr. Cardan caught her by the arm and held her up. This was going to be worse, he thought, than he had imagined ; more Stavroginesque. To faint when he kissed her hand—kissed it almost ironically—that was too much. But probably, he reflected, nothing of the kind had ever happened to her before. How many men had ever so much as spoken to her ? It was understandable.

'My good child—really now.' He slightly shook her arm. 'Pull yourself together. If you 're going to faint like this I shall never be able to trust you with a bear. Come, come.'

Still, the understanding of a thing does not alter it. It remains what it was when it was still uncomprehended. Seventeen hundred and fifty per annum—but at this rate it looked as though that would hardly be enough.

Miss Elver opened her eyes and looked at him. Into their blankness had come that look of anxious, unhappy love with which a child looks at his mother when he thinks that she is going to leave him. Mr. Cardan could not have felt more remorseful if he had committed a murder.

> What every weakness, every vice ?
> Tom Cardan, all were thine.

All the same, there were certain things the doing of which one felt to be an outrage. Still, one had to think of those seventeen hundred and fifty pounds ; one had to think of old age in solitude and poverty.

Leaving Miss Elver to play by herself in the garden, Mr. Cardan went indoors. He found his host sitting behind closed jalousies in a greenish twilight, his head on his hand.

' Feeling better ? ' asked Mr. Cardan cheerfully ; and getting no answer, he went on to tell a long, bright story of how he had searched for the grocer's brother, only to find, at last, that he was away from home and would be away till to-morrow. ' So I hope you won't mind,' he concluded, ' if I trespass on your charming hospitality for another night. Your sister has most kindly told me that I might.'

Mr. Elver turned on him a glance of concentrated loathing and averted his eyes. He said nothing.

Mr. Cardan drew up a chair and sat down. ' There 's a most interesting little book,' he said, looking at his host with a genial twinkling expression, ' by a certain Mr. W. H. S. Jones called " Malaria : a factor in the history of Greece and Rome," or some such title. He shows how the disease may quite suddenly obtain a footing in countries hitherto immune and in the course of a few generations bring a whole culture, a powerful empire to the ground. Conversely he shows how it is got rid of. Drainage, quinine, wire-netting . . .' The other stirred uneasily in his chair ; but Mr. Cardan went on ruthlessly. When the bell rang for luncheon he was talking to Mr. Elver about the only way in which the Yellow Peril might be permanently averted.

' First,' he said, laying the forefinger of his right hand against the thumb of his left, ' first you must introduce malaria into Japan. Japan 's immune, so far ; it 's a crying scandal. You must start by remedying that. And secondly,' he moved on to the index, ' you must see that the Chinese never have a chance to stamp out the disease in their country. Four hundred million malarial Chinamen may be viewed with equanimity. But four hundred million healthy ones—that 's a very different matter. The spread of malaria among the yellow races—there 's a cause,' said Mr. Cardan, rising from his chair, ' a cause to which some good European might profitably devote himself. You, who take so much interest in the subject, Mr. Elver, you might find a much worse vocation. Shall we go into lunch?' Mr. Elver rose, totteringly. 'I have a tremendous appetite,' his guest went on, patting him on his bent back. 'I hope you have too.'

Mr. Elver at last broke silence. 'You're a damned bully,' he whispered in a passion of misery and futile rage, 'a damned stinking bully.'

'Come, come,' said Mr. Cardan. 'I protest against "stinking."'

CHAPTER IX

EARLY the next morning Mr. Cardan and his hostess left the house and walked rapidly away through the fields in the direction of the lake. They had told the old woman that they would be back to a late breakfast. Mr. Elver was not yet awake; Mr. Cardan had left instructions that he was not to be called before half-past nine.

The ground was still wet with dew when they set out; the poplar trees threw shadows longer than themselves. The air was cool; it was a pleasure to walk. Mr. Cardan strode along at four miles an hour; and like a diver out of water, like a soaring bird reduced to walk the earth, Miss Elver trotted along at his side, rolling and hopping as she walked, as though she were mounted, not on feet, but on a set of eccentric wheels of different diameters. Her face seemed to shine with happiness; every now and then she looked at Mr. Cardan with shy adoration, and if she happened to catch his eye she would blush, turn away her head and laugh. Mr. Cardan was almost appalled by the extent of his success and the ease with which it had been obtained. He might make a slave of the poor creature, might keep her shut up in a rabbit-hutch, and, provided he showed himself now and again to be worshipped, she would be perfectly happy. The thought made Mr. Cardan feel strangely guilty.

'When we're married,' said Miss Elver suddenly, 'shall we have some children?'

Mr. Cardan smiled rather grimly. 'The trouble about children,' he said, 'is that the bears might eat them. You can never be quite sure of bears. Remember Elisha's bears and those bad children.'

Miss Elver's face became thoughtful. She walked on for a long time in silence.

They came to the lake, lying placid and very bright under the pale early-morning sky. At the sight of it Miss Elver clapped her

I

49

hands with pleasure ; she forgot in an instant all her troubles. The fatal incompatibility between bears and children ceased to pre-occupy her. ' What lovely water ! ' she cried, and bending down she picked up a pebble from the path and threw it into the lake.

But Mr. Cardan did not permit her to linger. ' There 's no time to lose,' he said, and taking her arm he hurried her on.

' Where are we going to ? ' asked Miss Elver.

He pointed to the village on the further shore of the lake. ' From there,' he said, ' we 'll take some sort of cab or cart.'

The prospect of driving in a cart entirely reconciled Miss Elver to parting at such short notice with the lake. ' That 'll be lovely,' she declared, and trotted on so fast that Mr. Cardan had to quicken his pace in order to keep up with her.

While the little carriage was being made ready and the horse put in and harnessed—hastelessly, as these things are always done in Italy, with dignity and at leisure—Mr. Cardan went to visit the grocer's brother. Now that he had come so far it would be foolish to miss the opportunity of seeing the treasure. The grocer's brother was himself a grocer, and so like his relative that Mr. Cardan could almost fancy it was Miss Thriplow's virtuous and simple friend from the hill-top to whom he was now speaking in the plain. When Mr. Cardan explained his business the man bowed, wreathed himself in smiles, laughed and blew acetylene into his face just as his brother had done. He expatiated on the beauty and the antiquity of his treasure, and when Mr. Cardan begged him to make haste and show him the sculpture, he would not suffer himself to be interrupted, but went on lyrically with his description, repeating the same phrases again and again and gesticulating until he began to sweat. At last, when he considered Mr. Cardan worked up to a due state of preliminary enthusiasm, the grocer opened the door at the back of the shop and mysteriously beckoned to his visitor to follow him. They walked down a dark passage, through a kitchen full of tumbling children on whom one had to be careful not to tread, across a little yard and into a mouldering out-house. The grocer led the way, walking all the time on tip-toe and speaking only in a whisper—for what reason Mr. Cardan could not imagine, unless it was to impress him with the profound importance of the affair, and perhaps to suggest that the beauty and antiquity of the work of art were such that it was only barefoot and in silence that it should be approached.

'Wait there,' he whispered impressively, as they entered the out-house.

Mr. Cardan waited. The grocer tip-toed across to the further corner of the shed. Mysteriously draped in sacking, something that might have been an ambushed man stood motionless in the shadow. The grocer halted in front of it and, standing a little to one side so as to give Mr. Cardan an uninterrupted view of the marvel to be revealed, took hold of a corner of the sacking, and with a magnificently dramatic gesture whisked it off.

There emerged the marble effigy of what in the imagination of a monumental mason of 1830 figured as a Poet. A slenderer Byron with yet more hyacinthine hair and a profile borrowed from one of Canova's Greeks, he stood, leaning against a truncated column, his marble eyes turned upwards in pursuit of the flying Muse. A cloak hung lankly from his shoulders; a vine leaf was all the rest of his costume. On the top of the truncated column lay a half-opened marble scroll, which the Poet's left hand held down for fear it should be blown clean away by the wind of inspiration. His right, it was evident, had originally poised above the virgin page a stylus. But the hand, alas, and the whole forearm almost to the elbow were gone. At the base of the column was a little square tablet on which, if the figure had ever been put to its proper monumental use, should have been written the name and claims to fame of the poet upon whose tomb it was to stand. But the tablet was blank. At the time this statue was carved there had evidently been a dearth of lyrists in the principality of Massa Carrara.

'E bellissimo!' said the grocer's brother, standing back and looking at it with a connoisseur's enthusiasm.

'Davvero,' Mr. Cardan agreed. He thought sadly of his recumbent Etruscan, his sarcophagus by Jacopo della Quercia, his Romanesque demon. Still, he reflected, even a bas-relief by Giotto would hardly have brought him five-and-twenty thousand pounds.

CHAPTER X

MR. CARDAN returned to the palace of the Cybo Malaspina to find that the number of guests had been increased during his absence by the arrival of Mrs. Chelifer. Mrs. Aldwinkle had not been particularly anxious to have Chelifer's mother in the house, but finding that Chelifer was preparing to leave as soon as his mother should arrive, she peremptorily insisted on giving the lady hospitality.

'It's absurd,' she argued, 'to go down again to that horrible hotel at Marina di Vezza, stay there uncomfortably for a few days and then go to Rome by train. You must bring your mother here, and then, when it's time for Mr. Falx to go to his conference, we'll all go to Rome in the car. It'll be far pleasanter.'

Chelifer tried to object; but Mrs. Aldwinkle would not hear of objections. When Mrs. Chelifer arrived at the station of Vezza she found Francis waiting for her on the platform with Mrs. Aldwinkle, in yellow tussore and a floating white veil, at his side. The welcome she got from Mrs. Aldwinkle was far more effusively affectionate than that which she got from her son. A little bewildered, but preserving all her calm and gentle dignity, Mrs. Chelifer suffered herself to be led towards the Rolls-Royce.

'We all admire your son so enormously,' said Mrs. Aldwinkle. 'He's so—how shall I say?—so *post bellum*, so essentially one of *us*.' Mrs. Aldwinkle made haste to establish her position among the youngest of the younger generation. 'All that one only dimly feels he expresses. Can you be surprised at our admiration?'

So far Mrs. Chelifer was rather surprised by everything. It took her some time to get used to Mrs. Aldwinkle. Nor was the aspect of the palace calculated to allay her astonishment.

'A superb specimen of early baroque,' Mrs. Aldwinkle assured her, pointing with her parasol. But even after she knew the dates, it all seemed to Mrs. Chelifer rather queer.

Mrs. Aldwinkle remained extremely cordial to her new guest; but in secret she disliked Mrs. Chelifer extremely. There would have been small reason, in any circumstances, for Mrs. Aldwinkle to have liked her. The two women had nothing in common; their views of life were different and irreconcilable, they had lived in separate worlds. At the best of times Mrs. Aldwinkle would have found her guest *bourgeoise* and *bornée*. As things actually were she loathed her. And no wonder; for in his mother Chelifer had a permanent and unexceptionable excuse for getting away from Mrs. Aldwinkle. Mrs. Aldwinkle naturally resented the presence in her house of this cause and living justification of infidelity. At the same time it was necessary for her to keep on good terms with Mrs. Chelifer; for if she quarrelled with the mother, it was obvious that the son would take himself off. Inwardly chafing, Mrs. Aldwinkle continued to treat her with the same gushing affection as at first.

To Mrs. Aldwinkle's guests the arrival of Mrs. Chelifer was more welcome than to herself. Mr. Falx found in her a more sympathetic and comprehensible soul than he could discover in his hostess. To Lord Hovenden and Irene her arrival meant the complete cessation of Irene's duties as a spy; they liked her well enough, moreover, for her own sake.

'A nice old fing,' was how Lord Hovenden summed her up.

Miss Thriplow affected almost to worship her.

'She's so wonderfully good and simple and *integral*, if you understand what I mean,' Miss Thriplow explained to Calamy. 'To be able to be so undividedly enthusiastic about folk-songs and animals' rights and all that sort of thing—it's really wonderful. She's a lesson to us,' Miss Thriplow concluded, 'a lesson.' Mrs. Chelifer became endowed, for her, with all the qualities that the village grocer had unfortunately not possessed. The symbol of his virtues—if only he had possessed them—had been the white apron; Mrs. Chelifer's integrity was figured forth by her dateless grey dresses.

'She's one of Nature's Quakeresses,' Miss Thriplow declared.
'If only one could be born like that!' There had been a time,
not so long ago, when she had aspired to be one of Nature's Guardswomen. 'I never knew that anything so good and dove-coloured
existed outside of Academy subject-pictures of 1880. You know:
"A Pilgrim Mother on Board the Mayflower," or something of that
sort. It's absurd in the Academy. But it's lovely in real life.'

Calamy agreed.

But the person who most genuinely liked Mrs. Chelifer was
Grace Elver. From the moment she set eyes on Mrs. Chelifer,
Grace was her dog-like attendant. And Mrs. Chelifer responded
by practically adopting her for the time being. When he learned
the nature of her tastes and occupations, Mr. Cardan explained her
kindness to himself by the hypothesis that poor Grace was the nearest
thing to a stray dog or cat that Mrs. Chelifer could find. Conversely, Grace's love at first sight must be due to the realization by
that cat-like mind that here was a born protector and friend. In
any case, he was exceedingly grateful to Mrs. Chelifer for having
made her appearance when she did. Her presence in the house
made easy what would otherwise have been a difficult situation.

That Mrs. Aldwinkle would be impressed by the romantic story
of Grace's abduction Mr. Cardan had always been certain. And
when he told the story, she *was* impressed, though less profoundly
than Mr. Cardan had hoped; she was too much preoccupied with
her own affairs to be able to respond with her customary enthusiasm
to what, at other times, would have been an irresistible appeal.
About her reception of the story, then, Mr. Cardan had never
entertained a doubt; he knew that she would find it romantic.
But that was no guarantee that she would like the heroine of the
story. From what he knew of her, which was a great deal, Mr.
Cardan felt sure that she would very quickly find poor Grace
exceedingly tiresome. He knew her lack of patience and her
intolerance. Grace would get on her nerves; Lilian would be

unkind, and goodness only knew what scenes might follow. Mr. Cardan had brought her to the palace meaning to stay only a day or two and then take his leave, before Mrs. Aldwinkle had had time to get poor Grace on her nerves. But the presence of Mrs. Chelifer made him change his mind. Her affectionate protection was a guarantee against Mrs. Aldwinkle's impatience; more important still, it had the best possible effect on Grace herself. In Mrs. Chelifer's presence she behaved quietly and sensibly, like a child doing its best to make a good impression. Mrs. Chelifer, moreover, kept a tenderly watchful eye on her appearance and her manners; kept her up to the mark about washing her hands and brushing her hair, dropped a gentle hint when she was not behaving as well as she ought to at table, and checked her propensity to eat too much of the things she liked and not enough of those she didn't like. Mrs. Chelifer, it was obvious, had the best possible influence over her. When they were married, Mr. Cardan decided, he would frequently invite Mrs. Chelifer to stay—preferably, though she was a very nice old thing, while he was away from home. Meanwhile, secure that his residence at the palace of the Cybo Malaspina would be marred by no disagreeable incidents, he wrote to his lawyer to make the necessary arrangements about his marriage.

For her part, Mrs. Chelifer was delighted to have found Grace. As Mr. Cardan had divined, she missed her cats and dogs, her poor children and traditional games. It was very reluctantly that she had at last given up the old Oxford house; very reluctantly, though the arguments that Francis had used to persuade her were unanswerable. It was too large for her, it was full of those mediaeval labour-creating devices of which Mr. Ruskin and his architectural followers were so fond, it cost more to keep up than she could afford; moreover, it was unhealthy, she was regularly ill there every winter; the doctors had been urging her for years past to get out of the Thames valley. Yes, the arguments were quite unanswerable; but it had been a long time before she had finally made up her mind to leave the place. Forty years of her life had been passed there; she was loth to part with all those memories. And then there were the dogs and the poor children, all her old friends and her charities. In the end, however, she had allowed herself to be persuaded. The house was sold; it was arranged that she should spend the winter in Rome.

'Now you're free,' her son had said.

But Mrs. Chelifer rather mournfully shook her head. 'I don't know that I very much like being free,' she answered. 'I shall be without occupation in Rome. I look forward to it almost with dread.'

Francis reassured her. 'You'll soon find something,' he said. 'Don't be afraid of that.'

'Shall I?' Mrs. Chelifer questioned doubtfully. They were walking together in the little garden at the back of the house; looking round her at the familiar grass plot and flower beds, she sighed.

But Francis was right; dogs, poor children or their equivalents are fortunately not rare. At the end of the first stage of her journey Mrs. Chelifer had found, in Grace Elver, a compensation for what she had abandoned at Oxford. Attending to poor Grace she was happy.

For the rest of the party Miss Elver's arrival had no special or personal significance. For them she was just Mr. Cardan's half-wit; that was all. Even Mary Thriplow, who might have been expected to take an interest in so genuine a specimen of the simple soul, paid little attention to her. The fact was that Grace was really too simple to be interesting. Simplicity is no virtue unless you are potentially complicated. Mrs. Chelifer, being with all her simplicity a woman of intelligence, threw light, Miss Thriplow felt, on her own case. Grace was simple only as a child or an imbecile is simple; her didactic value was therefore nil. Miss Thriplow remained faithful to Mrs. Chelifer.

CHAPTER XI

IT was night. Half undressed. Irene was sitting on the edge of her bed stitching away at an unfinished garment of pale pink silk. Her head was bent over her work and her thick hair hung perpendicularly down on either side, making an angle with her tilted face. The light clung richly to her bare arms and shoulders, was reflected by the curved and glossy surfaces of her tight-drawn stockings. Her face was extremely grave ; the tip of her tongue appeared between her teeth. It was a difficult job.

Round her, on the walls of the enormous room which had once been the bedchamber of the Cardinal Alderano Malaspina, fluttered an army of gesticulating shapes. Over the door sat God the Father, dressed in a blue crêpe de Chine tunic and enveloped in a mantle of red velvet, which fluttered in the divine afflatus as though it had been so much bunting. His right hand was extended ; and in obedience to the gesture a squadron of angels went flying down one of the side walls towards the window. At a *prie-Dieu* in the far corner knelt Cardinal Malaspina, middle-aged, stout, with a *barbiche* and moustache, and looking altogether, Irene thought, like the current British idea of a French chef. The Archangel Michael, at the head of his troop of Principalities and Powers, was hovering in the air above him, and with an expression on his face of mingled condescension and respect—condescension, inasmuch as he was the plenipotentiary of the *Padre Eterno*, and respect, in view of the fact that His Eminence was a brother of the Prince of Massa Carrara —was poising above the prelate's head the red symbolic hat that was to make him a Prince of the Church. On the opposite wall the Cardinal was represented doing battle with the powers of darkness. Dressed in scarlet robes he stood undaunted on the brink of the bottomless pit. Behind him was a carefully painted view of the Malaspina palace, with a group of retainers and handsome coaches in the middle distance and, immediately behind their Uncle, whom they gallantly supported by their prayers, the Cardinal's nephews. From the pit came up legions of hideous devils who filled the air with the flapping of their wings. But the Cardinal was more than a match for them. Raising a crucifix above his head, he conjured them to return to the flames. And the foiled devils, gnashing their teeth and trembling with terror, were hurled back towards the pit. Head foremost, tail foremost, in every possible position they came hurtling down towards the floor. When she lay in bed, Irene could see half a dozen devils diving down at her; and when she woke up in the morning, a pair of plunging legs waved frantically within a foot of her opening eyes. In the wall space over the windows the Cardinal's cultured leisures were allegorically celebrated. Nine Muses and three Graces, attended by a troop of Hours, reclined or stood, or danced in studied postures; while the Cardinal himself, enthroned in the midst, listened to their conversation and proffered his own opinions without appearing to notice the fact that all the ladies were stark naked. No one but the most polished and accomplished man of the world could have behaved in the circumstances with such perfect *savoir-vivre*.

In the midst of the Cardinal's apotheosis and entirely oblivious of it, Irene stitched away at her pink chemise. Undressing, just now, she had caught sight of it lying here in her work-basket; she hadn't been able to resist the temptation of adding a touch or two there and then. It was going to be one of her masterpieces when it was done. She held it out in her two hands, at arm's length, and looked at it, lovingly and critically. It was simply too lovely.

Ever since Chelifer's arrival she had been able to do a lot of work on her underclothes. Mrs. Aldwinkle, absorbed by her unhappy passion, had completely forgotten that she had a niece who ought to be writing lyrics and painting in water-colours. Irene was free to devote all her time to her sewing. She did not neglect the opportunity. But every now and then her conscience would suddenly prick her and she would ask herself whether, after all, it was quite fair to take advantage of poor Aunt Lilian's mournful preoccupation to do what she did not approve of. She would wonder if she oughtn't, out of loyalty to Aunt Lilian, to stop sewing and make a sketch or write a poem. Once or twice in the first days she even acted on the advice of her conscience. But when in the evening she brought Aunt Lilian her sketch of the temple, and the lyric beginning ' O Moon, how calmly in the midnight sky . . .' —brought them with a certain triumph, a consciousness of virtuous actions duly performed—that distracted lady showed so little interest in these artistic tokens of niecely duty and affection that Irene felt herself excused henceforward from making any further effort to practise the higher life. She went on with her stitching. Her conscience, it is true, still troubled her at times ; but she did nothing about it.

This evening she felt no conscientious qualm. The garment was so lovely that even Aunt Lilian, she felt sure, would have approved of it. It was a work of art—a work of art that deserved that honourable title just as richly as ' O Moon, how calmly in the midnight sky ' ; perhaps even more richly.

Irene folded up the unfinished masterpiece in rose, put it away, and went on with her undressing. To-night, she decided, as she brushed her hair, she would tell Aunt Lilian how right she had been about Hovenden. That ought to please her. ' How grateful I am,' she would say. And she 'd tell her how much she liked him —almost, almost in *that* way. Not quite yet. But soon ; she felt somehow that it might happen soon. And it would be the real thing. Real and solid. Not flimsy and fizzy and imaginary, like the episodes with Peter and Jacques and the rest of them.

She put on her dressing-gown and walked down the long corridor to Mrs. Aldwinkle's room. Cardinal Alderano was left alone with his devils and the obsequious angels, his nine naked Muses and the Eternal Father.

When Irene came in, Aunt Lilian was sitting in front of her looking-glass, rubbing skin food into her face.

' It appears,' she said, looking at herself in the glass, critically, as Irene had looked at her masterpiece of fine sewing, ' that there 's such a wonderful electric massage machine. I forget who told me about it.'

' Was it Lady Belfry ? ' Irene suggested. The image of Lady Belfry's face floated up before her mind's eye—smooth, pink, round, youthful looking, but with that factitious and terribly precarious youthfulness of beauty scientifically preserved.

' Perhaps it was,' said Mrs. Aldwinkle. ' I must certainly get one of them. Write to Harrods' about it to-morrow, will you, darling ? '

Irene began the nightly brushing of her aunt's hair. There was a long silence. How should she begin about Hovenden ? Irene was thinking. She must begin in some way that would show how really and genuinely serious it all was. She must begin in such a way that Aunt Lilian would have no possible justification for taking up a playful tone about it. At all costs, Aunt Lilian must not be allowed to talk to her in that well-known and dreaded vein of bludgeoning banter ; on no account must she be given an opportunity for saying : ' Did she think then that her silly old auntie didn't notice ? ' or anything of that kind. But to find the completely fun-proof formula was not so easy. Irene searched for it long and thoughtfully. She was not destined to find it. For Aunt Lilian, who had also been thinking, suddenly broke the silence.

' I sometimes doubt,' she said, ' whether he takes any interest in women at all. Fundamentally, unconsciously, I believe he 's a homosexualist.'

' Perhaps,' said Irene gravely. She knew her Havelock Ellis.

For the next half-hour Mrs. Aldwinkle and her niece discussed the interesting possibility.

CHAPTER XII

MISS THRIPLOW was writing in her secret note-book. 'There are people,' she wrote, ' who seem to have no capacity for feeling deeply or passionately about anything. It is a kind of emotional impotence for which one can only pity them profoundly. Perhaps there are more of these people nowadays than there were. But that's only an impression; one has no facts to go on, no justifying documents. But if it's the case, it's due, I suppose, to our intellectualizing education. One has to have a strong emotional constitution to be able to stand it. And then one lives so artificially that many of the profounder instincts rarely get an opportunity for displaying themselves. Fear, for example, and all the desperate passions evoked by the instinct of self-preservation in face of danger or hunger. Thousands of civilized people pass through life condemned to an almost complete ignorance of these emotions.'

Miss Thriplow drew a line under this paragraph and began again a little further down the page.

' To love primitively, with fury. To be no more civilized, but savage. No more critical, but whole-heartedly passionate. No more a troubled and dubious mind, but a young, healthy body certain and unwavering in its desires. The beast knows everything, says Uncle Yerochka in Tolstoy. Not everything; no. But he knows, at any rate, all the things the mind does not know. The strong complete spirit must know what the beast knows as well as what the mind knows.'

She drew another line.

' His hands are so strong and firm, and yet touch so softly. His lips are soft. Where his neck joins his body, in front, between the two strong tendons, where they converge towards the collar bone, is a boldly marked depression in the flesh that looks as though it had been made by the thumb of an artist god, so beautiful it is. So beautiful . . .'

It occurred to Miss Thriplow that there would be an excellent article to be written round the theme of masculine beauty. In the Song of Solomon it is described as lyrically as feminine beauty. It is rare to find modern poetesses expressing so frank an admiration. In the Paris Salons it is the female nude which prevails ; the male is exceptional and, when complete, seems a little shocking. How different from the state of things in Pompeii ! Miss Thriplow bit the end of her pen. Yes, decidedly, it would make a capital article.

' His skin is white and smooth,' she went on writing. ' How strong he is ! His eyes are sleepy ; but sometimes they seem to wake up and he looks at me so piercingly and commandingly that I am frightened. But I like being frightened—by him.'

Another line. Miss Thriplow would have written more on this subject ; but she was always apprehensive that somebody might find her note-book and read it. She did not want that to happen till she was dead. Miss Thriplow made an asterisk by the side of the first of the evening's notes. In the margin of the blank page opposite she scratched a similar sign, to indicate that what she was going to write now was in the nature of an appendix or corollary to what she had written in the first note.

' Certain people,' she wrote, ' who have no natural capacity for profound feeling are yet convinced, intellectually, that they ought to feel profoundly. The best people, they think, have formidable instincts. They want to have them too. They are the emotional snobs. This type, I am sure, is new. In the eighteenth century people tried to make out that they were rational and polished. The cult of the emotions began in the nineteenth. It has had a new turn given to it by Bergsonism and Romain-Rollandism in the twentieth century. It is fashionable now to be exactly the opposite of what it was fashionable to be in the eighteenth century. So that you get emotionally impotent people simulating passion with their minds. Hypocrites of instinct, they often more than half deceive themselves. And, if they are intelligent, they completely deceive all but the most observant of those around them. They act the emotional part better than those who actually feel the emotions. It is Diderot's paradox of the comedian, in real life; the less you feel, the better you represent feeling. But while the comedian on the stage plays only for the audience in the theatre, those in real life perform as much for an inward as an outward gallery; they ask for applause also from themselves and, what is more, they get it; though always, I suppose, with certain secret reservations. What a curious type it is! I have known many specimens of it.'

Miss Thriplow stopped writing and thought of the specimens she had known. There was a surprisingly large number of them. Every human being is inclined to see his own qualities and weaknesses in others. Inevitably: since his own mental and moral attributes are the only ones of which he has any personal experience. The man who visualizes his multiplication table in a fantastic and definite picture imagines that all other men must do the same; the musician cannot conceive of a mind that is irresponsive to music. Similarly the ambitious man presumes that all his fellows are actuated by his own desire to achieve distinction and power. The sensualist sees sensuality everywhere. The mean man takes it for granted that everybody else is mean. But it must not be thought that the possessor of a vice who sees his own weakness in all his fellows therefore condones that weakness. We rarely give our own weaknesses their specific name, and are aware of them only in a vague and empirical fashion. The conscious and educated part of us condemns the vice to which we are congenitally subject. At the same time, our personal knowledge of the vice—a knowledge not conscious or intellectual, but obscure, practical and instinctive—tends to direct the attention of the superficial, educated part of the mind to manifestations of this particular weakness, tends even to make it detect such manifestations when they do not exist; so that we are constantly struck by the ludicrous spectacle of the avaricious passionately condemning avarice in others much more generous than themselves, of the lascivious crying out on lasciviousness, the greedy criticizing greed. Their education has taught them that these vices are blameworthy, while their personal and empirical knowledge of them causes them to take a special interest in these weaknesses and to see signs of them everywhere.

If the number of Miss Thriplow's friends who belonged to the type of the emotionally impotent was surprisingly large, the fact was due to a tendency in Miss Thriplow herself towards precisely this spiritual weakness. Being by nature a good deal more acute and self-analytic than most of the men and women who indignantly castigate their own inveterate sins, Miss Thriplow was not unaware, while she criticized others, of the similar defect in herself. She could not help suspecting, when she read Dostoievsky and Tchehov, that she was organized differently from these Russians. It seemed to her that she felt nothing so acutely, with such an intricate joy or misery as did they. And even before she had started reading the Russians, Miss Thriplow had come to the painful conclusion that if the Brontë sisters were emotionally normal, then she must be decidedly sub-normal. And even if they weren't quite normal, even if they were feverish, she desired to be like them ; they seemed to her entirely admirable. It was the knowledge of her sub-normality (which she had come, however, to attribute to a lack of opportunities—we lead such sheltered, artificial lives—for the display of her potential passions and emotions) that had made Miss Thriplow so passionate an admirer of fine spontaneous feelings. It caused her at the same time to be willing and anxious to embrace every opportunity that presented itself for the testing of her re-actions. It is experience that makes us aware of what we are ; if it were not for contacts with the world outside ourselves we should have no emotions at all. In order to get to know her latent emotional self, Miss Thriplow desired to have as much experience, to make as many contacts with external reality as possible. When the external reality was of an unusual character and offered to be particularly fruitful in emotional revelations, she sought it with a special eagerness. Thus, a love affair with Calamy had seemed to her fraught with the most interesting emotional possibilities. She would have liked him well enough even if his drowsiness had concealed no inward fires. But the conviction that there was something ' queer,' as Mrs. Aldwinkle would say, and dangerous about the man made her imagine at every stage of their intimacy that she liked him better than she actually did ; made her anxious to advance to further stages in the hope that, as he revealed himself, ampler and more interesting revelations of her own hidden soul might there be awaiting her. She had had her reward ; Calamy had already genuinely frightened her, had revealed himself as excitingly brutal.

' You exasperate me so much,' he had said, ' that I could wring your neck.'

And there were moments when she half believed that he really would kill her. It was a new kind of love. She abandoned herself to it with a fervour which she found, taking its temperature, very admirable. The flood of passion carried her along ; Miss Thriplow took notes of her sensations on the way and hoped that there would be more and intenser sensations to record in the future.

CHAPTER XIII

CALAMY lay on his back, quite still, looking up into the darkness. Up there, he was thinking, so near that it's only a question of reaching out a hand to draw back the curtaining darkness that conceals it, up there, just above me, floats the great secret, the beauty and the mystery. To look into the depths of that mystery, to fix the eyes of the spirit on that bright and enigmatic beauty, to pore over the secret until its symbols cease to be opaque and the light filters through from beyond—there is nothing else in life, for me at any rate, that matters; there is no rest or possibility of satisfaction in doing anything else.

All this was obvious to him now. And it was obvious, too, that he could not do two things at once; he couldn't at the same time lean out into the silence beyond the futile noise and bustle—into the mental silence that lies beyond the body—he couldn't at the same time do this and himself partake in the tumult; and if he wanted to look into the depths of mind, he must not interpose a preoccupation with his bodily appetites.

He had known all this so well and so long; and still he went on in the same way of life. He knew that he ought to change, to do something different, and he profoundly resented this knowledge. Deliberately he acted against it. Instead of making an effort to get out of the noise and bustle, to break away from his enslavement and do what he ought to do, what he knew that, really and profoundly, he wanted to do, he had more than once, when his bonds had seemed on the point of falling away of themselves, deliberately tightened them. He resented this necessity of changing, even though it was a necessity imposed on him, not from without, but by what he knew to be the most intelligent part of his own being. He was afraid, too, that if he changed he would be making himself ridiculous. It was not that he desired to live as he had until a year ago. That dreary and fatiguing routine of pleasure had become intolerable; he had broken definitely with that. No; he pictured a sort of graceful Latin compromise. An Epicurean cultivation of mind and body. Breakfast at nine. Serious reading from ten till one. Luncheon prepared by an excellent French cook. In the afternoon a walk and talk with intelligent friends. Tea with crumpets and the most graceful of female society. A frugal but exquisite supper. Three hours' meditation about the Absolute, and then bed, not unaccompanied. . . . It sounded charming. But somehow it wouldn't do. To the liver of this perfect Life of Reason the secret, the mystery and the beauty, though they might be handled and examined, refused to give up their significance. If one really wanted to know about them, one must do more than meditate upon them of an evening between the French chef's masterpiece of maigre cooking and the night's rest, not in solitude. In these delightful Latin circumstances the secret, the mystery and the beauty reduced themselves to nothing. One thought of them only because they were amusing and to pass the time; they were really no more important than the tea with crumpets, the vegetarian supper and the amorous repose. If one wanted them to be more than these, one must abandon oneself completely to the contemplation of them. There could be no compromise.

Calamy knew this. But all the same he had made love to Mary Thriplow, not because he had felt an overwhelming passionate necessity to do so; but because she amused him, because her prettiness, her air of unreal innocence exasperated his senses, more than all because he felt that a love affair with Mary Thriplow would keep him thoroughly occupied and prevent him from thinking about anything else. It had not. The beauty and the mystery still hung just above him when he lay alone in the darkness. They were still there; his affair with Mary Thriplow merely prevented him from approaching them.

Down in the valley a clock struck one. The sound reminded

him that he had promised to go to her to-night. He found himself thinking of what would happen when they met, of the kisses, the caresses given and received. Angrily he tried to turn his thoughts to other themes; he tried to think of the mystery and the beauty that floated there, above him, on the further side of the curtaining darkness. But however vehemently he strove to expel them, the charnel images kept returning again and again to his mind.

'I won't go,' he said to himself; but he knew while he was saying it that he would. With an extraordinary vividness he imagined her lying on the crook of his arm, extenuated, limp and shuddering, like one who has been tormented on the rack. Yes, he knew that he would go.

The notion of torture continued to haunt his mind. He thought of those poor wretches who, accused of sorcery, admitted after the third day's torment that they had indeed flown along the wind, passed through keyholes, taken the form of wolves and conjoined themselves with incubi; who would admit, not only these things, but also, after another hour on the rack, that they had accomplices, that this man, that woman, that young child were also sorcerers and servants of the devil. The spirit is willing, but the flesh is weak. Weak in pain, but weaker still, he thought, more inexcusably weak, in pleasure. For under the torments of pleasure, what cowardices, what betrayals of self and of others will it not commit! How lightly it will lie and perjure itself! How glibly, with a word, condemn others to suffer! How abjectly it will surrender happiness and almost life itself for a moment's prolongation of the delicious torture! The shame that follows is the spirit's resentment, its sad indignation at its bondage and humiliation.

Under the torment of pleasure, he thought, women are weaker than men. Their weakness flatters their lover's consciousness of strength, gratifies his desire for power. On one of his own sex a man will vent his love of power by making him suffer; but on a

woman by making her enjoy. It is more the pleasurable torment
he inflicts than what is inflicted upon him that delights the
lover.

And since man is less weak, Calamy went on thinking, since
pleasure with him is never so annihilating that he cannot take
greater pleasure in the torment of his tormentor, is he not therefore
the less excusable for breaking faith with himself or others under
the delicious torture or the desire and anticipation of it ? Man
has less physical justification for his weakness and his enslavement. Woman is made by nature to be enslaved—by love, by
children. But every now and then a man is born who ought to
be free. For such a man it is disgraceful to succumb under the
torture.

If I could free myself, he thought, I could surely do something ;
nothing useful, no doubt, in the ordinary sense, nothing that would
particularly profit other people ; but something that for me would
be of the last importance. The mystery floats just above me. If
I were free, if I had time, if I could think and think and slowly
learn to plumb the silences of the spirit . . .

The image of Mary Thriplow presented itself again to his mind's
eye. Limply she lay in the crook of his arm, trembling as though
after torment. He shut his eyes ; angrily he shook his head. The
image would not leave him. If I were free, he said to himself,
if I were free . . .

In the end he got out of bed and opened the door. The corridor
was brightly illumined ; an electric light was left burning all night.
Calamy was just about to step out, when another door a little
further down the passage was violently thrown open and Mr. Falx,
his legs showing thin and hairy below the hem of a night-shirt,
impetuously emerged. Calamy retired into the shadowed em-
brasure of his door. With the anxious, harrowed expression on his
face of one who suffers from colic, Mr. Falx hurried past, looking
neither to the left hand nor to the right. He turned down another

passage which entered the main corridor a few yards away and disappeared; a door slammed. When he was out of sight, Calamy walked softly and rapidly down the corridor, opened the fourth door on the left and disappeared into the darkness. A little later Mr. Falx returned, at leisure, to his room.

PART IV

THE JOURNEY

Chapter I

LORD HOVENDEN detached from his motor car was an entirely different being from the Lord Hovenden who lounged with such a deceptive air of languor behind the steering-wheel of a Vauxhall Velox. Half an hour spent in the roaring wind of his own speed transformed him from a shy and diffident boy into a cool-headed hero, daring not merely in the affairs of the road, but in the affairs of life as well. The fierce wind blew away his diffidence ; the speed intoxicated him out of his self-consciousness. All his victories had been won while he was in the car. It was in the car—eighteen months ago, before he came of age—that he had ventured to ask his guardian to increase his allowance ; and he had driven faster and faster until, in sheer terror, his guardian had agreed to do whatever he wished. It was on board the Velox that he had ventured to tell Mrs. Terebinth, who was seventeen years older than he, had four children and adored her husband, that she was the most beautiful woman he had ever seen ; he had bawled it at her while they were doing seventy-five on the Great North Road. At sixty, at sixty-five, at seventy, his courage had still been inadequate to the achievement ; but at seventy-five it reached the sticking-point : he had told her. And when she laughed and told him that he was an impudent young shrimp, he felt not a whit abashed, but laughed back, pressed the accelerator down a little further, and when the needle of the speedometer touched eighty, shouted through the wind and the noise of the engine : ' But I love you.' Unfortunately, however, the drive came to an end soon after ; all drives must come to an end, sooner or later. The *affaire* Terebinth went no further. If only, Lord Hovenden regretfully sighed, if only one could spend all one's life in the Velox ! But the Velox had its disadvantages. There were occasions when the heroic, speed-intoxicated self had got the timorous pedestrian into awkward scrapes. There was that time, for example, when, rolling along at sixty, he had airily promised one of his advanced political friends to make a speech at a meeting. The prospect, while one was doing sixty, had seemed not merely unalarming, but positively attractive. But what agonies he suffered when he was standing on the solid earth again, at his journey's end! How impossibly formidable the undertaking seemed! How bitterly he cursed himself for his folly in having accepted the invitation! In the end he was reduced to telegraphing that his doctor had ordered him peremptorily to the south of France. He fled, ignominiously.

To-day the Velox had its usual effect on him. At Vezza, when they started, he was all shyness and submission. He assented meekly to all the arrangements that Mrs. Aldwinkle made and re-made every five minutes, however contradictory and impossible. He did not venture to suggest that Irene should come in his car; it was through no good management of his own, but by the mere luck of Mrs. Aldwinkle's final caprice before the actual moment of starting, that he did in fact find her sitting next him when at last they moved off from before the palace doors. At the back sat Mr. Falx, in solitude, surrounded by suit-cases. To him Lord Hovenden had even dutifully promised that he would never go more than five-and-twenty miles an hour. Pedestrian slavishness could hardly go further.

Heavily loaded, Mrs. Aldwinkle's limousine started first. Miss Elver, who had begged to be granted this special favour, sat in front, next the chauffeur. An expression of perfect and absolute bliss irradiated her face. Whenever the car passed any one by the roadside, she made a shrill hooting noise and waved her handker-chief. Luckily she was unaware of the feelings of disgust and indignation which her conduct aroused in the chauffeur; he was English and enormously genteel, he had the reputation of his country and his impeccable car to keep up. And this person waved handkerchiefs and shouted as though she were on a char-à-banc. Miss Elver even waved at the cows and horses, she shouted even to the cats and the chickens.

In the body of the car sat Mrs. Aldwinkle, Mrs. Chelifer, Chelifer and Mr. Cardan. Calamy and Miss Thriplow had decided that they had no time to go to Rome and had been left—without a word of objection on Mrs. Aldwinkle's part—at the palace. The landscape slid placidly past the windows. Mr. Cardan and Mrs. Chelifer talked about traditional games.

Meanwhile, a couple of hundred yards behind, Lord Hovenden disgustfully sniffed the dusty air. ' How intolerably slowly old Ernest drives !' he said to his companion.

' Aunt Lilian doesn't allow him to do more than thirty miles an hour,' Irene explained.

Hovenden snorted derisively. ' Firty ! But must we eat veir filthy dust all ve way ? '

' Perhaps you might drop back a bit,' Irene suggested.

' Or perhaps we might pass vem ? '

' Well . . .' said Irene doubtfully. ' I don't think we ought to make poor Aunt Lilian eat our dust.'

' She wouldn't eat it for long, if old Ernest is only allowed to do firty.'

' Well, in that case,' said Irene, feeling that her duty towards Aunt Lilian had been done, ' in that case . . .'

Lord Hovenden accelerated. The road was broad, flat and straight. There was no traffic. In two minutes Mrs. Aldwinkle had eaten her brief, unavoidable meal of dust ; the air was clear again. Far off along the white road, a rapidly diminishing cloud was all that could be seen of Lord Hovenden's Velox.

' Well, fank God,' Lord Hovenden was saying in a cheerful voice, ' now we can get along at a reasonable rate.' He grinned, a young ecstatic giant.

Irene also found the speed exhilarating. Under her grey silk mask, with its goggling windows for the eyes, her short lip was lifted in a joyful smile from the white small teeth. ' It 's lovely,' she said.

' I 'm glad you like it,' said Hovenden. ' Vat 's splendid.'

But a tap on his shoulder reminded him that there was somebody else in the car besides Irene and himself. Mr. Falx was far from finding the present state of affairs splendid. Blown by the wind, his white beard shook and fluttered like a living thing in a state of mortal agitation. Behind the goggles, his dark eyes had an anxious look in them. ' Aren't you going rather fast ? ' he shouted, leaning forward, so as to make himself heard.

' Not a bit,' Hovenden shouted back. ' Just ve usual speed. Perfectly safe.' His ordinary pedestrian self would never have dreamed of doing anything contrary to the wishes of the venerated master. But the young giant who sat at the wheel of the Velox cared for nobody. He went his own way.

They passed through the sordid outskirts of Viareggio, through the pinewoods beyond, solemn with dark green shadow, and aromatic. Islanded in their grassy meadow within the battlemented walls, the white church, the white arcaded tower miraculously poised on the verge of falling, the round white baptistery seemed to meditate in solitude of ancient glories—Pisan dominion, Pisan arts and thoughts—of the mysteries of religion, of inscrutable fate and unfathomed godhead, of the insignificance and the grandeur of man.

' Why ve deuce it shouldn't fall,' said Hovenden, as the Leaning Tower came in sight, ' I can't imagine.'

They drove past the house on the water, where Byron had bored himself through an eternity of months, out of the town. After Pontedera the road became more desolate. Through a wilderness of bare, unfertile hills, between whose yellowing grasses showed a white and ghastly soil, they mounted towards Volterra. The landscape took on something of an infernal aspect ; a prospect of

275

parched hills and waterless gulleys, like the undulations of a petrified ocean, expanded interminably round them. And on the crest of the highest wave, the capital of this strange hell, stood Volterra— three towers against the sky, a dome, a line of impregnable walls, and outside the walls, still outside but advancing ineluctably year by year towards them, the ravening gulf that eats its way into the flank of the hill, devouring the works of civilization after civilization, the tombs of the Etruscans, Roman villas, abbeys and mediaeval fortresses, renaissance churches and the houses of yesterday.

' Must be a bit slow, life in a town like vis,' said Hovenden, racing round the hairpin turns with an easy virtuosity that appalled Mr. Falx.

' Think if one had been born there,' said Irene.

' Well, if we 'd both been born vere,' replied Lord Hovenden, flushed with insolence and speed, ' it wouldn't have been so bad.'

They left Volterra behind them. The hellish landscape was gradually tempered with mundane greenness and amenity. They descended the headlong street of Colle. The landscape became once more completely earthly. The soil of the hills was red, like that from which God made Adam. In the steep fields grew rows of little pollard trees, from whose twisted black arms hung the festooned vines. Here and there between the trees shuffled a pair of white oxen, dragging a plough.

' Excellent roads, for a change,' said Lord Hovenden. On one straight stretch he managed to touch eighty-eight. Mr. Falx's beard writhed and fluttered with the agonized motions of some captive animal. He was enormously thankful when they drew up in front of the hotel at Siena.

' Wonderful machine, don't you fink ? ' Lord Hovenden asked him, when they had come to a standstill.

' You go much too fast,' said Mr. Falx severely.

Lord Hovenden's face fell. ' I 'm awfully sorry,' he apologized. The young giant in him was already giving place to the meek pedestrian. He looked at his watch. ' The others won't be here for another three-quarters of an hour, I should fink,' he added, in the hope that Mr. Falx would be mollified by the information.

Mr. Falx was not mollified, and when the time came, after lunch, for setting out on the Perugia road, he expressed a decided preference for a seat in Mrs. Aldwinkle's limousine. It was decided that he should change places with Miss Elver.

Miss Elver had no objection to speed; indeed, it excited her. The faster they went, the more piercing became her cries of greeting and farewell, the more wildly she waved her handkerchief at the passing dogs and children. The only trouble about going so fast was that the mighty wind was always tearing the handkerchiefs from between her fingers and whirling them irretrievably into receding space. When all the four handkerchiefs in her reticule had been blown away, Miss Elver burst into tears. Lord Hovenden had to stop and lend her his coloured silk bandana. Miss Elver was enchanted by its gaudy beauty; to secure it against the assaults of the thievish wind, she made Irene tie one corner of it round her wrist.

' Now it 'll be all right,' she said triumphantly; lifting her goggles, she wiped away the last traces of her recent grief.

Lord Hovenden set off again. On the sky-line, lifted high above the rolling table-land over which they were travelling, the solitary blue shape of Monte Amiata beckoned from far away. With every mile to southward the horns of the white oxen that dragged the carts became longer and longer. A sneeze—one ran the risk of a puncture; a sideways toss of the head—one might have been impaled on the hard and polished points. They passed through San Quirico; from that secret and melancholy garden within the walls of the ruined citadel came a whiff of sun-warmed box. In Pienza they found the Platonic idea of a city, the town with a capital T; walls with a gate in them, a short street, a piazza with a cathedral and palaces round the other three sides, another short street, another gate and then the fields, rich with corn, wine and oil; and the tall blue peak of Monte Amiata looking down across the fertile land. At Montepulciano there were more palaces and more churches; but the intellectual beauty of symmetry was replaced by a picturesque and precipitous confusion.

'Gosh!' said Lord Hovenden expressively, as they slid with locked wheels down a high street that had been planned for pack-asses and mules. From pedimented windows between the pilasters of the palaces, curious faces peered out at them. They tobogganed down, through the high renaissance, out of an arch of the Middle Ages, into the dateless and eternal fields. From Montepulciano they descended on to Lake Trasimene.

'Wasn't there a battle here, or something?' asked Irene, when she saw the name on the map.

Lord Hovenden seemed to remember that there had indeed been something of the kind in this neighbourhood. 'But it doesn't make much difference, does it?'

Irene nodded; it certainly didn't seem to make much difference.

'Nofing makes any difference,' said Lord Hovenden, making himself heard with difficulty in the teeth of a wind which his speedo-meter registered as blowing at forty-five miles an hour. 'Except' —the wind made him bold—'except you.' And he added hastily, in case Irene might try to be severe. 'Such a bore going down-hill on a twiddly road like vis. One can't risk ve slightest speed.'

But when they turned into the flat highway along the western shore of the lake, his face brightened. 'Vis is more like it,' he said. The wind in their faces increased from a capful to half a gale, from half a gale to a full gale, from a full gale very nearly to a hurricane. Lord Hovenden's spirits rose with the mounting speed. His lips curved themselves into a smile of fixed and permanent rapture. Behind the glass of his goggles his eyes were very bright. 'Pretty good going,' he said.

' Pretty good,' echoed Irene. Under her mask, she too was smiling. Between her ears and the flaps of her leather cap the wind made a glorious roaring. She was happy.

The road swung round to the left following the southern shore of the lake.

' We shall soon be at Perugia,' said Hovenden regretfully. ' What a bore ! '

And Irene, though she said nothing, inwardly agreed with him.

They rushed on, the gale blew steadily in their faces. The road forked ; Lord Hovenden turned the nose of his machine along the leftward branch. They lost sight of the blue water.

' Good-bye, Trasimene,' said Irene regretfully. It was a lovely lake ; she wished she could remember what had happened there.

The road began to climb and twist ; the wind abated to a mere half-gale. From the top of the hill, Irene was surprised to see the blue waters, which she had just taken leave of for ever, sparkling two or three hundred feet below on the left. At the joyous sight Miss Elver clapped her hands and shouted.

' Hullo,' Irene said, surprised. ' That 's odd, isn't it ? '

' Taken ve wrong road,' Hovenden explained. ' We 're going norf again up ve east side of ve lake. We 'll go right round. It 's too much bore to stop and turn.'

They rushed on. For a long time neither of them spoke. Behind them Miss Elver hooted her greetings to every living creature on the road.

They were filled with happiness and joy ; they would have liked to go on like this for ever. They rushed on. On the north shore of the lake the road straightened itself out and became flat again. The wind freshened. Far off on their respective hills Cortona and Montepulciano moved slowly, as they rushed along, like fixed stars. And now they were on the west shore once more. Perched on its jutting peninsula Castiglione del Lago reflected itself complacently in the water. 'Pretty good,' shouted Lord Hovenden in the teeth of the hurricane. 'By the way,' he added, 'wasn't it Hannibal or somebody who had a battle here? Wiv elephants, or somefing.'

'Perhaps it was,' said Irene.

'Not vat it matters in ve least.'

'Not in the least.' She laughed under her mask.

Hovenden laughed too. He was happy, he was joyful, he was daring.

'Would you marry me if I asked you?' he said. The question followed naturally and by a kind of logic from what they had been saying about Hannibal and his elephants. He did not look at her as he asked the question; when one is doing sixty-seven one must keep one's eyes on the road.

'Don't talk nonsense,' said Irene.

'I'm not talking nonsense,' Lord Hovenden protested. 'I'm asking a straightforward question. Would you marry me?'

'No.'

'Why not?'

'I don't know,' said Irene.

They had passed Castiglione. The fixed stars of Montepulciano and Cortona had set behind them.

'Don't you like me?' shouted Lord Hovenden. The wind had swelled into a hurricane.

'You know I do.'

'Ven why not?'

'Because, because . . . Oh, I don't know. I wish you'd stop talking about it.'

The machine rushed on. Once more they were running along the southern shore. A hundred yards before the forking of the roads, Lord Hovenden broke silence. 'Will you marry me?' he asked.

'No,' said Irene.

Lord Hovenden turned the nose of his machine to the left. The road climbed and twisted, the wind of their speed abated.

' Stop,' said Irene. ' You 've taken the wrong turn again.'

But Hovenden did not stop. Instead, he pressed down the accelerator. If the car got round the corners it was more by a miracle than in obedience to the laws of Newton or of nature.

' Stop ! ' cried Irene again. But the car went on.

From the hill-top they looked down once more upon the lake.

' Will you marry me ? ' Lord Hovenden asked again. His eyes were fixed on the road in front of him. Rapturously, triumphantly he smiled. He had never felt happier, never more daring, more overflowing with strength and power. ' Will you marry me ? '

' No,' said Irene. She felt annoyed ; how stupidly he was behaving !

They were silent for several minutes. At Castiglione del Lago he asked again. Irene repeated her answer.

' You 're not going to do this clown's trick again, are you ? ' she asked as they approached the bifurcation of the roads.

' It depends if you 're going to marry me,' he answered. This time he laughed aloud ; so infectiously that Irene, whose irritation was something laid on superficially over her happiness, could not help laughing too. ' *Are* you going to ? ' he asked.

' No.'

Lord Hovenden turned to the left. ' It 'll be late before we get to Perugia,' he said.

' Oo-ooh ! ' cried Miss Elver, as they topped the long hill. ' How lovely ! ' She clapped her hands. Then, leaning forward, she touched Irene's shoulder. ' What a lot of lakes there are here ! ' she said.

On the north shore Lord Hovenden asked again. Cortona and Montepulciano presided at the asking.

' I don't see why I should be bullied,' said Irene. Lord

Hovenden found the answer more promising than those which had gone before.

'But you 're not being bullied.'

'I am,' she insisted. 'You 're trying to force me to answer all at once, without thinking.'

'Now really,' said Hovenden, 'I call vat a bit fick. Forcing you to answer all at once! But vat 's exactly what I 'm not doing. I 'm giving you time. We 'll go round ve lake all night, if you like.'

A quarter of a mile from the forking of the road, he put the question yet once more.

'You 're a beast,' said Irene.

'Vat 's not an answer.'

'I don't want to answer.'

'You needn't answer definitely if you don't want to,' he conceded. 'I only want you to say vat you 'll fink of it. Just say perhaps.'

'I don't want to,' Irene insisted. They were very close, now, to the dividing of ways.

'Just perhaps. Just say you 'll fink of it.'

'Well, I 'll think,' said Irene. 'But mind, it doesn't commit . . .'

She did not finish her sentence; for the car, which had been heading towards the left, swerved suddenly to the right with such violence that Irene had to clutch at the arm of her seat to prevent herself from being thrown sideways bodily out of the machine. 'Goodness!'

'It 's all right,' said Lord Hovenden. They were running smoothly now along the right-hand road. Ten minutes later, from the crest of a little pass, they saw Perugia on its mountain, glittering in the sunlight. They found, when they reached the hotel, that the rest of the party had long since arrived.

'We took ve wrong turning,' Lord Hovenden explained. 'By

ve way,' he added, turning to Mr. Cardan, ' about vat lake we passed
—wasn't it Hannibal or some one . . .'

' Such a lot of lakes,' Miss Elver was telling Mrs. Chelifer.
' Such a lot ! '

' Only one, surely, my dear,' Mrs. Chelifer mildly insisted.

But Miss Elver wouldn't hear of it.   ' Lots and lots.'

Mrs. Chelifer sighed compassionately.

Before dinner Irene and Lord Hovenden went for a stroll in the
town.   The huge stone palaces lowered down at them as they
passed.   The sun was so low that only their highest windows, their
roofs and cornices took the light.   The world's grey shadow was
creeping up their flanks ; but their crests were tipped with coral
and ruddy gold.

' I like vis place,' said Lord Hovenden.   In the circumstances
he would have liked Wigan or Pittsburg.

' So do I,' said Irene.   Through the window in her thick hair
her face looked smiling out, merry in its childishness.

Leaving the stately part of the town, they plunged into the
labyrinth of steep alleys, of winding passage-ways and staircases
behind the cathedral.   Built confusedly on the hill-side, the tall
houses seemed to grow into one another, as though they were the
component parts of one immense and fantastical building, in which
the alleys served as corridors.   The road would burrow through
the houses in a long dark tunnel, to widen out into a little well-like
courtyard, open to the sky.   Through open doors, at the head of
an outside staircase, one saw in the bright electric light a family
sitting round the soup tureen.   The road turned into a flight of
stairs, dipped into another tunnel, made cheerful by the lights of
a subterranean wine shop opening into it.   From the mouth of the
bright cavern came up the smell of liquor, the sound of loud voices
and reverberated laughter.

And then, suddenly emerging from under the high houses, they
found themselves standing on the edge of an escarped slope, looking

out on to a huge expanse of pale evening sky, scalloped at its fringes by the blue shapes of mountains, with the round moon, already bright, hanging serene and solemn in the midst. Leaning over the parapet, they looked down at the roofs of another quarter of the city, a hundred feet below. The colours of the world still struggled against the encroaching darkness ; but a lavish municipality had already beaded the streets with yellow lights. A faint smell of wood-smoke and frying came up through the thin pure air. The silence of the sky was so capacious, so high and wide, that the noises of the town—like so many small, distinctly seen objects in the midst of an immense blank prairie—served but to intensify the quiet, to make the listener more conscious of its immensity in comparison with the trivial clatter at its heart.

' I like vis place,' Lord Hovenden repeated.

They stood for a long time, leaning their elbows on the parapet, saying nothing.

' I say,' said Hovenden suddenly, turning towards his companion a face on which all the shyness, the pedestrian's self-deprecation had reappeared, ' I 'm most awfully sorry about vat silly business of going round vat beastly lake.' The young giant who sat at the wheel of the Vauxhall Velox had retired with the machine into the garage, leaving a much less formidable Hovenden to prosecute the campaign which he had so masterfully begun. The moon, the enchanting beauty of the face that looked out so pensively through its tress-framed window, the enormous silence with the little irrelevant noises at its heart, the smell of wood-smoke and fried veal cutlets—all these influences had conspired to mollify Lord Hovenden's joyous elation into a soft and sugary melancholy. His actions of this afternoon seemed to him now, in his changed mood, reprehensibly violent. He was afraid that his brutality might have ruined his cause. Could she ever forgive him for such behaviour ? He was overwhelmed by self-reproach. To beg forgiveness seemed to be his only hope. ' I 'm awfully sorry.'

' Are you ? ' Irene turned and smiled at him. Her small white teeth showed beneath the lifted lip ; in the wide-set, childish eyes there was a shining happiness. ' I 'm not. I didn't mind a bit.'

Lord Hovenden took her hand. ' You didn't mind ? Not at all ? '

She shook her head. ' You remember that day under the olive trees ? '

' I was a beast,' he whispered remorsefully.

' I was a goose,' said Irene. ' But I feel different now.'

' You don't mean . . . '

She nodded. They walked back to their hotel hand in hand. Hovenden never stopped talking and laughing all the way. Irene was silent. The kiss had made her happy too, but in a different way.

CHAPTER II

TIME and space, matter and mind, subject, object—how inextricably they got mixed, next day, on the road to Rome! The simple-minded traveller who imagines himself to be driving quietly through Umbria and Latium finds himself at the same time dizzily switchbacking up and down the periods of history, rolling on top gear through systems of political economy, scaling heights of philosophy and religion, whizzing from aesthetic to aesthetic. Dimensions are bewilderingly multiplied, and the machine which seems to be rolling so smoothly over the roads is travelling, in reality, as fast as forty horses and the human minds on board can take it, down a score of other roads, simultaneously, in all directions.

The morning was bright when they left Perugia. In the blue sky above Subasio floated a few large white clouds. Silently they rolled away down the winding hill. At the foot of the mountain, secure from the sunlight in the delicious cool of their family vault, the obese Volumni reclined along the lids of their marble ash-bins, as though on couches round the dinner-table. In an eternal anticipation of the next succulent course they smiled and for ever went on smiling. We enjoyed life, they seemed to say, and considered death without horror. The thought of death was the seasoning which made our five and twenty thousand dinners upon this earth yet more appetizing.

A few miles further on, at Assisi, the mummy of a she-saint lies in a glass case, brilliantly illumined by concealed electric lights. Think of death, says the she-saint, ponder incessantly on the decay of all things, the transience of this sublunary life. Think, think; and in the end life itself will lose all its savour; death will corrupt it; the flesh will seem a shame and a disgustfulness. Think of death hard enough and you will come to deny the beauty and the holiness of life; and, in point of fact, the mummy was once a nun.

‘ When Goethe came to Assisi,’ said Mr. Cardan, as they emerged from the vaults of St. Clare, ' the only thing he looked at was the portico of a second-rate Roman temple. Perhaps he wasn't such a fool as we think him.'

' An admirable place for playing halma,' said Chelifer, as they entered the Teatro Metastasio.

Upon that rococo stage art was intended to worship itself. Everywhere now, for the last two hundred years and more, it has been worshipping itself.

But in the upper and the lower churches of St. Francis, Giotto and Cimabue showed that art had once worshipped something other than itself. Art there is the handmaid of religion—or, as the psycho-analysts would say, more scientifically, anal-erotism is a frequent concomitant of incestuous homosexuality.

' I wonder,' said Mr. Cardan pensively, ' if St. Francis really managed to make poverty seem so dignified, charming and attractive as they make out. I know very few poor people nowadays who cut a particularly graceful figure.' He looked at Miss Elver, who was waddling along the road like a water-bird on land, a few yards ahead. The end of one of Lord Hovenden's bright bandanas trailed behind her in the dust ; it was tied by one corner to her wrist and she had forgotten its existence. Twenty-five thousand pounds, thought Mr. Cardan, and sighed. St. Francis, Gotama Buddha—they managed their affairs rather differently. But it was difficult nowadays to beg with any degree of dignity.

They got into the cars once more ; waving the red bandana, Miss Elver said good-bye to the saints who thought so much of death that they were forced to mortify their lives. In their cool summer-house the obese Volumni smiled contemptuously. We thought not of death, we begat children, multiplied our flocks, added acre to acre, glorified life. . . . Lord Hovenden accelerated ; the two wisdoms, the new and the ancient law, receded into the distance.

Spello came tumbling down the hill to look at them. In Foligno it was market day. There were so many people that Miss Elver exhausted herself in continuous wavings and greetings. Trevi on its conical mountain was like the picture of a city in an illuminated book. By the side of the road, in the rich plain, stood factories; their tall chimneys were the slenderer repetitions of the castle towers perched high on the slopes of the hills above. In these secure and civilized times the robbers come down from their mountain fastnesses and build their watch-towers in the valleys. They were driving through progress; through progress at a mile a minute. And suddenly the cool and sparkling miracle of Clitumnus was at their right hand. The sacred spring came rushing out of the flank of the hill into a brimming pool. The banks were green with an almost English grass. There were green islands in the midst; and the weeping willow trees drooping over the water, the little bridges, transformed the Roman site into the original landscape from which a Chinese artist first drew a willow pattern.

'More lakes,' cried Miss Elver.

At Spoleto they stopped for lunch and the frescoes of Filippo Lippi, a painter Mrs. Aldwinkle particularly admired for having had the strength of mind, though a friar, to run off with a young girl at a Convent School. The shadowy apse was melodious with pious and elegant shapes and clear, pure colours. Anal-erotism was still the handmaid of incestuous homosexuality, but not exclusively. There was more than a hint in these bright forms of anal-erotism for anal-erotism's sake. But the designer of that more than Roman *cinquecento* narthex at the west end of the church, he surely was a pure and unmixed coprophilite. How charming is divine philosophy! Astrology, alchemy, phrenology and animal magnetism, the N-rays, ectoplasm and the calculating horses of Elberfield —these have had their turn and passed. We need not regret them; for we can boast of a science as richly popular, as easy and as all-explanatory as ever were phrenology or magic. Gall and Mesmer have given place to Freud. Filippo Lippi once had a bump of art. He is now an incestuous homosexualist with a bent towards anal-erotism. Can we doubt any longer that human intelligence progresses and grows greater ? Fifty years hence, what will be the current explanation of Filippo Lippi ? Something profounder, something more fundamental even than faeces and infantile incestuousness ; of that we may be certain. But what, precisely what, God alone knows. How charming is divine philosophy !

' I like vese paintings,' Lord Hovenden whispered to Irene.

They set out again. Over the pass of the Somma, down the long winding gorge to Terni.

On across the plain (the mountains bristling jaggedly all round) and up the hill to Narni ; Narni that hangs precariously on the brink of its deep precipitous valley ; on into the Sabine hills.

Sabine, Sabine—how wildly the mere word deviated the machine from its course ! *Eheu, fugaces,* how the days draw in—was not that first said, first elegantly and compellingly said, in a Sabine farm ? And the Sabine women ! Only Rubens knew what they looked like and how they ought to be raped. How large and blonde they were ! What glossy satin dresses they had on, what pearls ! And their Roman ravishers were tanned as brown as Indians. Their muscles bulged ; their eyes, their polished armour flashed. From the backs of their prancing horses they fairly dived into the foaming sea of female flesh that splashed and wildly undulated around them. The very architecture became tumultuous and orgiastic. Those were the high old times. Climbing from Narni, they drove into the heart of them.

But other artists than Peter Paul had passed this way. He painted only the Sabine name ; they, the scene. An ancient shepherd, strayed from one of Piranesi's ruins, watched them from a rock above the road, leaning on his staff. A flock of goats, kneeling ruminatively in the shade of an oak tree, their black bearded faces, their twisted horns sharply outlined against the bright blue sky, grouped themselves professionally—good beasts ! they had studied the art of pictorial composition under the best masters—

K*

in momentary expectation of Rosa da Tivoli's arrival. And the same Italianizing Dutchman was surely responsible for that flock of dusty sheep, those dogs, those lads with staves and that burly master shepherd, dressed like a capripede in goatskin breeches and mounted on the back of a little donkey, whose smallness contributed by contrast to the portly dignity of its rider. Nor were Dutchmen and Flemings the only foreign painters in this Italian scene. There were trees, there were glades in the woods, there were rocks that belonged by right of conquest to Nicolas Poussin. Half close the eyes, and that grey stone becomes a ruined sepulchre : *Et ego in Arcadia* . . . ; the village there, on the hill-top, across the valley, flowers into a little city of colonnades and cupolas and triumphal arches, and the peasants working in the fields are the people of a transcendental Arcadia gravely and soberly engaged in pursuing the True, the rationally Good and Beautiful. So much for the foreground and the middle distance. But suddenly, from the crest of a long descent, the remote wide background of Poussin's ideal world revealed itself : the vale of the Tiber, the broken plain of the Campagna, and in the midst—fantastic, improbable—the solitary cone of Mount Soracte, dim and blue against the blue of the sky

CHAPTER III

FROM the heights of the Pincio Mr. Falx denounced the city that lay spread out below him.

'Marvellous, isn't it?' Mrs. Aldwinkle had said. Rome was one of her private properties.

'But every stone of it,' said Mr. Falx, 'raised by slave labour. Every stone! Millions of wretches have sweated and toiled and died'—Mr. Falx's voice rose, his language became richer and richer, he gesticulated as though he were addressing a public meeting—'in order that these palaces, these stately churches, these forums, amphitheatres, cloaca maximas and what-nots might be here to-day to gratify your idle eyes. Is it worth it, I ask you? Is the momentary gratification of a few idlers a sufficient reason for the secular oppression of millions of human beings, their brothers, their equals in the eyes of God? Is it, I ask again? No, a thousand times no.' With his right fist Mr. Falx thumped the open palm of his left hand. 'No!'

'But you forget,' said Mr. Cardan, 'there's such a thing as a natural hierarchy.' The words seemed to remind him of something. He looked round. At one of the little tea-tables grouped round the band-stand at the other side of the road, Miss Elver, dressed in her sack of flowered upholstery, was eating chocolate éclairs and meringues, messily, with an expression of rapture on her cream-smeared face. Mr. Cardan turned back and continued: There are a few choice Britons who never never will be slaves, and a great many who not only will be slaves, but would be utterly lost if they were made free. Isn't it so?'

'Specious,' said Mr. Falx severely. 'But does the argument justify you in grinding the life out of a million human beings for the sake of a few works of art? How many thousand workmen and their wives and children lived degraded lives in order that St. Peter's might be what it is?'

'Well, as a matter of fact, St. Peter's isn't much of a work of art,' said Mrs. Aldwinkle scornfully, feeling that she had scored a decided point in the argument.

'If it's a question of degraded lives,' put in Chelifer, 'let me make a claim for the middle classes rather than the workers. Materially, perhaps, they may live a little better ; but morally and spiritually, I assure you, they stand at the very heart of reality. Intellectually, of course, they are indistinguishable from the workers. All but a negligible, freakish minority in both classes belong to the three lowest Galtonian categories. But morally and spiritually they are worse off ; they suffer from a greater reverence for public opinion, they are tortured by snobbery, they live perpetually in the midst of fear and hate. For if the workers are afraid of losing their jobs, so too are the burgesses, and with almost better reason—for they have more to lose, have further to fall. They fall from a precarious heaven of gentility into the abysses of unrelieved poverty, into the workhouse and the glutted labour exchanges ; can you wonder that they live in fear ? And as for hate—you can talk about the hate of the proletariat for the bourgeoisie, but it's nothing, I assure you, to the hate that the bourgeoisie feel for the proletariat. Your burgess loathes the worker because he is afraid of him ; he is terrified of the revolution that may pull him down from his genteel heaven into hell. How enviously, with what a bitter resentment, your burgess regards the slightest amelioration of the worker's existence ! To him it always seems an amelioration made at his expense. Do you remember, during the war and in the prosperous time immediately following, when the workers for the first time in history were paid a wage that enabled them to live in something like comfort, do you remember how furiously, with what a black atrabilious overflow of hatred, the middle classes denounced the riotous excesses of the idle poor ? Why, the monsters even bought pianos—pianos ! The pianos have all been sold again, long since. The spare furniture has gone the way of all superfluities. Even the winter overcoat is pawned. The burgess, for all that the times are hard for him too, feels happier; he is revenged. He can live in a comparative tranquillity. And what a life! He lives according to his lusts, but timorously and in a conventional way; his diversions are provided for him by joint stock companies. He has no religion, but a great respect for genteel conventions which have not even the justification of a divine origin. He has heard of art and thought, and respects them because the best people respect them; but his mental capacities and his lack of education do not allow him to get any real satisfaction out of them. He is thus poorer than the savage, who, if he has never heard of art or science, is yet rich in religion and traditional lore. The life of a wild animal has a certain dignity and beauty; it is only the life of a domesticated animal that can be called degraded. The burgess is the perfectly domesticated human animal. That is why,' added Chelifer, ' that is why any one who wants to live really at the heart of human reality must live in the midst of burgessdom. In a little while, however, it won't be necessary to make any invidious distinctions between the classes. Every one will soon be bourgeois. The charm of the lower classes in the past consisted in the fact that they were composed of human animals in a state of relative wildness. They had a traditional wisdom and a traditional superstition; they had ancient and symbolical diversions of their own. My mother can tell you all about those,' he put in parenthetically. ' That Tolstoy should have preferred the Russian peasants to his rich and literary friends is very comprehensible. The peasants were wild; the others, just as brutish at bottom, were disgustingly tame. Moreover, they were lap-dogs of a perfectly useless breed; the peasants at any rate did something to justify their existence. But in the other countries of Europe and the New World the wild breed is rapidly dying out. Million-sale newspapers and radios are domesticating them at a prodigious rate. You can go a long way in England nowadays before you find a genuine wild human animal. Still, they do exist in the country and even in the more fetid and savage parts of towns. That's why, I repeat, one must live among the suburban bourgeoisie. The degraded and domesticated are the typical human animals of the present time; it's they who will inherit the earth in the next generation; they're the characteristic modern reality. The wild ones are no longer typical; it would be ludicrous to be a Tolstoyan now, in western Europe. And as for the genuine men and women, as opposed to the human animals, whether wild or tame—they're so fabulously exceptional that one has no right to think of them at all. That cupola,' he pointed to the silhouette of St. Peter's, rising high above the houses on the other side of the city, ' was designed by Michelangelo. And very nice too. But what has it or he to do with us ? '

' Blasphemy ! ' cried Mrs. Aldwinkle, flying to the defence of Buonarroti.

Mr. Falx harked back to an earlier grievance. ' You malign human nature,' he said.

' All very true and indeed obvious,' was Mr. Cardan's comment. ' But I can't see why you shouldn't allow us to amuse ourselves with Michelangelo if we want to. God knows, it's hard enough for a man to adapt himself to circumstances ; why should you deprive him of his little assistants in the difficult task ? Wine, for example, learning, cigars and conversation, art, cooking, religion for those that like it, sport, love, humanitarianism, hashish and all the rest. Every man has his own recipe for facilitating the process of adaptation. Why shouldn't he be allowed to indulge in his dope in peace ? You young men are all so damned intolerant. How often have I had occasion to say it ? You 're nothing but a set of prohibitionists, the whole lot of you.'

' Still,' said Mrs. Chelifer in her gentle and musical voice, ' you can't deny that prohibition has done a great deal of good in America.'

They strolled back to the tea-table, which they had left a few minutes before to look at the view. Miss Elver was just finishing an éclair. Two empty dishes stood in front of her.

' Had a good tea ? ' asked Mr. Cardan.

Miss Elver nodded ; her mouth was too full to speak.

' Perhaps you 'd like some more cakes ? ' he suggested.

Miss Elver looked at the two empty dishes, then at Mr. Cardan. She seemed on the point of saying yes. But Mrs. Chelifer, who had taken the chair next hers, laid a hand on her arm.

' I don't think Grace really wants any more,' she said.

Grace turned towards her ; a look of disappointment and melancholy came into her eyes, but it gave place after a moment to a happier expression. She smiled, she took Mrs. Chelifer's hand and kissed it.

' I like you,' she said.

On the back of Mrs. Chelifer's hand her lips had left a brown print of melted chocolate. ' I think you 'd better just give your face a little wipe with your napkin,' Mrs. Chelifer suggested.

' Perhaps if you dipped the corner of it first into the hot water . . .'

There was a silence. From the open-air dancing-floor, a hundred yards away beneath the trees, came the sound, a little dimmed by the intervening distance and the pervading Roman noise, of the jazz band. Monotonously, unceasingly, the banjos throbbed out the dance rhythms. An occasional squeak indicated the presence of a violin. The trumpet could be heard tooting away with a dreary persistence at the tonic and dominant ; and clear above all the rest the saxophone voluptuously caterwauled. At this distance every tune sounded exactly the same. Suddenly, from the band-stand of the tea-garden a pianist, two fiddlers and a 'cellist began to play the Pilgrims' Chorus out of *Tannhäuser*.

Irene and Lord Hovenden, locked in one another's arms, were stepping lightly, meanwhile, lightly and accurately over the con-

crete dance-floor. Obedient to the music of the jazz band, forty
other couples stepped lightly round them. Percolating insidiously
through the palisade that separated the dance-floor from the rest
of the world, thin wafts of the Pilgrims' Chorus intruded faintly
upon the jazz.

'Listen,' said Hovenden. Dancing, they listened. 'Funny
it sounds when you hear bof at ve same time!'

But the music from beyond the palisade was not strong enough
to spoil their rhythm. They listened for a little, smiling at the
absurdity of this other music from outside; but they danced on
uninterruptedly. After a time they did not even take the trouble
to listen.

CHAPTER IV

MR. FALX had expected to find no difficulty, once they were arrived in Rome, in recalling his pupil to what he considered a better and more serious frame of mind. In the bracing atmosphere of an International Labour Conference Lord Hovenden, he hoped, would recover his moral and intellectual tone. Listening to speeches, meeting foreign comrades, he would forget the corrupting charms of life under Mrs. Aldwinkle's roof and turn to nobler and more important things. Moreover, on a young and generous spirit like his the prospect of possible persecution at the hands of the Fascists might be expected to act as a stimulant; the fact of being in opposition ought to make him feel the more ardently for the unpopular cause. So Mr. Falx calculated.

But it turned out in the event that he had calculated badly Arrived in Rome, Lord Hovenden seemed to take even less interest in advanced politics than he had during the last two or three weeks at Vezza. He suffered himself, but with a reluctance that was only too obvious to Mr. Falx, to be taken to a few of the meetings of the conference. Their bracing intellectual atmosphere had no tonic effect upon him whatsoever, and he spent his time at the meetings yawning and looking with an extraordinary frequency at his watch. In the evenings, when Mr. Falx wanted to take him to see some distinguished comrade, Lord Hovenden either made some vague excuse or, more frequently, was simply undiscoverable. The next day Mr. Falx learned with distress that he had passed half the night at a Dancing Club with Irene Aldwinkle. He could only look forward hopefully to the date of Mrs. Aldwinkle's return journey. Lord Hovenden—it had been arranged before they left England—would stay on with him in Rome till the end of the conference. With the removal of all temptations to frivolity he might be relied upon to re-become his better self.

Lord Hovenden's conscience, meanwhile, occasionally troubled him.

' I sometimes feel I've raver left old Mr. Falx in ve lurch,' he confided uneasily to Irene on the evening of their second day in Rome. ' But still, he can't really expect me to spend all ve day wiv him, can he ? '

Irene agreed that he really couldn't.

' Besides,' Lord Hovenden went on, reassuring himself, ' I'd really be raver out of it wiv his friends. And it's not as if he were lonely. Vere's such a lot of people he wants to talk to. And, you know, I fink I'd really be in ve way more van anyfing.'

Irene nodded. The band struck up again. Simultaneously the two young people got up and, united, stepped off on to the floor. It was a sordid and flashy cabaret, frequented by the worst sort of international and Italian public. The women were mostly prostitutes; a party of loud and tipsy young Englishmen and Americans were sitting in one corner with a pair of swarthy young natives who looked altogether too sober ; the couples who took the floor danced with an excessive intimacy. Irene and Lord Hovenden were discussing the date of their wedding ; they thought the cabaret delightful.

In the day-time, when Hovenden could get off going to the conferences, they wandered about the town buying what they imagined to be antiques for their future home. The process was a little superfluous. For, absorbed in the delights of shopping, they forgot that their future home was also a highly ancestral home.

' Vat looks an awfully nice dinner-service,' Lord Hovenden would say ; and darting into the shop they would buy it out of hand. ' A bit chipped '—he shook his head. ' But never mind.' Among the twenty-three valuable dinner-services with which their future home was already supplied was one of solid gold and one of silver gilt for less important occasions. Still, it was such fun buying, such fun to poke about in the shops ! Under the pale blue sky of autumn the city was golden and black—golden where the sunlight fell on walls of stucco or travertine, black in the shadows, deeply black under archways, within the doors of churches, glossily black where the sculptured stone of fountains shone wet with the unceasing gush of water. In the open places the sun was hot; but a little wind from the sea blew freshly, and from the mouth of narrow alleys, sun-proof these thousand years, there breathed forth wafts of a delicious vault-like coolness. They walked for hours without feeling tired.

Mrs. Aldwinkle meanwhile went the round of the sights with Chelifer. She had hopes that the Sistine Chapel, the Appian Way at sunset, the Coliseum by moonlight, the gardens of the Villa d'Este might arouse in Chelifer's mind emotions which should in their turn predispose him to feel romantically towards herself. The various emotions, she knew by experience, are not boxed off from one another in separate pigeon-holes; and when one is stimulated it is likely that its neighbours will also be aroused. More proposals are made in the taxi, on the way home from a Wagner opera, in the face of an impressive view, within the labyrinth of a ruined palace, than in drab parlours or the streets of West Kensington. But the Appian Way, even when the solitary pine trees were black against the sunset and the ghosts were playing oboes, not for the sensual ear, in the ruined sepulchres; the Coliseum, even under the moon; the cypresses, the cascades and the jade-green pools of Tivoli—all were ineffective. Chelifer never committed himself; his behaviour remained perfectly courteous.

Seated on a fallen column in the ruins of Hadrian's Villa, Mrs. Aldwinkle even went so far as to tell him about certain amorous passages in her past life. She told him, with various little modifications of the facts, modifications in which she herself had long ago come implicitly to believe, the story of the affair with Elzevir, the pianist—such an artist! to his finger-tips; with Lord Trunion—such a *grand seigneur* of the old school! But concerning

Mr. Cardan she was silent. It was not that Mrs. Aldwinkle's mythopoeic faculties were not equal to making something very extraordinary and romantic out of Mr. Cardan. No, no; she had often described the man to those who did not know him; he was a sort of village Hampden, a mute inglorious What's-his-name, who might have done anything—but anything—if he had chosen to give himself the trouble. He was a great Don Juan, actual in this case, not merely potential. He was a mocking devil's advocate, he was even a devil. But that was because he was misunderstood—misunderstood by everybody but Mrs. Aldwinkle herself. Secretly he was so sensitive and kind-hearted. But one had to be gifted with intuition to find it out. And so on; she had made a capital mythical figure out of him. But an instinct of caution restrained her from showing off her myths too freely before people who were well acquainted with the originals. Chelifer had never met Lord Trunion or the immortal Elzevir. He *had* met Mr. Cardan.

But the effect of the confidences was as small as that of the romantic scenery and the stupendous works of art. Chelifer was not encouraged by them either to confide in return or to follow the example of Elzevir and Lord Trunion. He listened attentively, gave vent, when she had finished, to a few well-chosen expressions of sympathy, such as one writes to acquaintances on the deaths of their aged grandmothers, and after a considerable silence, looking at his watch, said he thought it was time to be getting back : he had promised to meet his mother for tea, and after tea, he added, he was going to take her to look at *pensions*. Seeing that she was going to stay in Rome the whole winter, it was worth taking some trouble about finding a nice room. Wasn't it ? Mrs. Aldwinkle was forced to agree. They set off through the parched Campagna towards the city. Mrs. Aldwinkle preserved a melancholy silence all the way.

On their way from the hotel to the tea-shop in the Piazza Venezia Mrs. Chelifer, Miss Elver and Mr. Cardan passed through the forum of Trajan. The two little churches lifted their twin domes of gold against the sky. From the floor of the forum, deep-sunk beneath the level of the road—a foot for every hundred years—rose the huge column, with tumbled pillars and blocks of masonry lying confusedly round its base. They paused to look round.

' I 've always been a Protestant,' said Mrs. Chelifer after a moment's silence ; ' but all the same I 've always felt, whenever I came here, that Rome was somehow a special place ; that God had marked it out in some peculiar way from among other cities as a place where the greatest things should happen. It 's a significant place, a portentous place—though I couldn't tell you exactly why. One just feels that it is portentous ; that 's all. Look at this piazza, for example. Two florid little counter-Reformation churches, all trumpery pretentiousness and no piety ; a mixed lot of ordinary houses all round, and in the hole in the middle a huge heathen memorial of slaughter. And yet for some reason it all seems to me to have a significance, a spiritual meaning ; it 's important. And the same applies to everything in this extraordinary place. You can't regard it with indifference as you can an ordinary town.'

' And yet,' said Mr. Cardan, ' a great many tourists and all the inhabitants contrive to do so with complete success.'

' That 's only because they 've never looked at the place,' said Mrs. Chelifer. ' Once you 've really looked . . .'

She was interrupted by a loud whoop from Miss Elver, who had wandered away from her companions and was looking over the railing into the sunken forum.

' What is it ? ' called Mr. Cardan. They hurried across the street towards her.

' Look,' cried Miss Elver, pointing down, ' look. All the cats ! '

And there they were. On the sun-warmed marble of a fallen column basked a large tabby. A family of ginger kittens were playing on the ground below. Small tigers stalked between the blocks of masonry. A miniature black panther was standing up on its hind legs to sharpen its claws on the bark of a little tree. At the foot of the column lay an emaciated corpse.

'Puss, puss,' Miss Elver shrilly yelled.

'No good,' said Mr. Cardan. 'They only understand Italian.'

Miss Elver looked at him. 'Perhaps I'd better learn a little, then,' she said. 'Cat's Italian.'

Mrs. Chelifer meanwhile was looking down very earnestly into the forum. 'Why, there are at least twenty,' she said. 'How do they get there?'

'People who want to get rid of their cats just come and drop them over the railing into the forum,' Mr. Cardan explained.

'And they can't get out?'

'So it seems.'

An expression of distress appeared on Mrs. Chelifer's gentle face. She made a little clicking with her tongue against her teeth and sadly shook her head. 'Dear, dear,' she said, 'dear, dear. And how do they get fed?'

'I've no idea,' said Mr. Cardan. 'Perhaps they feed on one another. People throw things down from time to time, no doubt.'

'There's a dead one there, in the middle,' said Mrs. Chelifer; and a note of something like reproach came into her voice, as though she found that Mr. Cardan was to blame for the deadness of the little corpse at the foot of the triumphal column.

'Very dead,' said Mr. Cardan.

They walked on. Mrs. Chelifer did not speak; she seemed preoccupied.

CHAPTER V

'AN *pris caruns flucuthukh*'; Mr. Cardan beckoned to the guide. 'Bring the lamp a little nearer,' he said in Italian, and when the light had been approached, he went on slowly spelling out the primitive Greek writing on the wall of the tomb : '*flucuthukh nun tithuial khues khathc anulis mulu vizile ziz riin puiian acasri flucuper pris an ti ar vus ta aius muntheri flucuthukh.*' He straightened himself up. 'Charming language,' he said, 'charming ! Ever since I learned that the Etruscans used to call the god of wine Fufluns, I 've taken the keenest interest in their language. Fufluns —how incomparably more appropriate that is than Bacchus, or Liber, or Dionysos ! Fufluns, *Fufluns,*' he repeated with delighted emphasis. 'It couldn't be better. They had a real linguistic genius, those creatures. What poets they must have produced ! "When Fufluns *flucuthukhs* the *ziz* "—one can imagine the odes in praise of wine which began like that. You couldn't bring together eight such juicy, boozy syllables as that in English, could you ? '

'What about " Ale in a Saxon rumkin " then ? ' suggested Chelifer.

Mr. Cardan shook his head. 'It doesn't compare with the Etruscan,' he said. 'There aren't enough consonants. It 's too light, too fizzy and trivial. Why, you might be talking about soda water.'

'But for all you know,' said Chelifer, '*flucuthukh* in Etruscan may mean soda water. Fufluns, I grant you, is apposite. But perhaps it was just a fluke. You have no evidence to show that they fitted sound to sense so aptly in other words. " When Fufluns *flucuthukhs* the *ziz* " may be the translation of " When Bacchus drowns the hock with soda." You don't know.'

'You 're quite right,' Mr. Cardan agreed. 'I don't. Nor does any one else. My enthusiasm for Fufluns carried me away. *Flucuthukh* may not have the fruity connotation that a word with a sound like that ought to have; it may even, as you say, mean soda water. Still, I continue to hope for the best; I believe in my Etruscans. One day, when they find the key to this fossilized language, I believe I shall be justified; *flucuthukh* will turn out to be just as appropriate as Fufluns—you mark my words! It's a great language, I insist; a great language. Who knows? A couple of generations hence some new Busby or Keat may be drumming Etruscan syntax and Etruscan prosody into the backsides of British boyhood. Nothing would give me greater satisfaction. Latin and Greek have a certain infinitesimal practical value. But Etruscan is totally and absolutely useless. What better basis for a gentleman's education could possibly be discovered? It's the great dead language of the future. If Etruscan didn't exist, it would be necessary to invent it.'

'Which is precisely what the pedagogues will have to do,' said Chelifer, 'there being no Etruscan literature beyond the inscriptions and the rigmarole on the mummy-wrappings at Agram.'

'So much the better,' replied Mr. Cardan. 'If we wrote it ourselves, we might find Etruscan literature interesting. Etruscan literature composed by Etruscans would be as boring as any other ancient literature. But if the epics were written by you, the Socratic dialogues by me, the history by some master of fiction like Miss Thriplow—then we'd possess a corpus in which the rare schoolboys who can derive some profit from their education could take a real interest. And when, a generation hence, we have become as much out of date in our ideas as Tully or Horace, the literature of Etruria will be rewritten by our descendants. Each generation will use the dead language to express its own ideas. And expressed in so rich an idiom as I take Etruscan to be, the ideas will seem the more significant and memorable. For I have often noticed that an idea which, expressed in one's native language, would seem dull, commonplace and opaque, becomes transparent to the mind's eye, takes on a new significance when given a foreign and unfamiliar embodiment. A cracker-motto in Latin sounds much weightier and truer than the same motto in English. Indeed, if the study of dead languages has any use at all, which I should be sorry to admit, it consists in teaching us the importance of the verbal medium in which thoughts are expressed. To know the same thing in several languages is to know it (if you have any sense at all) more profoundly, more richly, than if it were known only in one. The youth who learns that the god of wine is called, in Etruscan, Fufluns has a profounder knowledge of the attributes of that divine personality than the youth who only knows him under the name of Bacchus. If I desire that archaeologists should discover the key to the Etruscan language, it is merely in order that I may have a deeper insight into the thing or idea connoted by such sumptuous words as *flucuthukh* or *khathc*. For the rest I care nothing. That they should discover the meaning of these inscriptions is a matter to me of the most complete indifference. For after all, what would they discover? Nothing that we don't already know. They would discover that before the Romans conquered Italy men ate and drank, made love, piled up wealth, oppressed their weaker neighbours, diverted themselves with sports, made laws and so on. One could have divined as much by walking down Piccadilly any day of the week. And besides, we have their pictures.' He threw out his hand. The guide, who had been listening patiently to the incomprehensible discourse, responded to the gesture by raising his acetylene lamp. Called magically into existence by the bright white light, a crowd of gaily coloured forms appeared on the walls of the vault in which they were standing. Set in a frame of conventionalized trees, a pair of red-brown wrestlers with Egyptian eyes and the profiles of the Greeks who disport themselves round the flanks of the earliest vases were feeling for a hold. On either side of them, beyond the trees, stood two couples of long-legged black horses. Above them, in the segment of a circle between the upper line of this band of paintings and the vaulted roof, a great leopard lay couchant, white-

skinned, with a pattern of black spots arranged like those on the
china dogs and cats of a later age. On the wall to the left they were
feasting : red-brown Etruscans reclined on couches ; porcelain-
white women, contrasting as voluptuously with their tanned companions as the pale, plump nymphs of Boucher with their brown
pastoral lovers, sat by their sides. With hieratic gestures of mutual
love they pledged one another in bowls of wine. On the opposite
wall the fowlers were busy—here with slings, there with nets. The
sky was alive with birds. In the blue sea below they were spearing
fish. A long inscription ran from right to left across the wall. The
vaulted roof was painted with chequers, red, black and white.
Over the low, narrow door that led from the tomb into the ante-
chamber there knelt a benevolent white bull. Two thousand five
hundred years ago they had wept here over the newly dead.

'You see them,' continued Mr. Cardan, 'hunting, drinking,
playing, making love. What else could you expect them to do ?
This writing will tell us no more than we know already. True, I
want to know what it means, but only because I hope that the brown
man may be saying to the white lady : " *Flucuthukh* to me only
with thine eyes," or words to that effect, " and I will *flucuthukh*
with mine." If that was what they really were saying, it would
throw an entirely new light on the notion of drinking. An entirely new light.'

'It would throw no new light on love, if lovers they are,' said
Mrs. Aldwinkle mournfully.

'Wouldn't it ?' Mr. Cardan queried. 'But imagine if
flucuthukh turned out to mean, not drink, but love. I assure you
that the feelings denoted by such a word would be quite different
from those we sum up by " love." You can make a good guess
from the sound of the word in any language what the people who
speak it mean when they talk of love. *Amour*, for example—that
long ou sound with the rolled r at the end of it, how significant it is !
Ou—you have to push your lips into a snout-like formation, as

though you were going to kiss. Then, briskly, rrr—you growl like a dog. Could anything be more perfectly expressive of the matter-of-fact lasciviousness which passes for love in nine-tenths of French fiction and drama ? And *Liebe*—what a languishing, moonlit, sentimental sound the long ie has ! And how apt, too, is the bleating labial by which it is followed !—be,—be. It is a sheep whose voice is choked by emotion. All German romanticism is implied in the sound of the word. And German romanticism, a little *détraqué*, turns quite logically into expressionismus and the wild erotic extravagance of contemporary German fiction. As for our *love*—that's characteristically non-committal and diffident. That dim little monosyllable illustrates our English reluctance to call a spade a spade. It is the symbol of our national repressions. All our hypocrisy and all the beautiful platonism of our poetry is there. Love . . .' Mr. Cardan whispered the word, and holding up his finger for silence cocked his ear to catch the faint echoes of his voice reverberating from wall to wall under the sepulchral vault. ' Love. . . . How utterly different is our English emotion from that connoted by *amore* ! *Amore*—you fairly sing the second syllable, in a baritone voice, from the chest, with a little throaty tremolo on the surface to make it sound more palpitating. *Amori* —it's the name of the quality that Stendhal so much admired in the Italians and the absence of which in his own countrymen, and more especially countrywomen, made him rank Paris below Milan or Rome—it's the apt and perfectly expressive name of passion.'

' How true ! ' said Mrs. Aldwinkle, brightening for a moment through her gloom. This compliment to her Italian language and Italian character touched and pleased her. ' The very sound of *amore* is passionate. If the English knew what passion meant, they'd have found a more expressive word than love. That's certain. But they don't know.' She sighed.

' Quite so,' said Mr. Cardan. ' *Amore*, we see, can mean nothing else than Southern passion. But now, suppose that *flucuthukh* should turn out to be the Etruscan for love—what then ? *Amour* connotes lasciviousness, *Liebe* sentiment, *amore* passion. To what aspect of the complex phenomenon of love can *flucuthukh* refer ? The microbe Staphylococcus pyogenes produces in some patients boils, in others sties in the eye ; in certain cases it is even responsible for *keratitis punctata*. It is the same with love. The symptoms vary in different individuals. But owing to the boundless suggesti-bility and imitativeness of man, the commonest symptoms at any given period tend to become universal in any one society. Whole peoples take the disease in the same way ; one suffers from *amour*, another from *Liebe* and so on. But now imagine a people to whom love was *flucuthukh*. What can have been the particular symptoms of the general amorous disease to which such a name was given ? One cannot guess. But at least it is fascinating to speculate.'

One after the other the party filed out through the narrow door into the ante-room of the sepulchre and up the steep flight of steps leading to the surface of the ground. Blinking in the bright after-noon light, they stepped out on to the bare and windy down.

It was a solitary place. The arches of a ruined aqueduct went striding along the ridge, and following their long recession the eye came at last to rest on the walls and tall towers of Corneto. To the left the hog-backed down sloped seawards ; on the further side of the narrow plain at its foot stretched the Mediterranean. On the right lay a deep valley, shut in on the further side by a great round hill. Its grassy flanks were furrowed and pitted with what had once been the works of man. Once, on that hill, had stood the sacred city, Tarquinii of the Etruscans. The long bare down on which they were standing had been, through how many centuries ? its necropolis. In little houses hollowed out of the chalky stone slept the innumerable dead. Here and there the top of a vault was broken through ; from the hollow darkness within came up even at high summer an immemorial coolness. Here and there the surface of the down swelled up into round grass-grown barrows.

It was from the heart of one of these tumuli that they had now emerged. The guide put out his lamp and shut the door upon the Etruscan ghosts. They walked for a few hundred yards through geological time—between the sea and the hills, under the floating clouds; on the sky-line the Middle Ages pricked up their towers; the smudged and flattened relics of Etruria undulated almost imperceptibly under the grass; from the Roman road in the plain below came up the distant hooting of a motor car.

The sound of the motor horn aroused Irene from the thoughtful trance in which, sad-faced and childish, this time, pathetically, she was walking. She had been silent and melancholy ever since, yesterday morning, they had left Rome; Lord Hovenden had stayed behind with Mr. Falx. The long-drawn hooting of the electric horn seemed to remind her of something. She looked down towards the sea-board plain. A cloud of white dust was advancing along the Maremman road from the direction of Civita Vecchia. It hung, opaque, over half a mile of road, fading slowly to transparency towards the tail. At the head, where the dust was thickest, a small black object moved like a rapidly crawling insect across the map-like expanse of plain, drawing the cloud after it. From the opposite direction came another black-headed comet of dust. Like two white serpents they approached one another, as though rushing to battle. Nearer, nearer they came. Irene stopped still to look at them. She was filled with a horrible apprehension. It seemed impossible that they should not crash together. Nearer, nearer. The heads of the two serpents seemed almost to be touching one another. Suppose, just suppose that one of the cars was his. . . . Inevitably they must collide. Crash and smash—oh, the horror of it! Irene shut her eyes. A few seconds later she opened them. The two white snakes had merged together into one very thick opaque snake. It was impossible to see the little black heads at all. For one horrible moment she thought that they must have destroyed one another. But they reappeared after a little, receding now one from the other, no more approaching. The two serpents were still one serpent, but two-headed, a long amphisbaena. Then, gradually, the middle of the amphisbaena began to grow thin, to fade; a little clump of trees showed through it, dimly at first, mistily, then clearly. The amphisbaena had fallen in half and the two white snakes crawled on, one northwards, the other towards the south, and between their fading tails was a wide and ever wider gap. Irene heaved a deep sigh of relief and ran on after the others. It seemed to her that she had been the witness of a catastrophe miraculously averted. She felt much happier than she had felt all day. On a wide road two automobiles had passed one another. That was all.

The guide was unlocking the door that gave entrance to another excavated barrow. He relit his lamp and led the way down the steep steps into the tomb. On one wall they were horse-racing and wrestling, hieratically, all in profile. A goddess—or perhaps it was merely the Lady Mayoress of the city—wearing that high bonnet-shaped coiffure which the Roman matrons were afterwards to borrow from their neighbours, was distributing the prizes. On the other walls they were feasting. The red-brown men, the white-skinned ladies reclined along their couches. A musician stood by, playing on his double flute, and a female dancer, dressed in what looked rather like a Persian costume, was dancing a shawl dance for the diversion of the diners.

'They seem to have had simple tastes,' said Mr. Cardan. 'There's nothing very sophisticated or *fin de siècle* here—no bull-baiting by naked female acrobats, as at Cnossos; no gladiatorial fights, no wholesale butchering of animals, no boxing matches with brass knuckle-dusters, as in the Roman arenas. A nice school-boyish sort of people, it looks to me. Not quite civilized enough to be *exigeant* about their pleasures.'

'And not yet quite civilized enough,' added Chelifer, 'to be really vulgar. In that respect they fall a long way behind the later

Romans. Do you know that huge mosaic in the Lateran museum ? It comes from one of the Imperial baths, I forget which, and consists of portraits of the principal sporting heroes of the epoch—boxers and wrestlers—with their trainers and backers. These last are treated very respectfully by the mosaic-maker, who represents them wearing togas and standing in the noblest attitudes. One sees at a glance that they are the *gens bien*, the sportsmen, the amateurs—in a word, the monied interest. The athletes are portrayed in a state of nature, and are indeed so excessively natural that one could easily mistake the heavy-weight boxers for gorillas peeled of their superfluous hair. Under each portrait is a caption with the name of the hero represented. The whole thing reminds one very much of the sporting page in a picture paper—only it is a page that is forty feet long by thirty wide, and made, not of wood-pulp, but of the most durable materials ever devised by the ingenuity of man for the embodiment and visible eternization of his thoughts. And it is, I think, precisely the size and everlastingness of the frightful thing that makes it so much worse than the similar page from our picture papers. To make ephemeral heroes of professional sports-men and prize-fighters is bad enough; but that a people should desire to immortalize their fame is surely indicative of a profounder vulgarity and abjection. Like the Roman mob, the mobs of our modern capitals delight in sports and exercises which they themselves do not practise; but at any rate, the fame of our professionals lasts only a day after their triumph. We do not print their effigies on marble pavements made to live down a hundred generations of men. We print them on wood-pulp, which is much the same as printing them on water. It is comforting to think that by the year two thousand one hundred the whole of contemporary journal-ism, literature and thought will have crumbled to dust. The mosaic, however, will still be in its present state of perfect preserva-tion. Nothing short of dynamite or an earthquake will ever totally destroy the effigies of those Imperial boxers. And a very good thing, too, for the future historians of Rome. For no man can claim that he has really understood the Roman empire till he has studied that mosaic. That pavement is a vessel filled with the quintessence of Roman reality. A drop of that reality is enough to shrivel up all the retrospective Utopias that historians have ever made or ever can make out of the chronicles of ancient Rome. After looking at that mosaic a man can have no more generous illusions about the people who admired it or the age in which it was made. He will realize that Roman civilization was not merely just as sordid as ours, but if anything more sordid. But in these Etruscan vaults,' Chelifer added, looking round at the frescoed walls, ' one gets no such impression of organized and efficient beastliness as one gets from the Roman mosaic. There's a freshness, as you say, Mr. Cardan, a certain jolly schoolboyishness about all the fun they represent. But I have no doubt, of course, that the impression is entirely fallacious. Their art has a certain archaic charm ; but the artists were probably quite as sophisticated and quite as repulsive as their Roman successors.'

' Come, come,' said Mr. Cardan, ' you forget that they called Bacchus Fufluns. Give them at least the credit that is due to them.'

' But the Romans too had a fine language,' Chelifer objected. ' And yet they laid down immense enlargements of the sporting page of the *Daily Sketch* in marble tesserae on a foundation of cement.'

They climbed again towards the light. The steps were so high and her legs so short that Miss Elver had to be helped up. The tomb resounded with her laughter and shrill whooping. They emerged at last out of the ground.

On the top of a high barrow some two or three hundred yards away stood the figure of a man, distinct against the sky. He was shading his eyes with his hand and seemed to be looking for something. Irene suddenly became very red.

' Why, I believe it's Hovenden,' she said in a voice that was as casual as she could make it.

Almost simultaneously the man turned his face in their direction. The shading hand went up in a gesture of greeting. A glad 'Hullo!' sounded across the tombs; the man skipped down from his barrow and came running across the down towards them. And Hovenden it was; Irene had seen aright.

'Been looking for you all over ve place,' he explained breathlessly as he came up. With the greatest heartiness he shook the hands of all present except—diplomatically—Irene's. 'Vey told me in ve town vat a party of foreigners was out here looking at ve cemetery or somefing. So I buzzed after you till I saw old Ernest wiv ve car at ve side of ve road. Been underground, have you?' He looked into the dark entrance of the tomb. 'No wonder I couldn't . . .'

Mrs. Aldwinkle cut him short. 'But why aren't you in Rome with Mr. Falx?' she asked.

Lord Hovenden's boyish, freckled face became all at once exceedingly red. 'Ve fact is,' he said, looking at the ground, 'vat I didn't feel very well. Ve doctor said I ought to get away from Rome at once. Country air, you know. So I just left a note for Mr. Falx and . . . and here I am.' He looked up again, smiling.

CHAPTER VI

'BUT at Montefiascone,' said Mr. Cardan, concluding the history of the German bishop who gave the famous wine of Montefiascone its curious name, ' at Montefiascone Bishop Defuk's servant found good wine at every shop and tavern ; so that when his master arrived he found the prearranged symbol chalked up on a hundred doors. *Est, Est, Est*—the town was full of them. And the Bishop was so much enraptured with the drink that he decided to settle in Montefiascone for life. For life—but he drank so much that in a very short time it turned out that he had settled here for death. They buried him in the lower church, down there. On his tombstone his servant engraved the Bishop's portrait with this brief epitaph : " *Est Est Jo Defuk. Propter nimium hic est. Dominus meus mortuus est.*" Since when the wine has always been called Est Est Est. We 'll have a flask of it dry for serious drinking. And for the frivolous and the feminine, and to sip with the dessert, we 'll have a bottle of the sweet *moscato*. And now let 's see what there is to eat.' He picked up the menu and holding it out at arm's length—for he had the long sight of old age—read out slowly, with comments, the various items. It was always Mr. Cardan who ordered the dinner (although it was generally Lord Hovenden or Mrs. Aldwinkle who paid), always Mr. Cardan ; for it was tacitly admitted by every one that Mr. Cardan was the expert on food and wine, the professional eater, the learned and scholarly drinker.

Seeing Mr. Cardan busy with the bill of fare, the landlord approached, rubbing his hands and cordially smiling—as well he might on a Rolls-Royce-full of foreigners—to take orders and give advice.

' The fish,' he confided to Mr. Cardan, ' the fish is something special.' He put his fingers to his lips and kissed them. ' It comes from Bolsena, from the lake, down there.' He pointed out of the window at the black night. Somewhere, far down through the darkness, lay the Lake of Bolsena.

Mr. Cardan held up his hand. 'No, no,' he objected with decision and shook his head. 'Don't talk to me of fish. Never safe in these little places,' he explained to his companions. 'Particularly in such hot weather. And then, imagine eating fish from Bolsena—a place where they have miracles, where holy wafers bleed for the edification of the pious and as a proof of the fact of transubstantiation. No, no,' Mr. Cardan repeated, 'fishes from Bolsena are altogether too fishy. Let's stick to fried eggs, with fillet of veal to follow. Or a little roast capon . . .'

'I want fish,' said Miss Elver. The passionate earnestness of her tone contrasted strikingly with the airiness of Mr. Cardan's banter.

'I really wouldn't, you know,' said Mr. Cardan.

'But I like fish.'

'But it may be unwholesome. You never can tell.'

'But I want it,' Miss Elver insisted. 'I love fish.' Her large lower lip began to tremble, her eyes filled with tears. 'I *want* it.'

'Well, then, of course you shall have it,' said Mr. Cardan, making haste to console her. 'Of course, if you really like it. I was only afraid that it mightn't perhaps be good. But it probably will be.'

Miss Elver took comfort, blew her long nose and smiled. 'Thank you, Tommy,' she said, and blushed as she pronounced the name.

After dinner they went out into the piazza for coffee and liqueurs. The square was crowded and bright with lights. In the middle the band of the local Philharmonic Society was giving its Sunday evening concert. Planted on the rising ground above the piazza Sammicheli's great church solemnly impended. The lights struck up, illuminating its pilastered walls. The cupola stood out blackly against the sky.

'The choice,' said Mr. Cardan, looking round the piazza, ' seems

315

to lie between the Café Moderno and the Bar Ideale. Personally, I should be all for the ideal rather than the real if it wasn't for the disagreeable fact that in a bar one has to stand. Whereas in a café, however crassly materialistic, one can sit down. I'm afraid the Moderno forces itself upon us.'

He led the way in the direction of the café.

'Talking of Bars,' said Chelifer, as they sat down at a little table in front of the café, ' has it ever occurred to you to enumerate the English words that have come to have an international currency ? It's a somewhat curious selection, and one which seems to me to throw a certain light on the nature and significance of our Anglo-Saxon civilization. The three words from Shakespeare's language that have a completely universal currency are Bar, Sport and W.C. They're all just as good Finnish now as they are good English. Each of these words possesses what I may call a family. Round the idea " Bar " group themselves various other international words, such as Bitter, Cocktail, Whiskey and the like. " Sport " boasts a large family—Match, for example, Touring Club, the verb to Box, Cycle-Car, Performance (in the sporting sense) and various others. The idea of hydraulic sanitation has only one child that I can think of, namely Tub. Tub—it has a strangely old-world sound in English nowadays ; but in Yugo-Slavia, on the other hand, it is exceedingly up-to-date. Which leads us on to that very odd class of international English words that have never been good English at all. A Smoking for example, a Dancing, a Five-o'clock —these have never existed except on the continent of Europe. As for High-Life, so popular a word in Athens, where it is spelt iota, gamma, lambda, iota, phi—that dates from a remote, mid-Victorian epoch in the history of our national culture.'

'And Spleen,' said Mr. Cardan, ' you forget Spleen. That comes from much further back. A fine aristocratic word, that ; we were fools to allow it to become extinct. One has to go to France to hear it uttered now.'

'The word may be dead,' said Chelifer, 'but the emotion, I fancy, has never flourished more luxuriantly than now. The more material progress, the more wealth and leisure, the more standardized amusements—the more boredom. It's inevitable, it's the law of Nature. The people who have always suffered from spleen and who are still the principal victims, are the prosperous, leisured and educated. At present they form a relatively small minority; but in the Utopian state where everybody is well off, educated and leisured, everybody will be bored; unless for some obscure reason the same causes fail to produce the same effects. Only two or three hundred people out of every million could survive a lifetime in a really efficient Utopian state. The rest would simply die of spleen. In this way, it may be, natural selection will work towards the evolution of the super-man. Only the intelligent will be able to bear the almost intolerable burden of leisure and prosperity. The rest will simply wither away, or cut their throats—or, perhaps more probably, return in desperation to the delights of barbarism and cut one another's throats, not to mention the throats of the intelligent.'

'That certainly sounds the most likely and natural ending,' said Mr. Cardan. 'If of two possible alternatives one is in harmony with our highest aspirations and the other is, humanly speaking, absolutely pointless and completely wasteful, then, you may be sure, Nature will choose the second.'

At half-past ten Miss Elver complained that she did not feel very well. Mr. Cardan sighed and shook his head. 'These miraculous fishes,' he said. They went back to the hotel.

'Luckily,' said Mrs. Aldwinkle that evening while Irene was brushing her hair, 'luckily I never had any babies. They spoil the figure so frightfully.'

'Still,' Irene ventured to object, 'still . . . they must be rather fun, all the same.'

Mrs. Aldwinkle pretexted a headache and sent her to bed almost at once. At half-past two in the morning Irene was startled out of her sleep by a most melancholy groaning and crying from the room next to hers. 'Oo, Oo! Ow!' It was Grace Elver's voice. Irene jumped out of bed and ran to see what was the matter. She found Miss Elver lying in a tumbled bed, writhing with pain.

'What is it?' she asked.

Miss Elver made no articulate answer. 'Oo, Oo,' she kept repeating, turning her head from side to side as though in the hope of escaping from the obsessing pain.

Irene ran to her aunt's bedroom, knocked at the door and, getting no answer, walked in. 'Aunt Lilian,' she called in the darkness, and louder, 'Aunt Lilian!' There was still no sound. Irene felt for the switch and turned on the light. Mrs. Aldwinkle's bed was empty. Irene stood there for a moment looking dubiously at the bed, wondering, speculating. From down the corridor came the repeated 'Oo, Oo!' of Grace Elver's inarticulate pain. Roused by the sound from her momentary inaction, Irene turned, stepped across the passage and began knocking at Mr. Cardan's door.

CHAPTER VII

Selections from Francis Chelifer

IN the sporting calendar the most interesting events are booked for the autumnal months. There is no hunting in the spring. And even in Italy there is a brief close season for song-birds that lasts from the coming of the nightingales to the departure of the last swallow. The fun, the real fun, starts only in the autumn. Grouse-shooting, partridge-shooting—these are the gay preliminaries. But the great day is the First of October, when the massacre of the gaudy pheasant begins. Crack! crack!—the double barrels make music in the fading woods. And a little later the harmonious dogs join in and the hoof, as the Latin poet so aptly puts it, the hoof shakes the putrid field with quadrupedantical sound. Winter is made gay with the noise of hunting.

It is the same in the greater year of certain feminine lives. . . . Pop! pop!—on the First of October they go out to shoot the pheasant. A few weeks later, tally-ho, they hunt the fox. And on Guy Fawkes's day the man-eating season begins. My hostess, when she picked me up on the beach of Marina di Vezza, had reached a point in her year somewhere between pheasant-shooting and man-eating. They say that foxes enjoy being hunted; but I venture to doubt the truth of this comforting hypothesis. Experientia does it, as Mrs. Micawber's papa (ha ha! from Mr. Toft) . . . Etcetera.

If loving without being loved in return may be ranked as one of the most painful of experiences, being loved without loving is certainly one of the most boring. Perhaps no experience is better calculated to make one realize the senselessness of the passion. The spectacle of some one making a fool of himself arouses only laughter. When one is playing the fool oneself, one weeps. But when one is neither the active imbecile nor the disinterested spectator, but the unwilling cause of somebody else's folly—then it is that one comes to feel that weariness and that disgust which are the proper, the human reaction to any display of the deep animal stupidity that is the root of all evil.

Twice in my life have I experienced these salutary horrors of boredom—once by my own fault, because I asked to be loved without loving ; and once because I had the misfortune to be picked up on the beach, limp as sea-weed, between the First of October and Guy Fawkes's day. The experiences were disagreeable while they lasted ; but on the other hand, they were highly didactic. The first of them rounded off, so to speak, the lesson I had learned from Barbara. The second episode was staged by Providence, some few years later, to remind me of the first and to print what the Americans would call its ' message ' still more indelibly upon my mind. Providence has been remarkably persistent in its efforts to sober me. To what end I cannot imagine.

Poor Miss Masson ! She was a very good secretary. By the end of 1917 she knew all that it was possible to know about rubber tubing and castor oil. It was unfortunate for every one concerned that Providence should have destined her to instruct me yet more deeply in the fearful mysteries of love. True, I brought it on myself. Providence, on that occasion, elected to act indirectly and threw the blame on me. I accept it all—all the more willingly since my act shows in the most illuminating manner what are the consequences, the frightful consequences, of stupidity. There is a certain satisfaction to be derived from having personally proved the truth of one's own wisdom by acting in defiance of its precepts.

Yes, I brought it on myself. For it was I who made the first advances. It was I who, out of pure wantonness, provoked the sleeping, or at least well-disciplined tiger that lay hidden in Dorothy Masson's heart—put my walking-stick between the bars and, against all the rules, poked it rudely in the ribs. I got what I asked for.

I was like that wanton Blackamoor in one of old Busch's mis-anthropically comic picture-books.

> Ein Mohr aus Bosheit und Pläsier
> Schiesst auf das Elefantentier.

With his little arrow he punctures the placid pachyderm; and the pachyderm takes his revenge, elaborately, through fourteen subsequent woodcuts.

My only excuse—the recentness of that ludicrous catastrophe with which the tragedy of Barbara had concluded—was an excuse that might equally have served as an additional reason against doing what I did; I ought, after having once been bitten, to have shown myself twice shy. But in the state of misery in which I found myself I hoped that a second bite might distract my attention from the anguish of the first. And even this is not precisely accurate; for I never anticipated that the second would really be a bite at all. I looked forward merely to a kind of playful diversion, not to anything painful. True, when I found how serious the affair threatened to become for Dorothy Masson, I might have guessed that it would soon be serious also for myself, and have drawn back. But, inspired by that high-spirited irresponsibility which I have come since then so highly to admire in the natural, brutish human specimen, I refused to consider possible consequences and went on in the course I had begun. I was not in the least in love with the woman; nor did her person inspire me with any specific desire. My motive forces were misery, mingled with a kind of exasperation, and the vague itch of recurrent appetite. More than half of the world's 'affairs' have no more definite reasons for occurring. Ennui and itch are their first causes. Subsequently imagination may come into play and love will be born. Or experience may beget specific desires and in so doing may render one party necessary to the happiness of the other, or each to each. Or perhaps there will be no development at all and the affair will end placidly as it began, in itch and ennui.

But there are cases, of which mine was one, where one party may be inspired by the mere indefinite wantonness I have been describing, while the other is already imagination-ridden and in love. Poor Dorothy! There came into her eyes when I kissed her a look such as I had never seen in any other human eyes before or since. It was the look one sees in the eyes of a dog when its master is angry and raises his whip—a look of absolute self-abasement mingled with terror. There was something positively appalling in seeing those eyes staring at one out of a woman's face. To see a human being reduced in one's arms to the condition of a frightened and adoring dog is a shocking thing. And the more so in this case since it was completely indifferent to me whether she was in my arms or not. But when she raised her face and looked at me for a moment with those abject and terrified eyes of hers, it was not merely indifferent to me; it was even positively distasteful. The sight of those large-pupilled eyes, in which there was no glimmer of a human rational soul, but only an animal's terror and abasement, made me feel at once guilty and, complementarily, angry, resentful and hostile.

'Why do you look at me like that?' I asked her once. 'As though you were frightened of me.'

She did not answer; but only hid her face against my shoulder, and pressed me more closely in her arms. Her body shook with involuntary startings and tremblings. Casually, from force of habit, I caressed her. The trembling became more violent. 'Don't,' she implored me in a faint hoarse whisper, 'don't.' But she pressed me still closer.

She was frightened, it seemed, not of me but of herself, of that which lay sleeping in the depths of her being and whose awakening threatened to overwhelm, to blot for a moment out of existence that well-ordered, reasonable soul which was the ruler at ordinary times of her life. She was afraid of the power within her that could make her become something other than her familiar self. She was fearful of losing her self-mastery. And at the same time there was nothing else that she desired. The sleeping power within her had begun to stir and there was no resisting it. Vainly, hopelessly, she continued to attempt the impossible. She went on trying to resist, and her resistance quickened her desire to yield. She was afraid and yet invited my awakening kisses. And while she whispered to me imploringly, like one who begs for mercy, she pressed me in her arms. I, meanwhile, had begun to realize all the potentialities for boredom implicit in the situation. And how boring it did in fact turn out to be ! To be pursued by restless warmth when all that one desires is cool peace ; to be perpetually and quite justly accused of remissness in love and to have to deny the accusation, feebly, for the sake of politeness ; to be compelled to pass hours in tedious company—what an affliction, what a martyrdom it is ! I came to feel extremely sorry for those pretty women who are perpetually being courted by a swarm of men. But the pretty women, I reflected, had this advantage over me : that they were by nature a good deal more interested in love than I. Love is their natural business, the reason of their existence ; however distasteful their suitors may personally be to them, they cannot find them as completely boring and insufferable as would, placed in similar circumstances, a person to whom love as such is fundamentally rather uninteresting. The most tedious lover atones a little, in the eyes of the courted lady, for his personal insupportableness by the generic fact of being a lover. Lacking a native enthusiasm for love, I found it more difficult to support the martyrdom of being loved by Miss Masson.

But such an affair, you will object, is a typical piece of reality. True ; but at that time I was not quite such a believer in the real and earnest side of life as I am now. And even now I should regard it as something of a work of supererogation to associate with realities of so exceptionally penetrative a nature. A sober man, if he is logical and courageous, is bound to pass his life between Gog's

Court and Miss Carruthers's. But he is not bound to make love to Miss Carruthers or to provoke the clinging affections of Fluffy. That would be too much—so it seems to me, at any rate at present; though perhaps the time may come when I shall feel strong enough to take my reality in these stiff doses. There is an electric machine used by masseurs for driving iodine into stiffened joints. Love acts like this machine; it serves to drive the lover's personality into the mind of the beloved. I am strong enough at present to be able to bathe in the personalities of ordinary human animals; but I should be suffocated, I should faint away, if the muddy swill were to be pumped into my spiritual system by the penetrating electricity of love.

Miss Masson stood one Galtonian class higher than Miss Carruthers or Fluffy. One out of every four people is a Fluffy; only one out of every six is a Dorothy Masson. It makes a slight but perceptible difference. None the less, how much I suffered! When I brought her a few orchids as a present, remarking as I gave them to her that they looked so delightfully like artificial flowers, she would thank me and say she adored orchids, adding after a moment's pause for thought that she liked them because they looked so like artificial flowers. And she laughed softly to herself, she looked up at me for confirmatory applause. For that little habit alone I sometimes felt that I could have murdered her. But her solicitude, her reproaches, expressed or more often mute (for she rarely made scenes, but only looked at me with those sad brown eyes), her incessant desire to be close to me, to touch me, to kiss and be kissed—these were almost enough to drive me to suicide. It lasted for more than a year, an eternity. And technically it still lasts; for I never broke with her, never dramatically quitted her, but only quietly and gradually faded out of her life like the Cheshire Cat. Sometimes, even, we still meet. And still, as though nothing had happened, I take her in my arms and kiss her, till that strange expression of abject terror comes again into her eyes, till she implores me, in a voice made faint with excessive desire, to spare her well-disciplined everyday soul and not deliver it into the power of the fearful thing that is waking darkly within her. And still as she speaks she presses me closer, she offers her stretched throat to my kisses. And before and after, we talk about politics and common friends. And still as of old she echoes the last phrase I have spoken, still softly laughs and still expects me to admire her original thoughts. Finally I take my leave.

' You 'll come again soon ? ' she asks, looking up into my face with eyes that are full of sadness and apprehension, of questions unuttered, of unexpressed reproaches. I kiss her hand. ' Of course,' I say. And I go away, taking pains as I walk down the street not to speculate on the subject of her thoughts.

But Providence seems to have thought my connection with Dorothy inadequately instructive. Dorothy, after all, was only twenty-six when the episode began. Hers was that vernal and flowery season during which, even in Italy, warblers are not shot. It would be another twenty years before she reached her First of October ; thirty, perhaps, before the man-eating season should begin. And it was I who had made the first advances. But for my exhibition of *Bosheit und Pläsier* the boring history would never have unrolled itself. But Providence, anxious, for some inscrutable reason, to teach me a yet more memorable lesson, went so far as almost to drown me, so determined was it that I should fall into the hands of the suitable schoolmistress. I was to learn how ludicrously dreadful, as well as how boring, love can be.

I made no advances on this occasion. From the first I did nothing but retreat. Mrs. Aldwinkle's blue danger signals bore down on me ; like an agile pedestrian in the London traffic, I stepped aside. When she asked what women had inspired me, I answered that nothing inspired me but the London slums and the vulgarity of Lady Giblet. When she said that one could see by my face that I had been unhappy, I said that that was odd ; I had always been perfectly happy. When she talked about experience, meaning, as women generally do when they use that word, merely love, I replied with a discussion of experience in relation to the Theory of Knowledge. When she accused me of wearing a mask, I protested that I paraded my naked soul for every one to see. When she asked if I had ever been in love, I shrugged my shoulders and smiled : not to speak of. And when she asked, at very close range, if I had ever been loved, I answered quite truthfully that I had, but that it bored me.

But still, indomitably, she renewed the attack. There might have been something grand about her unwavering determination— something grand, if it had not been grotesque. Providence was teaching me yet once more that the unsapient life is a dreary and hopeless business, and that it is, for all practical purposes, the only life—lived everywhere by all but a negligibly few exceptions. At least I presume that that is what Providence was trying to impress on me. But in the process it was using Mrs. Aldwinkle, I thought, rather hardly. I felt sorry for the poor lady. Some hidden irrational force within herself was compelling her to cut these capers, throw herself into these ludicrous postures, say these stupid words and contort her face into these grimaces ; she was helpless. She just obeyed orders and did her best ; but her best was ludicrous. And not merely ludicrous but appalling. She was like a buffoon carrying a skull.

Unflaggingly she played the deplorable part assigned to her. Every day she brought me flowers. ' I want them to blossom in your verses,' she said. I assured her that the only scent which provoked me to write was that of the butchers' shops on a winter's evening along the Harrow Road. She smiled at me. ' Don't think I can't understand you,' she said. ' I do. I do.' She leaned forward ; her eyes shone, her perfume enveloped me, she breathed heliotrope in my face. I could see with extraordinary distinctness the little wrinkles round her eyes, the careless smear of rouge at the corners of the mouth. 'I do understand you,' she repeated.

She did understand me. . . . One night (it was at Monte-fiascone, on our way back from Rome), when I was reading in bed, I heard a sound; I looked up, and saw Mrs. Aldwinkle carefully closing the door behind her. She was wearing a dressing-gown of sea-green silk. Her hair hung in two thick plaits over her shoulders. When she turned round, I saw that her face had been coloured and powdered with more than ordinary care. In silence she advanced across the room, she sat down on the edge of my bed. An aura of ambergris and heliotrope surrounded her.

I smiled politely, closed my book (keeping a finger, however, between the pages to mark my place) and slightly raised my eyebrows in interrogation. To what, I made my face inquire, do I owe the honour? . . .

I owed it, it seemed, to my hostess's urgently felt need to tell me yet once more that she understood me.

'I couldn't bear,' she said breathlessly, 'couldn't bear to think of you here alone. With your secret misery.' And when I made as though to protest, she held up her hand. 'Oh, don't think I haven't seen through your mask. Alone with your secret misery . . .'

'No, really . . .' I managed to put in. But Mrs. Aldwinkle would not suffer herself to be interrupted.

'I couldn't bear to think of your terrible loneliness,' she went on. 'I wanted you to know there was at least one person who understood.' She leaned towards me, smiling, but with lips that trembled. All at once her eyes filled with tears, her face contorted itself into the terrible grimace of misery. She made a little moaning noise and, letting herself fall forward, she hid her face against my knees. 'I love you, I love you,' she repeated in a muffled voice. Her body was shaken by recurrent spasms of sobbing. I was left wondering what to do. This was not in the programme. When one goes out man-eating or pheasant-shooting, one has no business to weep over the victim. But the trouble is, of course, that the man-eater sees herself as the victim. *Hinc illae lacrimae.* It is impossible for two human beings to agree completely about anything. *Quot homines,* for now that the Dictionary of Familiar Quotations has been opened I may as well continue to make use of it, *quot homines, tot disputandum est.* There is no agreement even about the truths of science. One man is a geometrician ; the other can only understand analysis. One is incapable of believing in anything of which he cannot make a working model ; the other wants his truth as abstract as it is possible to make it. But when it comes to deciding which of two people is the victim and which the man-eater, there is nothing to be done but abandon the attempt. Let each party stick to his own opinion. The most successful men are those who never admit the validity of other people's opinions, who even deny their existence.

' My dear Lilian,' I said (she had insisted on my calling her Lilian within a day or two of my arrival), ' my dear Lilian . . .' I could find nothing more to say. A successful man, I suppose, would have said something frankly brutal, something that would have made it clear to Mrs. Aldwinkle which of the two, in his opinion, was the victim and which the carnivore. I lacked the force. Mrs. Aldwinkle went on sobbing.

' I love you. Couldn't you love me a little ? A little only ? I would be your slave. Your slave ; I 'd be your slave,' she kept repeating.

What things she said ! I listened to her, feeling pity—yes, pity no doubt—but still more, a profound embarrassment, and with it anger against the person who had thrust me into this untenable position.

' It 's no good,' I protested. ' It 's impossible.'

She only began again, desperately.

How much further the scene might have prolonged itself and

what might have happened if it had been protracted, I do not know. Luckily, however, an extraordinary commotion suddenly broke loose in the hotel. Doors slammed, voices were raised, there was the noise of feet along the corridors and on the stairs. Startled and alarmed, Mrs. Aldwinkle got up, went to the door, opened it a crack and looked into the passage. Some one hurried past; hastily she closed it again. When the coast was clear, she slipped out into the passage and tip-toed away, leaving me alone.

The commotion was caused by the beginning of Miss Elver's death-agony. Providence, having decided that my education had gone far enough, had broken off the lesson. The means it employed were, I must say, rather violent. A vain man might have been gratified by the reflection that one woman had been made miserable in order that he might be taught a lesson, while another had died—like King John, of a surfeit of lampreys—in order that the lesson might be interrupted before it was carried too disagreeably far. But as it happens, I am not particularly vain.

CHAPTER VIII

FROM the first nobody put very much faith in the local doctor; the mere look of him was enough to inspire mistrust. But when across the patient's prostrate and comatose body he chattily confided that he had taken his degree at the University of Siena, Mr. Cardan decided that it was time to send for somebody else.

'Siena's notorious,' he whispered. 'It's the place where the imbeciles who can't get their degrees at Bologna, or Rome, or Pisa go and have themselves made doctors.'

Mrs. Aldwinkle, who in the middle of the tumult had suddenly reappeared (Irene did not know from where), expressed her horror. Doctors were one of her specialities; she was very particular about doctors. Mrs. Aldwinkle had had a number of interesting maladies in the course of her life—three nervous break-downs, an appendicitis, gout and various influenzas, pneumonias and the like, but all of them aristocratic and avowable diseases; for Mrs. Aldwinkle distinguished sharply between complaints that are vulgar and complaints of a gentlemanly sort. Chronic constipation, hernia, varicose veins (' bad legs ' as the poor so gruesomely call them)— these, obviously, were vulgar diseases which no decent person could suffer from, or at any rate, suffering, talk about. Her illnesses had all been extremely refined and correspondingly expensive. What she did not know about doctors, English, French, Swiss, German, Swedish and even Japanese, was not worth knowing. Mr. Cardan's remarks about the University of Siena impressed her profoundly.

'The only thing to do,' she said decisively, 'is for Hovenden to drive straight back to Rome and bring back a specialist. At once.' She spoke peremptorily. It was a comfort for her, in her present distress of mind, to be able to do something, to make arrangements, to order people about, even herself to carry and fetch. 'The Principessa gave me the name of a wonderful man. I've got it written down somewhere. Come.' And she darted off to her room.

Obediently Lord Hovenden followed her, wrote down the talismanic name and took himself off. Chelifer was waiting for him at the bottom of the stairs.

' I may as well come with you, if you don't mind,' he said. ' I think I should only be in the way here.'

It was nearly half-past five when they started. The sun had not yet risen, but it was already light. The sky was pale grey with dark clouds low down on the horizon. There were mists in the valleys and the Lake of Bolsena was hidden from view under what seemed the waters of a milky sea. The air was cold. Driving out of the town, they met a train of pack mules climbing slowly, in the midst of a jingle of bells, up the steep street towards the market-place.

Viterbo was still asleep when they drove through. From the crest of the Ciminian mountains they first saw the sun. By seven o'clock they were in Rome. The sun-tipped obelisks, the gilded roofs and cupolas reached up out of shadow into the pale blue sky. They drove up the Corso. In the Piazza di Venezia they stopped at a café, ordered some coffee, and while it was being brought looked up in a directory the address of Mrs. Aldwinkle's doctor. He lived, they found, in the new quarter near the station

' I leave all ve talking to you,' said Hovenden, as they sipped their coffee. ' I 'm no good at ve language.'

' How did you manage the other day when you had to see the doctor yourself ? ' Chelifer inquired.

Lord Hovenden blushed. ' Well,' he said, ' as a matter of fact, ve doctor I saw was English. But he 's gone away now,' he added hastily, for fear that Chelifer might suggest their bringing the English doctor along too ; ' gone to Naples,' he further specified, hoping by the accumulation of circumstantial details to give greater verisimilitude to his story, ' for an operation.'

' He was a surgeon, then ? ' Chelifer raised his eyebrows.

Hovenden nodded. ' A surgeon,' he echoed, and buried his face in his coffee-cup.

They drove on. As they turned out of the Piazza into Trajan's Forum, Chelifer noticed a little crowd, mostly of street boys, pressing against the railings on the further side of the forum. At its centre stood a pale thin woman in dove-grey clothes whom even at this distance one could not fail to recognize as English, or at any rate definitely not Italian. The lady in grey was leaning over the railings, lowering very carefully at the end of a string, to which it was ingeniously attached by four subsidiary strings passed through holes bored in the rim, a large aluminium pannikin filled with milk. Slowly revolving as it went down, the pannikin was lowered to the floor of the sunken forum. Hardly had it touched the ground when, with simultaneous mewings and purrings, half a dozen thirsty cats came running up to it and began to lap at the white milk. Others followed ; every cranny gave up its cat. Lean toms jumped down from their marble pedestals and trotted across the open with the undulating, bounding gait of a running leopard. Month-old kittens staggered up on tottering legs. In a few seconds the pannikin was besieged by a horde of cats. The street boys whooped with delight.

' Well, I 'm blowed,' said Lord Hovenden, who had slowed up to watch the curious scene. ' I believe it 's your mover.'

' I think it is,' said Chelifer, who had recognized her long ago.

' Would you like me to stop ? ' asked Hovenden.

Chelifer shook his head. ' I think we 'd better get to the doctor as quickly as possible,' he said.

Looking back as they drove out of the forum, Chelifer saw that his mother, faithful to her vegetarian principles, was throwing down into the den of cats bread and cold potatoes. In the evening he imagined she would come again. She had not taken long to find her Roman occupation.

CHAPTER IX

THE funeral was not due to take place before sunset. The bearers, the choristers, the sexton, the priest himself, most likely, were all in the fields, picking the grapes. They had something more important to do, while the light lasted, than to bury people. Let the dead bury their dead. The living were there to make wine.

Mr. Cardan sat alone in the empty church. Alone; what had once been Grace Elver lay, coffined, on a bier in the middle of the aisle. That did not count as company; it was just so much stuff in a box. His red knobbly face was as though frozen into stillness, all its gaiety, its twinkling mobility were gone. It might have been the face of a dead man, of one of the dead whose business it is to bury the dead. He sat there grim and stony, leaning forward, his chin in his hand, his elbow on his knee.

Three thousand six hundred and fifty days more, he was thinking; that is, if I live another ten years. Three thousand six hundred and fifty, and then the end of everything, the tunnelling worms.

There are such horrible ways of dying, he thought. Once, years ago, he had a beautiful grey Angora cat. She ate too many black-beetles in the kitchen and died vomiting shreds of her shard-torn stomach. He often thought of that cat. One might die like that oneself, coughing up one's vitals.

Not that one eats many black-beetles, of course. But there is always putrid fish. The effects are not so very different. Wretched moron! he thought, looking at the coffin. It had been a disgusting sort of death. Pains, vomiting, collapse, coma, then the coffin—and now the busy ferments of putrefaction and the worms. Not a very dignified or inspiring conclusion. No speeches, no consoling serenities, no Little Nells or Paul Dombeys. The nearest approach to the Dickensian had been when, in a brief spell of lucidity, she asked him about the bears he was going to give her after they were married.

'Will they be grown up?' she asked. 'Or puppies?'

'Puppies,' he answered, and she had smiled with pleasure.

Those had been almost the only articulate words she had uttered. Through that long death-agony they were the only witnesses to the existence of her soul. For the rest of the time she had been no more than a sick body, mindlessly crying and muttering. The tragedy of bodily suffering and extinction has no catharsis. Punctually it runs its dull, degrading course, act by act to the conclusion. It ennobles neither the sufferer nor the contemplator. Only the tragedy of the spirit can liberate and uplift. But the greatest tragedy of the spirit is that sooner or later it succumbs to the flesh. Sooner or later every soul is stifled by the sick body; sooner or later there are no more thoughts, but only pain and vomiting and stupor. The tragedies of the spirit are mere struttings and posturings on the margin of life, and the spirit itself is only an accidental exuberance, the products of spare vital energy, like the feathers on the head of a hoopoo or the innumerable populations of useless and foredoomed spermatozoa. The spirit has no significance; there is only the body. When it is young, the body is beautiful and strong. It grows old, its joints creak, it becomes dry and smelly; it breaks down, the life goes out of it and it rots away. However lovely the feathers on a bird's head, they perish with it; and the spirit, which is a lovelier ornament than any, perishes too. The farce is hideous, thought Mr. Cardan, and in the worst of bad taste.

Fools do not perceive that the farce is a farce. They are the more blessed. Wise men perceive it and take pains not to think about it. Therein lies their wisdom. They indulge themselves in all the pleasures, of the spirit as of the body—and especially in those of the spirit, since they are by far the more varied, charming and delightful—and when the time comes they resign themselves with the best grace they can muster to the decay of the body and the extinction of its spiritual part. Meanwhile, however, they do not think too much of death—it is an unexhilarating theme; they do not insist too much upon the farcical nature of the drama in which they are playing, for fear that they should become too much disgusted with their parts to get any amusement out of the piece at all.

The most ludicrous comedies are the comedies about people who preach one thing and practise another, who make imposing claims and lamentably fail to fulfil them. We preach immortality and we practise death. Tartuffe and Volpone are not in it.

The wise man does not think of death lest it should spoil his pleasures. But there are times when the worms intrude too insistently to be ignored. Death forces itself sometimes upon the mind, and then it is hard to take much pleasure in anything.

This coffin, for instance—how can a man take pleasure in the beauty of the church in which this boxful of decaying stuff is lying? What can be more delightful than to look up the aisle of a great church and see at the end of a long dark vista of round-headed arches a brightly illumined segment of the drum of the cupola— the horizontal circle contrasting harmoniously with the perpendicular half-circles of the arches? There is nothing lovelier among all the works of man. But the coffin lies here under the arches, reminding the connoisseur of beauty that there is nothing but the body and that the body suffers degradingly, dies and is eaten by maggots.

Mr. Cardan wondered how he would die. Slowly or suddenly? After long pain? Intelligent, still human? Or an idiot, a moaning animal? He would die poor, now, in any case. Friends would club together and send him a few pounds every now and then. Poor old Cardan, can't let him die in the workhouse. Must send him five pounds. What a bore! Extraordinary how

he manages to last so long ! But he was always a tough old devil.
Poor old Cardan !

A door banged; in the hollow echoing church there was a
sound of footsteps. It was the sacristan. He came to tell
Mr. Cardan that they would soon be ready to begin. They
had hurried back from the fields on purpose. The grapes were
not so plentiful nor of quite such good quality as they had been
last year. But still, one thanked God for His mercies, such as
they were.

Blessed are the fools, thought Mr. Cardan, for they shall see
nothing. Or perhaps they do see and, seeing, nevertheless comfortingly believe in future compensations and the justice of eternity.
In either case—not seeing, or seeing but believing—they are fools.
Still, believing is probably the best solution of all, Mr. Cardan
went on to reflect. For it allows one to see and not to ignore. It
permits one to accept the facts and yet justify them. For a believer
the presence of a coffin or two would not interfere with the apprecia-
tion of Sammicheli's architecture.

The bearers filed in, bringing with them from the fields a
healthy smell of sweat. They were dressed for the occasion in
garments that ought, no doubt, to have been surplices, but which
were, in point of fact, rather dirty and crumpled white dust-coats.
They looked like a cricket eleven entirely composed of umpires.
After the bearers came the priest, followed by a miniature umpire
in a dust-coat so short that it did not hide his bare knees. The
service began. The priest reeled off his Latin formulas as though
for a wager; the bearers, in ragged and tuneless unison, bawled
back at him the incomprehensible responses. During the longer
prayers they talked to one another about the vintage. The boy
scratched first his head, then his posterior, finally picked his nose.
The priest prayed so fast that all the words fused together and
became one word. Mr. Cardan wondered why the Catholic
Church did not authorize prayer wheels. A simple little electric

motor doing six or eight hundred revolutions a minute would get through a quite astonishing amount of pious work in a day and cost much less than a priest.

' Baa baba, baa baa, Boo-oo-baa,' bleated the priest.

' Boooo-baa,' came back from the bawling flock.

Not ceasing for a moment to pick his nose, the diminutive umpire, who seemed to know his part as perfectly as a trained dog in a music hall, handed the priest a censer. Waving it as he went, and rattling off his pious Latin, he walked round and round the bier. Symbolic and religious perfume ! It had smoked in the stable of Bethlehem, in the midst of the ammoniac smell of the beasts, the sign and symbol of the spirit. The blue smoke floated up and was lost along the wind. On the surface of the earth the beasts unremittingly propagate their kind ; the whole earth is a morass of living flesh. The smell of it hangs warm and heavy over all. Here and there the incense burns ; its smoke soon vanishes. The smell of the beasts remains.

' Baa baba,' went the priest.

' Baa,' the choristers retorted, a fifth lower down the scale.

The boy produced water and a kind of whisk. Once more the priest walked round the bier, sprinkling the water from the end of the wetted whisk ; the little umpire followed in his train, holding up the tail of his outer garment. The bearers, meanwhile, talked to one another in serious whispers about the grapes.

Sometimes, Mr. Cardan thought, the spirit plays its part so solemnly and well that one cannot help believing in its reality and ultimate significance. A ritual gravely performed is overwhelmingly convincing, for the moment at any rate. But let it be performed casually and carelessly by people who are not thinking of what the rite is meant to symbolize ; one perceives that there is nothing behind the symbols, that it is only the acting that matters —the judicious acting of the body—and that the body, the doomed, decaying body, is the one, appalling fact.

The service was over; the bearers picked up the coffin and carried it to the hearse that stood at the church door. The priest beckoned to Mr. Cardan to follow him into the sacristy. There, while the little umpire put away his censer and the whisk, he presented his bill. Mr. Cardan paid.

PART V

CONCLUSIONS

Chapter I

'WHAT are you thinking of?'

'Nothing,' said Calamy.

'Yes, you were. You must have been thinking about something.'

'Nothing in particular,' he repeated.

'Tell me,' Mary insisted. 'I want to know.'

'Well, if you really want to know,' Calamy began slowly . . .

But she interrupted him. 'And why did you hold up your hand like that? And spread out the fingers? I could see it, you know; against the window.' Pitch dark it was in the room, but beyond the unshuttered windows was a starlit night.

Calamy laughed—a rather embarrassed laugh. 'Oh, you saw it, did you—the hand? Well, as a matter of fact, it was precisely about my hand that I was thinking.'

'About your hand?' said Mary incredulously. 'That seems a queer thing to think about.'

'But interesting if you think about it hard enough.'

'Your hands,' she said softly, in another voice, 'your hands. When they touch me . . .' With a feminine movement of gratitude, of thanks for a benefit received, she pressed herself more closely against him; in the darkness she kissed him. 'I love you too much,' she whispered, 'too much.' And at the moment it was almost true. The strong complete spirit, she had written in her note-book, must be able to love with fury, savagely, mindlessly. Not without pride, she had found herself complete and strong. Once, at a dinner party, she had been taken down by a large black and lemon coloured Argentine; unfolding his napkin, he had opened the evening's conversation, in that fantastic trans-Pyrenean French which was his only substitute for the Castilian, by saying, with a roll of his black eyes and a flashing ivory smile: ' Jé vois qué vous avez du

339

temmperramenk.' 'Oh, à revendre,' she had answered gaily, throwing herself into the light Parisian part. How marvellously amusing! But that was Life—Life all over. She had brought the incident into a short story, long ago. But the Argentine had looked with an expert's eye; he was right. 'I love you too much,' she whispered in the darkness. Yes, it was true, it was nearly true, at the moment, in the circumstances. She took his hand and kissed it. 'That's all *I* think about your hand,' she said.

Calamy allowed his hand to be kissed, and as soon as it was decently possible gently withdrew it. Invisibly, in the darkness, he made a little grimace of impatience. He was no longer interested in kisses, at the moment. 'Yes,' he said meditatively, 'that's one way of thinking of my hand, that's one way in which it exists and is real. Certainly. And that was what I was thinking about— all the different ways in which these five fingers'—he held them up again, splayed out, against the window's oblong of paler darkness —'have reality and exist. All the different ways,' he repeated slowly. 'If you think of that, even for five minutes, you find yourself plunged up to the eyes in the most portentous mysteries.' He was silent for a moment; then added in a very serious voice. 'And I believe that if one could stand the strain of thinking really hard about one thing—this hand, for example—really hard for several days, or weeks, or months, one might be able to burrow one's way right through the mystery and really get at something— some kind of truth, some explanation.' He paused, frowning. Down and down, through the obscurity, he was thinking. Slowly, painfully, like Milton's Devil, pushing his way through chaos; in the end, one might emerge into the light, to see the universe, sphere within sphere, hanging from the floor of heaven. But it would be a slow, laborious process; one would need time, one would need freedom. Above everything, freedom.

'Why don't you think about me?' Mary Thriplow asked. She propped herself up on one elbow and leaned over him; with her

other hand she ruffled his hair. ' Don't I bear thinking about ? '
she asked. She had a fistful of his thick hair in her hand ; softly
she tugged at it, testingly, as though she were preparing for something worse, were assuring her grip for a more violent pull. She
felt a desire to hurt him. Even in her arms, she was thinking,
he escaped her, he simply wasn't there. ' Don't I bear thinking
about ? ' she repeated, tugging a little harder at his hair.

Calamy said nothing. The truth was, he was reflecting, that she
didn't bear thinking about. Like a good many other things. All
one's daily life was a skating over thin ice, was a scampering of
water-beetles across the invisible skin of depths. Stamp a little
too hard, lean a shade too heavily and you were through, you were
floundering in a dangerous and unfamiliar element. This love
business, for example—it simply couldn't be thought of ; it could
only support one on condition that one never stopped to think.
But it was necessary to think, necessary to break through and sink
into the depths. And yet, insanely and desperately, one still went
skating on.

' Do you love me ? ' asked Mary.

' Of course,' he said ; but the tone of his voice did not carry
much conviction.

Menacingly she tugged at the tuft of hair she held twined round
her fingers. It angered her that he should escape her, that he
should not give himself up completely to her. And this resentful
feeling that he did not love her enough produced in her a comple-
mentary conviction that she loved him too much. Her anger
combined with her physical gratitude to make her feel, for the
moment, peculiarly passionate. She found herself all at once playing the part of the *grande amoureuse*, the impassioned de Lespinasse,
playing it spontaneously and without the least difficulty. ' I could
hate you,' she said resentfully, ' for making me love you so much.'

' And what about me ? ' said Calamy, thinking of his freedom.
' Haven't I a right to hate too ? '

' No. Because you don't love so much.'

' But that 's not the question,' said Calamy, neglecting to record his protest against this damning impeachment. ' One doesn't resent love for its own sake, but for the sake of what it interferes with.'

' Oh, I see,' said Mary bitterly. She was too deeply wounded even to desire to pull his hair. She turned her back on him. ' I 'm sorry I should have got in the way of your important occupations,' she said in her most sarcastic voice. ' Such as thinking about your hand.' She laughed derisively. There was a long silence. Calamy made no attempt to break it ; he was piqued by this derisive treatment of a subject which, for him, was serious, was in some sort sacred. It was Mary who first spoke.

' Will you tell me, then, what you were thinking ? ' she asked submissively, turning back towards him. When one loves, one swallows one's pride and surrenders. ' Will you tell me ? ' she repeated, leaning over him. She took one of his hands and began to kiss it, then suddenly bit one of his fingers so hard that Calamy cried out in pain.

' Why do you make me so unhappy ? ' she asked between clenched teeth. She saw herself, as she spoke the words, lying face downward on her bed, desperately sobbing. It needs a great spirit to be greatly unhappy.

' Make you unhappy ? ' echoed Calamy in a voice of irritation ; he was still smarting with the pain of that bite. ' But I don't. I make you uncommonly happy.'

' You make me miserable,' she answered.

' Well, in that case,' said Calamy, ' I 'd better go away and leave you in peace.' He slipped his arm from under her shoulders, as though he were really preparing to go.

But Mary enfolded him in her arms. ' No, no,' she implored. ' Don't go. You mustn't be cross with me. I 'm sorry. I behaved abominably. Tell me, please, what you were thinking about your hand. I really am interested. Really, really.' She spoke eagerly, childishly, like the little girl at the Royal Institution lecture.

Calamy couldn't help laughing. ' You 've succeeded in rather damping my enthusiasm for that subject,' he said. ' I 'd find it difficult to begin now, in cold blood.'

' Please, please,' Mary insisted. Wronged, it was she who asked pardon, she who cajoled. When one loves . . .

' You 've made it almost impossible to talk anything but nonsense,' Calamy objected. But in the end he allowed himself to be persuaded. Embarrassed, rather awkwardly—for the spiritual atmosphere in which these ideas had been ruminated was dissipated, and it was in the void, so to speak, in the empty cold that his thoughts now gasped for breath—he began his exposition. But gradually, as he spoke, the mood returned ; he became at home once more with what he was saying. Mary listened with a fixed attention of which, even in the darkness, he was somehow conscious.

' Well, you see,' he started hesitatingly, ' it 's like this. I was thinking of all the different ways a thing can exist—my hand, for example.'

' I see,' said Mary Thriplow sympathetically and intelligently. She was almost too anxious to prove that she was listening, that she was understanding everything ; she saw before there was anything to see.

' It 's extraordinary,' Calamy went on, ' what a lot of different modes of existence a thing has, when you come to think about it. And the more you think, the more obscure and mysterious everything becomes. What seemed solid vanishes ; what was obvious and comprehensible becomes utterly mysterious. Gulfs begin opening all around you—more and more abysses, as though the ground were splitting in an earthquake. It gives one a strange sense of insecurity, of being in the dark. But I still believe that, if one went on thinking long enough and hard enough, one might somehow come through, get out on the other side of the obscurity.

343

But into what, precisely into what ? That 's the question.' He was silent for a moment. If one were free, he thought, one could go exploring into that darkness. But the flesh was weak ; under the threat of that delicious torture it turned coward and traitor.

'Well ? ' said Mary at last. She moved closer to him, lightly, her lips brushed across his cheek. She ran her hand softly over his shoulder and along his arm. 'Go on.'

'Very well,' he said in a business-like voice, moving a little away from her as he spoke. He held up his hand once more against the window. 'Look,' he said. 'It 's just a shape that interrupts the light. To a child who has not yet learned to interpret what he sees, that 's all it would be, just a shaped blotch of colour, no more significant than one of those coloured targets representing a man's head and shoulders that one learns shooting on. But now, suppose I try to consider the thing as a physicist.'

'Quite,' said Mary Thriplow ; and from the movement of a floating tress of her hair which brushed against his shoulder he knew that she was nodding her head.

'Well then,' Calamy went on, 'I have to imagine an almost inconceivable number of atoms, each consisting of a greater or lesser number of units of negative electricity whirling several million times a minute round a nucleus of positive electricity. The vibrations of the atoms lying near the surface sift out, so to speak, the electro-magnetic radiations which fall upon them, permitting only those waves to reach our eyes which give us the sensation of a brownish-pink colour. In passing it may be remarked that the behaviour of light is satisfactorily explained according to one theory of electro-dynamics, while the behaviour of the electrons in the atom can only be explained on a theory that is entirely inconsistent with it. Inside the atom, they tell us now, electrons move from one orbit to another without taking any time to accomplish their journey and without covering any space. Indeed, within the atom there is neither space

nor time. And so on and so on. I have to take most of this on
trust, I'm afraid, for I understand next to nothing about these
things. Only enough to make me feel rather dizzy when I begin
to think about them.'

'Yes, dizzy,' said Mary, 'that's the word. Dizzy.' She
made a prolonged buzzing over the z's.

'Well then, here are two ways already in which my hand
exists,' Calamy went on. 'Then there's the chemical way.
These atoms consisting of more or fewer electrons whizzing round
a nucleus of greater or lesser charge are atoms of different elements
that build themselves up in certain architectural patterns into
complicated molecules.'

Sympathetic and intelligent, Mary echoed : ' Molecules.'

' Now if, like Cranmer, I were to put my right hand into the fire,
to punish it for having done something evil or unworthy (words, by
the way, which haven't much in common with chemistry), if I were
to put my hand in the fire, these molecules would uncombine themselves into their constituent atoms, which would then proceed to
build themselves up again into other molecules. But this leads me
on at once to a set of entirely different realities. For if I were to
put my hand in the fire, I should feel pain ; and unless, like Cranmer,
I made an enormous effort of will to keep it there, I should withdraw it ; or rather it would withdraw itself almost without my
knowledge and before I was aware. For I am alive, and this hand
is part of a living being, the first law of whose existence is to preserve
its life. Being alive, this hand of mine, if it were burnt, would
set about trying to repair itself. Seen by a biologist, it reveals
itself as a collection of cells, having each its appointed function,
and existing harmoniously together, never trespassing upon one
another, never proliferating into wild adventures of growth, but
living, dying and growing to one end—that the whole which they
compose may fulfil its purpose—and as though in accordance with
a preordained plan. Say that the hand is burnt. From all round

the burn the healthy cells would breed out of themselves new cells to fill in and cover the damaged places.'

' How wonderful life is ! ' said Mary Thriplow. ' Life . . .'

' Cranmer's hand,' Calamy went on, ' had done an ignoble thing. The hand is part, not merely of a living being, but of a being that knows good and evil. This hand of mine can do good things and bad things. It has killed a man, for example ; it has written all manner of words ; it has helped a man who was hurt ; it has touched your body.' He laid his hand on her breast ; she started, she trembled involuntarily under his caress. He ought to think that rather flattering, oughtn't he ? It was a symbol of his power over her—of her power, alas, over him. ' And when it touches your body,' he went on, ' it touches also your mind. My hand moves like this, and it moves through your consciousness as well as here, across your skin. And it 's my mind that orders it to move ; it brings your body into my mind. It exists in mind ; it has reality as a part of my soul and a part of yours.'

Miss Thriplow couldn't help reflecting that there was, in all this, the stuff for a very deep digression in one of her novels. "This thoughtful young writer . . ." would be quoted from the reviewers on the dust-cover of her next book.

' Go on,' she said.

Calamy went on. ' And so these,' he said, ' are some of the ways—and there are plenty more, of course, besides—these are some of the ways in which my hand exists and is real. This shape which interrupts the light—it is enough to think of it for five minutes to perceive that it exists simultaneously in a dozen parallel worlds. It exists as electrical charges ; as chemical molecules ; as living cells ; as part of a moral being, the instrument of good and evil ; in the physical world and in mind. And from this one goes on to ask, inevitably, what relationship exists between these different modes of being. What is there in common between life and chemistry ; between good and evil and electrical charges ; between a collection of cells and the consciousness of a caress ? It 's here that the gulfs begin to open. For there isn't any connection—that one can see, at any rate. Universe lies on the top of universe, layer after layer, distinct and separate . . .'

' Like a Neapolitan ice,' Mary's mind flew at once to the fantastic and unexpected comparison. "This witty young writer . . ." That was already on her dust-covers.

Calamy laughed. ' All right,' he agreed. ' Like a Neapolitan ice, if you like. What 's true in the chocolate layer, at the bottom of the ice, doesn't hold in the vanilla at the top. And a lemon truth is different from a strawberry truth. And each one has just as much right to exist and to call itself real as every other. And you can't explain one in terms of the others. Certainly you can't explain the vanilla in terms of any of the lower layers—you can't explain mind as mere life, as chemistry, as physics. That at least is one thing that 's perfectly obvious and self-evident.'

' Obvious,' Mary agreed. ' And what 's the result of it all ? I really don't see.'

' Neither do I,' said Calamy, speaking through an explosion of melancholy laughter. ' The only hope,' he went on slowly, ' is that perhaps, if you went on thinking long enough and hard enough, you might arrive at an explanation of the chocolate and the lemon by the vanilla. Perhaps it 's really all vanilla, all mind, all spirit. The rest is only apparent, an illusion. But one has no right to say so until one has thought a long time, in freedom.'

' In freedom ? '

' The mind must be open, unperturbed, empty of irrelevant things, quiet. There 's no room for thoughts in a half-shut, cluttered mind. And thoughts won't enter a noisy mind ; they 're shy, they remain in their obscure hiding-places below the surface, where they can't be got at, so long as the mind is full and noisy. Most of us pass through life without knowing that they 're there at all. If one wants to lure them out, one must clear a space for

M* 347

them, one must open the mind wide and wait. And there must be no irrelevant preoccupations prowling around the doors. One must free oneself of those.'

' I suppose I 'm one of the irrelevant preoccupations,' said Mary Thriplow, after a little pause.

Calamy laughed, but did not deny it.

' If that 's so,' said Mary, ' why did you make love to me ? '

Calamy did not reply. Why indeed ? He had often asked that question himself.

' I think it would be best,' she said, after a silence, ' if we were to make an end.' She would go away, she would grieve in solitude.

' Make an end ? ' Calamy repeated. He desired it, of course, above everything—to make an end, to be free. But he found himself adding, with a kind of submarine laughter below the surface of his voice : ' Do you think you *can* make an end ? '

' Why not ? '

' Suppose I don't allow you to ? ' Did she imagine, then, that she wasn't in his power, that he couldn't make her obey his will whenever he desired ? ' I *don't* allow you,' he said, and his voice quivered with the rising mirth. He bent over her and began to kiss her on the mouth ; with his hands he held and caressed her. What an insanity, he said to himself.

' No, no.' Mary struggled a little ; but in the end she allowed herself to be overcome. She lay still, trembling, like one who has been tortured on the rack.

CHAPTER II

ON their return, somewhat low-spirited, from Montefiascone, Mrs. Aldwinkle and her party found Mary Thriplow alone in the palace.

'And Calamy ? ' Mrs. Aldwinkle inquired.

'He 's gone into the mountains,' said Miss Thriplow in a serious, matter-of-fact voice.

'Why ? '

'He felt like that,' Mary answered. 'He wanted to be alone to think. I understand it so well. The prospect of your return filled him almost with terror. He went off two or three days ago.'

'Into the mountains ? ' echoed Mrs. Aldwinkle. 'Is he sleeping in the woods, or in a cave, or something of that kind ? '

'He 's taken a room in a peasant's cottage on the road up to the marble quarries. It 's a lovely place.'

'This sounds most interesting,' said Mr. Cardan. 'I must really climb up and have a look at him.'

'I 'm sure he 'd rather you didn't,' said Miss Thriplow. 'He wants to be left alone. I understand it so well,' she repeated.

Mr. Cardan looked at her curiously ; her face expressed a bright and serious serenity. 'I 'm surprised that you too don't retire from the world,' he said, twinkling. He had not felt as cheerful as this since before the dismal day of poor Grace's funeral.

Miss Thriplow smiled a Christian smile. 'You think it 's a joke,' she said, shaking her head. 'But it isn't really, you know.'

'I 'm sure it isn't,' Mr. Cardan made haste to protest. 'And believe me, I never meant to imply that it was. Never, on my word. I merely said—quite seriously, I assure you—that I was surprised that you too . . .'

'Well, you see, it doesn't seem to me necessary to go away bodily,' Miss Thriplow explained. 'It 's always seemed to me that one can live the hermit's life, if one wants to, in the heart of London, anywhere.'

'Quite,' said Mr. Cardan. 'You're perfectly right.'

'I think he might have waited till I came back,' said Mrs. Aldwinkle rather resentfully. 'The least he could have done was to leave a note.' She looked at Miss Thriplow angrily, as though it were she who were to blame for Calamy's impoliteness. 'Well, I must go and get out of my dusty clothes,' she added crossly, and walked away to her room. Her irritation was the disguise and public manifestation of a profound depression. They're all going, she was thinking, they're all slipping away. First Chelifer, now Calamy. Like all the rest. Mournfully she looked back over her life. Everybody, everything had always slipped away from her. She had always missed all the really important, exciting things; they had invariably happened, somehow, just round the corner, out of her sight. The days were so short, so few now. Death approached, approached. Why had Cardan brought that horrible imbecile creature to die in front of her like that? She didn't want to be reminded of death. Mrs. Aldwinkle shuddered. I'm getting old, she thought; and the little clock on the mantel-piece, ticking away in the silence of her huge room, took up the refrain: Getting old, getting old, getting old, it repeated again and again, endlessly. Getting old—Mrs. Aldwinkle looked at herself in the glass—and that electric massage machine hadn't arrived. True, it was on its way; but it would be weeks before it got here. The posts were so slow. Everything conspired against her. If she had had it before, if she'd looked younger . . . who knew? Getting old, getting old, repeated the little clock. In a couple of days from now Chelifer would be going back to England; he'd go away, he'd live apart from her, live such a wonderful, beautiful life. She'd miss it all. And Calamy had already gone; what was he doing, sitting there in the mountains? He was thinking wonderful thoughts, thoughts that might hold the secret she had always been seeking and had never found, thoughts that might bring the consolation and tranquillity of which she always so sorely stood in need. She was missing them, she 'd never know them. Getting old, getting old. She took off her hat and tossed it on to the bed. It seemed to her that she was the unhappiest woman in the world.

That evening, while she was brushing Mrs. Aldwinkle's hair, Irene, braving the dangers of Aunt Lilian's terrifying fun, screwed up her courage to say : ' I can never be grateful enough to you, Auntie, for having talked to me about Hovenden.'

' What about him ? ' asked Mrs. Aldwinkle, from whose mind the painful events of the last few weeks had quite obliterated such trivial memories.

Irene blushed with embarrassment. This was a question she had not anticipated. Was it really possible that Aunt Lilian could have forgotten those momentous and epoch-making words of hers ? ' Why,' she began stammering, ' what you said about . . . I mean . . . when you said that he looked as though . . . well, as though he liked me.'

' Oh yes,' said Mrs. Aldwinkle without interest.

' Don't you remember ? '

' Yes, yes,' Mrs. Aldwinkle nodded. ' What about it ? '

' Well,' Irene went on, still painfully embarrassed, ' you see . . that made me . . . that made me pay attention, if you understand.'

' Hm,' said Mrs. Aldwinkle. There was a silence. Getting old, getting old, repeated the little clock remorselessly.

Irene leaned forward and suddenly boiled over with confidences. ' I love him so much, Aunt Lilian,' she said, speaking very rapidly, ' so much, so much. It 's the real thing this time. And he loves me too. And we 're going to get married at the New Year, quite quietly ; no fuss, no crowds shoving in on what isn't their business ; quietly and sensibly in a registry office. And after that we 're going in the Velox to . . .'

' What are you talking about ? ' said Mrs. Aldwinkle in a furious voice, and she turned round on her niece a face expressive of such passionate anger that Irene drew back, not merely astonished, but positively afraid. 'You don't mean to tell me,' Mrs. Aldwinkle began; but she could not find the words to continue. 'What have you two young fools been thinking about?' she got out at last.

. . . old, getting old; the remorseless ticking made itself heard in every silence.

From being merry and excited in its childishness Irene's face had become astonished and miserable. She was pale, her lips trembled a little as she spoke. 'But I thought you'd be glad, Aunt Lilian,' she said. 'I thought you'd be glad.'

'Glad because you're making fools of yourselves?' asked Mrs. Aldwinkle, savagely snorting.

'But it was you who first suggested,' Irene began.

Mrs. Aldwinkle cut her short, before she could say any more, with a brusqueness that might have revealed to a more practised psychologist than Irene her consciousness of being in the wrong. 'Absurd,' she said. 'I suppose you're going to tell me,' she went on sarcastically, 'that it was I who told you to marry him.'

'I know you didn't,' said Irene.

'There!' Mrs. Aldwinkle's tone was triumphant.

'But you did say you wondered why I wasn't in love . . .'

'Bah,' said Aunt Lilian, 'I was just making fun. Calf loves . . .'

'But why shouldn't I marry him?' asked Irene. 'If I love him and he loves me. Why shouldn't I?'

Why shouldn't she? Yes, that was an awkward question. Getting old, getting old, muttered the clock in the brief ensuing silence. Perhaps that was half the answer. Getting old! they were all going; first Chelifer, then Calamy, now Irene. Getting old, getting old; soon she'd be quite alone. And it wasn't only that. It was also her pride that was hurt, her love of dominion that suffered. Irene had been her slave; had worshipped her,

352

taken her word as law, her opinions as gospel truth. Now she was
transferring her allegiance. Mrs. Aldwinkle was losing a subject
—losing her to a more powerful rival. It was intolerable. ' Why
shouldn't you marry him ? ' Mrs. Aldwinkle repeated the phrase
ironically two or three times, while she hunted for the answer.
' Why shouldn't you marry him ? '

' Why shouldn't I ? ' Irene asked again. There were tears in
her eyes ; but however unhappy she might look, there was something determined and indomitable in her attitude, something
obstinate in her expression and her tone of voice. Mrs. Aldwinkle
had reason to fear her rival.

' Because you 're too young,' she said at last. It was a very
feeble answer ; but she had been unable to think of a better one.

' But, Aunt Lilian, don't you remember ? You always said
that people ought to marry young. I remember so well, one time,
when we talked about Juliet being only fourteen when she first
saw Romeo, that you said . . .'

' That has nothing to do with it,' said Mrs. Aldwinkle, cutting
short her niece's mnemonic display. Irene's memory, Mrs. Aldwinkle had often had reason to complain, was really too good.

' But if you said . . .' Irene began again.

' Romeo and Juliet have nothing to do with you and Hovenden,'
retorted Mrs. Aldwinkle. ' I repeat : you 're too young.'

' I 'm nineteen.'

' Eighteen.'

' Practically nineteen,' Irene insisted. ' My birthday 's in
December.'

' Marry in haste and repent at leisure,' said Mrs. Aldwinkle,
making use of any missile, even a proverb, that came ready to hand.
' At the end of six months you 'll come back howling and complaining and asking me to get you out of the mess.'

' But why should I ? ' asked Irene. ' We love one another.'

' They all say that. You don't know your own minds.'

'But we do.'

Mrs. Aldwinkle suddenly changed her tactics. 'And what makes you so anxious all at once to run away from me ?' she asked. 'Can't you bear to stay with me a moment longer ? Am I so intolerable and odious and . . . and . . . brutal and . . . She clawed at the air. 'Do you hate me so much that . . .'

'Aunt Lilian !' protested Irene, who had begun to cry in earnest.

Mrs. Aldwinkle, with that tactlessness, that lack of measure that were characteristic of her, went on piling question upon rhetorical question, until in the end she completely spoiled the effect she had meant to achieve, exaggerating into ludicrousness what might otherwise have been touching. 'Can't you bear me ? Have I ill-treated you ? Tell me. Have I bullied you, or scolded you, or . . . or not given you enough to eat ? Tell me.'

'How can you talk like that, Aunt Lilian ?' Irene dabbed her eyes with a corner of her dressing-gown. 'How can you say that I don't love you ? And you were always telling me that I ought to get married,' she added, breaking out into fresh tears.

'How can I say that you don't love me ?' echoed Mrs. Aldwinkle. 'But is it true that you 're longing to leave me as soon as possible ? Is that true or not ? I merely ask what the reason is, that 's all.'

'But the reason is that we want to get married ; we love each other.'

'Or that you hate me,' Mrs. Aldwinkle persisted.

'But I don't hate you, Aunt Lilian. How can you say such a thing ? You know I love you.'

'And yet you 're anxious to run away from me as fast as you possibly can,' said Mrs. Aldwinkle. 'And I shall be left all alone, all alone.' Her voice trembled ; she shut her eyes, she contorted her face in an effort to keep it closed and rigid. Between her eyelids the tears came welling out. 'All alone,' she repeated brokenly. Getting old, said the little clock on the mantel-piece, getting old, getting old.

Irene knelt down beside her, took her hands between her own and kissed them, pressed them against her tear-wet face. ' Aunt Lilian,' she begged, ' Aunt Lilian.'

Mrs. Aldwinkle went on sobbing.

' Don't cry,' said Irene, crying herself. She imagined that she alone was the cause of Aunt Lilian's unhappiness. In reality, she was only the pretext ; Mrs. Aldwinkle was weeping over her whole life, weeping at the approach of death. In that first moment of agonized sympathy and self-reproach, Irene was on the point of declaring that she would give up Hovenden, that she would spend all her life with her Aunt Lilian. But something held her back. Obscurely she was certain that it wouldn't do, that it was impossible, that it would even be wrong. She loved Aunt Lilian and she loved Hovenden. In a way she loved Aunt Lilian more than Hovenden, now. But something in her that looked prophetically forward, something that had come through innumerable lives, out of the obscure depths of time, to dwell within her, held her back. The conscious and individual part of her spirit inclined towards Aunt Lilian. But consciousness and individuality—how precariously, how irrelevantly almost, they flowered out of that ancient root of life planted in the darkness of her being ! The flower was for Aunt Lilian, the root for Hovenden.

' But you won't be all alone,' she protested. ' We shall constantly be with you. You 'll come and stay with us.'

The assurance did not seem to bring much consolation to Mrs. Aldwinkle. She went on crying. The clock ticked away as busily as ever.

CHAPTER III

IN the course of the last few days the entries in Miss Thriplow's note-book had changed their character. From being amorous they had turned mystical. Savage and mindless passion was replaced by quiet contemplation. De Lespinasse had yielded to de Guyon.

'Do you remember, darling Jim,' she wrote, 'how, when we were ten, we used to discuss what was the sin against the Holy Ghost ? I remember we agreed that using the altar as a W.C. was probably the unforgivable sin. It's a great pity that it isn't, for then it would be so extremely easy to avoid committing it. No, I'm afraid it's not quite so straightforward as that, the sin against the Holy Ghost. And it's most perilously easy to fall into it. Stifling the voices inside you, filling the mind with so much earthy rubbish that God has no room to enter it, not giving the spirit its fair chance—that's the sin against the Holy Ghost. And it's unforgivable because it's irremediable. Last-minute repentances are no good. The sin and the corresponding virtue are affairs of a lifetime. And almost everybody commits the sin ; they die unforgiven, and at once they begin again another life. Only when they've lived in the virtue of the Holy Ghost are they forgiven, let off the pains of life and allowed to sink into unity with All. Isn't that the meaning of the text ? It's terribly difficult not to commit the sin. Whenever I stop to think, I am appalled by the badness of my own life. Oh, Jim, Jim, how easily one forgets, how unthinkingly one allows oneself to be buried under a mountain of little earthy interests ! The voices are muffled, the mind is blocked up, there's no place for the spirit of God. When I'm working, I feel it's all right ; I'm living in the virtue of the Holy Ghost. For then I'm doing the best I can. But the rest of the time, that's when I go wrong. One can't be doing all the time, one can't always give out. One must also be passive, must

CONCLUSIONS

receive. That's what I fail to do. I flutter about, I fill my mind
with lumber, I make it impossible for myself to receive. One
can't go on like this; one can't go on sinning against the Holy
Ghost—not if one once realizes it.'

There was a line. The next note began: 'To think steadily
and intensely of one thing is a wonderful mental exercise; it serves
to open up the mysteries that lie below the commonplace surface
of existence; and perhaps, if one went on thinking long enough
and hard enough, one might get through the mystery to its explanation. When I think, for example, of my hand . . .' The note
was a long one; it covered, in Miss Thriplow's clear, cultured
writing, more than two pages of the book.

'Recently,' she had written after that, 'I have been saying my
prayers again, as I used to when I was a child. Our Father which
art in heaven—the words help to clear out one's mind, to rid it of
the lumber and leave it free for the coming of the spirit.'

The next three notes had got there by mistake. Their place was
not in the secret, personal book, but in the other volume, wherein
she recorded little snippets that might come in useful for her novels.
Not, of course, that the entries in the secret book didn't also come
in useful for her fiction sometimes; but they were not recorded
expressly for that purpose.

'A man in riding breeches,' the first note ran: 'he makes a
little creaking noise as he walks along, whipcord rubbing against
whipcord, that is like the creaking noise that swans make, flying,
when they move their big white wings.'

Then followed two lines of comic dialogue.

'*Me.* I find the *Fall of the House of Usher* a most blood-
curdling story.

'*Frenchman.* Yes, yes, she bloods my curdle also.'

The third note recorded that 'moss after a shower on a sultry
day is like a sponge still damp from the hot bath.'

There followed a corollary to the note on prayer. 'There is no

357

doubt,' she had written, ' that the actual technique of prayer—the kneeling, the hiding the face in the hands, the uttering of words *in an audible voice*, the words being addressed into empty space—helps by its mere dissimilarity from the ordinary actions of everyday life to put one into a devout frame of mind. . . .'

To-night she sat for some time in front of the open book, pen in hand, without writing anything. She frowned pensively and bit the end of her pen. In the end she put it on record that ' St. Augustine, St. Francis and St. Ignatius Loyola lived dissolute lives before their conversions.' Then, opening her other, her un-secret note-book, she wrote:' X and Y are old friends from childhood. X dashing, Y timid ; Y admires X. Y marries, while X is at the war, a passionate creature who takes Y more out of pity (he is wounded) than from love. There is a child. X returns, falls in love with Y's wife, A. Great passion amid growing anguish of mind—on her part because she is deceiving Y, whom she likes and respects, and daren't undeceive him for fear of losing the child ; on his part because he feels that he ought to give up all this sort of thing and devote himself to God, etc.; in fact, he feels the premonitions of conversion. One night they decide that the time has come to part ; it can't go on—she because of the deception, he because of mysticism, etc. It is a most touching scene, lasting all a last chaste night. Unfortunately Y finds out for some reason —baby ill, or something of the kind—that A is not staying at her mother's as she said, but is elsewhere. Early in the morning Y comes to X's flat to ask him to help in the search for A. Sees A's coat and hat lying on the drawing-room sofa ; understands all. In a fury flies at X, who, defending himself, kills him. The end. Question, however ; doesn't it end with too much of a click ? too epigrammatically, so to speak ? I wonder whether in this twentieth century one can permit oneself the luxury of such effective dramatic devices. Oughtn't one to do it more *flatly*, somehow ? More terre-à-terreishly, more real-lifeishly ? I feel that a con-

clusion like that is almost an unfair advantage taken at the reader's
expense. One ought to arrange it differently. But the question
is, how? Can one let them separate and show them living, she
en bonne mère de famille, he as a coenobite? It would drag it
out terribly, wouldn't it? Must think of this carefully.'

She shut the book and put the cap on her fountain pen, feeling
that she had done a good evening's work. Calamy was now safely
laid down in pickle, waiting to be consumed whenever she should
be short of fictional provisions.

After having undressed, washed, brushed her hair, polished her
nails, greased her face and cleaned her teeth, Miss Thriplow turned
out the light, and kneeling down by the side of her bed said several
prayers, aloud. She then got into bed, and lying on her back, with
all her muscles relaxed, she began to think about God.

God is a spirit, she said to herself, a spirit, a spirit. She tried
to picture something huge and empty, but alive. A huge flat
expanse of sand, for example, and over it a huge blank dome of
sky; and above the sand everything should be tremulous and
shimmering with heat—an emptiness that was yet alive. A spirit,
an all-pervading spirit. God is a spirit. Three camels appeared
on the horizon of the sandy plain and went lolloping along in an
absurd ungainly fashion from left to right. Miss Thriplow made
an effort and dismissed them. God is a spirit, she said aloud.
But of all animals camels are really almost the queerest; when one
thinks of their frightfully supercilious faces, with their protruding
under lips like the last Hapsburg kings of Spain . . . No, no;
God is a spirit, all-pervading, everywhere. All the universes are
made one in him. Layer upon layer . . . A Neapolitan ice
floated up out of the darkness. She had never liked Neapolitan
ices since that time, at the Franco-British exhibition, when she had
eaten one and then taken a ride on Sir Hiram Maxim's Captive
Flying Machines. Round and round and round. Lord, how she
had been sick, afterwards, in the Blue Grotto of Capri! ' Sixpence

each, ladies and gentlemen, only sixpence each for a trip to the celebrated Blue Grotto of Capri, the celebrated Blue Grotto, ladies and gentlemen. . . .' How sick! It must have been most awkward for the grown-ups. . . . But God is a spirit. All the universes are one in the spirit. Mind and matter in all their manifestations—all one in the spirit. All one—she and the stars and the mountains and the trees and the animals and the blank spaces between the stars and . . . and the fish, the fish in the Aquarium at Monaco. . . . And what fish! What extravagant fantasies! But no more extravagant or fantastic, really, than the painted and jewelled old women outside. It might make a very good episode in a book—a couple of those old women looking through the glass at the fishes. Very beautifully and discreetly described; and the fundamental similarity between the creatures on either side of the glass would just be delicately implied—not stated, oh, not stated; that would be too coarse, that would spoil everything, but just implied, by the description, so that the intelligent reader could take the hint. And then in the Casino . . . Miss Thriplow brusquely interrupted herself. God is a spirit. Yes. Where was she? All things are one, ah yes, yes. All, all, all, she repeated. But to arrive at the realization of their oneness one must climb up into the spirit. The body separates, the spirit unites. One must give up the body, the self; one must lose one's life to gain it. Lose one's life, empty oneself of the separating Me. She clasped her hands tightly together, tighter, tighter, as though she were squeezing out her individual life between them. If she could squeeze it all out, make herself quite empty, then the other life would come rushing in to take its place.

Miss Thriplow lay quite still, hardly breathing. Empty, she said to herself every now and then, quite empty. She felt wonderfully tranquil. God was surely very near. The silence grew more profound, her spirit became calmer and emptier. Yes, God was very near.

Perhaps it was the distant roaring of a train in the valley far below that reminded her of the noise of the whirling drill; or perhaps the thin bright line of light that came in, through a chink in the top of the rickety old door, from the illuminated corridor, to reach half across the ceiling above her—perhaps it was this long sharp probe of brightness that reminded her of a surgical instrument. Whatever may have been the cause, Miss Thriplow suddenly found herself thinking of her dentist. Such a charming man; he had a china bull-dog on the mantel-piece of his consulting-room and a photograph of his wife and twins. His hair wouldn't lie down. He had such kind grey eyes. And he was an enthusiast. 'This is an instrument of which I'm particularly fond, Miss Thriplow,' he used to say, picking out a little curved harpoon from his armoury. 'A little wider, please, if you don't mind. . . .' What about a story of a dentist who falls in love with one of his patients? He shows her all the instruments, enthusiastically, wants her to like his favourites as much as he does. He pretends that there's more wrong with her teeth than there really is, in order to see her more often.

The dentist grew dim, he began the same gesture again and again, very slowly, but could never finish it, having forgotten, half-way through the act, what he meant to do. At last he disappeared altogether. Miss Thriplow had fallen into a profound and tranquil sleep.

CHAPTER IV

IT had been raining, stormily; but now the wind had fallen and between the heavy clouds the sun was brightly shining. The yellowing chestnut trees stood motionless in the still bright air, glittering with moisture. A noise of rapidly running water filled the ear. The grass of the steep meadows shone in the sunlight. Calamy stepped out from the dark and frowsty living-room of the cottage and walked up the steep path on to the road. He halted here and looked about him. The road at this point was terraced out of one of the sides of a deep valley. The ground rose steeply, in places almost precipitously, above it. Below it the green mountain meadows, brilliant in the sunshine and dotted here and there with clumps of chestnut trees, fell away into the depths of the valley, which the afternoon sun had left already in a vaporous smoky shadow. Profoundly shadowed, too, were the hills on the further side of the narrow cleft. Huge black masses, smoky with the same vapour as that which floated at the bottom of the valley, they rose up almost in silhouette against the bright light beyond. The sun looked down, over their clouded summits, across the intervening gulf, touching the green hillside, on the slope of which Calamy was standing, with a radiance that, in contrast to the dark hills opposite, seemed almost unearthly. To the right, at the head of the valley, a great pinnacle of naked rock, pale brown and streaked here and there with snow-white veins of marble, reached up into the clouds and above them, so that the summit shone like a precious stone in the sunlight, against the blue of the sky. A band of white vapour hung round the shoulders of the mountain. Beneath it appeared the lower buttresses of rock and the long slopes of hanging wood and meadowland falling away into the valley, all shadowy under the clouds, shadowy and dead, save where, here and there, a great golden beam broke through, touching some chosen tract of grass or woodland or rock with an intense and precarious life.

Calamy stood for a long time looking out at the scene. How beautiful it was, how beautiful! Glittering in the light, the withering trees seemed to have prepared themselves as though for a feast. For a feast—and yet it was winter and death that awaited them. Beautiful the mountains were, but menacing and terrible; terrible the deep gulf below him with its smoky vaporous shadows, far down, below the shining green. And the shadows mounted second after second as the sun declined. Beautiful, terrible and mysterious, pregnant with what enormous secret, symbolic of what formidable reality?

From the direction of the cottage below the road came a tinkle of bells and the shrill shouting of a child's voice. Half a dozen tall black and white goats, with long black beards, long twisted horns and yellow eyes, slitted with narrow pupils, came trotting up the slope, shaking their flat bells. A little boy scrambled after them, brandishing a stick and shouting words of command. To Calamy he touched his cap; they exchanged a few words in Italian, about the rain, the goats, the best pasture; then, waving his stick and peremptorily shouting at his little flock, the child moved on up the road. The goats trotted on in front, their hoofs clicking on the stones; every now and then they paused to pull a mouthful of grass from the bank at the side of the road; but the little boy would not let them pause. 'Via!' he shouted, and banged them with his stick. They bounded forward. Soon herdsman and flock were out of sight.

If he had been born that little boy, Calamy wondered, would he still be working, unquestioningly, among these hills: tending the beasts, cutting wood; every now and then carting his faggots and his cheeses down the long road to Vezza? Would he, still, un-questioningly? Would he see that the mountains were beautiful, beautiful and terrible? Or would he find them merely ungrateful land, demanding great labour, giving little in return? Would he believe in heaven and hell? And fitfully, when anything went

363

wrong, would he still earnestly invoke the aid of the infant Jesus, of the Blessed Virgin and St. Joseph, that patriarchal family trinity —father, mother and baby—of the Italian peasant? Would he have married? By this time, very likely, his eldest children would be ten or twelve years old—driving the goats afield with shrill yellings and brandished sticks. Would he be living quietly and cheerfully the life of a young patriarch, happy in his children, his wife, his flocks and herds? Would he be happy to live thus, close to the earth, earthily, an ancient, instinctive, animally sagacious life? It seemed hardly imaginable. And yet, after all, it was likely enough. It needs a very strong, a passionately ardent spirit to disengage itself from childish tradition, from the life which circumstances impose upon it. Was his such a spirit?

He was startled out of his speculations by the sound of his own name, loudly called from a little distance. He turned round and saw Mr. Cardan and Chelifer striding up the road towards him. Calamy waved his hand and went to meet them. Was he pleased to see them or not? He hardly knew.

'Well,' said Mr. Cardan, twinkling jovially, as he approached, 'how goes life in the Thebaïd? Do you object to receiving a couple of impious visitors from Alexandria?'

Calamy laughed and shook their hands without answering.

'Did you get wet?' he asked, to change the conversation.

'We hid in a cave,' said Mr. Cardan. He looked round at the view. 'Pretty good,' he said encouragingly, as though it were Calamy who had made the landscape, 'pretty good, I must say.'

'Agreeably Wordsworthian,' said Chelifer in his precise voice.

'And where do you live?' asked Mr. Cardan.

Calamy pointed to the cottage. Mr. Cardan nodded comprehendingly.

'Hearts of gold, but a little niffy, eh?' he asked, lifting his raised white eyebrow still higher.

'Not to speak of,' said Calamy.

'Charming girls?' Mr. Cardan went on. 'Or goitres?'

'Neither,' said Calamy.

'And how long do you propose to stay?'

'I haven't the faintest idea.'

'Till you 've got to the bottom of the cosmos, eh?'

Calamy smiled. 'That 's about it.'

'Splendid,' said Mr. Cardan, patting him on the arm, 'splendid. I envy you. God, what wouldn't I give to be your age? What wouldn't I give?' He shook his head sadly. 'And, alas,' he added, 'what could I give, in point of actual fact? I put it at about twelve hundred quid at the present time. My total fortune. Shouldn't we sit down?' he added on another note.

Calamy led the way down the little path. Along the front of the cottage, under the windows, ran a long bench. The three men sat down. The sun shone full upon them; it was pleasantly warm. Beneath them was the narrow valley with its smoky shadows; opposite, the black hills, cloud-capped and silhouetted against the brightness of the sky about the sun.

'And the trip to Rome,' Calamy inquired, 'was that agreeable?'

'Tolerably,' said Chelifer, with precision.

'And Miss Elver?' he addressed himself politely to Mr. Cardan.

Mr. Cardan looked up at him. 'Hadn't you heard?' he asked.

'Heard what?'

'She 's dead.' Mr. Cardan's face became all at once very hard and still.

'I 'm sorry,' said Calamy. 'I didn't know.' He thought it more tactful to proffer no further condolences. There was a silence.

'That 's something,' said Mr. Cardan at last, 'that you 'll find it rather difficult to contemplate away, however long and mystically you stare at your navel.'

'What?' asked Calamy.

'Death,' Mr. Cardan answered. 'You can't get over the fact that, at the end of everything, the flesh gets hold of the spirit, and squeezes the life out of it, so that a man turns into something that's no better than a whining sick animal. And as the flesh sickens the spirit sickens, manifestly. Finally the flesh dies and putrefies ; and the spirit presumably putrefies too. And there's an end of your omphaloskepsis, with all its by-products, God and justice and salvation and all the rest of them.'

'Perhaps it is,' said Calamy. 'Let's admit it as certain, even. I don't see that it makes the slightest difference. . . .'

'No difference ? '

Calamy shook his head. 'Salvation's not in the next world ; it's in this. One doesn't behave well here for the sake of a harp and wings after one is dead—or even for the sake of contemplating throughout eternity the good, the true and the beautiful. If one desires salvation, it's salvation here and now. The kingdom of God is within you—if you'll excuse the quotation,' he added, turning with a smile to Mr. Cardan. 'The conquest of that kingdom, now, in this life—that's your salvationist's ambition. There may be a life to come, or there may not ; it's really quite irrelevant to the main issue. To be upset because the soul may decay with the body is really mediaeval. Your mediaeval theologian made up for his really frightful cynicism about this world by a childish optimism about the next. Future justice was to compensate for the disgusting horrors of the present. Take away the life to come and the horrors remain, untempered and unpalliated.'

'Quite so,' said Chelifer.

'Seen from the mediaeval point of view,' Calamy went on, 'the prospect is most disquieting. The Indians—and for that matter the founder of Christianity—supply the corrective with the doctrine of salvation in this life, irrespective of the life to come. Each man can achieve salvation in his own way.'

' I 'm glad you admit that,' said Mr. Cardan. ' I was afraid you 'd begin telling us that we all had to live on lettuces and look at our navels.'

' I have it from no less an authority than yourself,' Calamy answered, laughing, ' that there are—how many ?—eighty-four thousand—isn't it ?—different ways of achieving salvation.'

' Fully,' said Mr. Cardan, ' and a great many more for going to the devil. But all this, my young friend,' he pursued, shaking his head, ' doesn't in any way mitigate the disagreeableness of slowly becoming *gaga*, dying and being eaten by worms. One may have achieved salvation in this life, certainly ; but that makes it none the less insufferable that, at the end of the account, one's soul should inevitably succumb to one's body. I, for example, am saved—I put the case quite hypothetically, mind you—I have been living in a state of moral integrity and this-worldly salvation for the last half-century, ever since I reached the age of puberty. Let this be granted. Have I, for this reason, any the less cause to be distressed by the prospect, in a few years' time, of becoming a senile imbecile, blind, deaf, toothless, witless, without interest in anything, partially paralysed, revolting to my fellows—and all the rest of the Burtonian catalogue ? When my soul is at the mercy of my slowly rotting body, what will be the use of salvation then ? '

' It will have profited during the fifty years of healthy life,' said Calamy.

' But I 'm talking about the unhealthy years,' Mr. Cardan insisted, ' when the soul 's at the mercy of the body.'

Calamy was silent for a moment. ' It 's difficult,' he said pensively, ' it 's horribly difficult. The fundamental question is this : Can you talk of the soul being at the mercy of the body, can you give any kind of an explanation of mind in terms of matter ? When you reflect that it 's the human mind that has invented space, time and matter, picking them out of reality in a quite arbitrary fashion—can you attempt to explain a thing in terms of something it has invented itself? That's the fundamental question.'

'It's like the question of the authorship of the *Iliad*,' said Mr. Cardan. 'The author of that poem is either Homer or, if not Homer, somebody else of the same name. Similarly, philosophically and even, according to the new physics, scientifically speaking, matter may not be matter, *really*. But the fact remains that something having all the properties we have always attributed to matter is perpetually getting in our way, and that our minds do, in point of fact, fall under the dominion of certain bits of this matter, known as our bodies, changing as they change and keeping pace with their decay.'

Calamy ran his fingers perplexedly through his hair. 'Yes, of course, it's devilishly difficult,' he said. 'You can't help behaving *as if* things really were as they seem to be. At the same time, there *is* a reality which is totally different and which a change in our physical environment, a removal of our bodily limitations, would enable us to get nearer to. Perhaps by thinking hard enough . . .' He paused, shaking his head. 'How many days did Gotama spend under the bo-tree? Perhaps if you spend long enough and your mind is the right sort of mind, perhaps you really do get, in some queer sort of way, beyond the limitations of ordinary existence. And you see that everything that seems real is in fact entirely illusory—*maya*, in fact, the cosmic illusion. Behind it you catch a glimpse of reality.'

'But what bosh your mystics talk about it,' said Mr. Cardan. 'Have you ever read Boehme, for example? Lights and darknesses, wheels and compunctions, sweets and bitters, mercury, salt and sulphur—it's a rigmarole.'

'It's only to be expected,' said Calamy. 'How is a man to give an account of something entirely unlike the phenomena of known existence in a language invented to describe these phenomena? You might give a deaf man a most detailed verbal description of the Fifth Symphony; but he wouldn't be much the wiser for it, and he'd think you were talking pure balderdash—which from his point of view you would be. . . .'

'True,' said Mr. Cardan; 'but I have my doubts whether any amount of sitting under bo-trees really makes it possible for any one to wriggle out of human limitations and get behind phenomena.'

'Well, I'm inclined to think that it does make it possible,' said Calamy. 'There we must agree to differ. But even if it is impossible to get at reality, the fact that reality exists and is manifestly very different from what we ordinarily suppose it to be, surely throws some light on this horrible death business. Certainly, as things seem to happen, it's as if the body did get hold of the soul and kill it. But the real facts of the case may be entirely different. The body as we know it is an invention of the mind. What is the reality on which the abstracting, symbolizing mind does its work of abstraction and symbolism? It is possible that, at death, we may find out. And in any case, what is death, *really* ?'

'It's a pity,' put in Chelifer, in his dry, clear, accurate voice, 'it's a pity that the human mind didn't do its job of invention a little better while it was about it. We might, for example, have made our symbolic abstraction of reality in such a way that it would be unnecessary for a creative and possibly immortal soul to be troubled with the haemorrhoids.'

Calamy laughed. 'Incorrigible sentimentalist !'

'Sentimentalist ?' echoed Chelifer, on a note of surprise.

'A sentimentalist inside out,' said Calamy, nodding affirmatively. 'Such wild romanticism as yours—I imagined it had been extinct since the deposition of Louis-Philippe.'

Chelifer laughed good-humouredly. 'Perhaps you're right,' he said. 'Though I must say I myself should have handed out the prize for sentimentality to those who regard what is commonly known as reality—the Harrow Road, for example, or the Café de la Rotonde in Paris—as a mere illusion, who run away from it and devote their time and energy to occupations which Mr. Cardan sums up and symbolizes in the word omphaloskepsis. Aren't they the soft-heads, the all-too-susceptible and sentimental imbeciles ? '

' On the contrary,' Calamy replied, ' in point of historical fact they 've generally been men of the highest intelligence. Buddha, Jesus, Lao-tsze, Boehme, in spite of his wheels and compunctions, his salt and sulphur, Swedenborg. And what about Sir Isaac Newton, who practically abandoned mathematics for mysticism after he was thirty ? Not that he was a particularly good mystic ; he wasn't. But he tried to be ; and it can't be said that he was remarkable for the softness of his head. No, it 's not fools who turn mystics. It takes a certain amount of intelligence and imagina- tion to realize the extraordinary queerness and mysteriousness of the world in which we live. The fools, the innumerable fools, take it all for granted, skate about cheerfully on the surface and never think of inquiring what 's underneath. They 're content with appearances, such as your Harrow Road or Café de la Rotonde, call them realities and proceed to abuse any one who takes an interest in what lies underneath these superficial symbols, as a romantic imbecile.'

' But it 's cowardice to run away,' Chelifer insisted. ' One has no right to ignore what for ninety-nine out of every hundred human beings is reality—even though it mayn't actually be the real thing. One has no right.'

' Why not ? ' asked Calamy. ' One has a right to be six foot nine inches high and to take sixteens in boots. One has a right, even though there are not more than three or four in every million like one. Why hasn't one the right to be born with an unusual sort of mind, a mind that can't be content with the surface-life of appearances ? '

But such a mind is irrelevant, a freak,' said Chelifer. ' In real life—or if you prefer it, in the life that we treat as if it were real—it 's the other minds that preponderate, that are the rule.

The brutish minds. I repeat, you haven't the right to run away from that. If you want to know what human life is, you must be courageous and live as the majority of human beings actually do live. It's singularly revolting, I assure you.'

'There you are again with your sentimentality,' complained Calamy. 'You're just the common variety of sentimentalist reversed. The ordinary kind pretends that so-called real life is more rosy than it actually is. The reversed sentimentalist gloats over its horrors. The bad principle is the same in both cases— an excessive preoccupation with what is illusory. The man of sense sees the world of appearances neither too rosily nor too biliously and passes on. There is the ulterior reality to be looked for ; it is more interesting. . . .'

'Then you'd condemn out of hand all the countless human beings whose life is passed on the surface ? '

'Of course not,' Calamy replied. 'Who would be such a fool as to condemn a fact ? These people exist ; it's obvious. They have their choice of Mr. Cardan's eighty-four thousand paths to salvation. The path I choose will probably be different from others. That's all.'

'Very likely,' said Mr. Cardan, who had been engaged in lighting a cigar, 'very likely they'll find the road to their salvation more easily than you will find the road to yours. Being simpler, they'll have within them fewer causes for disharmony. Many of them are still practically in the tribal state, blindly obeying the social code that has been suggested into them from childhood. That's the pre-lapsarian state ; they've not yet eaten of the tree of the knowledge of good and evil—or rather it's the whole tribe, not the individual, that has eaten. And the individual is so much a part of the tribe that it doesn't occur to him to act against its ordinances, any more than it occurs to my teeth to begin violently biting my tongue of their own accord. Those simple souls—and there are still a lot of them left, even among the motor buses—will find their way to salvation very easily. The difficulty begins when the individuals begin to get thoroughly conscious of themselves apart from the tribe. There's an immense number of people who ought to be tribal savages, but who have been made conscious of their individuality. They can't obey tribal morality blindly and they're too feeble to think for themselves. I should say that the majority of people in a modern educated democratic state are at that stage—too conscious of themselves to obey blindly, too inept to be able to behave in a reasonable manner on their own account. Hence that delightful contemporary state of affairs which so rejoices the heart of our friend Chelifer. We fall most horribly between two stools—the tribe and the society of conscious intelligent beings.'

'It's comforting to think,' said Chelifer, ' that modern civilization is doing its best to re-establish the tribal régime, but on an enormous, national and even international scale. Cheap printing, wireless telephones, trains, motor cars, gramophones and all the rest are making it possible to consolidate tribes, not of a few thousands, but of millions. To judge from the Middle Western novelists, the process seems already to have gone a long way in America. In a few generations it may be that the whole planet will be covered by one vast American-speaking tribe, composed of innumerable individuals, all thinking and acting in exactly the same way, like the characters in a novel by Sinclair Lewis. It's a most pleasing speculation—though, of course,' Chelifer added guardedly, ' the future is no concern of ours.'

Mr. Cardan nodded and puffed at his cigar. ' That's certainly a possibility,' he said. ' A probability almost ; for I don't see that it's in the least likely that we shall be able to breed a race of beings, at any rate within the next few thousand years, sufficiently intelligent to be able to form a stable non-tribal society. Education has made the old tribalism impossible and has done nothing—nor ever will do anything—to make the non-tribal society possible.

CONCLUSIONS

It will be necessary, therefore, if we require social stability, to create a new kind of tribalism, on the basis of universal education for the stupid, using the press, wireless and all the rest as the instruments by which the new order is to be established. In a generation or two of steady conscious work it ought to be possible, as Chelifer says, to turn all but two or three hundred in every million of the inhabitants of the planet into Babbitts.'

'Perhaps a slightly lower standard would be necessary,' suggested Chelifer.

'It's a remarkable thing,' pursued Mr. Cardan meditatively, 'that the greatest and most influential reformer of modern times, Tolstoy, should also have proposed a reversion to tribalism as the sole remedy to civilized restlessness and uncertainty of purpose. But while we propose a tribalism based on the facts—or should I say the appearances?'—Mr. Cardan twinkled amicably at Calamy—'of modern life, Tolstoy proposed a return to the genuine, primordial, uneducated, dirty tribalism of the savage. That won't do, of course; because it's hardly probable, once they have tasted it, that men will allow *le confort moderne*, as they call it in hotels, to be taken from them. Our suggestion is the more practicable—the creation of a planet-wide tribe of Babbitts. They'd be much easier to propagate, now, than moujiks. But still the principle remains the same in both projects—a return to the tribal state. And when Tolstoy and Chelifer and myself agree about anything, believe me,' said Mr. Cardan, 'there's something in it. By the way,' he added, 'I hope we haven't been hurting your susceptibilities, Calamy. You're not moujiking up here, are you? Digging and killing pigs and so on. Are you? I trust not.'

Calamy shook his head, laughing. 'I cut wood in the mornings, for exercise,' he said. 'But not on principle, I assure you, not on principle.'

'Ah, that's all right,' said Mr. Cardan. 'I was afraid you might be doing it on principle.'

'It would be a stupidity,' said Calamy. 'What would be the point of doing badly something for which I have no aptitude; something, moreover, which would prevent me from doing the thing for which it seems to me just possible I may have some native capacity.'

'And what, might I ask,' said Mr. Cardan with an assumed diffidence and tactful courtesy, 'what may that thing be?'

'That's rather biting,' said Calamy, smiling. 'But you may well ask. For it has certainly been hard to see, until now, what my peculiar talent was. I've not even known myself. Was it making love? or riding? or shooting antelopes in Africa? or commanding a company of infantry? or desultory reading at lightning speeds? or drinking champagne? or a good memory? or my bass voice? Or what? I'm inclined to think it was the first: making love.'

'Not at all a bad talent,' said Mr. Cardan judicially.

'But not, I find, one that one can go on cultivating indefinitely,' said Calamy. 'And the same is true of the others—true at any rate for me. . . . No, if I had no aptitudes but those, I might certainly as well devote myself exclusively to digging the ground. But I begin to find in myself a certain aptitude for meditation which seems to me worth cultivating. And I doubt if one can cultivate meditation at the same time as the land. So I only cut wood for exercise.'

'That's good,' said Mr. Cardan. 'I should be sorry to think you were doing anything actively useful. You retain the instincts of a gentleman; that's excellent. . . .'

'Satan!' said Calamy, laughing. 'But do you suppose I don't know very well that you can make out the most damning case against the idle anchorite who sits looking at his navel while other people work? Do you suppose I haven't thought of that?'

'I'm sure you have.' Mr. Cardan answered, genially twinkling.

374

'The case looks damning enough, no doubt. But it's only really cogent when the anchorite doesn't do his job properly, when he's born to be active and not contemplative. The imbeciles who rush about bawling that action is the end of life, and that thought has no value except in so far as it leads to action, are speaking only for themselves. There are eighty-four thousand paths. The pure contemplative has a right to one of them.'

'I should be the last to deny it,' said Mr. Cardan.

'And if I find that it's not my path,' pursued Calamy, 'I shall turn back and try what can be done in the way of practical life. Up till now, I must say I've not seen much hope for myself that way. But then, it must be admitted, I didn't look for the road in places where I was very likely to find it.'

'What has always seemed to me to be the chief objection to protracted omphaloskepsis,' said Mr. Cardan, after a little silence, 'is the fact that you're left too much to your personal resources; you have to live on your own mental fat, so to speak, instead of being able to nourish yourself from outside. And to know yourself becomes impossible; because you can't know yourself except in relation to other people.'

'That's true,' said Calamy. 'Part of yourself you can certainly get to know only in relation to what is outside. In the course of twelve or fifteen years of adult life I think I've got to know that part of me very thoroughly. I've met a lot of people, been in a great many curious situations, so that almost every potentiality latent in that part of my being has had a chance to unfold itself into actuality. Why should I go on? There's nothing more I really want to know about that part of myself; nothing more, of any significance, I imagine, that I could get to know by contact with what is external. On the other hand, there is a whole universe within me, unknown and waiting to be explored; a whole universe that can only be approached by way of introspection and patient uninterrupted thought. Merely to satisfy curiosity it would surely be worth exploring. But there are motives more impelling than curiosity to persuade me. What one may find there is so important that it 's almost a matter of life and death to undertake the search.'

' Hm,' said Mr. Cardan. ' And what will happen at the end of three months' chaste meditation when some lovely young temptation comes toddling down this road, " balancing her haunches," as Zola would say, and rolling the large black eye ? What will happen to your explorations of the inward universe then, may I ask ? '

' Well,' said Calamy, ' I hope they 'll proceed uninterrupted.'

' You hope ? Piously ? '

' And I shall certainly do my best to see that they do,' Calamy added.

' It won't be easy,' Mr. Cardan assured him.

' I know.'

' Perhaps you 'll find that you can explore simultaneously both the temptation and the interior universe.'

Calamy shook his head. ' Alas, I 'm afraid that 's not practicable. It would be delightful if it were. But for some reason it isn't. Even in moderation it won't do. I know that, more or less, by experience. And the authorities are all agreed about it.'

' But after all,' said Chelifer, ' there have been religions that prescribed indulgence in these particular temptations as a discipline and ceremony at certain seasons and to celebrate certain feasts.'

' But they didn't pretend,' Calamy answered, ' that it was a discipline that made it easy for those who underwent it to explore the inward universe of mind.'

' Perhaps they did,' objected Chelifer. ' After all, there 's no golden rule. At one time and in one place you honour your father and your mother when they grow old ; elsewhere and at other periods you knock them on the head and put them into the *pot-au-feu*. Everything has been right at one time or another and everything has been wrong.'

'That's only true with reservations,' said Calamy, 'and the reservations are the most important part. There's a parallel, it seems to me, between the moral and the physical world. In the physical world you call the unknowable reality the Four-Dimensional Continuum. The Continuum is the same for all observers; but when they want to draw a picture of it for themselves, they select different axes for their graphs, according to their different motions—and according to their different minds and physical limitations. Human beings have selected three-dimensional space and time as their axes. Their minds, their bodies and the earth on which they live being what they are, human beings could not have done otherwise. Space and time are necessary and inevitable ideas for us. And when we want to draw a picture of that other reality in which we live—is it different, or is it somehow, incomprehensibly, the same ?—we choose, unescapably—we cannot fail to choose, those axes of reference which we call good and evil; the laws of our being make it necessary for us to see things under the aspects of good and evil. The reality remains the same; but the axes vary with the mental position, so to speak, and the varying capacities of different observers. Some observers are clearer-sighted and in some way more advantageously placed than others. The incessantly changing social conventions and moral codes of history represent the shifting axes of reference chosen by the least curious, most myopic and worst-placed observers. But the axes chosen by the best observers have always been startlingly like one another. Gotama, Jesus and Lao-tsze, for example; they lived sufficiently far from one another in space, time and social position. But their pictures of reality resemble one another very closely. The nearer a man approaches these in penetration, the more nearly will his axes of moral reference correspond with theirs. And when all the most acute observers agree in saying that indulgence in these particular amusements interferes with the exploration of the spiritual world, then one can be pretty sure it's true. In itself, no doubt, the natural and moderate satisfaction of the sexual instincts is a matter quite indifferent to morality. It is only in relation to something else that the satisfaction of a natural instinct can be said to be good or bad. It might be bad, for example, if it involved deceit or cruelty. It is certainly bad when it enslaves a mind that feels, within itself, that it ought to be free—free to contemplate and recollect itself.'

'No doubt,' said Mr. Cardan. 'But as a practical man, I can only say that it's going to be most horribly difficult to preserve that freedom. That balancing of haunches . . .' He waved his cigar from side to side. 'I shall call again in six months and see how you feel about it all then. It's extraordinary what an effect the natural appetites do have on good resolutions. Satiated, one thinks regeneration will be so easy; but when one's hungry again, how hard it seems.'

They were silent. From the depths of the valley the smoky shadows had climbed higher and higher up the slope. The opposite hills were now profoundly black and the clouds in which their peaks were involved had become dark and menacing save where, on their upper surfaces, the sun touched them with, as it declined, an ever richer light. The shadow had climbed up to within a hundred feet of where they were sitting, soon it would envelop them. With a great jangling of bells and a clicking of small hard hoofs the six tall piebald goats came trotting down the steep path from the road. The little boy ran behind them, waving his stick. 'Eia-oo!' he shouted with a kind of Homeric fury; but at the sight of the three men sitting on the bench outside the house he suddenly became silent, blushed and slunk unheroically away, hardly daring to whisper to the goats while he drove them into their stable for the night.

'Dear me,' said Chelifer, who had followed the movements of the animals with a certain curiosity, ' I believe those are the first goats I have seen, or smelt, in the flesh since I took to writing about them in my paper. Most interesting. One tends to forget that the creatures really exist.'

' One tends to forget that anything or any one really exists, outside oneself,' said Mr. Cardan. ' It 's always a bit of a shock to find that they do.'

' Three days hence,' said Chelifer meditatively, ' I shall be at my office again. Rabbits, goats, mice ; Fetter Lane ; the family *pension*. All the familiar horrors of reality.'

' Sentimentalist ! ' mocked Calamy.

' Meanwhile,' said Mr. Cardan, ' Lilian has suddenly decided to move on to Monte Carlo. I go with her, of course ; one can't reject free meals when they 're offered.' He threw away his cigar, got up and stretched himself. ' Well, we must be getting down before it gets dark.'

' I shan't see you again for some time, then ? ' said Calamy.

' I shall be here again at the end of six months, never fear,' said Mr. Cardan. ' Even if I have to come at my own expense.'

They climbed up the steep little path on to the road.

' Good-bye.'

' Good-bye.'

Calamy watched them go, watched them till they were out of sight round a bend in the road. A profound melancholy settled down upon him. With them, he felt, had gone all his old, familiar life. He was left quite alone with something new and strange. What was to come of this parting ?

Or perhaps, he reflected, nothing would come of it. Perhaps he had been a fool.

The cottage was in the shadow now. Looking up the slope he could see a clump of trees still glittering as though prepared for a festival above the rising flood of darkness. And at the head of the valley, like an immense precious stone, glowing with its own inward fire, the limestone crags reached up through the clouds into the pale sky. Perhaps he had been a fool, thought Calamy. But looking at that shining peak, he was somehow reassured.

Printed in Great Britain
by T. and A. CONSTABLE LTD., Hopetoun Street,
Printers to the University of Edinburgh